To She ... Enjoy! Rebecca x

False Widow

by

Rebecca Xibalba and Tim Greaves

(from an original idea by Rebecca Xibalba)

False Widow

Copyright © 2023 Rebecca Xibalba and Tim Greaves
TimBex Productions

I

CHAPTER 1

Marie Shaw checked her watch for the umpteenth time; it felt as if she had been standing and waiting for ages, yet the hands had hardly moved.

She jutted out her bottom lip and exhaled irritably. 'Come on!'

As the main doors of the junior school opened wide and a swarm of small children hurried out into the afternoon sunshine, Marie's eyes darted back and forth. Then she spotted her younger sister walking slowly down the steps and

1

across the playground, dragging her satchel behind her. 'Lucy, come *on*!' she seethed.

Her sister strolled lazily up to her. 'I'm hot.'

'Where's Thomas?' Marie asked, surveying the rapidly-emptying playground.

'I dunno.'

Marie rolled her eyes and let out a sigh. 'As if I haven't been kept waiting here long enough. If he…'

'Here he comes!' Lucy shouted.

As he approached his two sisters, Thomas stopped, frowned, then turned back. 'I forgot my coat,' he called out as he ran off towards the school doors.

'For God's sake!' Marie hissed.

Thomas returned a minute later, his coat slung over his shoulder. Marie grabbed each of them by their wrists and took off at speed along the pavement.

'Owww!' Lucy yelled. 'You're hurting me!'

Without slowing down, Marie looked down at her younger sister. 'Well, hurry up then!' She dug her nails deep into Lucy's little hand, causing the girl to shriek again. Then she picked up the pace, all but dragging her siblings along behind her.

The frenzied dash from her last class at college every day had become a mind-numbing chore for Marie. When, five years earlier, her parents had bestowed upon her the task of collecting Thomas and Lucy from school, she had been delighted. After all, in her eyes, it was an acknowledgement on their part that she was mature enough to be trusted with the responsibility. It had filled her with pride. Yet the excitement of hanging around waiting for the children outside the school gates in all weathers, walking them home – dear God, how they dawdled! – and preparing their tea had quickly worn off.

Now, at the age of 16 – mere months away from 17, in fact – and approaching the end of her first year at Fellbury College, the rigmarole had become a thorn in her side. No matter that the school was half a mile from the college and she had to pass it to get home anyway, now she finished earlier, she felt that her bonus half hour of freedom was being stolen from her. There was no disputing it: Thomas and Lucy cramped her style and, on those occasions when anyone she knew from college spotted her with them, she was embarrassed beyond words and wanted the ground to open up and swallow her.

It was all her stupid parents fault, of course. They were neglecting *their* responsibilities by offloading the youngsters' needs on her. Marie worked hard at college. Was it really so much to expect that her free time was her own, unshackled by obligations that weren't really hers?

Why have kids if you're unable, or indeed unwilling to look after them? So what if her parents ran their own company? That made them the bosses, didn't it? They could dictate their own hours, allowing them to be available for family commitments – commitments of *their* own making. Calling on Marie to do it all was a bare-faced liberty.

The facts were plain and simple: Lucy and Thomas were Gareth and Lynda Shaw's children, not Marie's!

Today in particular there was additional stress. Her best friend, Emily, had managed to secure a pair of tickets for them to see Status Quo playing live at the Hammersmith

Odeon. There would barely be enough time as it was to get her brother and sister home and cook up their meal, before she would have to get changed and be out the door again to catch the train to London. So she could really have done without Thomas faffing around over a forgotten coat.

'Can we stop and get some sweets?' Lucy asked, dragging her heels as they approached the newsagent on the corner.

'No!'

'Why not?' Thomas asked, pouting.

'We haven't got time.'

'*Please*,' Thomas whined, stopping outside the shop door and idly kicking away a discarded ice lolly wrapper with the toe of his shoe. 'Can we have an ice lolly instead? I'm so hot.'

'Oh, yes please!' Lucy chimed in.

The wrapper stuck to the bottom of the boy's shoe and, leaning on the door to steady himself, he lifted his foot to peel it off.

'I said *no*!' Marie exclaimed crossly. 'Besides, I haven't got any money with me.' That was the truth, but just to be spiteful, she added, 'Even if I did, it's your own fault we don't have time. If you'd bucked your ideas up and not left your coat behind, there *might* have been time.'

The shop door opened and an elderly woman with a shopping bag on wheels appeared. Marie grabbed Thomas's hand to pull him out of the way and screwed up her face; his fingers were sticky with the residue from the wrapper.

'Oh, for God's sake, Thomas!'

Angrily corralling the two children, she hustled them off up the road towards home.

Marie had just set down two plates of chicken nuggets, baked beans and slightly undercooked chips in front of Lucy and Thomas when the front doorbell rang. She opened up to find her friend standing on the step.

Emily was wearing an off-the-shoulder sky-blue top and orange parachute pants. She'd had her long, naturally blonde hair crimped especially for the occasion. Marie thought she looked fabulous, but she would never have deigned to tell her so.

Her face flushed with excitement, Emily threw her hands in the air. '*Here we gooooo-oh…*'

'*Rockin' all over the world!*' Marie sang back to her. She giggled. 'Come in, quick, I'm just going up to change. Wait in the kitchen. There's Pepsi in the fridge if you want some.' She sped off upstairs.

In her room, she threw open the wardrobe, all plans of wearing her new, bright yellow parachute pants abandoned; Emily's choice of attire had seen to that. Marie was confident she was more attractive than her friend, and she certainly had longer, shapelier legs. But Emily had a larger chest, and wasn't that what men looked at first? If she had any chance of making eye-contact with the knee-weakeningly gorgeous Francis Rossi that evening, she didn't want him looking past her and staring at Emily Marks's boobs!

Stripping off, she settled on a bright pink mini-skirt that barely covered her bottom and a matching pink crop top that she knew would best accentuate her negligible assets. She was just about to slip on the top, when a thought crossed her mind. Removing her bra and throwing it on the bed – *Francis can't fail to notice me now*, she thought, smiling to herself – she quickly got dressed. Applying some eye-shadow and her favourite cherry-red lipstick, she squirted a handful of mousse into the palm of her hand, scrunched it into her hair, then hurried back downstairs.

'You look amazing!' Emily exclaimed when Marie walked into the kitchen.

Marie smiled. 'Don't I though!'

Thomas sniggered. 'I can see your knickers.' He had baked bean sauce around his mouth.

Lucy threw a chip at him.

Marie shot her brother a warning look. 'Shut up and eat your tea, you little troll!' She looked up at the clock on the wall beside the fridge and frowned. It was seven minutes after five. 'Mum and Dad said they'd be home by five. What time's the train?'

'Five forty-seven,' Emily replied. 'We've got plenty of time.'

At that moment, the sound of the front door opening heralded the arrival home of Marie's parents.

'Coo-ee,' Mrs Shaw called out. 'Sorry we're a bit late.' She caught sight of Marie with her hands on her hips, standing glaring at them from the kitchen doorway. 'Dad got caught talking to a client on the phone,' she added apologetically.

'You said you'd be in by five!' Marie snapped. 'You know we've got a train to catch!'

6

'Well we're here now,' Mr Shaw said, setting down his briefcase beside the coat-stand inside the door. He paused and stared disapprovingly at his daughter. 'What on *earth* do you think you're wearing?'

'Clothes, obviously' Marie said sarcastically.

'Not *those* clothes you're not. At least not if you intend leaving the house this evening.'

'Don't start on her, Gareth,' Mrs Shaw said, stepping past her daughter into the kitchen. She saw Emily standing beside the counter and smiled. 'Hello, Em. You're looking nice. Happy Birthday.'

Emily beamed. 'Aww, thank you, Mrs Shaw.'

'No,' Mr Shaw continued. 'I'm not having a daughter of mine going out looking like, like...' – he seemed to be struggling to find the right word.

'Like *what*, Dad?'

'Like... *that*!'

'You look lovely, dear,' Mrs Shaw whispered to Marie.

'Just go and get changed,' Mr Shaw said.

'I haven't got *time*, Dad!'

Mr Shaw shrugged. 'You either get changed into something more respectable, or you're not setting foot out of the door.' There was a note of finality in his voice.

'That's *so* unfair!'

'Your choice.'

Huffing, Marie ran back up the stairs.

'And put a bra on!' Mr Shaw called after her. He walked through to the kitchen and smiled at Emily. 'You're looking very pretty, Miss Marks. Are you having a nice birthday?'

Emily blushed. She always did when Mr Shaw addressed her so formally. 'I am, thank you, Mr Shaw.'

A couple of minutes later, Marie reappeared wearing a Status Quo T-Shirt and the yellow parachute pants. 'Better?'

Her father nodded. 'Much.'

'Very nice,' Mrs Shaw said

Marie looked at Emily. 'We need to get going.'

Her father glanced at the clock. 'Do you girls need a run to the station?'

'No, we're fine.' Marie grabbed Emily by the arm and pulled her down the hall, 'Come on.'

'Enjoy the show,' Mrs Shaw called after them.

Marie grabbed up her shoulder bag from the foot of the stairs and the pair disappeared through the front door, slamming it behind them.

As they hurried down the path, Emily said, 'You should have let your Dad give us a lift. We're really going to have to shuffle now or we'll miss the train.'

'Relax,' Marie said. 'We've got time. Besides, I didn't want him to see this.' She opened the top of her bag to show her friend the pink miniskirt and top inside.

'You sneaky little thing!'

Marie grinned. 'I'll get changed on the train. Then it's Marguerita Time!'

They hightailed it to the station, only to arrive on the platform at five forty-three as the tannoy crackled into life: 'The five forty-seven to London Waterloo is running ten minutes late. We apologise for the delay this will cause to your journey.'

8

'I don't believe it!' Marie panted. She clutched her side and winced. 'Now I've got a stitch.'

'Me too,' Emily replied breathlessly. 'My legs are killing me.'

'If my bloody Dad hadn't made me get changed, we wouldn't have had to run.' She pointed to the Ladies' toilets. 'We've got a few minutes to spare now. I'm going to go and change. It'll be easier than trying to do it in the loo on the train.'

Marie reappeared a couple of minutes later wearing her pink miniskirt and crop top. Standing beside a door stencilled **STAFF ONLY**, a station porter was leaning on a broom, observing the two girls lecherously.

'What d'you think *you're* looking at?' Marie said testily.

A look of oafish embarrassment crossed the man's face and he hastily busied himself sweeping the platform.

Marie rolled her eyes. 'Flippin' perv.'

Emily smiled at her. 'You can't blame him really. That outfit is pretty revealing.'

'He's old enough to be my granddad!'

'But if you dress like that, it's a red-letter day for guys. You can't choose who gets to look and who doesn't.'

'You sound like my Dad!'

'What do you mean?'

'Lecturing me on what I like to wear,' Marie said peevishly.

'I'm not lecturing you,' Emily said quietly. 'You look great.' She had known Marie since they were at playschool together and always knew when it was advisable to withdraw. 'I just meant…'

'*What*?'

'That if he had been forty years younger and super-hot you'd have been happy to let him have an eyeful.'

Marie grinned. 'You got *that* right! But he'd be out of luck.' She put a hand over her heart and patted it. 'I belong to Francis.'

The pair burst out laughing.

The train arrived and they boarded. It was heaving with early evening passengers, but they walked through the carriages and managed to find two empty seats. Emily was about to sit down, but Marie grabbed her shoulder. 'Oi! You know *I* like the window seat!'

Emily politely stepped back and let her friend in first, then sat down beside her. 'Where are we going to eat?'

'We're not. I want to go straight to the gig. We can eat after.'

Emily frowned. 'But we'll be in London in twenty minutes. I thought our plan was to grab some food before the show.'

'Er, excuse me, *your* plan, not mine. We have to get there before the doors open, then we can get a spot right at the front.' She adjusted her crop top, which was riding up. 'I want Francis to be able to get a good look at my outfit.'

'Surely we could at least stop quickly and have a milkshake?' Emily pressed. 'I'm hungry and the doors don't open till seven-thirty.'

'Listen up cloth-ears.' Marie flicked Emily's earlobe. I *said* we're going straight to the gig.

Emily sighed. There was no point arguing. 'Okay.' They fell silent for a couple of minutes, then she said, 'So what do you reckon they'll play tonight?'

Marie giggled. 'Francis could sing *The Wheels on the Bus* and I'd be happy.'

Emily's eyes lit up. 'Hey, I wonder if we found someone at the venue and had a word, they might be able to arrange for them to sing Happy Birthday to me?'

'Don't be ridiculous!' Marie scoffed.

'It's not ridiculous. You hear about bands doing that for their fans.'

'Not the Quo. They're way too cool to do something cheap like that.'

Emily nodded. 'Yeah, I suppose.' She smiled wistfully. 'It would be *so* great if they did though. It'd be the best present *ever*. Can you imagine it? Francis looking *right* at me and…'

'Well it's not happening, so there's not much point creaming yourself dreaming about it.'

Emily's smile faded. 'So what *do* you think they'll play then?'

Marie thoughtfully twisted a lock of her chestnut brown hair around her index finger. 'The standards, obviously. *Down Down*. *Rockin' All Over the World* is pretty much a cert. *Whatever You Want*.'

'As long as they do *What You're Proposing* I'll be well pleased. That's still my favourite. Mickey loves that one too.'

Marie rolled her eyes. 'I don't know what you see in him. He's so… average.'

The fact of the matter was, there were few girls at Fellbury College whose hearts didn't flutter when Mickey Bird smiled at them, Marie included, although she would never admit it. Mickey was a second year business studies student and captain of the rugby team, with rugged good looks, dark come-to-bed eyes and a smile that could charm the birds out of the trees.

'Have you seen his new haircut?' Marie continued.

'No?'

Marie chuckled. 'I saw it today. He's gone all skinhead.'

Emily's eyes widened. 'Oh no!'

'Yep.'

'That's a real shame. I loved his long hair. It really suited him.' She smiled. 'I bet he still looks sexy-as though.'

'He looks daft if you ask me.'

'Mickey Bird could *never* look daft.'

'I don't understand why you give him the time of day.' Marie looked at Emily judgmentally. 'He could have any girl he wants, you know. He wouldn't go out with someone as plain as you in a million years.'

'Yeah, I suppose.' Emily looked sadly down at her lap. It was 1984, she was 17-years old, and as confident and self-assured as any girl of her age could be. Yet, in Marie's presence, she was always made to feel inferior. She was perfectly used to her friend's insensitive remarks and, although she took them in her stride, she did sometimes wonder whether the putdowns were unwitting or, more perplexingly, born of calculated malice. It made Emily question how they had remained friends for so long.

Couldn't they have just one evening out together without a sarcastic comment or a barbed jibe? It *was* her birthday, after all. But Marie's behaviour was really taking the shine off the evening ahead, and already Emily couldn't wait to be back on the train and on her way home.

CHAPTER 2

It had been one of Marie's myriad of childhood aspirations to see a koala bear in its natural habitat, and so it was, that in November 1985, she set out on a long-planned gap year to backpack around Australia. Her mother and father had suggested she wait until the New Year to go, so that she could spend Christmas at home, but Marie was adamant she wanted to get her adventures underway.

Her parents, though initially unwilling to let her go alone, were compelled to make good on a promise; perhaps of the thinking it would never actually happen, they had told her that, if she excelled in her studies, they would fund her flight, along with any associated essentials. When Marie had walked out of Fellbury College at the end of her second year clutching a fistful of distinctions and honours, they had to put their hands in their pockets.

'Who knows,' Emily had ribbed her on the day she helped Marie to pack. 'You might end up getting married to a surfer!'

Despite the fact she was making light of the matter, Emily was extremely sad to see Marie leave. During the fourteen years they'd been friends – fortnight holidays abroad notwithstanding – it was seldom that more than a few days had ever passed without them seeing each other. Part of her wished she was going too. Indeed, Marie had asked her several times if she would, and her own parents had given their consent should she wish to. But she'd been offered – and had accepted – a summer job in admin for a local company that supplied arcade machines to the gaming industry. The bottom line was that she had always been a home bird, and the mere thought of being separated from her family for so long filled her with severe anxiety.

Marie laughed. 'Don't worry about *that*. I'm going to Australia to have a good time and see the koala bears. I won't be messing around with airhead surfer dudes.'

Along with two or three other friends, the night before Marie flew out to Perth, they went for a farewell meal together.

Later that evening, when it came time to say goodbye, Emily had tears in her eyes.

'You won't forget about me, will you?'

'Don't be daft!' Marie exclaimed.

'And you will write to me?'

'Of course! You'll get so many postcards you won't know what to do with them all.'

'And you'll phone? Whenever you get a chance, I mean.'

Marie put her arms around her friend and held her tightly. 'You're my best friend and you always will be. Of course I'll phone.'

'I'll miss you.'

'And I'll miss you too.' Marie kissed her cheek. 'But a year isn't so long. It'll be over in a blink and I'll be back before you know it.'

Emily pulled a tissue from her handbag and blew her nose. 'Unless you marry that surfer dude.'

Marie laughed. 'Well, *obviously*!'

Marie's first night in Australia was spent at the guesthouse her parents had booked her in to. On her first full day, she visited the Cohuna Koala Park on the outskirts of Perth, where she got to realise her childhood dream.

On day two, she collected some refreshments from a store. The girl serving at the till made Marie smile to herself; although it shouldn't have been a surprise, she was thrilled to hear that she sounded exactly like the stars from the Australian TV shows that she had seen. With plenty to eat and drink loaded in her backpack, she set off on an extended walk along the coastline.

When she had departed England, the country was in the grip of a cold, damp November, and it initially felt bizarre to step back into early summer temperatures, practically overnight; with the thermometers touching 22°, the promise of several sweltering months ahead was already in the air. Marie didn't mind. She thrived in hot weather; it made her feel alive.

At the end of the week, it was time to leave, and she took a flight from Perth on the east coast to Sydney on the west, where the real adventure got underway.

In her head, Marie had always seen herself hiring a camper van to travel up the coast to Brisbane and beyond; the fact that she hadn't yet learned to drive put pay to that idea. Her parents had given her sufficient funds for using public transport, but although Greyhound buses were numerous, it wasn't her plan to see Australia from the window of a bus. She wanted to do as much as possible on foot.

Before heading north out of Sydney, she took a day trip by train south to Wollongong, for no other reason than the name made her laugh and she really wanted to send Emily and her parents a postcard each from a place called Wollongong.

In the middle of her second week, she set off towards Brisbane and the Gold Coast. Stopping overnight at guesthouses on the way, in places with names like Tuggerah, Buladelah and Coolongolook, she sent her family and Emily a postcard from every one of them. At each stop, she hung around for a day or two taking in the sights, before moving on.

Doing as much walking as she could, she did make use of the occasional bus, and in order to save a few dollars, on two occasions she did the one thing her parents had vehemently instructed her against: she hitchhiked.

The first time, she was a little nervous, but a middle-aged woman who introduced herself as Abigail, accompanied by a sweet Miniature Schnauzer named Dougie, picked her up and they had a pleasant enough conversation during the time they spent together. Her confidence fortified, Marie did the same thing again a couple of days later, but this time it wasn't such a nice experience. A man named Mick, with twin girls – maybe only three or four years old – sitting quietly on the back seat of his truck, said he could drive her as far as Port Macquarie. He was genial enough, but Marie became increasingly uncomfortable after noticing the man kept furtively glancing at her legs and every time he laughed, she could smell beer on his breath. When he dropped her off, much to her alarm, Mick leant over and tried to kiss her, and

17

then seemed quite put out when she swore at him and made a hasty exit. That brought her hitchhiking escapades to an abrupt end.

Marie spent Christmas Day at Corindi Beach, missing the comforts of family life for the first time since she had left. Although she had made a point of phoning home weekly, she was aware that, despite her promise to do so, she hadn't actually spoken to Emily once. So, after a tearful call that evening with her family, she dialed Emily's number. It felt really good to hear her best friend's voice after so long and they laughed and cried and caught up with their respective news.

A random decision in Brisbane a few weeks later changed Marie's traveling plans, and, subsequently, her life.

On the day she arrived in the city, the Greyhound deposited her across the street from a bar named The Redback Tavern. It was the large, neon-lit effigy of a spider over the door that initially drew her attention. Desperate for something to drink after several hours on the bus, she crossed over and went inside. The hubbub and the music – emanating from an old-style jukebox – were noisily vying for superiority, but the atmosphere was largely convivial and Marie's ice cold glass of Foster's slipped down a treat.

She was sitting near the jukebox, alongside which there was a noticeboard mounted on the wall. As she quenched her thirst and soaked up the atmosphere, she idly cast her eyes over the brightly coloured pieces of paper pinned on the board. Along with a poster advertising live music at The Redback – twice weekly, Tuesdays and Saturdays – and several handwritten advertisements seeking guitarists to help form bands, an A5 sheet caught her eye:

Earn big $$$s!
WAITRESS WANTED
Five evenings a week. Perks.
Ask at the bar.

Marie had already decided she would probably spend a couple of weeks in and around Brisbane, and the opportunity to earn some cash was too good to ignore. Furthermore, integrating herself into the Australian nightlife – and in a place where the staff appeared to be of a similar age to her – filled her with anticipation. When she finished her drink, she returned to the bar and spoke with the barman, and ten minutes later, she left The Redback Tavern having been offered the job.

She found a small guesthouse, The Swagman's Rest, just a few minutes' walk away from the bar, where she was able to secure a room for two weeks, with an option to extend if she wanted to.

Work at The Redback Tavern wasn't the breeze that she thought it would be, but the money was as good as the poster had indicated and she quickly found her stride. It transpired that the place was a popular watering hole with surfers, who would pour into the city at night after a day riding the rollers out on North Stradbroke Island.

One evening Marie was caught up in an argument with an inebriated customer who had been dining alone and decided he wasn't going to pay for his tasteless – so he claimed –

sizzling shrimp platter. Despite Marie's apology and her offer to see if she could arrange for some money off the price of the meal, the man had worked up a head of steam and was just starting to become abusive, when a young man in his early twenties stepped up behind him and spoke.

'Is there a problem here?'

The customer, his eyes still angrily locked on Marie, didn't look round. 'Too bloody right there's a problem!' He angrily shoved the empty plate in front of him across the table towards Marie. 'The food here is disgusting and I'm not paying for it!'

'But you ate it all anyway, mate?'

'What?' The man turned his head and sized up the young lad standing beside him.

'You cleared your plate. Gotta say, that's not what I'd do if I got served food that tasted bad. I mean, I'd have sent it straight back. But it takes all sorts, I guess.'

The man sized him up, trying to work out who he was and why he had barged his way into his dispute with the waitress. 'What the fuck's it got to do with *you*?'

The lad was wearing a Bermuda shirt, from the sleeves of which poked bronzed, muscular arms, and tight shorts out of which protruded similarly well-toned legs. He had blonde, shoulder-length, wavy hair, swept back and held away from his tanned face by a bright green bandana. He shrugged. 'Just sayin', mate.'

Marie was standing rooted to the spot, awkwardly watching the drama unfold, relieved that the heat had now been diverted away from her, but unsure what was going to happen next.

The customer's attention was completely focused on the young interloper now.

'And I reckon you owe this young lady an apology for your brusque tone,' the lad continued. 'After all, it's not her fault you're a bilker, is it?'

'What did you call me?' the man blustered. He started to get up, but the younger man took hold of his shoulder and forced him back down into his seat.

Still gripping the man's shoulder, the lad bent towards him and spoke calmly. 'A twister. You know full well there was nothing wrong with that food. I bet you try this lark on a lot, and pick on young girls too afraid to argue back.'

The irate customer had started to sweat and he struggled to break free of the lad's grip. 'Get your filthy hands off me!'

'Here's the thing,' the lad said, maintaining his coolness and still effortlessly pinning the man to his seat with one hand. 'You should thank your lucky stars that it was *me* who overheard you being rude to this young lady and not my father. He owns this place and he doesn't take kindly to steaming great galahs like you abusing his staff. He takes even less kindly to being accused of providing anything less than the very best cuisine. You want to know what happened to the last guy who started shouting his mouth off about the food he'd been served being off?'

The lad leaned in close and whispered something into the man's ear. As he listened, his eyes grew wider and the colour appeared to drain from his face. He swallowed hard. 'I'm sorry.'

'Don't say sorry to me, mate. Say sorry to this innocent young girl.' The lad afforded Marie a wink.

21

The man looked up at her. 'I'm very sorry, Miss.'

'That's better. Now get on and pay for your meal.' The lad released his hold on the man's shoulder. 'And be sure you don't forget to add a generous tip.'

The lad stood over the man while he counted out several dollar bills to settle his check, and waited until he had gone before he addressed Marie.

'You okay?'

Marie smiled at him. 'I'm fine. Thanks for that. My guardian angel!'

The lad laughed. 'Is that an English accent I detect?'

Marie smiled. 'It is.'

He punched the air. 'I knew it! I *love* British chicks! Say something else.'

Marie giggled. 'Like what?'

'Forget it.' The lad extended his hand. 'I'm Kai.'

'Kai Ferris?' Marie took hold of his hand and shook it politely.

'Excuse me?'

'My boss, Mr Ferris. You're his son?'

Kai grinned. 'Oh, yeah, about that. I've got a confession to make.'

'Oh?'

'My surname is Garrett and my father works for the Attack Creek Historical Reserve.'

Marie frowned. 'But you told that man…' She trailed off as the penny dropped, and she nodded approvingly. 'Nice one.'

'I just don't like seeing men like that getting their rocks off belittling women.'

'Well, thank you again, I really appreciate it. Where is Attack Creek?'

'In the Northern Territories. You haven't told me your name.'

'Sorry. I'm Marie Shaw.'

'Good to know you, Marie. Listen, what time do you knock off?'

Marie smiled at him coyly. 'Ten.'

'What do you say we go somewhere together and get a bevvy?'

'Marie!' The impatient shout came from the bar. 'Drinks for table fifteen.'

'Sorry. I've got to get back to work.'

'But what about the bevvy?'

Marie nodded. 'Okay. Why not?'

CHAPTER 3

Kai had been drinking with two friends, but just before ten o'clock, Marie saw them get up and bump fists, and they all disappeared. When she finished her shift, Marie found him waiting outside for her, smoking a cigarette. When he saw her, he took a final puff, dropped it on the ground and stamped it out.

'Ready to go?'

'Where are we going?' Marie asked.

'It's a surprise. I thought we'd take a little drive.'

Marie frowned. 'You've been drinking all evening. I don't think driving is a very good idea.'

'It's cool. I switched to soft drinks an hour ago. And I'd only had a couple before that.' Kai winked at her. 'All set then?'

Marie hesitated. 'I don't mean to be a killjoy, but I'd really like to know where it is you're taking me.'

Kai smiled. 'Sure. I thought we might take a run up to Kookaburra Point. There's a terrific view over the city and out to sea. It looks amazing at night.' He saw the look of doubt on Marie's face. 'But, hey, if you'd rather go find a bar, that's cool. I mean, you don't know me. I totally get it. And, honestly, it would be a bit weird if you weren't unsure about getting into a camper van with a virtual stranger.'

'Oh my God!' Marie exclaimed. 'I always wanted to tour Australia in a camper van!'

'Well, I wouldn't say we were going touring,' Kai said breezily. 'Unless you reckon a ten-minute drive up to the Point constitutes a tour.'

Marie smiled. 'Kookaburra Point sounds really great.'

Kai grinned, showing perfect white teeth. 'Your chariot awaits.'

He led her up the street to where a beaten-up camper van was parked beside the kerb. Marie saw that there were two surfboards bungee-strapped to a rack on the roof and she sniggered.

'What's funny?'

'Nothing,' Marie replied. 'I was just thinking about a conversation I had with a friend before I came out here. About surfers.'

'Nothing derogatory, I hope? We get a lot of that.'

Marie shook her head and discreetly crossed her fingers. 'Absolutely not.'

'This time of year, me and my mates are out on our boards most days.'

'You don't work?'

'I do, but I'm what you'd call a jack-of-all-trades. A bit of this, a bit of that, you know? But there's always time for surfing.' Kai held open the passenger door for her.

'Where do you go?' Marie asked, getting in.

'Cylinder Beach out on North Stradroke Island mostly. That's where we were today. Sometimes we go up the coast to Ocean Beach. That's on Bribie Island.' He shut the door, walked around the driver's side and climbed in. 'Occasionally we'll do Moreton Island,' he continued. 'That's a little further out across the Bay though, and there are no lifeguards, so you're kind of on your own if you run into trouble.'

'It sounds a bit dangerous,' Marie said, recalling her remark to Emily about airhead surfers. 'Surely it's not a good idea to surf with no lifeguards around.'

Kai grinned. 'Doesn't phase me. I get a real buzz out of going rogue. I mean, sure, waves aren't always predictable, but it's only really dangerous if you don't know what you're doing.' He turned the key in the ignition. The motor coughed twice and kicked in. 'And, trust me, I've been surfing for a long time and I know *exactly* what I'm doing.'

They were on the road for only a few minutes before the streetlights petered out and they were driving in darkness. All Marie could see up ahead in the beams from the headlights was the winding road, which soon took them on a steady incline.

'How much further is it?' she asked.

'Not far.'

In the glow of the lights from the dashboard, was it Marie's imagination that Kai's smile suddenly didn't look so friendly? She was beginning to question her decision to come. What had she been thinking, getting into a van with a strange man in the middle of the night? She glanced nervously over her shoulder at the bedding laying in the back of the van and felt a bit sick.

Her fears were quelled a little when a sign flashed past that read: **Kookaburra Point ½ km**. At the top of the slope, the road opened out into an expanse of open ground, where she was further relieved to see several cars parked up and a number of young couples strolling along a ridge at the far end.

Kai parked away from the other vehicles and they got out. 'Come look at this.' He took Marie's hand and led her up a grassy bank to the top of the ridge, and there, spread out before them, was what looked like the whole of Brisbane.

The sight was so magical, it made Marie catch her breath. 'Oh, wow!'

'Pretty cool, eh?' Kai pointed at a tall building to their right. 'Over there, that's AMP Place, the Gold Tower. Tallest building in Briz. Although it'll be second tallest when Riverside Centre is completed next year. That's gonna be like 40 storeys high.'

Marie shivered. It had been a typically hot summer's day, but up here, at ten-thirty at night, the temperature had plummeted.

Kai put an arm around her shoulders. 'You cold?'

Marie took a step away from him. 'I'm okay.'

'If you look over there,' Kai continued, 'they're building an even higher skyscraper. No idea when they'll finish it, but I've heard it's gonna be 44 storeys. Mental!'

Marie rubbed her bare arms to warm them up. 'Everything looks so beautiful from here.'

'Including you.'

Marie turned her head. Kai was staring at her. 'Sorry,' he said. 'That was very forward of me.'

'It's fine,' Marie said, hoping that the darkness was hiding her blushes. She rubbed her arms more briskly.

'You *are* cold.'

'A bit. I should have brought a sweater with me. I have one at work, I just thought we were going for a drink and I wouldn't need it.'

'Sorry. We can go back to the van if you like.'

'No, I want to stay and enjoy the view a bit longer.'

'Let's at least sit down then. We'll be out of the breeze over there.' Kai took her hand and led her over to a nearby bench. They sat down and this time, when he slipped his arm around her, she let him.

'What was it you said to that guy in the bar tonight?'

Kai looked at her vacantly.

'The guy who didn't want to pay for his food. You whispered something to him.'

'Oh!' Kai laughed. 'I told him that my Dad not only owned The Redback, but he was also one of the Bandidos.'

'I don't know what that means.'

'The Bandidos are a bike gang. They were originally founded in the States back in the sixties, I think, but the Australian chapter was involved in Milperra Massacre a couple of years back.'

Marie looked at him blankly. 'I've not heard of that. But massacre doesn't sound good.'

'It was a shoot-out in Sidney between the Bandidos and a rival gang, The Comancheros. Seven people died and a shit-load more got hurt. It might not have made the news outside of Australia, I guess, but I doubt there's anyone over here that didn't hear about it. So I told him my Dad was a Bandido.'

Marie smiled. 'Well, it did the trick. He looked like he was going to faint!' They sat in silence for a moment, then she said, 'So, do you bring all the girls here?'

'*All* the girls?' Kai chuckled. 'What sort of a guy do you think I am?'

'A very good-looking one.' Now it was Marie's turn to apologise. 'Sorry, I shouldn't have said that.' She stared out at the twinkling lights below.

'Why not? I mean, unless you don't *really* think that.'

'No, I *do* think that. If I didn't, I suppose I wouldn't be here.'

'So you fancy me and I fancy you.' Kai's fingers had been drawing little circles on her shoulder. Now she felt them tighten and give it a little squeeze. 'What are we going to do about that?'

Marie turned her face towards him and was about to say she had no idea when he leaned over and pressed his lips firmly against hers. Closing her eyes, she responded to the kiss, which quickly increased in urgency. Kai still had his left arm across her shoulders, and she felt his other hand brush across the front of her shirt. As they continued to embrace, his hand dropped lower, slipped underneath the bottom of her shirt and came to rest over her left breast. Feeling herself tingle as his fingers slipped inside the cup of her bra, her brain did a reality check. She broke away from him and put her hand over his. 'No.'

'Why not?'

'Evening.' The voice startled them both. They looked up to see a middle-aged couple, hand-in-hand, walking past. Kai quickly withdrew his hand from beneath Marie's shirt. 'Fantastic view,' the man said as the passed by.

'Bonzer, mate. Bonzer.' Kai waited until they were far enough away and tried to worm his hand back under Marie's shirt.

'I said no.' She shuffled away from him.

Kai looked flustered. 'Why not? I like you and you like me. I don't see what the problem is here. You *do* like me, don't you?'

'I don't even know you.' Marie sighed. 'But yes, I do.'

'Then let's just go with our feelings.'

Marie stood up and straightened her shirt. 'Not tonight. It's too cold. Would you mind taking me home.' She rather expected Kai to protest further, but he didn't.

'Sure.' He smiled up at her warmly. 'Where *is* home?'

'The Swagman's Rest. It's a guesthouse on Valetta Street. It's not actually that far from The Redback.'

Kai stood up. 'I know Valetta Street. Near the marina.'

'That's it, yes,'

'Come on then.' He put his arm around her shoulders again. 'Let's get you home.'

They went back to the van and the return journey passed in silence.

As they pulled up outside The Swagman's Rest, Marie said, 'I'm sorry about back there. It's just I don't really know you. But…'

Kai reached over and placed a hand on her knee. 'No apology necessary. I totally get it.'

Marie smiled. 'I was just about to say, but I'd like to *get* to know you. That is, if you want to see *me* again.'

Kai grinned. Showing the two rows of perfect white teeth. 'I absolutely want to see you again. What about tomorrow night?'

CHAPTER 4

'Petal, you have *got* to be kidding me! Kookaburra Kai? *Already*?'

It was the following evening and Marie was on a mid-shift break, sitting in the small yard to the rear of The Redback Tavern and sharing a pitcher of fresh lemonade and a round of sandwiches with Sasha, one of her colleagues. Still riding on a high after her trip up to Kookaburra Point, she hadn't been able to resist telling Sasha about it.

She frowned. 'What do you mean?'

Sasha took a sip of lemonade and chuckled. 'That bastard doesn't waste any time, does he? You've only been here a few weeks!'

Marie got along well with most of the girls she worked with. But Sasha was a couple of years older than the others and on Marie's first day she had taken Marie under her wing and showed her the ropes. As they got closer, she found she could confide in the older woman, who had provided her with sound advice on some personal matters on more than one occasion. Marie looked upon her as she might an older sister. Even so, it niggled her that she was being laughed at.

'I don't understand. Is there something I need to know about him?'

'Only that you ought to keep your distance.'

'I don't see why. He was really nice. He took me up to…'

'Don't tell me. Kookaburra Point.'

Marie smiled. 'Well, yes actually. He wanted to show me the lights.'

Sasha laughed and rolled her eyes. 'I bet that isn't all he wanted to show you.' She bit into a sandwich. 'Mmm, this salmon is good.'

'He was a perfect gentleman,' Marie said haughtily, remembering how quickly Kai had manoeuvred his hand up her shirt. She decided to keep that particular detail to herself.

'There's a first then. Honestly, petal, ask any of the girls here about him and they'll all tell you the same thing: he's bad news. There's fifteen of us working the rota here…' – she paused and mouthed silently as she counted on her fingers – '…no, sixteen counting Crissy, but she calls in sick so often she doesn't really count. Anyway, out of sixteen, there's only two that haven't been out with Kookaburra Kai.'

'Why do you keep calling him that?'

'Because that's what he's known as among us all here. He always takes girls he fancies to the Point. And it doesn't cost him a penny, avoids having to foot a bar bill. Did I mention he's cheap too?'

'But it's so lovely up there. Seeing the city all lit up is magical. Romantic.'

'I'm not saying it isn't. But that sort of atmos has a way of loosening knicker elastic, and he bloody well capitalises on it. There was a girl working here a couple of years ago – I didn't know her, she was gone by the time I started – but I was told Kai got her up the duff. She kind of vanished and nobody knows how that ended up, but he just carried on playing the field like nothing had ever happened.' Sasha looked at Marie. 'You didn't let him…?'

'No! It's like I said, he was a gentleman.' She chewed at her bottom lip. 'Actually, I'm seeing him again tonight.'

Sasha couldn't hide the look of concern on her face, but she said, 'Well, you just be careful, petal.'

'I will.' Marie picked up her tumbler of lemonade and held the cool glass against her cheek. 'So, if he's so awful, how come all the girls have been out with him?'

'Isn't it obvious? He's bloody gorgeous! But it's not *all* the girls. Despite his best efforts, he hasn't had his wicked way with me or Marlene. You know she likes girls, right?'

Marie nodded and drank some lemonade. 'But weren't you tempted? Just a bit?'

Sasha finished off her sandwich and emptied her glass. 'He's tried it on with me a couple of times, even though he knows I'm going steady with my Ethan. That alone should tell you what a creep he is. But no. Gorgeous or not, he's a predator, the lowest of the low, and as soon as he gets what he wants, he'll dispose of you faster than the condom he spaffed his load in.'

Marie screwed up her face. 'Eww. That's disgusting.'

'So is he.' Sasha placed a hand over Marie's. 'Trust me, petal. Behind the handsome, tanned face, the voluminous hair and the dazzling smile, there's one nasty asshole waiting to shit on you. Go out with him again if you want – I'm not your ma, I can't tell you what to do – but just be careful, yeah?'

The back door opened and Jim Ferris appeared carrying a crate of empty beer bottles. 'Come on, ladies, gabbing time's over.' He bent and set the crate down beside the wall alongside a row of others.

34

Marie liked Ferris a lot, and not just because he'd been kind enough to give her the job. He was also a British emigrant, a down-to-earth, wiry little man – skeletal, some might say –in his late forties or early fifties, at least in Marie's estimation. He took everything in his stride and she had never once seen him get angry. He also had a cheeky sense of humour. Marie smiled as she remembered Kai telling Mr Awkward Customer that Ferris was some kind of murderous biker. With a thinning head of hair, a friendly, wrinkled face that reminded Marie of Sid James, a pencil moustache and rimless, circular-lensed spectacles, he couldn't have looked less intimidating if he tried.

Sasha got up from the table. 'Coming, Jimbo.'

Ferris frowned. 'How many times have I told you, it's *Mister* Ferris?'

Sasha stood to attention and saluted. 'Yes, sir, Mister Ferris sir.'

The frown melted into a smile. 'Come on with you. There's customers dying of thirst in there.'

Sasha looked at Marie. 'I hope you have a lovely time tonight, I really do. Just be sure you approach with extreme caution.'

Marie's shift ended at seven that evening and when she came out of the front door of The Redback with Sasha, she saw Kai waiting for her across the street, where he'd managed to find a parking space. Leaning against the hood of the van smoking, he caught sight of the girls and put up a hand and waved. The pair of them crossed over and, as they approached, he quickly stubbed out the cigarette.

'You did that last night too,' Marie said. 'I don't mind if you want to smoke.'

'Nah, it's cool. I was just killing time.' He looked at Sasha. 'Hiya, Sash. How's it hanging?' If he felt even remotely awkward, he didn't show it.

'Kai,' Sasha responded with a nod. She didn't make eye contact with him and it was evident she felt uncomfortable in his presence. Leaning in close to Marie, she whispered to her: 'Remember, petal, extreme caution.' Then she kissed her on the cheek and said, less secretively, 'See you tomorrow night.'

'I'm off tomorrow.'

'Thursday then.'

As she started to walk away, Kai called after her, 'You can come with if you like, Sash.' There was a mocking tone to his voice.

Sasha didn't look back. 'No thanks. Two's company, three's…'

'*Way* more fun!' Kai chuckled.

Deeming the remark unworthy of a response, Sasha kept walking and crossed back over the street. When she was far enough away that she was well out of earshot, Marie looked at Kai irritably. 'You didn't really want her to come, did you?'

'Of course not.'

'Then why did you invite her?' Marie folded her arms petulantly.

'I was just teasing. I knew she'd say no.'

'But what if she'd said yes?'

'Relax.' Kai leant forward and she allowed him to give her a peck on the cheek. 'She didn't.'

Marie unfolded her arms. 'Where are we going tonight then?'

'I figured on taking a run up to Nudgee Beach. We can pick up some tucker and a few tinnies on the way. It's usually kinda quiet there in the evenings. If we're lucky we might even have the whole beach to ourselves.'

Sasha's words of warning were still playing on Marie's mind. She raised an eyebrow. 'Really?'

'Yeah. We can take a swim too. You like swimming?'

'I do.'

'Excellent. Shall we do that then?' He grinned at her.

Behind the dazzling smile..., Marie thought. But she nodded. 'Sounds great.'

When they arrived, the beach was actually quite busy, but they found a spot on the sand away from most of the other people, and as the evening wore on the numbers dwindled until they were pretty much alone.

It was approaching ten o'clock and an elderly husband and wife with a yappy dachshund had arrived an hour or so after them, and they were still loitering nearby. Marie was laying on the sand, gazing up at the night sky, but Kai was sat up with his arms wrapped round his knees and he kept glancing over at the couple, evidently willing them to pack up and go. Marie, on the other hand, was actually quite pleased they were there, unwittingly having assumed the role of chaperones.

Eventually, after a lot of faffing and a squabble – stimulated by the fact that the man hadn't folded the towel they had been sitting on properly – the couple left.

'Thank Christ for that,' Kai exclaimed. 'I thought they were never gonna go.'

'They weren't doing any harm,' Marie said. 'And their dog was quite sweet.'

'Yeah, I guess.' He flopped back on the sand and propped his head up on his hand. 'But I've been wanting to get to know you all night and they were cramping my style.'

'Get to know me? We've been talking for ages. I think you know everything there is to know.'

'I don't mean getting to know you. I mean getting to *know* you. I've been aching to kiss you since we got here.'

Marie smiled up at him. 'Well?'

'Well what?'

'They're gone now, aren't they? What are you waiting for?'

Kai moved towards her and Marie closed her eyes, anticipating the feel of his lips pressed to hers. But instead, she felt his chin brush across the side of her face and he planted a soft kiss on her earlobe.

'You have really sexy ears, do you know that?'

'*Seriously*?!'

'Yeah. I mean, like, *really* sexy.' He kissed her ear again.

'So you've been waiting all night to kiss my ear?!'

They stared at each other in silence for a few seconds.

'Not just your ear.'

Marie reached up and placed a hand behind his head, drawing him down for a kiss. After only a few seconds Kai broke away and abruptly sat up.

'What's the matter?'

'I don't know about you, but I suddenly feel really cold.'

'I'm not too bad.' Marie smiled. 'Come here and have a cuddle then, I'll warm you up.'

No.' Kai stood up. 'I think we ought to make a move.

'Marie rested herself up on her elbows. 'But we haven't had our swim yet.'

'Another time. There's a breeze picking up.' He held out a hand and helped her up.

She playfully pushed out her bottom lip. 'Have I done something wrong? I thought you fancied me.'

'I do. But look.' Kai held out his arms and even in the darkness she could see they were covered with goosebumps. He bent and picked up their towels. 'Come on, I'll drive you home.'

Half an hour later, they pulled up outside The Swagman's Rest. Kai switched off the engine and swiveled in his seat to face Marie. 'Listen, I've got a gardening job on in the morning, but it shouldn't take more than about an hour. As you've got the day off, maybe I can swing by and pick you up and we can do something.'

Marie was still annoyed that he had curtailed their evening on the beach so abruptly. She didn't doubt that he'd been genuinely cold, but she had a feeling something else was wrong. 'Won't you be out surfing with your mates?' she asked slightly huffily.

39

'Yeah, usually I would be, but I'll blow them off.'

'That's not very nice on your mates.'

'I'd much rather go out somewhere with you.'

Marie couldn't contain her smile. 'Then that would be lovely.'

'What do your reckon to the Koala Sanctuary?'

'The Lone Pines?'

'That's right, over on Jesmond Road. You know it?'

Marie's face lit up. 'Koala bears are my most favourite animals in the world. They're adorable! The very first thing I did when I arrived in Australia was visit the Cohuna Koala Park in Perth. That's the one I'd always dreamed of going to. And I've been to Lone Pines twice since I've been in Brisbane.' She noticed that Kai had an odd look on his face. 'What?'

'Nothing. I was just thinking about how beautiful you are.'

Marie put a hand to her face. 'Oh. Well, I'm not really, but thank you.'

'Trust me, you really are.' He leant over and kissed her lightly on the lips, then he sat back and sighed. 'I'll have a think about somewhere else we can go then,' he said, scratching his head. 'If you like animals, there are several zoos around here. Tell you what, the Australia Zoo up in Beerwah is pretty decent. It's not too far a hike.'

'I'm happy to go to Lone Pines again.' Marie laughed. 'Honestly, I'd move in and live there permanently if I could!'

Kai grinned. 'Yeah, it's a beautiful place. I actually do a bit of work there a couple of Saturdays every month.'

Marie's eyes widened. '*Really?*'

'Don't sound so surprised. I told you, I'm a jack-of-all-trades, me. The guy who runs it is an old mate of my Dad's.'

'That's *so* cool.'

'Pick you up about ten-thirty then?'

'Yes please.'

They kissed goodnight and Marie started to get out.

'Would you like me to walk you to the door?'

Marie turned back and rolled her eyes. 'It's, like, ten yards! I think I can just about make it on my own.' Her eyes widened. 'Unless there are crocodiles around here!'

Kai chuckled. 'On Valetta Street? Don't worry, you're safe. No crocs. You need to watch out for gators though.'

Marie laughed. 'Goodnight.'

Kai nodded at her. 'I'll wait just to make sure you get there safely. Just in case, y'know?'

'Of the gators?'

'Yep. Those and the funnelwebs.'

Marie frowned. 'Funnelwebs?'

'Spiders.' Kai sucked air through his teeth. 'Horny little bastards, they are. The males roam about in the summer looking for females to mate with. They'd eat a pretty thing like you for breakfast.'

Marie smiled. 'See you in the morning, Kai.'

He laughed. 'G'night.'

She shut the door and he watched as she walked up the short flight of stone steps to the porch. She seemed to loiter on the doorstep for a moment and looked back towards him. He put up a hand and blew her a kiss, but rather than

41

reciprocating and going inside, she came back down the steps.

Kai leaned over and wound down the passenger side window. 'What's up?'

She leant on the frame. 'What's the time?'

Kai looked at his watch. 'Ten after twelve.'

'Damn it!'

'What's the problem?'

'The door's locked and I can't get in,' Marie said exasperatedly. 'I remember now, when I first got the room, the landlord stressed I needed to be in by midnight or I'd be sleeping on the pavement.'

'Well that sucks!'

'He said something about gremlins and being indoors by midnight, so I kind of thought he was joking. Obviously he wasn't.'

Kai grinned. 'Wasn't it don't *feed* the gremlins after midnight?'

'He got that wrong. But it doesn't matter now. What the heck am I going to do?'

'Can't you bang on the door and wake him up?'

'I could I suppose. He's a nice enough guy, but I bet he won't be very happy. I don't want to fall out with him.'

'Listen, I tend to kip in the van over the summer, so I keep a mattress in the back. It's not exactly The Ritz, but it's somewhere to get your head down. There's room enough for two if you want to share.' Kai could see Marie was thinking about it. 'No funny stuff, I promise.'

Marie made doe eyes at him. 'That's a shame.'

'Huh?'

'Never mind. Yes, sure. Thank you.'

Kai smiled. 'Okay, hop in. We'll scoot up to Wynnum Mangrove Boardwalk. There's free overnight parking there. I'll drop you back here first thing in the morning and you can freshen up while I'm working.'

A short while later they parked up and sat talking and drinking the last of the beers they had bought for the beach. It had turned one-thirty by the time they climbed into the back of the van. Kai politely turned his back while Marie stripped down to her underwear and scrambled beneath the blanket. She watched while he removed his shirt and socks and began to unzip his shorts, but then he appeared to think better of it. When he got under the blanket she felt his leg brush against hers.

'Sorry,' he said, promptly shifting himself over to the edge.

'It's okay. I don't mind if you want to... you know.'

Marie had never had sex before. The nearest she had come to doing so was at Emily's sixteenth birthday party in the back bedroom of her parents' house with a boy from their school, Peter Welles; it had been little more than curious fumbling, which had ended almost before it had begun when Peter made a funny noise and hastily excused himself.

Kai rolled on to his side so that he was facing her. He was so close that Marie could feel his warm breath on her ear. 'Can I be straight up with you?'

'Of course.'

'Fact is, I'd like nothing more than make love with you. But you've had a few drinks – so have I for that matter – and it would be wrong of me to take advantage.'

43

Everything Sasha had warned Marie about was rushing through her head, but she didn't care. She yearned for him now. 'I haven't had *that* much to drink. And you wouldn't be taking advantage if I wanted it too.'

She tried to feel for him under the blanket, but he placed a hand over hers to stop her.

'Please, don't,' he said.

Marie pulled her hand out from under the blanket and sighed deeply. 'You *don't* fancy me, do you? First you made an excuse about it being too cold at the beach, now it's that we've had too much to drink.'

'Firstly, I *do* fancy you,' Kai said. 'Big time. And, yes, I admit I was making excuses at the beach. But it was really for the same reason. We've both had a lot to drink tonight and it would be so easy to abuse this little cohabiting situation we find ourselves in. You have no idea how much I want you, but I just think we both deserve better. And now I think we'd better stop talking about it and get some kip.' He chuckled. 'Or else you'll discover that your extraordinarily loveliness is matched only by the extraordinary weakness of my resolve.'

Now he's trying to make light of it, Marie thought. *If he really fancied me, we'd be doing it by now.* 'Okay,' she said flatly and rolled over, putting her back to him. 'Goodnight.'

Detecting her peevishness, Kai rested a hand on her shoulder. 'Please don't be mad. Honestly, I think we'll both regret it if we do it. We'll be seeing a lot of each other from now on – at least, I hope we will – and there'll be time enough for that once we get to know each other better.'

Marie thought about all the things Sasha had told her about Kookaburra Kai. It seemed that the stories couldn't have been further from the truth. She put a hand over his. 'It's fine. It's just not what I was expecting.'

'Expecting?'

'Sasha was telling me that you're a bit of a ladies man.'

'Was she now?'

'Yes,' Marie said. 'You've got a bit of a reputation with the girls at The Redback.' Kai fell silent. She could hear his rhythmic breathing. She waited for a moment and whispered, 'Is it true?'

'I'll make no bones about the fact I like girls. Heck, I'm a normal, red-blooded guy. And, sure, I've dated a few of them there – quite a lot, I guess, truth be told. But I know what they all think of me, and what they don't know, they make up.'

Smiling to herself in the darkness, Marie squeezed his hand. 'Goodnight,' she said softly.

Kai moved his body up close against hers, slid his arm around her and before long they were both sound asleep.

CHAPTER 5

The following morning, Kai dropped Marie off at The Swagman's Rest early and told her he'd be back to pick her up in an hour and a half.

She showered and spent twenty minutes trying to decide what to wear, eventually deciding on a Status Quo T-shirt, denim shorts and her favourite pink Nike trainers. Then she went downstairs and had a light breakfast in the dining room.

'Can't say as I heard you come in last night,' the landlord, Mr Bishop remarked as he brought in her tea and toast. 'I said to the missus when I locked up, I don't think Miss Shaw is in. Truth be told, I was a bit worried about you.'

Mr Bishop was a kindly soul, but as he had been so explicit about lights-out protocol, Marie felt awkward admitting her mistake. 'No, sorry,' she said, thinking on the hoof. 'I should have let you know, I'd intended staying over with a friend.' She felt more foolish lying than had she told him the truth.

'No harm done,' Mr Bishop said, smiling. 'Enjoy your breakfast, sweetheart.'

Kai returned for her just after ten and when he spotted Marie's shirt he gasped. 'You're in to the Quo!'

'They're the greatest. I went to see them live in London with my friend Emily a couple of years ago. That's where I got the shirt.' Mentioning Emily's name filled her with guilt. She hadn't spoken to her since Christmas, let alone sent any more postcards, and she made a mental note to give her a ring immediately after her regular weekly phone call home at the weekend.

'Oh, man, I'm so jealous,' Kai said. 'They haven't played Australia since seventy-eight. I wanted to go but I was too young.'

'They are *so* great live! You must try to see them if they come back.'

Marie enjoyed her third visit to the Lone Pines Koala Sanctuary even more than she did the first two. Having someone with her made the experience more fun. Kai insisted on paying the entrance charge too; Marie told him she was surprised that he couldn't get in for free as he knew the owner, but he said he wanted to support the cause by paying. Later, he bought them both popcorn and sodas too, slowly but surely nixing Sasha's claim that he was tight-fisted. He even shelled out to have a professional photo taken of the pair of them holding Banjo, one of the sanctuary's oldest resident bears. As they walked around the park's beautiful, natural landscaping, they held hands and Kai chatted away, telling her all about the history of the place.

'Did you know it was established in 1927? Almost sixty years ago.'

Marie did know that, but she claimed otherwise; she didn't want to undermine the fun he was having playing tour guide.

That evening they went for food in a little beachside bistro at Redland Bay. Marie, whose experience of burgers amounted to a Wimpy grill, thought the mountain of food on the plate in front of her was out of this world and she said so.

Kai chuckled. 'Well, the greenery is pretty much a given,' he said, tucking in. 'But it's not a proper Australian burger unless you've got bacon, pineapple, beetroot and a fried egg in your bun.'

'I've never seen a burger like it!'

'And the egg has to be super-runny,' Kai added as some yolk dribbled down his chin. He laughed. 'Just like this one.'

Marie reached over and wiped off the egg with a tissue.

Kai grinned. 'Thanks, mum.'

That night they walked out along Hillier Beach and found a secluded spot where they went swimming in their underwear beneath the soft glow of a full moon. The water was cold and they weren't in long. Afterwards, they toweled themselves off and huddled up close to get warm, sharing passionate kisses until it was time to leave. Once again, Marie felt slightly deflated that beyond fondling her breasts, Kai hadn't made a move to initiate sex. Nevertheless, she didn't allow it to tarnish what had otherwise been a wonderful day. And Kai dropped her off at the guesthouse with five minutes to spare before Mr Bishop locked up for the night.

She had a strange dream that night. She was sitting an exam in which the questions were ridiculously simple and she completed the paper with ease, feeling exceptionally pleased with herself. She was then standing in a library with Emily, who told her that they needed to send their answers through to the moderator to get the results. They did this by placing the test papers on a photocopier beside one of the bookshelves that was heaving with old, dust-covered books. Emily sent hers first and, when she lifted it off the platen, the result was already there, stamped on it in big red letters was the word **DISTINCTION**. Looking inordinately pleased with herself, she urged Marie to hurry up and send hers. Feeling reluctant to do so, Marie acceded and her assurance was crushed when she lifted the paper again to find the words **AVERAGE** and **NEEDS MORE POSTCARDS** and something else handwritten in brackets underneath that she couldn't decipher at first, but when she looked again it was very clear: Stay away from men! and it was signed, Sasha. Emily asked Marie why she was being so distant and questioned her on her results. Feeling ashamed, she lied and said they were the same as hers, and when Emily tried to take the test paper from her to see, she whipped it away and shouted, 'Don't you trust me? I thought we were friends!'

It was an innocuous enough dream in essence. Her twinge of guilt the previous day over her lack of staying in touch with Emily had presumably stimulated the bit about postcards and the remark signed by Sasha spoke for itself. Beyond that, Marie couldn't place any real significance on it. Why a test? And what was the significance of a library? Significant or otherwise, she felt extremely uncomfortable in the pit of her stomach when she woke and the dream was still lingering on her mind later that day.

On her way to work, she stopped at her usual call box and dialled her friend's number. It was five o'clock in the afternoon in Brisbane, which meant it was eight o'clock in the morning back in England, and Marie was hoping she might catch Emily before she went off to work. She let it ring for over a minute, but there was no reply. Needing to get to The Redback Tavern to begin her shift, she decided she would try again at the weekend as she'd originally intended.

When she took her break at eight, she had no sooner sat down than Sasha appeared and sat opposite her looking expectant.

'How did it go then, petal?'

'What?'

Sasha pursed her lips. 'Don't give me "what", with that innocent look on your face. You look like the cat that got the cream tonight. I've noticed you laughing and joking with the customers.'

'Isn't that part and parcel of the job?'

'Sure it is, but you've been *exceptionally* bubbly tonight. So, come on, are you going to spill the beans about your date with you know who the other night? I assume it went well.'

'It was good. *Really* good. And it's two dates now. We spent the whole day together yesterday too. Actually I suppose that makes it number three if you count the flying visit to see the lights. Anyway, we went to the koala sanctuary.'

'*Again*? How many times is that you've been now?'

Marie looked sheepish. 'Three.'

Sasha shook her head. 'I tell you, I've been living in Brisbane for years and I haven't visited it once.'

'You really should.'

'I'm sure I will one day.' Sasha looked her in the eye. 'So, it sounds like he's got his hooks in you good and proper. I just hope that's *all* he's got in you.'

At that moment, the back door of the inn opened and two of the other waitresses, Trudy and Marlene appeared.

Marie shook her head. 'You've all got him wrong.'

Trudy planted herself in the seat next to her. 'Who's got who wrong?'

'Marie was just telling me about her date with Kookaburra Kai.'

Marie frowned. 'Please don't keep calling him that.'

'Sorry.' Sasha filled two glasses of lemonade and passed them to Trudy and Marlene.

Trudy took a sip of lemonade. 'Oh my God, that is *so* good. My throat's dustier than a drongo's dong tonight.' She smiled at Marie. 'So what did you get up to?'

'Kai took me to the koala sanctuary, we had some dinner and later on we went for a swim. It was lovely.'

Trudy nodded approvingly. 'Nice one. And did you let him in your pants?'

Marlene rolled her eyes. 'Jeez, why don't you just say what you mean, Trude?!'

Trudy gave her a dismissive look and turned her attention back to Marie. 'Well? Did you put out or not?'

'No I did not!' Marie exclaimed. 'Honestly, this is like living in an episode of *Crown Court*!'

'What's that?' Marlene asked.

'A soap on British TV. Each episode is set in a courtroom and...' Marie trailed off. 'What the heck does it matter what it is? We didn't have sex and that's all I'm saying on the matter.'

Sasha and Trudy exchanged glances.

'Good on you, missy.' Marlene chuckled. 'Speaking for m'self, I'd rather sleep with Edith Cowan than Kai Garrett.'

'You'd bed anyone as long as there wasn't a pecker involved,' Trudy said.

Marlene grinned. 'Guilty as charged.'

'Who's Edith Cowan?' Marie asked.

Marlene swallowed a mouthful of lemonade. 'The first Australian woman to serve as a member of parliament.' She shook her head sorrowfully. 'God, she was one sour-faced old bird.'

'I've no idea who that is,' Marie said.

'No reason you should have, petal,' Sasha said. 'Likes her politics does our Marlene.'

Trudy laughed. 'And a bit of mummified cooch by the sound of it.' She saw the look of disgust on Marie's face. 'She died years ago, babe.'

'Nineteen-thirty-two,' Marlene chipped in.

'But well done you for keeping your lady bits a Garrett-free zone,' Trudy continued. 'There's not many here can lay claim to such moral resilience.' She emptied her glass. 'Self included,' she muttered.

Marie had a fleeting mental image of Kai and Trudy together. The thought made her feel ill and she had a sudden urge to retaliate somehow. 'We did do a few things together, obviously. Private stuff, I mean. But it's like I was trying to say to Sasha just now, he's not like everyone in this place seems to think he is. He was a consummate gentleman.'

Trudy glanced at Marlene with a smirk on her face. Then she stood up and rested a hand on Marie's shoulder. 'Whatever you say. Just don't come crying that you weren't warned when he does the dirty on you, eh?' She walked back to the door and held it open. 'Come on, Marls, back to the salt mines.'

When the two girls had gone, Sasha came over and put her arm around Marie. 'Don't let Trudy get under your skin, eh?'

'She hasn't.'

'Well, you don't look so happy now. Honestly, petal, all the girls here are the kiss and tell sort. They love to brag, and Trudy's the worst. She's all mouth that one. If Kai's the gent you say he is – and, like I told you, to be fair I've never actually been out with him for first hand experience one way or the other – the chances are she didn't get to sleep with him. Girls like her don't take rejection kindly, they feel humiliated, so they think it's better to let people believe they've done the deed.'

'So all that stuff you warned me about the other day might not be true then.'

Sasha shrugged. 'I was looking out for you, telling you what I'd heard. But no, I guess maybe not.'

Marie smiled. 'I appreciate you looking out for me.'

'Cool. Come on then, let's get back to work before Jimbo comes hunting for us.'

CHAPTER 6

The first time that she and Kai made love wasn't exactly the idyllically romantic interlude she had imagined it would be. He was gentle and attentive enough, putting her pleasure before his own, but – perhaps predictably – it happened on the mattress in the back of his camper van; it was humid and sweaty, and she was actually quite relieved when it was over. The second time was more enjoyable and as they got to know each other's bodies, the experience improved every time thereafter.

The next three months drifted past in a bit of a blur. It had never been Marie's intention to stay in Brisbane for more than a few weeks, a couple of months at most. But meeting Kai Garrett had changed everything. When she called her parents to tell them she had revised her plans and was now going to be staying on for a bit longer and the reasons why, they expressed deep concern:

How old was this lad? ('*Four* years your senior? That's a significant gap at your age, Marie.')

How long had she known him? ('Only a week and you're abandoning your trip? That's foolishly impulsive.')

What does he do for a living? ('This and that hardly sounds like a stable career plan, does it? And he's a *surfer* too? Oh, Marie, please think this over before you do anything rash.')

Both her mother and father tried to impress on her that she was young and it would be a terribly wasted opportunity not to see as much of the country as possible before returning home at the end of the year.

But Marie was adamant: she intended to remain in Brisbane to be with Kai. She even made noises that, if things worked out between them, she might not actually be coming home at all; she had been rethinking university, and the whole idea of continuing her education simply didn't appeal to her any more. Her parents were horrified, telling her that it was a preposterous thing to say and she needed to sort her ideas out pronto.

The phone call ended in anger when Marie hung up on them.

The visa that Marie had obtained to travel around the country was valid for a period of twelve months and hadn't been inexpensive. Infuriated by the way her parents had spoken to her, she immediately started to look at options to extend her stay. It wasn't quite as difficult as she thought it might be, but there were still hoops to jump through. Emigration worked on a points system and she scored high on most of the requisite criteria: her age certainly worked in her favour, then there was standard of education, a proficiency in the English language, sponsorship – Kai's parents stepped up to the plate on that one – work experience, and several other minutiae. The fact that she was in a relationship with an Australian national, with a view to possible marriage (which had been an exaggeration, but not beyond the realms of possibility), also added weight to her case.

Kai had no place of his own. As he'd told Marie, he mostly slept in the van during the summer months, but for the rest of the year he would crash at his parents' house in Mango Hill on the northern reaches of Brisbane. His Uncle Wally and Aunt Liz owned premises at Woorim Ocean Beach on Bribie Island, where they had established a small but thriving business renovating and selling pleasure boats and marine equipment. There was a small, unoccupied flat above Woorim Watercraft, which, although he didn't really need to, Wally took advantage of for additional storage space.

One day, Kai approached Wally with a proposal he couldn't refuse and a financial arrangement was reached between them. He worked hard to clear the flat and make it habitable, and in April – as summer gave way to autumn and temperatures dipped to the high-end teens – he and Marie moved in together.

Two weeks after they did so, Marie received the paperwork approving her Australian citizenship.

Business at Woorim Watercraft tended to tail off after the summer, but Wally, having just lost one of his two full-time employees, offered Kai the position.

'Having a young, good-looking fella like you around the place, a bit of extra trade is a cert.' Wally guffawed. 'And I'm guessing you could use the extra scratch too. After all, you've got that pretty young Sheila of yours to feed now.'

It wasn't actually the first time Wally had tried to schmooze his nephew into working for him, and he was delighted when Kai accepted.

Marie carried on working part-time at The Redback Tavern where, in her presence, Kai's name was seldom ever mentioned. Now that he and Marie were officially a couple, it was almost as if the other girls working there were envious. And why wouldn't they be? Contrary to his unfounded reputation, Kai was an extremely desirable catch.

The only one among them who ever spoke to Marie about him was Sasha. One day, as they were finishing their shift, she called her to one side.

'So how are things going between you two lovebirds?'

'Great.'

'It must be a couple of months already since you moved in.'

'Almost three.'

Sasha laughed. 'And they said it wouldn't last!' She saw Marie frown. 'I'm joshing you, petal. I'm really glad it's working out for you.' A look of doubt crossed her face. 'And it really *is* working out, isn't it?'

'I said, it's great. Why?'

'Oh, I don't know. It's just that I've noticed you haven't been quite your usual sparkling self the last few weeks. And you seem to be tired all the time. I guess I'm kind of worried about you.'

Marie smiled. 'Oh, there's nothing to worry about; I'm fine. I *have* been a bit tired though. Kai works all hours now. He does most days for his Uncle in the store, but he still flits about doing oddments for other people too and he's often out pretty late. I don't like going to bed before he's home safe and sound. It can be one or two in the morning some nights. And even though it's late, he's usually still feeling a bit...' – she suddenly looked a little uncomfortable – '...well, you know. Guys will be guys.'

Sasha grinned. 'When my Ethan's bushed, it's hard to get him to raise his eyebrows, let alone anything useful! The honeymoon period definitely ended for us months ago. But speaking of honeymoons, Ethan finally asked me to marry him last night.'

Marie's face lit up and, with a squeal, she threw her arms around Sasha and hugged her tightly. 'That's *amazing* news. Congratulations!' She released her from her hold and took a step back. 'It *is* amazing news, isn't it? I mean, I'm assuming you said yes?'

'Nah, I told him to go and suck on a bushman's goolies.'

Marie's mouth dropped open. 'Oh my God, you *didn't*?!'

Sasha chortled and gave her a playful shove. 'Don't be a drongo, of course I didn't!' She held out her hand to show Marie the diamond band on her ring finger. 'What do you think?'

'That's gorgeous!'

'Isn't it though? We've been together for four years. I've only been waiting for the dopey bastard to propose like, *forever*!'

Marie smiled at her warmly. 'I'm really pleased for you, Sash.'

'Thanks, petal. Listen, we're having a little party weekend after next. There probably won't be more than a dozen of us, but you and Kai are invited.'

'We'd love to come!'

'Cool.'

'No way!' Kai stripped off his T-shirt, mopped the sweat off his face with it and walked into the bathroom.

Marie followed him in. 'But I've already said we'd go. Sash is my best friend.'

'Exactly. She's *your* friend, not mine.' Kai spun the hot tap and ran some water into the sink. 'She's done me no favours. If you'd listened to her, we'd never have gotten past our first date.'

'But she's really nice. I've only met Ethan a couple of times briefly when he dropped Sash off at work, but he seemed nice too. Please, Kai.'

'You can go on your own if you like, I'm not stopping you, but there's Buckley's chance of you dragging me there.'

'*Please*,' Marie repeated imploringly. 'It's an important night for them. I don't want to let them down.'

Kai bent over the sink and splashed water over his face. 'It's been a pig of a day and I'm knackered. We'll talk about it tomorrow.'

Quickly unbuttoning the top of her nightgown, Marie moved in close and snaked her arms around him, pressing her breasts against his back. 'Can't we talk about it *now*?' She dropped a hand down and deftly released the button on the top of his jeans, lowering the zip and sliding her hand inside. 'I don't want to go on my own,' she said despondently. 'I want my man there with me.' Peering over Kai's shoulder, she could see his face looking back at her from the bathroom mirror. 'Please say you'll come.' She softly kissed his neck. 'It would make me really happy.'

Kai sighed and lifted her arms away so that he could turn around and face her. 'Alright, I'll think about it, okay?'

He moved to kiss her, but she turned her face away and lowered her hand to the front of his jeans, feeling him through the material, her fingers toying with the swelling. Then, abruptly, she withdrew them. 'Well, don't think about it for *too* long.'

Kai grinned. 'You little…!'

Pouting at him provocatively, Marie backed slowly away, then turned and scampered out of the bathroom and across the living room.

Kai chased after her, catching up at the bedroom door and effortlessly whisking her off her feet with his muscular arms. Carrying her over to the bed, he roughly deposited her on the blankets.

She gazed up at him, wide-eyed and breathless with excitement. 'Well?'

Kai loomed over her, his eyes filled with desire. 'We'll go to the bloody party, okay? Happy now?'

Smiling jubilantly, Marie threw her arms around his shoulders and drew him towards her. 'Very.'

Marie regretted coaxing Kai to join her at the party. He made no bones about the fact he didn't want to be there and was in a sulk from the moment they arrived. While everybody else was standing around chatting, he stubbornly refused to be sociable, stepping away from the throng and sitting by himself beside a table where Sasha had laid out a selection of tasty nibbles. Marie tried a couple of times to get him involved, even physically pulling him to his feet when the Berlin number *Take My Breath Away* came on and getting him to slow-dance with her: 'Come on, you *love* this one.' Kai obliged, but as soon as the song finished he went and sat back down.

Finally, Marie couldn't bite her tongue any longer and, pulling over a chair, she sat down beside him.

'What's the matter?' she said, trying to temper her ire.

Kai didn't look at her. 'You have to ask?' he replied sullenly.

'I know you didn't really want to come, but…'

'Too right I didn't want to come. I hardly know anyone here and those I do know I don't like. I just want to go home.'

'Well, we're here, so can't you just grit your teeth and smile for a couple of hours instead of sitting here on your own with a face like a wet weekend? We don't have to stay until the end.'

'Thank Christ for that.' Reaching over, Kai selected a small savoury from one of the plates on the table and pushed it into his mouth whole.

'Come on,' Marie said, her tone softening. 'Why don't you go and speak to Ethan?'

'Why?' Kai said, spitting crumbs.

'To be sociable. Talk to him about surfing, or the store, or… oh, I don't know, *anything*! But please don't just sit here moping. You're making me look bad.'

Kai shot her a withering look. 'Well, pardon me, God forbid I should make *you* look bad.'

'I didn't mean it like that. I just meant…'

'I'm not in the mood to be sociable. Just leave me alone.'

Marie exploded. 'For God's sake, Kai, don't be such a fucking bore!'

At that precise moment the music fell silent between tracks. Mortified, Marie looked up to see that everyone had stopped talking and all eyes were on her. She felt herself colouring up and then, blessedly, the next track on the turntable started, killing the silence in the room and conversations resumed as if nothing had happened.

'Thanks for making me look a total prat,' Marie hissed at Kai.

He shrugged. 'That one's on you, not me.' He stood up. 'I'm going out for a ciggy.'

Marie was incensed. 'Fine. Don't bother coming back!'

As Kai disappeared through the patio doors, she felt the tears well in her eyes.

Sasha appeared and took Kai's empty seat beside her. 'Is everything okay, petal?'

'Not really. Look, I'm sorry about that outburst just now. I didn't mean to ruin the party.'

'You haven't ruined anything.'

'It's just Kai's behaving like a spoilt child.' She put a finger to the corner of her eye and dabbed away a tear.

'Don't cry,' Sasha said, grinning. 'Your mascara will run and you'll look like a right clown.'

Marie sniffed. 'Yes, sorry.'

'Don't apologise. Come and have a cuddle.' Sasha put an arm around her.

Marie rested her head on her friend's shoulder. 'That's the first time we've argued since we've been together,' she said sadly.

'Seriously?' Sasha said incredulously. 'What *are* you two, bloody saints or something?'

'Well, we did bicker once when we were out food shopping, but other than that, yes, that was the first.'

Sasha kissed the top of Marie's head. 'Don't worry, petal, it won't be the last. Me and Ethan argue all the time and it's usually about stuff that doesn't matter a shit. But you know what the best part of arguing is?'

Marie sat up. 'What?'

Sasha winked at her. 'Making up of course! Look, I know he didn't want to come tonight and I know it's because of me. But he made the effort, didn't he? And, I tell you, that's more than Ethan would have done if it had been your party and he didn't like you. You've got yourself a keeper there, girl. Go on, go out and speak to him, and if you need to leave, that's totally cool.'

Marie smiled at her warmly. 'Thanks, Sash.'

'What for?'

'Being my friend.'

'Don't be a drongo!'

They hugged and kissed each other on the cheek. At that moment, as if on cue, Marlene appeared and stood looking down at them with a grin on her face. 'Hello, hello, what's with all the canoodling?' She sounded tipsy. 'Can anyone join in?'

Marie and Sasha stood up. 'Go on,' Sasha said. 'I'll see you Monday night.'

As Marie left through the patio doors, Sasha turned her attention to Marlene. 'Come on then, you! You look like you could use a top-up.' She hooked an arm through her friend's and led her over to the drinks cabinet.

CHAPTER 7

Sasha had certainly been right about arguments – and the making up. But over the next couple of years the spats between Marie and Kai increased in frequency and the making up afterwards less pleasurable. They were usually initiated by something that didn't really matter and ended up as full-blown shouting matches. And, as their tolerance of one another's irksome little habits gradually deteriorated, the most trivial things were enough to trigger yet another dispute; forks repeatedly put in the tray for the knives in the cutlery drawer; a bra left on the floor at the end of the bed; the fact Marie sat around watching TV in the afternoons – she had become addicted to a new soap, *Home and Away* – instead of keeping the flat tidy; the Hoover bag not having been emptied – again!

Marie's parents were still less than enchanted with what they deemed to be their daughter's insouciantly impulsive life choice, but they hadn't wanted her to become estranged to them. As such, they had made every effort, however patently reluctant, to accept it.

So it was that, in the summer of 1988, a month before Christmas, Marie's family visited. She was glad to see them, especially Thomas and Lucy, who had both grown up beyond belief in the three years since she had last set eyes on them.

They stayed in a hotel not far from Woorim Ocean Beach and Marie met up with them every day, showing them around the sights of Brisbane. Kai joined them whenever work commitments permitted.

Although Kai made a half-hearted effort to get along with Mr and Mrs Shaw, he was patently uncomfortable in their presence and the conversations they shared always felt awkward. Meanwhile, for no other reason than the circumstances under which their lives had intersected, Marie's father took an immediate dislike to Kai. Nevertheless, as best as they could be, differences were holstered for the duration and they had a reasonably pleasant, if occasionally strained couple of weeks together, which was only blighted on the day before her family were due to leave.

Marie had prepared a farewell meal. Kai had taken on additional work, almost as if he wanted to spend as much time away from her as possible. His current project was extensively landscaping a garden for the Baileys, a wealthy family with a property up near Pelican Waters. He hadn't returned when it was time to eat and they had their food without him. When he finally rolled in an hour later, after the table had been cleared, Marie let rip on him and a blazing row ensued. Rather than getting involved, her mother and father left them to it, rounding up Thomas and Lucy and taking them out for ice cream.

The family had an early flight back to England the next morning, so when they returned an hour later to say their farewells, they found Marie in tears and Kai had gone out. There was an uneasy air of unspoken grievances hanging over everyone, and when Marie's father took the children downstairs to wait for their taxi, her mother hung back for a moment and had a quiet word. She told Marie that both she and her father had been shocked by the argument, that they believed Kai to be totally unsuitable to her, and implored her to consider returning to England, further adding that her father had claimed he would disown her if she didn't.

'You really don't get it, do you, Mum? I love Kai and he loves me. Sure, we have the occasional argument – heck, who doesn't? But my life is here now and if you and Dad can't accept that... well, I'm sorry, but I'm not coming back to the UK and that's that.'

When Marie accompanied her mother downstairs to say a last goodbye, her father was waiting with her brother and sister, idly looking in the window of Woorim Watercraft. He looked expectantly at her mother and Marie saw her give him a little shake of her head.

At that moment, the taxi they'd booked to take them back to the hotel appeared and pulled up at the kerb. Thomas and Lucy hugged Marie goodbye, but neither of her parents embraced her and, without even looking at her again, they ushered the children into the cab and climbed in behind them.

Marie watched sadly as the car pulled away, paused at the junction at the end of the street and then disappeared around the corner.

Her family were gone.

Marie had never once doubted her decision to stay in Australia with Kai back in 1986. But after her parents' visit in 1988 the arguments between them worsened and they shared less and less moments of intimacy. He would often spend the night away too, under the pretext that he was working into the evenings on the Bailey's landscaping and it was better to take advantage of their generous hospitality than journey back from Pelican Waters so late. Marie didn't believe a word of it and as his overnight absences became more frequent she started to wonder if he might be playing away.

Her fears were consolidated one evening at work when Trudy happened to mention that she had seen Kai out at the beach that afternoon with a stunning blonde wearing a bikini that barely covered her modesty. Marie tried to hide the hurt in her eyes, but Trudy could see her candour had upset her and, instead of backing off, she maliciously twisted the knife:

'Honestly, what I wouldn't give to have perfect tits like that girl.' She cupped her own breasts. 'They made mine look like two aspirins on a surfboard!'

That night Kai actually came home and Marie tackled him about it. She had expected blunt denial, but instead he admitted it. Yes, he had been with a girl at the beach, but she was the Bailey's eighteen-year-old daughter, Tonia, and he was simply making good on a promise to take her surfing. When Marie accused him of messing around behind her back, he took her in his arms, told her he loved her and would never do that, let alone with "a kid" like Tonia.

They made love that night for the first time in months, although to Marie it felt as if they were merely going through the motions. Afterwards, as she lay in the darkness listening to Kai gently snoring beside her, she made up her mind that she was going to take steps to ensure he would never abandon her.

67

Her old friend, Emily, had been on her mind and the following morning, she picked up the telephone and made a call to England.

The voice on the end of the line didn't sound particularly pleased to hear from her: 'Marie? What do you want? It's almost eleven, I was just going to bed.'

'I'm *so* sorry I haven't been in touch, Em.'

'Haven't been in *touch*?! I haven't heard a peep out of your for, like, eighteen months!'

'I'm sorry, okay? Life here kind of got busy.'

'Yes, so I heard. I bumped into your Mum in town just after Christmas. She told me you're shacked up with some surfer.' Emily imbued the word surfer with an unbridled note of derision.

'Yes, his name's Kai. And he's not just some airhead surfer.'

Marie went on to outline how she and Kai had met and moved in together, how happy she had been, but how things between them had deteriorated so badly in recent months. Emily listened in silence, and only when Marie concluded – 'I can't be certain, but I think he's cheating on me, Em!' – did she speak.

'Have you finished?'

Marie was slightly taken aback by the coldness in her old friend's voice. 'Yes.'

'I don't care, Marie. I don't hear from you for months on end and you're only calling now because you've got a problem.'

'I apologised, didn't I?'

'Oh, and that makes everything okay, does it? You were my best friend, we did *everything* together, but the moment something better came along you threw it all away.'

'But I wanted your advice.'

'You see? *Still* it's all about you. Have you asked me how *I'm* getting on? What might be happening in *my* life?'

Marie fell silent for a moment. 'Sorry. What is happening in your life?'

'Not that it really has anything to do with you, but I just got a promotion at work – 'I'm an assistant manager now – and I'm dating Mickey Bird.'

'Mickey *Bird*?' Marie laughed. 'You've got to be kidding me!'

Emily didn't laugh. 'What's so funny about that? We're very happy together, we make each other laugh and we've been talking about maybe getting engaged.'

'I'm sorry,' Marie said. 'I wasn't making fun of you.'

'Make all the fun you want. Like I said, I don't care.'

'Please, Em, I had an idea about Kai, but I wanted someone to hear me out.'

'You haven't got friends over there?'

'I have, but…'

'Then ask them. If you think he's cheating on you, just dump him. Or don't. But please don't call me again.'

Before Marie could respond, there was a click and the line went dead.

Although a lingering twinge of doubt remained, Marie wanted to believe Kai about Tonia Bailey. But he was a good-looking man and a natural-born charmer. Even if

Trudy's sighting of him with Tonia had been innocent, she was certain it was only going to be a matter of time before some floozy turned his head and he would be gone. Their relationship was reaching crisis level and she was beginning to fear that her life in Australia was under threat. She needed to take action without delay.

The day after her call with Emily, she popped her birth control pill out of its foil packet and flushed it down the toilet. She wasn't due to work that evening and, having told Kai that she had a surprise for him and making him promise he would be home, she cooked up one of his favourite meals: pan-seared fillet of barramundi with rustic fregola sarda pasta in a sweet and tangy agrodolce sauce made with aromatic shallots and plump raisins. Neither she nor Kai were big drinkers and, although they both enjoyed a glass of wine, they seldom indulged. However, Marie bought a bottle of chardonnay.

Kai was delighted when he saw what she had prepared for them. While they ate, they talked, and they both apologised for the way they had been behaving to one another in recent months. They vowed to make more of an effort to be less critical of each other's foibles and when they went to bed that night they made love. Kai treated Marie as tenderly as he had done the first time they were together, while she, responding to his attentiveness with the requisite moans of pleasure, lay wondering how long it might take her to conceive.

It took considerably longer than she anticipated.

One particularly chilly evening in July, when Marie was serving a customer at The Redback Tavern, she started to feel faint. Sasha – who happened to be attending the neighbouring table – had noticed Marie was looking peaky when she arrived to start her shift and she had been keeping half an eye on her. Sasha saw her sway and put a hand to her brow and she reacted swiftly. Excusing herself to the man who had been umming and ahing over whether to have the king prawn salad or the pork chops, Sasha ran over and put an arm around Marie's waist just as her legs started to buckle.

'You okay, petal?'

'I don't feel so good.' Marie mumbled.

'Pauline!' Sasha called out. 'Can you come and serve table six? Gail, can you see to 7.'

Two of the other waitresses hurried over. Apologising to the young couple on the table Marie had been tending, Sasha helped her out to the staff bathroom where she was promptly sick.

After Marie had cleaned up, Sasha took her out back and made her a cup of tea to settle her stomach.

'How are you feeling now?'

'A bit fragile,' Marie replied, rubbing her stomach.

'I knew you weren't well. You should have cried off tonight.'

'I didn't want to let Mr Ferris down.'

'Bugger Jimbo,' Sasha scoffed. 'We'd have managed. Hell, we've had to cope with as many as three off in the past. Do you reckon it's something you ate?'

'I don't know.'

'Or a bug?'

'Could be, I guess.'

Sasha laughed. 'You're not preggers, are you?'

The words cut through Marie like a knife and she felt a rush of excitement and fear all balled into one. Could it possibly be true? Her period was a couple of days late, but she was well used to that. She forced a nervous smile. 'Of course not. Don't be daft.' Finishing her tea, she said, 'I feel a bit better now, I'd better get back to work.'

Sasha frowned. 'I still think you ought to go home.'

'Honestly, I'm fine.'

She didn't sleep a wink that night. The following morning, as soon as Kai had headed out to work, Marie threw on her clothes and ran to the pharmacy three streets away. Purchasing a pregnancy testing kit, she ran all the way back home and breathlessly ripped open the packaging and scanned the accompanying leaflet. She went through to the bathroom and, even though there was nobody else in the flat, locked the door. Having done what the instruction sheet had informed her she needed to do, she sat back on the toilet seat, staring impatiently at the test stick and willing it to reward her with the result she wanted.

CHAPTER 8

Although Kai and Marie's relationship had improved since their heart-to-heart, arguments between them were still frequent. His work for the Baileys had ended and he was back to dividing his time working in Woorim Watercraft and his usual round of cash-in-hand odd-jobs, some of which still seemed to command overnight stays, much to Marie's chagrin.

When Kai arrived home that evening, Marie had prepared another special meal. He was surprised to see her.

'I thought you were working tonight.'

She smiled. 'No, I phoned in sick.'

'You're sick?' His face filled with concern. 'What's wrong?'

'I *phoned in* sick, I'm not *actually* sick.'

'Okay.' Kai looked confused. 'So what gives?'

'Sit down and I'll tell you.'

'Alright. As it happens, I've got something to tell you too.' He took a seat and Marie laid out the food and took a seat opposite him. 'Man, this looks great. What is it?'

'Chicken Parmigiana.'

Kai forked some into his mouth. 'Mmm, that's amazing! So, what's going on? Why did you call in sick?'

Marie felt her heartbeat quickening. She smiled. 'You said you had some news. You go first.'

'Okay.' Kai took another mouthful of food. 'You remember the landscape job I did for the Baileys?'

'Of course.'

'Well, they were so chuffed they recommended me to some friends of theirs who need some work done.'

'That's great!'

'I need to drive over and assess what they need before I commit.'

'That's fair enough.'

Kai shifted awkwardly in his seat. 'Yeah, but the thing is, these people live over in Lightning Ridge.'

'I have no idea where that is.'

'It's about an hour south of Goodooga.'

Marie laughed. 'Did you just make that name up?'

'No.'

'Then stop messing with me. I have no idea where any of those places are.'

'Lightning Ridge is, like, a little over seven hundred kilometres west of Brisbane.'

Marie's smile faded. 'That's insane. Surely these people must have someone living there who can do the work for them?'

'Based on Jack Bailey's glowing recommendation, they want me. They're offering scratch we can't afford to turn down, love, *and* they've said they'll pay my travelling expenses to go over and size things up. It's Wednesday tomorrow, isn't it?'

'Yes,' Marie said solemnly.

'Cool. I'm figuring I'll head up there tomorrow, then I can be back Friday. If I accept their proposal – and right now I can't think of a good reason why I wouldn't – they want me to start work in September.'

'I'm assuming that means you'll be staying away from home?'

Kai laughed. 'Obviously. It's like an eight-hour drive each way. I'll be back whenever I can though.'

'How long is this job likely to take?'

'I can't be sure until I know exactly what it is they want. A couple of months I'd guess.'

Marie's eyes widened. 'A couple of *months*?!'

'Maybe less. I don't know right now.'

They fell silent.

Kai chewed on a piece of chicken. 'Are you mad with me?'

'No. It's just… I don't know. Two months is a hell of a long time.'

'They're expecting me tomorrow, but if you really don't want me to do it, I'll tell them I can't.' He reached over and placed a hand over Marie's. 'Honestly, I'll go give them a call right now.'

Marie sighed. 'No, it's fine. Like you said, we can use the money, especially…' she trailed off.

Kai grinned. 'Thanks, love. It'll be worth it.' His expression changed. 'Sorry, you had something to tell me too?'

Marie's face brightened. 'Yes, well, you know how you were saying just now we could use some extra money.'

'Yeah, sure.'

'Well…' – Marie took a deep breath – '…it'll come in handy when we have an extra mouth to feed.'

Kai's was about to take another mouthful of food. He paused his fork at his mouth and frowned. 'What?'

'An extra mouth to feed.'

'I heard you. What are you talking about?'

'We're going to be a mummy and daddy!'

Kai stared at her for a moment, then he threw down his cutlery, got up from the table and walked over to the window where he stood with his back to her.

Marie suddenly felt nauseous. 'What's the matter? Aren't you pleased?' Kai didn't reply. She stood up and went over to him. 'Kai? I said aren't you pleased?'

He didn't look at her. 'How far gone are you?'

'I don't know, I haven't spoken to the doctor yet. I only found out this morning when I did a pee test.'

'Then you *might* not be?' Kai turned to face her.

'I did it twice to be sure. I think I am.'

'Pissing on sticks doesn't make you pregnant, Marie!' Kai grabbed her by her shoulders, his eyes searching hers for answers. 'You're on the bloody pill. You can't get pregnant when you're on the pill. Unless…'

She shrugged his hands away. 'I don't know, do I? I'm just telling you what the test said.'

Kai huffed. 'Well, you need to be absolutely sure before you go laying shit like that on me.'

'I told you I'll speak to the doctor, didn't I?'

'Well make sure you do. Soon as.'

Marie looked at him tearfully. 'I thought you'd be over the moon. You always said you wanted to be a daddy.'

'Sure I do, *one* day. But not yet. I'm way too young to be dealing with a rug-rat. You just speak to the bloody doc and get it confirmed one way or the other.'

'And if I am?'

Kai scowled at her. 'Get rid of it.'

Marie gasped. 'Please say you don't mean that!'

'Too bloody right I mean it. We're not having a kid and that's final.'

'If I am pregnant, I'm having it.'

Kai walked over to the door. 'Then you're on your own.' He slipped on his coat. 'I'm not talking about this any more tonight. I'm gonna sleep in the camper.'

'You can't, it's freezing out there tonight!'

Kai paused at the open door. 'Remember, make sure you see the doc in the morning. I'm heading up to Lightning Ridge first thing, I'll give you a call when I get there.'

'Please, Kai, you can't just go off like this. Not now.'

'I'll see you on Friday evening.'

For the second night in a row, Marie hardly slept at all. All sorts of options were jostling for attention in her head. The obvious solution to her problem screamed out at her from the photo of her family on the bedside table, but she didn't want to acknowledge the fact. Had her parents been right after all and she simply hadn't been able, or willing to see it? Perhaps Kai wasn't right for her and she didn't belong in Australia.

By the time the morning light began to peep through the curtains, she had made up her mind. Even though she was in little doubt that she was pregnant, she would make an appointment to see the doctor that morning and speak to Kai again once she knew for sure one way or another.

Marie's visit to the surgery that afternoon confirmed what she already knew in her heart; she was approximately seven weeks pregnant. The doctor congratulated her and gave her the requisite details so that she could register with the nearby clinic.

She worked her shift that night in a trance, getting orders wrong and spilling a gin and tonic down an older lady's best dress. When Jim Ferris lost his temper with her, she apologised profusely and said she wasn't feeling well, so he sent her home. She expected to find a message from Kai on the answer machine, but there was nothing. Waiting up until after midnight, she was about to give up and go to bed when the phone rang. She answered on the second ring and it was him.

'Where have you been?' Marie asked angrily. 'I thought you were going to call when you got there?'

'And that's what I'm doing,' Kai replied curtly. 'I've only just arrived an hour ago.'

'But you were going to set off first thing this morning.'

'I did. But I got a flat thirty kilometres out of Lightning Ridge. Had to wait for five hours for a tow truck and the bastard charged me a hundred bucks. Calvin – that's Mr Jessop, the guy who wants me to do his garden – said he'll reimburse me though.' He sighed. 'Anyway, doesn't matter now, I'm here.'

'I'm sorry we argued last night.'

If Marie was expecting a reciprocal apology, it didn't come.

'Did you see the doc?'

'Yes.'

'And?'

The line went silent.

'Well that answers that,' Kai said irritably. 'How far gone?'

'Seven weeks,' Marie whispered.

'Not too late to do something about it then.'

'I told you I'm not terminating it.'

'You need to think long and hard about that, Marie. It's me or the kid. You can't have both.'

'What sort of horrible ultimatum is that?' Marie sobbed. 'Please don't let this tear us apart. You'd be such a great father. I was hoping it would pull us closer together, that's why…'

'Why you stopped taking the pill without consulting with me first.'

'You knew!'

'Of course I didn't know, but I'm not a galah. I had a lot of time to think driving out here and I figured it out. How else could you get pregnant? You should have told me before you did that, Marie. We could have discussed it like adults.'

'But clearly you'd have said no.'

'Damned right. But I'd have had a chance to explain my side of things rather than have it sprung on me that you were knocked up.'

'So is that it then? Your final word?'

Kai sighed. 'Yes. Listen, I'm not going to come back on Friday. Mr Jessop has offered me a bonus if I'll start right away and I said I would. I'll come back week after next, it'll give us both time to cool off.'

Marie wanted to say *I won't be here*, because in that moment she knew that she wouldn't. Instead, she simply said, 'Sure.'

'I'll call at the weekend. Goodnight, Marie.'

'Goodbye, Kai.'

Marie put down the receiver and went through to the bathroom to get ready for bed. Midway through brushing her teeth, her legs gave out beneath her and she crumpled to the carpet and sobbed until there were no more tears left to cry.

The following morning, when she had eaten breakfast – a simple slice of buttered toast, which she still found difficult to stomach – she called and booked a flight back to England late the following Tuesday afternoon, then spent the rest of the day tidying her affairs.

Before she set off for her shift at The Redback Tavern, she tried calling her parents to let them know what was happening, but there was no reply.

When she handed in her resignation, Jim Ferris – who was busy in the kitchen checking over a delivery of vegetables – was initially a little sniffy with her.

'It's a pretty poor show, Marie,' he said testily. 'You know the score: a minimum one weeks' notice. It's not much to ask, a lot of places expect a month.'

'I'm really sorry, Mr Ferris. Something unexpected has come up.'

Ferris had always liked Marie. The annoyance on his face softened. 'Are you alright?'

'Yes, I'm fine. I just have to… move on. I wouldn't be dropping this on you so suddenly unless I had to.'

'Well, there's no harm done, I guess. We do what we have to do, eh?'

Marie smiled. 'Yes.'

'It's been an absolute pleasure having you here. We're going to miss your smiling face at The Redback – staff *and* customers. Me too. Just you take care of yourself and be sure you don't forget us.'

'Never.' Marie put her arms around him. He was a little surprised by the display of affection, but he put an arm around her shoulders and returned the gesture.

'Thank you, Mr Ferris. For everything.'

During break, Sasha sat listening in silence, an expression of disbelief on her face, as Marie explained everything to her.

'Jeez.' Sasha puffed out her cheeks and exhaled slowly. 'And you're absolutely positive you've got a bun in the oven?'

'The doctor confirmed it.'

'No doubt?'

'None.'

Sasha shook her head. 'Well that explains you puking your guts up the other night I guess. And Kai would honestly rather split up with you than have the sprog?'

'It seems that way, yes.'

'Oh, petal, I'm so sorry.' Sasha came over and sat down beside Marie. 'Is there no way you can try and make him see sense?'

Marie shook her head. 'As far as he's concerned, it's not open for discussion.'

'So when are you leaving?'

'I'm booked to fly out on Tuesday.'

'Without even telling him? Just like that?'

Marie shrugged. 'Just like that.'

'He won't be happy about that.'

'Too bad. It was him who handed out the ultimatum. Listen, I'm going to leave him a note, and I know it isn't likely, but if by chance he comes sniffing around asking, just say all you know is, I handed in my notice and I've gone back to the UK. Don't let on that I've told you everything. And please don't say anything to the other girls.'

Sasha put a hand on Marie's knee and gave it a squeeze. 'I won't breathe a word. Cross my heart.' She sighed. 'It won't be the same around here without you.'

Marie smiled. 'That's what Mr Ferris said.'

'Well, he's right!' A thought suddenly occurred to her and her face fell. 'Shit, you're gonna miss my wedding! I was going to ask you to be a bridesmaid too.'

'I'm sorry.' Marie could feel herself beginning to well up. 'You've been such a good friend to me.'

'You'll keep in touch, won't you? I know calls can get costly, but maybe once in a while? And a Christmas card?'

'You can count on it.'

They hugged.

'Love you,' Sasha said tearfully.

'Love you too.'

Marie was putting on her coat and scarf at the end of her shift when there was a soft tap on the door and Marlene appeared.

'Sash just told me you're going back to England. Say it isn't true!'

Marie just looked at her blankly.

'It *is* true?! Balls! It's so sudden though. What's happened? Sash says she doesn't know. If you…'

82

'Personal reasons.'

Marlene gave her a big hug. 'I'll miss you.'

'I'll miss you too,' Marie said.

'Can I let you into a little secret? I mean, I suppose it doesn't hurt to say it now I'm not going to see you again.'

'Go on.'

Marlene grinned. 'It's a shame you're into guys. I always rather fancied you.'

'I know.'

Marlene looked slightly flustered. 'Really?'

Marie smiled gave her a peck on the cheek. 'Take care of yourself, Marlene.'

'You too.'

Kai didn't telephone over the weekend. Although she was a little surprised, curiously, Marie realised that she didn't particularly care. To hell with him; if he didn't want to be father to their child, then she didn't want to be with *him*. Already, she was mentally disengaging.

Surprised by how few of her possessions actually held any significance, on the Tuesday morning she packed a single suitcase to within breaking point. Then she put through a call to her parents in England.

Her father answered the phone. When he heard the voice, he immediately passed Marie on to her mother.

'I'm coming home, Mum.'

There was an awkward silence, then her mother said, 'I see. When?'

'Today. You were right. I made a bad choice staying. It's just taken me all this time to realise it. I should have listened to you and Dad. I'm sorry.'

'So you're coming home for good then?'

'Yes.'

'You know you can't come back here, don't you.'

Marie sighed. 'I was hoping I might be able to speak to Dad about that.'

Mrs Shaw lowered her voice. 'He won't speak to you, Marie. You broke his heart when you threw away your plans for university to stay in Australia and live with... that boy.'

'Kai, Mum. He has a name. And he's hardly a boy.'

'Whatever. You broke mine too. Your father's a proud man and what you did... I don't think he'll ever forgive you.'

'Couldn't you speak to him for me?'

There was another pause. 'It's late. We're just going to bed. I'll see if he'll listen, but don't set your hopes too high.'

'Thanks, Mum.'

'What time is your flight due in?'

'It's twenty hours, so I think I'll be landing at Heathrow around three o'clock Wednesday morning – your time.'

'Safe journey then.'

'I'll see you soon.'

'Maybe.'

The soft click on the line ended the call.

Marie left a letter on the kitchen counter and weighed it down with the salt and pepper cruet set that had been one of the first things she and Kai had bought together when they moved into the flat. Then, casting a last, sad look around the ιoom, she closed the door on the past couple of years of her life and went downstairs and out onto the street, where a taxi was waiting.

Upstairs in the flat, the telephone rang four times before the answer machine kicked in and Kai's voice filled the room.

'Marie, are you there? Pick up will you?' There was a pause. 'Okay, I guess you're out. I'm sorry I didn't call at the weekend, but I've been laid up for a couple of days. Jessop ordered a ton of rocks for the rockery he wants me to build and I put my bloody back out shifting them off the truck.' He laughed. 'It's okay, I'm fine. Er… Anyway, sorry again for not calling and, er… Well, I guess I'll try again later. I love you.'

When Kai called again twice the following day, he got the answer machine on both occasions. Starting to worry, he called The Redback Tavern. Jim Ferris answered and Kai's concerns were exacerbated when the man casually informed him that Marie had handed in her notice a few days earlier and, no, she hadn't given him a reason why and he had no idea where she was. When Kai started to get shirty, Ferris hung up on him.

Making his excuses to Ed Jessop, Kai covered the eight hundred kilometres from Lightning Ridge to Brisbane in record time, where he found the flat deserted and many of Marie's possessions gone. Then he spotted the envelope on the kitchen counter with his name written neatly on the front. Taking a seat at the table, he opened it.

Kai.

(*not* "Dear *Kai*", he thought.)

> By the time you read this I will be back in the UK.
> I had <u>so</u> hoped that you would embrace the idea
> of fatherhood and I ~~honstly~~ honestly believe you
> would have been a brilliant dad. Hopefully one day
> you still will be, but it won't be with me. I realise
> now that what I hoped would bring us together
> was a foolish pipe dream and it has actually driven
> us apart. But I cannot and <u>will</u> not destroy the
> new life that is growing inside of me, it's <u>our</u> baby!
> Thank you for the past few years, you made me so
> happy. I loved you and I know I probably always
> will a bit. But if you care anything for me at all,
> please don't try to contact me. I won't be
> returning to Australia and it's better that we
> separate cleanly than get ~~embruled~~ embroiled in a
> painful attempt to repair the unrepairable. You
> made your decision and I have made mine.
> Marie.

Kai pulled out a tissue, wiped his eyes and blew his nose. He returned the letter to the envelope, folded it neatly in two and dropped it in the pedal bin. Opening the fridge, he fished out the remains of the bottle of wine they had opened the previous week and poured himself a large glass. Sitting back down at the table, he raised it and said, to nobody in particular, 'Cheers.'

II

CHAPTER 9

After her flight landed at Heathrow, by the time Marie had retrieved her suitcase from the baggage carousel, it was just after four in the morning. It was too early to call home, so she negotiated her way through to the arrivals lounge wheeling her suitcase behind her. She found a coffee shop where she could kill some time and ordered a hot chocolate and an apple Danish.

When she checked her watch again, it was almost five-fifteen. Assuming her father would probably be up for work, she found a phone booth in the arrivals lounge and then she called home.

The phone rang four times and mother answered and whispered, 'Hello?'

Marie frowned. 'Why are you whispering?'

'Because your father's asleep and I don't want to wake him.'

'I'm sorry, I thought he would be getting ready for work by now.'

'He's on holiday this week and he's having a lay in.'

'I already waited over a hour. I told you what time my flight was due in. So what about Dad?'

'I told you, he's asleep.'

Marie rolled her eyes. 'I meant did you talk to him for me?'

'You see? All you think about is yourself!'

'Mum, did you *talk* to him?'

There was an awkward silence, then Mrs Shaw said, 'Yes, I did.'

'*And*?!' Marie was started to feel irritable. The flight back from Brisbane had been interminable and she was tired. 'What did he say?'

'He hasn't changed his mind. You're not welcome here.'

Marie inhaled sharply. 'Is that how you feel too?'

'It doesn't matter how I feel. Your father's word is final. It's his house, he pays the bills.'

Marie didn't want to get into an argument about household politics. Maybe if she could at least speak to them face to face, she might be able convince them to give her a chance. Trying not to let her annoyance filter through to her tongue, she said, 'Can't you at least come and pick me up?'

'No.'

'*Please*, Mum!'

'You have money with you, don't you?'

'Of course I do.'

'Then get a taxi.'

'A taxi?' Marie snapped. 'It's fifty miles to home, it'll cost a…'

'I said not to come home.'

'Where *am* I supposed to go then?'

'Anywhere but here.'

'I thought that if I could just *see* Dad, talk to him, maybe…'

'You'd be wasting your breath. I'm sorry, Marie, he won't budge.'

'Well, I'm coming anyway,' Marie said angrily, and without waiting for her mother to reply, she hung up.

The taxi dropped her at the kerb outside the row of terraced houses in Warrington Gardens at six-twenty.

The driver counted out the cash that Marie handed him with an expression of disenchantment on his face. 'No tip?'

Marie glared at him. 'I've just paid you a fortune! You've done nothing but prattle on all the way here – I'd have thought after the first few miles you'd have picked up on the fact I wasn't saying much and I didn't want to chat, but no, on and on and on you went. And don't try to tell me you took the quickest route, because you didn't. So if you want a tip, go and find some other mug!'

The man folded the banknotes and dropped them in this shirt pocket. 'Bitch.'

As the taxi pulled away, Marie stood for a moment looking at the house, remembering the last time she had stood here and everything that had happened since. Being in Australia already felt like a lifetime ago. There was something different about the house, but she couldn't figure out what. Pulling her suitcase behind her, she walked up the path to the front step, where she rifled through her handbag to find her door key and tried to put it in the lock. It wouldn't fit. Suddenly, she realised it wasn't her parents' front door. Incredulous at her own foolishness, she took a step back –

I know I'm tired and all these houses look the same, she thought, *but how stupid can you get, Marie?*

– only then did she spot the chrome-effect numbers screwed to the wall and the penny dropped. It *was* her parents house, they had merely replaced the front door.

She was about to ring the bell, when the door opened and her father appeared. He stood in the open doorway, and they looked at each other in silence for a few seconds. Then he took a pace forward and, for a fleeting moment, Marie thought he was going to embrace her, but he shooed her back and bent down to straighten the doormat. Then he stood up and put his hands on his hips, staring at her with indifference.

Marie broke the silence. 'You got a new front door.'

'Last year. What do you want, Marie?'

'I wanted a chance to say I'm sorry.'

Her father frowned. 'You'd best get on and say it then.'

'I'm *really* sorry. I…'

'Doesn't change a thing,' Mr Shaw said tersely. 'Is that all?'

Marie adopted an expression of contrition. 'Can't I come in for a few minutes? Just to talk?'

'No, you can't.'

'Where's Mum?'

'Fixing breakfast. Here…' Mr Shaw turned away from her and bent to pick something up. When he turned back, he had a suitcase in one hand and a bulging rucksack in the other.

'What's that?' Marie said, knowing full well what it was.

'Your belongings. Your mother packed them for you an hour ago.' He set the two bags down in the open doorway, almost as if he were forming a symbolic barrier between her life before she went off to Australia and her life now. 'Go on,' he urged her. 'Take them.'

Marie looked down at the bags forlornly. 'What if there's stuff missing?'

'You've lived without your things quite happily for the past four years, I don't think it's going to prove too much hardship now. Go on, make yourself scarce. And please don't come round here bothering us again. It'll upset your brother and sister.'

'Can't I even say a quick hello to Thomas and Lucy?'

'They're getting dressed for school.'

'So that's it then. You're disowning me?'

'You disowned *us*, Marie.'

'I didn't mean to. I…'

Mr Shaw shut the door in her face.

Although Marie had been certain that, given the opportunity, she would be able to sweet-talk her father into changing his mind, it had turned out he was even more stubborn than she had anticipated. She stood on the doorstep for a moment trying to decide what to do. Then a thought flashed through her head. Of course! Her Aunt Harriet lived just around the corner.

As she hoisted the rucksack onto her back, one of the straps got tangled and caught on the drawstring of her hooded sweatshirt, pulling it tight across her throat. Cursing under her breath, she managed to adjust it, then she took the handle of each of the two suitcases and, with the wheels rumbling loudly, set off up the road.

Harriet Palmer was ten years older than Marie's mother. Even with the age gap – when Harriet was fifteen, Lynda was only five – they had been extremely close as children, as close as two sisters could be in fact. Yet, even though they had lived just five streets away from one another for the past ten years, Harriet and Gareth Shaw had never seen eye to eye and as a result, the sisters seldom spoke. Being Lynda Shaw's firstborn, Marie had always been Harriet's favourite of the Shaw's three children and she doted on her. Marie loved her "Harri", her three-year-old self's pronunciation of her aunt's name, which had stuck long after she had grown up.

Looking at her watch – it was almost seven o'clock – Marie rang the doorbell of the imposing house at number nine, Ogilvie Crescent and waited. She had just pressed the bell again when she heard a muffled voice coming from inside the house.

'Alright, keep your hair on, I'm just coming.'

The door opened to the point that the steel safety chain jerked it to a stop and Harriet Palmer peered warily out. Although her graying hair was in rollers, it looked tangled and one roller was hanging down over her ear. She looked half asleep. 'Who is it?' she asked crossly. 'What do you want?'

'It's me, Harri.'

The woman squinted at her. 'Who's "me"?'

'Marie. Your niece.'

For a moment, there was no trace of recognition on the woman's face, but then her eyes widened and her thin lips broadened into a smile. 'Marie? What on earth are you doing here. I thought you'd gone off to live down under.'

'I did, but I'm home now.'

'How wonderful to see you. Come in, my love, come in. Oops, just a moment.'

She closed the door and Marie heard Harriet fiddling to unlatch the safety chain. Then the door opened again.

'Sorry about that,' Harriet chuckled. She wiggled her fingers in the air. 'Onset arthritis. It's a real bugger first thing in the morning.' She beckoned to Marie. 'Don't stand out there getting cold, come on in.'

'Can I bring my stuff?'

'Of course.' Harriet glanced at the two suitcases and chuckled again. 'It looks like you've brought everything with you but the kitchen sink!'

'It's a long story.'

'Well come in and tell me all about it.'

Marie stepped inside and was immediately greeted by the familiar scent of violets.

'Is it okay if I use the loo? I haven't been since I got off the plane and I'm busting.'

'Mi casa es su casa, my dear. I'll pop the kettle on.'

By the time Marie came back downstairs, Harriet had prepared tea and toast and they sat down together at the kitchen table to have breakfast.

'Well now,' Harriet exclaimed, slathering a generous spoonful of thick cut marmalade on a slice of toast, 'aren't you a sight for sore eyes!'

'It's good to see you too.'

'So what have you been up to since we last had a good old chinwag? It must be ten years or more.'

Marie smiled. 'It's only four.'

Harriet frowned. 'Only four? It seems so much longer. But then I seem to have trouble keeping track of what day of the week it is these days! Anyway, tell me about your travels. I did hear from your mother some time ago that you'd met a young man.'

As if Harriet had pressed a button, Marie burst into tears.

'What on earth's the matter, my love?'

'I'm sorry. It's just I've been under a lot of stress recently.'

'Well that won't do, will it?' Harriet pulled out a lace handkerchief from her sleeve and handed it over. 'Dry your eyes and tell me all about it.'

Marie gave her a bare bones account of her time in Australia. Deciding to keep quiet for now about her pregnancy, she concluded by explaining that the reason for her return to England was essentially irreconcilable differences with Kai.

'It's very sad when relationships break down. But we pick ourselves up and dust ourselves off and move on, don't we? You're young and there are plenty more fish in the sea.'

Marie went on to explain that her father had refused to forgive her for her decision to abandon her plans for university and stay overseas, and was adamant that she was no longer welcome in the house. 'So I came here. I'm sorry, I didn't have anywhere else to go.'

'Well, I for one am pleased to see you, even if Gareth isn't.' Harriet tutted and topped up their teacups from the brown earthenware pot decorated with a smiling pig's face that she'd had for as long as Marie could remember. 'He's a hard man, your father. But as for not having anywhere else to go, don't you go worrying your pretty little head about that. You're more than welcome to stay here for as long as you like. It would be a pleasure to have you here.'

Marie smiled gratefully, 'Thank you, Harri.'

Harriet chuckled. 'I haven't been called that in many a year. How long has it been? Must be ten years or more now.'

Marie frowned. 'No, it's four. I told you that just now.'

Harriet looked a little surprised. '*Did* you? Silly me. Oh well, it still warms my heart to hear it.' A faraway look appeared in her eyes. 'It seems like only yesterday that you were a toddler and I used to take you to the park for ice cream. Happy, happy times. Anyway.' She stood up. 'I imagine you've had a tiring trip, why don't you go and have a nice long bath and freshen up and I'll make up the bed in the back bedroom for you.'

'Are you sure it's not an imposition?'

Harriet waved a hand at her. 'I've been living on my own since your Uncle Frank died. It gets a bit lonely rattling around in a big old house like this, so it'll be a treat to have some company.'

The following morning, after the best night's sleep she'd had in days, Marie got up early and put the kettle on. She found half a packet of Rich Tea biscuits in the cupboard and laid out a couple on a saucer. Having made the tea, she carried a tray upstairs and tapped lightly on Harriet's bedroom door.

'Who's that?' her muffled voice called from the other side of the door.

'It's Marie. I've brought you a cup of tea.'

Harriet muttered something that Marie couldn't understand.

'Is it alright if come in?'

'Yes, yes, come in, dear.'

Marie pushed open the door and saw her aunt sitting up in bed with a pillow propped behind her.

'How very kind. Ooh, biscuits too!'

Marie set down the tray on the bedside table and handed over the cup.

With slightly trembling fingers, Harriet took it and had a sip. 'Hmm. Nothing quite like the first cup of the day.' She glanced back at the tray. 'Aren't you having one, dear?'

Marie perched herself on the end of the bed. 'No, I'll wait until breakfast. I've been thinking, I'm going to have to get down to the council offices and see if I can make an appointment to speak with someone in the housing department.'

Harriet laughed. 'Good luck with that, dear.'

'I don't know what else to do.'

'A right old shower, they are. You won't get much help from them.'

'I will if I tell them I'm pregnant.'

Marie's statement hung heavy in the air for a few second, then Harriet's face lit up.

'You're *not*?!'

Marie nodded. 'I am.'

'Oh, my dear, what wonderful news!' Harriet set down her cup and got out of bed. She sat down beside Marie and gave her a hug. 'I bet your young man is over the moon.'

Marie shook her head. 'Not really. That's why I came back to England. He doesn't want to know.'

'That's a shame. Never mind, eh?'

Harriet's remark was so offhand that Marie wasn't sure that she'd understood. She decided to let it go.

'Do your Mum and Dad know?' Harriet continued.

'I haven't told them yet. I didn't really get a chance.'

'Well, I'm sure they'll be cock-a-hoop when you do.'

Marie sighed. 'I'm not going to. Not yet anyway. What with Dad being so obstinate and everything.'

Harriet patted her shoulder. 'Very wise. But listen, don't you worry about where you're going to live. You can stay here for as long as you like.'

'But what about when the baby comes?'

Harriet shrugged. 'We'll turn the box room into a nursery.'

Marie looked at her aunt sadly. 'That's really kind, but I can't ask you to do that. I've not got much money and…'

'Oh pish.' Harriet flapped a hand. 'You just shoosh yourself about money now. You're staying with me and I'll not hear another word said about it.'

Marie smiled and kissed her aunt's cheek. 'Thank you so much, Harri.'

Leaving her aunt to get dressed, Marie took the tea tray downstairs, smiling to herself. She had been hoping that Harriet might let her stay for a few days, but now it looked as if she would be here considerably longer.

CHAPTER 10

Harriet had retired from her job as a seamstress when her husband, Frank passed away and thanks to the money he left her she'd had no need to work again. She spent a lot of time out with her small circle of friends, with whom she enjoyed knit and natter get-togethers, coffee mornings, trips to the theatre and occasionally days out by coach visiting National Trust sites.

All this pretty much left Marie to her own devices, and when she wasn't out having a good time with her own friends, she would fall into a couch potato routine, wasting away the hours sitting in front of the television. Harriet gave her niece a generous weekly allowance, most of which she managed to fritter away. When the baby started to show, just as Harriet had promised, she took Marie out in Old Mabel, her Jeep Cherokee – behind the wheel of which she looked comically tiny – to buy furnishings, with which they were able to transform the box room into a nursery together.

The days turned into weeks and the weeks into months and the night that Marie's waters broke, Harriet hurried her to the hospital. When Marie had originally been asked if she would like to know the sex of the baby, she had declined; she was so sure in her head that it would be a girl, she had already decided to call her Melissa. When, three hours later, she gave birth and the midwife announced it was a 7lb and 9oz baby boy, it quite startled her. She hadn't even considered boys' names, but before long she decided upon Donovan.

Marie's family came to visit her in hospital. Her mother, Thomas and Lucy cooed over the infant. Her father, however, took one look at the tiny thing laying in the crib, made a grunting sound of disapproval, and went over to the window, where he remained watching the activity in the car park below until everyone was ready to leave.

When Marie brought the baby home two days later, she couldn't help feeling a little superfluous; Harriet had already unpacked and set up everything they had purchased for the nursery without giving her any say in where the cot or the rocking chair with the giant teddy bear on it were positioned, or where the ceiling mobiles were hung.

Harriet, generous to a fault, paid for everything that the baby needed. Yet although, up until Donovan arrived, Marie's freedom to do as she pleased had been largely confined to her bedroom, she started to put her mark on other parts of the house. Although it bothered Harriet a little, being far too soft and forgiving, she let her niece get on with it.

Things finally came to a head the day after Donovan's second birthday. With the allowance that Harriet continued to give her and her single parent child benefits combined, Marie had plenty of disposable cash. On impulse, she had bought herself a milkshake blender and in order to create some space for it on the kitchen counter, she'd consigned Harriet's old 1970s Magimix food processor to the dustbin.

When Harriet arrived home from afternoon tea with her friends, she noticed it was missing, she felt compelled to confront her. She found Marie in the lounge with the television on and her head buried in a magazine.

'I see you've bought yourself a fancy blender, dear.'

100

Marie looked up from her gossip magazine. 'Yes, it's pretty great, isn't it? You can whip up a shake in seconds. I love it.'

'You didn't need to go spending money on that. My Magimix would have done the job just as well.'

'That manky old thing?' Marie scoffed. 'I don't think so.'

'There's nothing wrong with it!'

'It was filthy and it's so old I'm surprised it wasn't in the Natural History Museum.'

'It was perfectly clean!'

Shaking her head, Marie returned her attention to the magazine. 'If you thought that was clean, you need to get your eyes tested.'

Harriet looked at her niece uncomfortably. 'Marie, dear,' she said hesitatingly. 'About the Magimix. What have you done with it? I don't mind if you want to have your milkshake thingy on the counter, if you're going to be using it regularly I mean, but I've looked in all the cupboards and I can't find it.'

Marie didn't look up. 'I told you, it was manky. I chucked it. And, to be honest, I don't think I've seen you use it once since I've been here.'

Harriet looked taken aback. 'Frank gave me that for an anniversary present. And I *did* use it.'

Marie shrugged. 'Buy yourself a new one then. You can afford it.'

Harriet bent down and picked up a discarded toy monkey. 'I do wish you would keep Donovan's toys tidied away, dear. I trod on one of his little plastic cars yesterday and hurt my toe.'

'You should put your slippers then,' Marie muttered. 'I gave you a pair for your birthday. Waste of money that was if you're not going to wear them.'

'The point is, there's plenty of room in the nursery for his toys. I'd rather they weren't scattered all over the place.'

Finally, Marie looked up from her magazine. 'I thought this was my home as well.'

'It is, dear. But…'

'Then stop moaning all the time. You're giving me a headache.'

'I didn't mean to sound as if I'm moaning. It's just with Donovan's toys and the general mess around the house, especially when you've had your friends from the mother and toddler group round, it would be nice if it could be kept a little tidier.'

'So I'm not allowed to have my friends round now?'

Harriet shook her head. 'That's not what I said, dear.'

'It sure as hell sounded like it. It's not like they're bothering you, I always pick a day to invite them when you're going to be out.'

Not wishing their conversation to escalate into an argument, Harriet said, 'Well, I didn't mean it to sound as if I was complaining.'

'Well, it does.'

'Sorry.' Harriet turned away and went out to the kitchen to put the kettle on.

'You making tea?'

'Yes.'

'Make us one, would you?'

When Harriet returned with their drinks, she nodded at the television. 'If you're not watching that, my programme is due on in a minute.' She handed Marie her tea.

'It's *Neighbours*,' Marie said stubbornly. 'You know I never like to miss it.'

'But you were reading, dear, I didn't think you were really paying any attention. And I do like to watch...'

Marie tossed the magazine aside. 'Happy now?'

Harriet looked sadly at her niece. 'Sorry, I didn't mean to upset you.'

Marie looked up at her aunt and her attitude appeared to change. 'It's fine. I'm just so flippin' tired at the moment. Donovan has been keeping me up at night with that constant crying. I don't know what to do about him. Nothing seems to calm him down.'

'It's just a phase, dear. It'll pass. I must say though, he's been keeping me awake too.'

Marie sighed. 'I'm sorry, but like I said, I don't know what I can do.'

'I'm only getting a couple of hours sleep every night and I'm exhausted. I was having tea with my friends the other day and I nodded off in the chair. It was so embarrassing. I've been thinking I might make an appointment with the doctor, see if he can prescribe some sleeping tablets.'

Marie smiled. 'That's a good idea.'

'Do you think so? I wasn't sure. Maybe just short term until Donovan settles a bit.'

'Absolutely.'

Harriet nodded. 'Very well. I'll give them a call tomorrow.'

Leaving Marie to watch the television, she returned to the kitchen and sat down at the table, where she drank her tea alone.

Harriet was able to get the prescription she wanted. A single tablet with the bedtime Horlicks prepared by Marie frequently afforded her eight hours' solid sleep, which even Donovan's most extreme tantrums failed to disrupt. She would often sleep so deeply that, when she awoke in the morning, she would initially be disoriented and incoherent. But Marie would bring her a cup of tea in bed and she would soon return to her usual self. Often, however, she wouldn't feel like going out and was starting to spend more time around the house, making it more difficult for Marie to have her friends over.

She suggested to her aunt if they came for just an hour or two, she might like to go up to her room with a cup of tea and have an afternoon nap. Harriet was very accommodating, and so it became routine for Marie to make the tea, into which she would stealthily drop a couple of Nytol tablets that she'd picked up in Boots to ensure that Harriet didn't disturb them.

The cumulative effect was that, when she got up after a couple of hours of deep slumber, Harriet would often be woolly-headed and uncommunicative. Over time, she started retiring to bed every night progressively earlier, giving Marie more and more freedom to do as she wished around the house; she started inviting friends round for evening drinks.

A month passed and, early one evening when Marie was helping her aunt to get ready for bed, it registered that there were only a matter of days' worth of the sleeping pill prescription left and then they would be gone.

'Harri,' she said, as she placed the tray with the mug of Horlicks on the bedside table, 'you're almost out of sleeping pills. You need to make an appointment with Doctor Quimby to arrange a repeat.'

Harriet, leaning against her pillow, looked up sleepily from the book on her lap. 'Actually, dear, I've been thinking about not taking them any more.'

Marie frowned. 'Oh? I thought they were helping.'

'They are and I've been sleeping really well. But since I've been taking them I feel tired pretty much all the time. I haven't even had tonight's pill yet and I could close my eyes now without it and I think I'd go out like a light.' She half chuckled. 'Honestly, my brain these days. It's ridiculous, most of the time I don't even know what day of the week it is.'

Marie sat down on the edge of the bed beside her. 'I don't think it's a good idea to stop a prescription without completing the course. And you're obviously sleeping well, so they must be proving beneficial. Donovan kicked up such a fuss last night that the people at the end of the street must have heard. But it didn't wake you, did it?'

'No. No, it didn't.'

'There you go then. The pills are obviously doing their job. It's perfectly normal for our bodies to take time to adjust to new medicine and you've only been taking them for a few weeks.'

Harriet looked at her niece uncertainly. 'I suppose so.' She thought for a moment. 'How many is it I take?'

'One every night. You know that. Here...' – Marie reached for the mug on the tray and handed it over – '...have your warm drink and get a good night's sleep.' She passed over the small, white tablet and smiled. 'I wouldn't suggest you do anything that wasn't good for you, would I? You're my Harri and I love you.'

Marie stood up and watched Harriet swallow the pill with a mouthful of Horlicks.

'Thank you, dear. I'll have a think about speaking to the doctor.'

'Don't worry yourself about that' Marie could see Harriet's eyes beginning to droop. She took the mug from her and put her book on the table. 'If you're not feeling up to it in the morning, I'll call the surgery and make your appointment for you.'

Marie looked at her watch: it read seven-thirty. Crossing to the door, she reached for the light switch. 'Goodnight,' she whispered.

The only response was the soft sound of snoring.

Smiling, she went downstairs to call her friends.

CHAPTER 11

'I'm rather surprised to hear that.' Doctor Edith Quimby looked at the woman sitting meekly opposite her desk in her consulting room. 'You have been taking them as prescribed, Mrs Palmer? One a day?'

'Yes, doctor,' Harriet responded emphatically. 'One every night with a hot drink just before bedtime.'

Doctor Quimby studied at the PC screen in front of her. 'They're a low enough dosage, they shouldn't leave you feeling drowsy during the day.' She spoke without actually addressing Harriet, as if she were thinking aloud.

''My niece was saying that it can take our bodies a while to get used to new medication.'

'Hmm,' the doctor said absent-mindedly, still looking at the screen.

'It's not *too* bad,' Harriet continued, wishing she hadn't mentioned her inordinate tiredness over the past few weeks. 'I'm probably exaggerating a bit when I said I'm tired *all* day. I'm sure it's nothing to worry about.' She could sense a refusal for a repeat prescription was brewing.

Doctor Quimby scrolled down the screen. 'I see you haven't had a blood test since nineteen...' – she scrolled a little further – '...nineteen eighty-eight.'

Harriet felt her stomach constrict. 'Is that a bad thing?'

The doctor looked up at her reassuringly. 'No, no. There can be all sorts of reasons for extreme fatigue. On a simple-to-address level, it could be hormonal. Or dietary, perhaps. Are you eating normally?'

'Normal for me.'

'What would be normal for you?'

'Well, I don't eat a lot. I never have done. Small amounts, that's me.'

'I see. But what you do eat, is it healthy?'

'Reasonably healthy, I would say, yes.' Harriet smiled. 'I confess, I do like my sweeties though.'

The doctor returned her smile. 'I think most of us do, Mrs Palmer. As long as it's kept in moderation.'

'What could it be then?'

Doctor Quimby stroked her chin. 'Are you under any undue stress at the moment? That you're aware of, I mean?'

'Not really. I suppose my niece's little one is a bit of a handful, especially at night. That's why the pills are so helpful. Do you think it could be something more serious?'

'Let's not hypothesise any more. A blood test is merely a formality to ensure there isn't an underlying problem.' She smiled and added, none too convincingly, 'Which I'm sure there isn't.' She tapped on the keyboard. 'Let's just book you in for that now.'

'What about the sleeping pills though?' Harriet asked. 'Honestly, I've been finding them *so* beneficial.'

The doctor's fingers paused, hovering over the keys. 'Under the circumstances, I'm reluctant to consent to a repeat prescription…'

Harriet's face dropped. 'But, doctor, I…'

Doctor Quimby held up a finger. 'Please, Mrs Palmer, hear me out. I will, however, just this one time, administer a short course on an even lower dosage than the one you have been taking.'

Harriet smiled. 'Thank you, that's a great weight off my mind.'

When Harriet arrived home, she found Marie with her feet up on the sofa, reading a magazine and drinking a glass of Pepsi.

'Where's Donovan?'

'Having his afternoon nap,' Marie replied with a note of disinterest. 'How did you get on at the doc's?'

'Not so well. Doctor Quimby wants me to have a blood test.'

Frowning, Marie put aside her magazine. 'Oh? Didn't you get the repeat prescription then?'

'Not a repeat, but she's given me something else not quite as strong as the others.'

Marie sat up. 'Why?'

Harriet looked awkward. 'Well, I know what we discussed, but I felt I had to tell her how tired I've been feeling lately.'

Marie scowled. 'I thought we'd agreed you weren't going to mention that. Now you've probably ended up with something less effective.'

'We don't actually know they're less effective, I haven't tried them yet, it's just…'

'And a blood test.' Marie rolled her eyes. 'I bet you're looking forward to that.'

'No, not really. I'm not keen on needles.'

'Me neither.' Marie's mind was turning over. She didn't think that a blood test would be likely to reveal any evidence of the additional barbiturates she'd been surreptitiously

109

administering on top of Harriet's regular prescription tablets, but she couldn't be a hundred percent certain.

'I must say, I do wish I hadn't said anything now,' Harriet said regretfully.

Seeing an opportunity, Marie ceased it. She smiled. 'Then why bother? It strikes me it's a bit pointless now you've got the tablets.'

'The doctor wants to be sure there isn't something untoward going on.'

'You're fit as a fiddle, Harri. You don't feel unwell, do you?'

'No, not at all. Just tired.'

Marie got up off the sofa and pushed her feet into her slippers. 'There you go then. When is it you're supposed to be having this blood test?'

'Next Thursday.'

'It's entirely your decision, of course, but if I were you I'd get on the phone to them tomorrow and say something has come up and you can't make it.'

Harriet looked doubtful. 'Do you think that's wise?'

'Absolutely. You're not ill, you don't like needles and it means another trip all the way down there for nothing.'

'But what if they want me to make one for a later date?'

'Just tell them you need to check your diary and you'll call back. That makes sense, doesn't it?'

Harriet still didn't look convinced, but she nodded anyway. 'I suppose.'

'Of course it does.' Marie put her arms around her aunt and gave her a hug. 'Now, you go and take your coat off and I'll make us a nice cup of tea. And let's take a look at these new tablets the doctor has given you.' She walked through to the kitchen.

Harriet took off her coat and hung it on the stand in the hall. 'I haven't got them yet. I was too weary to stop in town today. I'll get them tomorrow.'

'Actually,' Marie called back from the kitchen, 'I was thinking I might go into town myself this afternoon. I can pick them up for you if you like.'

'No, it's fine. I still have a couple of the others left. I'll go and get them after I've had my lunch with the ladies tomorrow.' Harriet sat down in the armchair.

Marie made a mug of tea and then, glancing over her shoulder to be sure that Harriet couldn't see what she was doing from the living room, she emptied the remainder of the carton of milk down the sink. There was another unopened carton in the fridge. Taking it out, she emptied that too, quickly running the cold-water tap to swill away the evidence.

When she came back into the living room, Harriet saw that she was only carrying one mug.

'Oh, aren't you having one too, dear?'

'No, we're out of milk.' Marie handed Harriet the mug. 'I just used the last drop for yours.'

'Oh my word, I didn't realise we were so low.'

'Don't worry about it.'

'But I do. I'm certain I bought one when I was out yesterday. Is there not a fresh pint in the fridge?'

Marie gave her aunt a sympathetic smile. 'Are you *sure* about that, Harri?' she asked teasingly.

'Well, I *thought* I had, but suppose I could be mistaken.'

111

'If you did, Mr Nobody must have drunk it,' Marie said laughing. 'It's certainly not there now. Anyway, that's an extra reason for me to pop down to the shops. I can get us some fresh milk and drop in to get your prescription too.'

'Well, if it isn't too much trouble.'

'Of course it isn't. Just keep half an ear on Donovan for me, will you? He probably won't wake up, but if he does, you'll find his dummy on the windowsill in his room, just give him that.'

'I will. You'll find the prescription in my handbag.'

Marie went out into the hall, found the prescription in her aunt's bag and slipped on her coat. Reappearing in the living room doorway, she patted her pockets and said, 'Money. I don't have any cash.'

'Oh, you can take a fiver from my purse, dear. It's in my bag on the hall table.'

Marie retrieved the purse and opened it up. Inside was some loose change, two five-pound notes, two tens and a twenty. Aware that Harriet could see her through the open doorway, she turned away a little and removed one of the fives and the twenty. Then, hastily tucking them into the back pocket of her jeans, she turned back to face her aunt. 'Right,' she said breezily, 'I'll only be a couple of hours. Is there anything else you need?'

Harriet shook her head. 'No, I don't think so. Unless you fancied something nice for supper.'

'That sounds good. How about I get us a pizza?'

'I'm not mad keen, but if that's what you'd like I don't mind too much. Take an extra fiver with you.'

'Pizza it is then.' Marie returned to Harriet's bag and removed the other five-pound note. 'While I'm out, why don't you give the doctor a quick call and cancel that silly blood test?'

'I will.'

Marie smiled. 'See you later then.'

Before doing anything else, Marie made a beeline for Boots and collected Harriet's prescription. Outside on the pavement, she tore open the top off the sealed paper bag and examined the contents. The label on the box identified the tablets as Doxepin. A quick read of the accompanying leaflet made it apparent that they were little more than mild sedatives. Annoyed, she went back into Boots and bought a box of twenty 50mg Nytol tablets. Then she made her way down to the end of the high street, where she ducked into Superdrug and bought another. Nipping across the road to Sainsbury's, she bought a pint of milk and a fresh pepperoni pizza, then spent the next hour browsing the CD shelves in HMV, where she used Harriet's twenty-pound note to buy herself Mariah Carey's latest album.

When Marie got back to the house, she found Harriet dozing in her armchair. After depositing the pint of milk in the fridge and leaving the pizza and Harriet's Doxepin on the kitchen counter, she went upstairs and dropped the CDs and the packets of Nytol on her bed. Then she took a quick look in on Donovan; he had been awake for hours the previous night, so she wasn't too surprised to find him still napping soundly. Although it was nearly time for his feed, she decided to leave him be a little longer. When she got back downstairs, Harriet had woken and was in the kitchen putting the kettle on.

'Did you call the doc?'

Sleepy-eyed, she nodded.

'And what about another appointment?'

'No, I did what you suggested and told them I'd ring them back another day.'

'Good for you.'

Harriet yawned. 'Thank you for getting my tablets, dear. And picking up the milk. You know, I was *so* sure I'd bought one yesterday. I just don't know where my head is these days.'

'Don't worry about it.' Marie gave her aunt a peck on the cheek. 'You're just tired. Are you hungry?'

'I was going to have a cup of tea, but now you mention it, I am a bit peckish, yes.'

'Me too. Shall I pop the pizza in the oven?'

Harriet nodded. 'Marie, dear…' She hesitated.

'Yes?'

'When you took the money from my purse, you did just take the two five pound notes, didn't you?'

Marie suddenly spotted her aunt's purse on the far end of the counter. Avoiding making eye contact, she picked up the pizza, removed the plastic wrapper and deposited it in the pedal bin. 'I like my pizza super-crispy.' She crossed to the oven. 'What gas mark do you reckon it needs?'

'Nine should cook it through well.'

Marie set the dial, slipped the pizza onto a baking tray and put it in the oven. She turned back to face Harriet. 'Damn, I should have thought to get some dessert too.'

Harriet was looking at her inquisitively. 'The money, dear.'

'Money?' Marie went to the cupboard and got out two plates.

'Yes, the money you took from my purse. It was just the two fives, wasn't it?'

'That's right.' Marie set the plates down on the kitchen table. 'I don't suppose you have a pizza cutter do you? You know, one of those rotating thingies on a handle?'

'You didn't happen to notice how much was left in there did you?'

'In your purse? Not really.' Marie adopted a thoughtful expression. 'One other note – a tenner, maybe. And a few coins.'

'Not a twenty?'

'I don't think so.' Marie frowned. 'Why are you asking?'

'I thought there was more than that, but…'

Marie scowled. 'Are you suggesting I took money from you?'

Harriet's tone immediately became apologetic. 'No, it's not that at all. It's just…'

'Just *what*?' Marie put her hands on her hips and stared at Harriet fiercely.

'Well, I only went to the bank yesterday and drew out some cash. I thought there was a twenty-pound note too.'

'Just like you thought you bought some milk yesterday, but you didn't?' Marie said mockingly.

'No! Well, yes. I mean…' – Harriet put a hand to her brow. – '…Oh, I don't know, dear. I can't understand what's wrong with me at the moment. I don't know whether I'm coming or going half the time.' There were tears in her eyes. 'Maybe there *is* something more serious wrong with me. Maybe I shouldn't have cancelled that blood test after all.'

Marie had been standing staring at her aunt dispassionately. Suddenly her demeanour changed. 'Here.' She took the older woman's arm and guided her to a chair at the table. 'Sit yourself down,' she said comfortingly. 'Take the weight off your feet.' Pulling a tissue from the box on the counter, she handed it to Harriet and took the seat opposite her 'You need to stop worrying about silly little things that don't matter. So you forgot to buy some milk. So you thought you had a bit more money in your purse than you actually do. So what? It's easy to get a bit confused. I do myself sometimes. But, honestly, you don't need a blood test. I'm here with you now and I'll look after you.'

Harriet dabbed away a tear with the tissue. 'I'm sorry, dear. It was wrong of me to question you. I know you have my best interests at heart.'

Marie reached over and squeezed the slender, liver-spotted hand. 'One hundred percent.' She stood up and went to the cutlery drawer. 'Why actually did you go checking your purse if it wasn't to see how much I'd taken?' she asked in a matter-of-fact manner as she pulled out two pairs of knives and forks.

'Oh, I just wanted to get the appointment card for the blood test that the receptionist at the doctor's gave me and put it in the bin.'

Marie smiled to herself. 'Best place for it,' she said.

CHAPTER 12

Several weeks passed, during which time the combination of the Doxepin prescribed by Dr Quimby and the Nytol that Marie had bought was having the desired effect on Harriet.

Occasionally – and mostly if she wanted to meet old friends for a coffee or a bite of lunch at one of their favourite haunts – Harriet would make a concerted effort to get out of the house for a few hours. But more and more often she began to make excuses to drop out, choosing instead to get up late, spend a large part of the day popping back to bed for a snooze, then retiring for the night no later than seven o'clock. The result was that Marie had total freedom of the house most of the time – and she loved it.

The day after their conversation over the missing money, Harriet had admitted that she was finding simple tasks like keeping the house tidy and doing the shopping extremely tiring and asked Marie if she minded doing it. To show that she trusted her niece implicitly – and again apologising for having become muddled over the amount of cash she thought was in her purse – Harriet had handed over her credit card, telling Marie to hang on to it and saying she could use it for any shopping that was required and anything that Donovan might need.

Of course, Marie did the bare minimum in the way of housework and allowed Donovan's toys – most of which he would play with for a few minutes before losing interest and discarding – to creep out of his bedroom and take up residence as part of the general décor. Harriet would

117

occasionally make noises about things getting under her feet, and warning Marie that they would be broken or cause someone to trip over, but her protestations fell on deaf ears and eventually she gave up.

Marie had half expected the doctor's surgery to pursue Harriet over the request for a blood test, but much to her surprise – and, even more so, her delight – the call never came. Increasingly woolly-headed, when the Doxepin ran out, Harriet wasn't even aware of the fact, and Marie certainly didn't draw her attention to it. Instead, she doubled the dosage on the Nytol she was administering and achieved the same effect.

With Harriet out of the way in the land of nod, she would often entertain friends and they would listen to music or watch a video, while enjoying expensive refreshments courtesy of an unwitting Aunt Harriet. When the monthly credit card bills arrived in the post, without letting her aunt see, Marie would tell her how much was due, often adding on another ten or fifteen pounds. Harriet would then write out a cheque for cash, which Marie would take to the bank, exchange for the money and pay off the credit card bill, tucking away the extra in her own purse.

One afternoon, with Christmas on the horizon, Harriet, out of bed and dressed for a change, was semi-dozing in her chair in the living room. The gas fire was on and the room was cosy and warm.

Her eyelids drooping, all she wanted to do was doze off, but Donovan was playing with a toy car, making loud *vroom-vroom* noises and she had to bite her tongue not to say anything; she knew it would solve nothing and only cause a stir. Slowly though, drowsiness won the battle, her head lolled to one side on the cushion propped up behind her and she began lightly snoring.

Marie was watching television with the sound down low, paying very little attention to Donovan, who crawled over to the hearth and started rolling his toy back and forth over the ceramic tiles, becoming more and more excited by the clattering noise the solid plastic wheels made.

On either end of the hearth there stood a matching pair of fifteen-inch tall Staffordshire spaniels. All of a sudden, Donovan bashed the toy car against the one on the left, it toppled over and hit the tiles.

Yawning, Marie looked over and tutted. 'Look what you've done now, Donny.' She didn't bother to get up off the sofa. Harriet, who had woken with a start at the sound of the breaking china, was taking a moment to grasp where she was and what was happening. 'That's *very* naughty,' Marie added as she realised her aunt was awake; the rebuke was impassive, as if she were reading the well-rehearsed words from a script she had become bored with. Nevertheless, Donovan started to cry.

Marie finally stood and scooped the little boy up in her arms. Still apparently disoriented, as Harriet started to get up, she was overcome with a wave of giddiness. 'Ooh, I feel a bit dizzy,' she muttered. As she put a hand on the arm of her chair to steady herself, she caught sight of the precious ornament laying on the hearth and her mouth fell open. 'Oh!' she exclaimed. 'Oh, no, not little Sammy.' She carefully got down on her knees in front of the fireplace and picked up the dog, rotating it in her hands and inspecting it for cracks.

'These belonged to my great grandmother,' she muttered, choking back tears of anger.

'Shoosh-shoosh now,' Marie said, trying to comfort the wailing child. 'Don't cry. It wasn't your fault.'

Harriet's head spun and she glared up at her niece. 'Of *course* it was his fault, Marie' she spat. 'And he deserves to be spanked, not told it wasn't his fault.' She was struggling to get back up off her knees.

'Don't you *dare* tell me I should spank my kid!' Marie retorted angrily. 'Who the hell do you think you are?'

Placing a hand on the mantle for support, Harriet managed to hoist herself into the standing position. She clutched the porcelain dog lovingly to her chest. 'He nearly smashed it!'

'But he didn't, did he?'

'No, but he *could* have! How do you think he's ever going to learn right from wrong if he misbehaves and gets rewarded with kisses and cuddles?'

Marie's eyes flashed. 'And you think spanking is the answer do you? He doesn't understand, he's only two!'

'Exactly. He *is* only two and he shouldn't be playing near the fire in the first place. And look.' She waved a hand at the scattering of toys on the carpet. 'His things are *everywhere*. I can't move in my own house for toys! If he wants to play he should do it in his own room.'

'So now he's supposed to stay in his room all day?'

'Don't twist my words, Marie, that's not what I said. But I spent a lot of money making that room nice for him and it looks like a tip. In fact, the whole house is a tip! And now…'

– she stifled a sob and held up the broken ornament – '…this!'

Marie shook her head. 'They're bloody horrible ugly things anyway. I don't know what you're making such a fuss about.'

Harriet's eyes widened. 'They are *not* ugly, they're beautiful. And they're worth a great deal of money! You know I have a lot of valuable things in this room.' She was still cradling the dog protectively. 'Sammy and Petra belonged to my great grandmother.'

'Yeah, so you said,' Marie countered with an undisguised note of couldn't-care-less. Donovan had stopped crying and was watching Harriet with mild curiosity. 'But being ancient doesn't mean it isn't tat. Christ, you *know* there's a child in the house, if you care so much about all this crap, you should put it away in your room out of harm's reach.'

'This is *my* house, young lady, and I'll put my things where I like!'

'Oh, I see, so it's *your* house now, is it? And there I was thinking it was mine and Donovan's too. Dumb, stupid old me!'

Harriet screwed up her face. 'Don't be facetious, girl. You know it's your home too. But you need to understand…'

'Oh, I understand alright.' Holding Donovan to her, Marie brushed past Harriet. 'Come on, Donny, we won't stay where we aren't welcome.'

'Don't be silly. Where are you going?'

'What do *you* care?' Marie shouted from the hall. 'You've made it quite clear you don't want us here.'

In an instant, the anger drained from Harriet's face. 'Of course I do. I'm sorry, I didn't mean to lose my temper. Please don't go, it's tipping down out there.'

Her appeal was greeted by the sound of the front door slamming shut.

Marie spent a couple of hours wheeling Donovan's pushchair around the shops. After they closed, she went into McDonald's, bought a cheeseburger, and took a seat in the window where she stayed, nursing a Pepsi, until almost seven o'clock. The rain had finally stopped and she decided it was time to make her way back to the house and apologise; not that she would mean a single word of it, of course, but extending an olive branch was all she could do; after all, she was painfully aware she had nowhere else to go. Added to which, she had invited a couple of friends over and they would be arriving at eight.

Harriet sat staring at the floor and listened in silence to Marie's seemingly heartfelt remorse over the angry words that had been exchanged between them. It was evident from the red rims around her eyes and the limp scrap of tissue scrunched-up in her hand that she had been crying.

Immediately, when she had come in, Marie had noticed that all the ornaments in the room that might have been in Donovan's reach had disappeared. She concluded her apology with the words, 'I love you, Harri.' Tickling Donovan's earlobe, she added, 'And so does Donny. You love your Harri, don't you, sausage?' The little boy giggled.

Marie stood and waited for a response, and after what seemed like an eternity – but was in fact only a matter of seconds – Harriet finally looked up.

'I'm sorry too, dear. I shouldn't have snapped like that. I don't know what possessed me, it's not like me at all. And I certainly shouldn't have said anything that made you think you aren't welcome here. This is your home now, just as much as it is mine. And of course I don't expect Donovan to be confined to his room either.'

'He honestly didn't mean to knock the little dog over.'

'I know he didn't, dear. As you can see, I've moved some of my things out now, just like you suggested.'

'Makes sense, doesn't it?'

Harriet nodded in agreement. 'It was remiss of me not to do it sooner.'

'No harm done then?'

'No.'

'And the dog thingy is okay?'

'Yes.'

'Good. Let me put Donny to bed and I'll make you some tea. After that I expect you'll be ready for bed.'

'Actually, I thought I might stay up and keep you company for a bit tonight. There's a programme on the television that sounded quite good. We don't seem to spend much time together.' Harriet saw Marie frown. 'That would be nice, wouldn't it? Watch some TV together?'

'Actually, would you mind having an early night? You could always read for a bit if you're not tired.'

'But I thought we might watch the programme together.'

'That would have been lovely.' There was a tone in Marie's voice that made it clear she thought watching TV with her aunt would be anything but lovely. 'The thing is though, I've got some friends coming over in a minute and we were going to put on a film. It's a bit too late to call and put them off, they'll be on their way by now.'

'Oh.' Harriet looked disappointed. 'I see.'

'Another night though, eh?' Without giving her aunt a chance to argue, she looked at Donovan. 'Give Harri a kiss night-night. Then we'll get you to bed.'

CHAPTER 13

Following an enjoyable, alcohol-fuelled evening with a couple of her friends, Marie lay awake in bed that night thinking for quite some while. She had been smart enough to paper over the cracks with her apology, but how long would it be before she and Harriet were at loggerheads again? And over something even more trifling than that stupid dog? The thought of being turfed out over some minor transgression filled her with trepidation and, more than anything else, she relished having the freedom of the house to do as she pleased. Her attempts to keep Harriet out of the way had been reasonably successful so far, but it had been awkward having to talk the woman into going to bed earlier; something stronger than the Nytol she'd been using might prove more efficacious.

There was something else that had crossed her mind a week or so back too; it was a little spiteful, which was why she had originally dismissed the notion, but maybe now was the right time to bring that little idea into play.

The following morning, while she was waiting for the kettle to boil, Marie went into the living room and found the remote control for the TV. Taking it back out to the kitchen, she went over to the fridge and popped the device inside on the top shelf.

After she'd eaten breakfast, she telephoned her doctor's surgery to make an appointment and was pleased that they were able to offer her one that afternoon with Doctor Golding.

Marie liked Doctor Robert Golding. He was at least twenty-five years older than her, possibly more, and she had heard stories when she first signed up at the practice about his brusque, no-nonsense manner. Yet, it was seldom that she wasn't able to engage him in pleasantries and make him smile. Although nothing had ever occurred that could be considered a breach of patient-doctor protocol, there was something she couldn't put her finger on that gave her the feeling he had an eye for her, which might – in some circumstances – be deemed unprofessional. Maybe he had eyes for all his attractive female patients; Marie had no idea. But either way, she had used this to her advantage on more than one occasion and had never come away from an appointment without what she went in for.

'What can I do for you today, Miss Shaw?' Doctor Golding asked with the familiar twinkle in his eye.

'I've been having trouble sleeping the past week or two. It's starting to make me irritable and I was hoping you might be able to give me something to help.'

'Is there any reason you're aware of that might be causing you to sleep badly?'

'Only looking after an energetic two-year-old.' Marie puffed out her cheeks. 'It's *exhausting*!'

Doctor Golding chuckled. 'Say no more. They talk about the terrible twos, but nobody mentions the terrible threes and fours and fives. I remember when my boy was two. I wasn't getting a wink of sleep.' He turned and looked at his PC screen. 'Sleeping tablets aren't a long-term remedy, of course, but I'm happy to prescribe you something to help for the short term. See how you get on.' He tapped on the computer keys.

Marie smiled sweetly. 'Thank you.'

'Not a problem. All of us need our beauty sleep, don't we?' He winked at her. 'I'm going to prescribe a two-week supply of a mild sedative.'

'That's great. I really need something that'll get me a few decent hours.'

'You need to take one, once a day about half an hour before bedtime. I suggest you don't take one *every* night, just every second or third night.'

Marie nodded. 'Okay.'

'Common side effects, you may find they make you a little lightheaded or less alert than normal, although that's usually in older people. But if you feel they're having any adverse effects – any at all – please stop taking them and make an appointment and come back and see me. Is that clear?'

'Crystal. Thank you, Doctor Golding.'

When Marie got home, she found Harriet sitting in the chair watching teatime television, with Donny sitting on the carpet at her feet looking at a picture book.

'Has he been good?' Marie asked, taking off her coat.

Harriet smiled. 'I've been struggling to stay awake, but he's been good as gold, dear. How did you get on at the dentist?'

'Doctor.'

'That's right, doctor.' Harriet rolled her eyes. 'Why on earth did I say dentist?'

'He said it's only a little mole and to keep an eye on it, but there's nothing to worry about.'

'That's a relief.'

'It is.' Marie's eyes fell upon the TV remote on the arm of Harriet's chair. 'Ah, brilliant, you found the buttons. I was looking for them earlier.'

'Oh, yes, er…' Harriet faltered.

'I looked high and low. Where were they?'

'It was the silliest thing, they er…' She faltered again.

'Silly?'

'They, er… yes, they got wedged down the side of the cushion.'

You lying cow, Marie thought, smiling to herself. 'Why's that silly, Harri? It happens all the time, I should have thought to check there myself.' She hung up her coat. 'Tea?'

One Thursday afternoon, just two weeks before Christmas, Marie was idly watching children's television with Donovan when the phone rang. It was Cassandra, one of her friends, calling to see if she fancied going to a Billy Ray Cyrus concert with her the following evening; she'd been intending to go with another friend who'd had to drop out due to family commitments.

'Oh, God, I'd have loved to. He's *so* fit! But I'm not really sure I can afford it, what with Christmas coming up. I've spent *so* much on toys for Donny.'

'It's all paid for,' Cassandra said. 'Jules said don't worry about it, just find someone else who can use it. What do you say?'

Marie grinned 'That's a yes then! I'll get my aunt to look after Donny. What time?'

'Pick you up at three. That'll give us time to get up to town and have something to eat first.'

Marie hung up and, leaving Donovan sitting on the sofa, she went out to the kitchen. On the counter, there was an envelope on which was written in spidery handwriting: Reg.

Harriet had employed Reg to tend the garden for her for years. He was no spring chicken – in his early 70s, Marie guessed – but five pounds and a cup of tea once every fortnight paid for two hours of the jovial man's time and he did an admirable job of keeping the modest garden at the rear of the property looking presentable. Each Christmas, as was Harriet's wont, she would give Reg a generous tip, and she had put the envelope out the night before, asking Marie to please give it to him if she wasn't about when he arrived for the last tidy up of the year.

Marie tore open the envelope and looked at the small card, on which was a picture of a robin perched on top of a snowman's head. She smirked as she read the message inside, written in tiny, spidery scrawl:

To dear Reg,

Many thanks for keeping my garden looking so lovely.
Best wishes for Christmas and the New Year.
From Harriet

Stuffing the enclosed twenty-pound note into her back pocket, she returned the card to the envelope, folded it in half and went out to the hall where she put it away in her handbag, to be disposed of later.

As she flopped back down on the sofa, Harriet appeared in the living room doorway.

'Who was that on the phone, dear?'

'Did it wake you?'

'It did.' Harriet shook her head. 'Just as well, I only went for a nap.' She looked at the clock on the mantelpiece. 'I've been asleep for over two hours.'

'You obviously needed it.'

Harriet sighed. 'I suppose. I'm going to make a hot drink. Would you like one.'

'No, I'm okay thanks.'

Harriet went out to the kitchen and reappeared a few minutes later with a mug of tea and a packet of Rich Tea biscuits.

'What time did Reg come?'

Marie kept her eyes on the television. 'Reg?'

'Yes, what time did he come?'

'He hasn't. Were you expecting him to?' Still Marie kept her eyes on the TV screen.

Taking a seat in her armchair, Harriet said, 'The envelope I left out for him has gone. He must have been.'

Marie didn't answer.

'Marie, dear…' Harriet waited for her niece to look at her. 'I said, he must have been if his envelope has gone.'

Marie turned her head. 'What *are* you talking about?'

'The envelope with Reg's Christmas Card and little gift. It's gone. I put it on the side last night and asked you to give it to him if I was asleep.'

'I remember you saying something about that, but I haven't seen an envelope. Are you sure he was coming today?'

Harriet put a hand to her face and rubbed her eyes. 'What day is it?'

'Thursday. I thought he usually comes Friday.'

Harriet looked confused. 'I... I'm suddenly not sure. What day is it again?'

'Thursday.'

'Oh, yes, it's tomorrow then. But what about the envelope?'

'I told you,' Marie said irritably, 'I haven't seen an envelope. Are you absolutely *certain* you put it out?'

Harriet's eyes filled with doubt. 'No, I'm not. I mean, I thought I had. I seem to remember writing a card. But I suppose I could have dreamt it... Oh, I don't know, my head is all over the place these days.'

'Well, why don't you do it now while we're talking about it? Where do you keep the cards?'

'In the top drawer of my writing desk.'

Resting the card on the back of a book, with a shaky hand, Harriet carefully wrote out a message, then she asked Marie to get her purse for her. 'Is there a twenty in there?'

Marie had a look inside. 'No, just a ten and half a dozen or so fivers.'

'Oh well, he'll just have to have it in bits this year,' Harriet muttered, asking Marie to put a ten and two fives inside the card and seal it in an envelope. 'Now,' she said, sitting back in her chair. 'I *know* I've done it this time and you saw me do it.'

Marie smiled. 'Shall I leave it in the kitchen for tomorrow?'

'Thank you, dear.'

Marie dropped the letter on the kitchen counter and sat back down, lifting Donovan onto her lap. 'So, I was wondering if I could ask you a little favour.'

'What?' Harriet had a sip of her tea.

'That phone call just now, it was Cass – she's one of my mates, I think you met her a few months back when she was round. Anyway, she's got a spare ticket for Billy Ray Cyrus tomorrow night and she's offered it to me.'

'Billy who?'

'Billy Ray Cyrus. He was on *Top of the Pops* the other night. The one dressed in dungarees, you know, with all the muscles.'

Harriet smiled. 'Oooh, yes, he's a bit of alright that one, isn't he?'

'More than a bit. Anyway, I said I'd go and I wondered if you'd be okay to look after Donny for me.'

Harriet looked at Marie uncertainly. 'Oh! Well, the thing is, I've not been feeling so well this week.'

'If you get a good night's sleep, I expect you'll be fine tomorrow.'

'I'm not sure, dear. I'm so tired and all muzzy-headed again today and little Donny... well, he can be a bit of a handful sometimes.'

'He'll be good as gold for his Harri, won't you, sausage?'

'Haweee-haweee!' Donovan shouted, clapping his hands together and dribbling.

Marie grinned. 'That's settled then.' Breaking into song, she started bouncing Donovan on her knee. 'But don't tell my heart, my achey-breaky heart…'

Donovan started giggling.

'Very well.' Harriet looked at her great nephew apprehensively. 'I'm sure we can find something nice to do to pass the time.'

'Thanks, Harri. You're an angel.'

Marie was pleased that she hadn't had to pay for the ticket; the seats were disappointing, Billy Ray Cyrus equally so. Nevertheless, she'd got to spend an evening out with Cassandra and that was always fun. They had plenty to drink, both before and after the show, and Marie arrived home a little after one o'clock the following morning feeling more than a little tipsy.

The house was in darkness and she went straight upstairs to the bathroom where she was sick twice. After stripping off her top – now streaked with vomit – she ran a sink of hot water and immersed the soiled garment in it. Then she crept along the landing to Donovan's room to check on him before crashing out.

To her surprise, he wasn't in his bed.

Wondering how badly he must have played up for Harriet to allow him to spend the night with her, she went into her room and, without even bothering to get undressed, fell headlong onto the duvet. Within a minute, she was sound asleep.

Some time later – she wasn't sure how long – she was woken by the sound of a banging door and voices coming from somewhere off downstairs. Bleary-eyed, she looked at the clock on her bedside table; it looked like it read four-fifteen, but her head felt as if it was splitting and she wasn't able to focus on it properly. She dragged herself up off the bed and, still feeling decidedly fragile, carefully made her way downstairs.

Marie's father was sitting on the sofa beside her mother.

'Oh, so you're home then!' Mr Shaw snapped. 'Look at the bloody state of you!'

Still fighting the niggling urge to be sick again, Marie rubbed her eyes. 'What are you doing here? What's going on?'

Before her father could answer, Harriet appeared in the kitchen doorway. 'Oh, Marie, dear, it's been awful, just awful!'

Marie's stomach tensed and she glanced around the room. 'Where's Donny?'

'He's in the hospital,' Harriet said. There were tears in her eyes. 'There was an accident.'

'What sort of...' Marie trailed off. 'I'm going to be sick.' Pushing past Harriet, she rushed over to the kitchen sink and threw up. Washing away the mess, she bent and took a gulp of cool water from the tap, quickly swooshed it around her mouth, gargled and spat. Then she went back into the living room, where Harriet had taken a seat in the armchair opposite her parents. 'What happened? Is Donny okay?'

'He'll be fine,' Mrs Shaw said.

Marie's father glared at her. 'With no thanks to you.'

'Tell me what happened.'

'It was all my fault,' Harriet said.

'Okay, but for Christ's sake, will someone *please* tell me what happened!'

Harriet's hands were trembling. 'I'm so sorry.'

Marie scowled. 'For the last time, what the fuck happened?'

'Watch your tongue, young lady!' Mr Shaw said tersely.

'We'd been looking at some of his little picture books,' Harriet said. 'And my eyes were getting so tired. I put one of his cartoon videos on to keep him occupied while I went out to the kitchen and put some water on to boil so we could have hard-boiled eggs for our supper. You know how Donny loves his dippy-soldiers. I needed the loo and, honestly, I was only gone a minute, but as I was coming back down I heard a crash in the kitchen and he screamed.' Harriet started to sob. 'He must have gone out looking for me and he'd pulled the water off the top of the stove. He scalded his arm.'

'Christ, Harri! How bad is it?'

'Not *too* bad, fortunately,' Mrs Shaw said.

'But bad enough he had to go to the hospital!' Marie glared at Harriet. 'Why the hell weren't you keeping an eye on him?'

'I *was*! It's like I said, I'd only turned my back for a moment to go to the loo…'

'I thought I could trust you to look after him!'

'I'm sorry. I don't know what else to say. It was an accident.'

Marie looked at her parents. 'And why actually are you here?' she said irritably. 'This hasn't got anything to do with you.'

Mr Shaw's face turned to thunder. 'We…'

'I phoned them,' Harriet cut in. 'I was in such a state, I couldn't trust myself to drive and I didn't know what else to do. Fortunately they came straight round and took us to A and E.' She looked at Gareth and Lynda Shaw appreciatively.

Marie shook her head. 'I can't believe you let this happen. I need to go to him.' She looked at her parents. 'I'll put some clothes on. Will you take me?'

'No,' Mr Shaw said emphatically.

Marie was slightly taken aback. 'Dad, please!'

'We can't go now,' Mrs Shaw replied. 'They're keeping Donny in under observation for a few hours. Obviously, we wanted to stay with him, but they said he's in the best place and it would be better if we go back at lunchtime and he should be able to come home. Honestly, Marie, they said he'll be fine, keeping him in is just as a precaution like.'

'You just want to be thankful it wasn't worse,' Mr Shaw said, getting up off the sofa. 'It makes me shudder to think. Poor little mite. Come on Lynda. I need to get some kip.'

'Hang on a minute, how exactly is it *my* fault?' Marie pointed at Harriet. 'She was supposed to be looking after him.'

'Don't blame your aunt. She's been telling us in the car how she's not been well lately. You must have known that, but you chose to go out on the town anyway. The kid is *your* responsibility, not hers. You're a mother and you need to grow up and start behaving like one.'

'It was *one* night out, for God's sake! Aren't I allowed that?'

136

'Not when you've a little one to look after,' Mrs Shaw said quietly. 'Your father and I had to make the same sacrifices for you and your brother and sister when you were small. It's what parents do.'

'And you need to sort yourself out,' Mr Shaw said angrily. 'Start getting your priorities right. You don't work, and when you aren't sat around on your arse all day doing bugger all, you're partying with your friends.'

Marie shot a glance at Harriet. 'Did *you* tell them that?'

Harriet opened her mouth to speak, but Mr Shaw cut her off. 'She didn't need to. You think I was born yesterday? You went off the rails when you shacked up with that loser in Australia. You're bone idle, girl, and you always have been. You think the world owes you a living? Well it bloody well doesn't and the sooner you realise it the better. That kiddie needs you to look after him properly and that means leading by example. Take a good look at yourself. You're a bloody mess.'

'I'm just tired.'

'Absolutely shit-faced, more like! I can smell the drink on you. You absolutely stink. Honestly, I'm ashamed of you girl, and you should be ashamed of yourself. Thoroughly bloody ashamed.'

Mrs Shaw put a hand on her husband's arm. 'I think you've said enough, Gareth. Now isn't the right time.'

Mr Shaw turned on her. 'When *is* the right time then, Lynda? Eh?'

'Please, Gareth…'

'No, no, when *is* the right bloody time? Come on, tell me, I'm dying to know. You can see the state of her. If it takes

137

something like this to give her a wake up call, then maybe it's a blessing.'

'That's an awful thing to say, Gareth. Poor little Donny!'

Mr Shaw looked as if he realised he'd gone too far. 'I don't mean it like that. You *know* I don't. But she needs to shape up and change her ways before something else really serious happens.'

Marie was about to fight her corner when Harriet suddenly screamed out – 'For God's sake, that's *enough*!' – and the room fell silent.

Mr and Mrs Shaw stared at her, both of them with a look of slight surprise on their faces. Except for the incident with the fireplace dogs, it was the first time Marie had seen her aunt riled.

'I'd like you to go now, please,' Harriet said, regaining her composure. 'I'm very grateful to you both for coming to my assistance. But I'm tired now and I'm going to bed.' Shakily, she rose from the armchair.

'Yes,' Mrs Shaw agreed. 'We *all* ought to get some sleep. Come on, Gareth.' She took her husband's arm and looked at Marie. 'I'll be back to pick you up at eleven and we'll go to the hospital and get Donovan.'

'Thanks, Mum.'

Marie led the way out into the hall and opened the front door to see them out.

'I'm sorry we argued,' Marie said. 'I do appreciate you taking Donny to the hospital.'

Her father paused on the doorstep. 'Just you remember what I said, girl. And let tonight be a lesson to you.'

When Marie returned to the sitting room, Harriet had already disappeared upstairs to bed. She sat down on the sofa, rested her head back against the cushions and stared up at the ceiling. *Let tonight be a lesson to you*, her father had said. Well, it had certainly been that. Harriet had become a serious millstone around her neck; a damned untrustworthy one at that. Things needed to change.

CHAPTER 14

Donovan had been lucky. The burns on his arm were first-degree and by the time Christmas arrived there was barely a sign of any injury ever having taken place.

Following the accident, however, Marie had seized upon every opportunity to ramp up her cruel campaign of deception. It was primarily only little things, but they were nevertheless having the cumulative effect of incrementally rendering Harriet ever more upset and confused. Marie would hide things she knew her aunt would notice had gone missing, later returning them as if they had never been moved. She would say things to the poor woman that she later vehemently denied having any recollection of. And whenever there was money involved, Harriet would end up paying for things twice, the initial outlay invariably finding its way into Marie's purse.

Although Harriet never spoke a word about it, she was quietly becoming increasingly concerned about her own mental faculties

Christmas itself was as pleasant as it could be given the air of mild friction that now existed between the two of them.

Marie had bought some gift tokens for her brother and sister and she met up in town on Christmas Eve to hand them over. She also gave them a card to pass to her parents.

'You do know Dad bins it every year, don't you?' Thomas remarked.

'Thomas!' Lucy exclaimed.

'Well, he does,' Thomas said defensively. 'The birthday cards too.'

'Mum keeps hers,' Lucy said, trying to sound positive.

Marie shrugged. 'Who cares? At least they can't accuse me of not having made any effort.'

'Have a nice Christmas, sis,' Thomas said, giving Marie a hug. 'We miss you, you know.'

Marie smiled. 'You have a good one too. Both of you.'

Harriet put in an appearance on Christmas Day at lunchtime. After they had eaten and exchanged small gifts, she returned to her bedroom. Marie told Harriet she would do the dishes, but ended up spending the rest of the afternoon and evening curled up on the sofa, drinking vodka that Cassandra had given her and watching the TV, while Donovan played contentedly with his mountain of new toys.

On Boxing Day morning, Donny was sitting on the living room carpet surrounded by an array of plastic dinosaurs that Marie's parents had bought for Christmas. Harriet, having finished the washing up that Marie denied having promised to do the day before, was napping in her chair.

Marie shook her shoulder to rouse her. 'Harri, I'm just going to the pub to meet Cass for a Christmas drinky. I won't be long. Keep an eye on Donny for a couple of hours, would you?'

Confused, Harriet looked up at her. 'Who?'

'Donny. I need you to look after him for half an hour.'

'Oh, yes, of course.' She yawned. 'Half an hour, you say?'

'No, an hour. Are you listening to me, Harri? *One* hour. One.'

'Yes, yes,' Harriet muttered groggily. 'I thought you said... oh, never mind. What time is it now?'

Marie glanced at the clock on the mantelpiece: it read eleven-eighteen. 'Ten-thirty,' she lied. 'I'll be back at eleven-thirty.'

Harriet's eyelids fluttered and her eyes closed. 'Eleven-thirty,' she mumbled almost inaudibly.

Marie sat on the arm of the sofa, watching her aunt closely and waiting until her breathing became rhythmic. Once she was positive she was sound asleep, she slipped her coat on, then went out to the kitchen. Rifling through the cutlery drawer, she located a pair of kitchen scissors and, returning to the living room, squatted down beside Donny.

'Hold these for Mummy for a moment, would you, sausage?'

Donny's eyes widened and he eagerly took the scissors from her. Marie stood up and stepped over to the doorway.

'Oh, for fuck's sake, Harri!' she shouted loudly.

Startled out of her slumber, Harriet's eyes shot open and she started to get up. 'What... what's happening?'

'I can't trust you for five minutes, can I?' Marie rushed over to Donovan and snatched the scissors out of his hand. As the child started to cry, she waved them angrily at Harriet.

Her aunt's eyes widened and she dropped back into the armchair. 'I... I don't understand. How on earth did he get those?'

142

'How the hell should I know? You were supposed to be keeping an eye on him!'

'I was… I mean, I thought I was… I must have closed my eyes for a few moments.'

'A few moments? I bet you've been asleep since I walked out the door an hour ago. Thank God I came back when I did!'

'I'm *so* sorry, Marie.'

'Sorry? *Sorry*?! First you let him tip boiling water over himself, now you let him get hold of a pair of scissors.'

'I *didn't* let him…'

'Have you *any* idea how irresponsible you are?'

Her face a picture of bewilderment, Harriet was struggling to speak, but the words wouldn't come.

'Right, that's it,' Marie said, standing up. 'That's the last time I'm ever asking you to look after him again. You're going ga-ga.'

'I… I can't… I mean. I don't…'

'Get out of my sight!'

Harriet looked even more confused. 'What?'

'I said get the hell out of my sight! Go on, go to your room and damned well stay there!'

As Harriet meekly did as she was told and retreated upstairs, Marie smiled at Donovan, who had stopped crying and was looking up at her curiously. 'She's a naughty Harri, isn't she?' Removing her coat, she bent and picked up the child. 'And you're my best boy!' Smiling, she planted a kiss on Donovan's cheek and he chuckled happily. 'Do you want to watch some cartoons with Mummy?'

143

Over the weeks that followed, the atmosphere in the house became increasingly frosty. The two women tended to keep out of each other's way, and when Marie did actually deign to speak to her aunt, the communication between them was functional and to the point. They stopped eating together and, due to Marie's disinclination to do anything that required effort, the housework fell by the wayside. The upshot of all this was that Harriet slipped into a depression. She stopped leaving the house to see her friends and only ever came out of her room to use the bathroom or to prepare a frugal plate of food for herself. She had a portable televison in her room, but she seldom bothered to put it on, choosing instead to lay on her bed, drifting in and out of slumber to the soothing sounds of the new Classic FM station on her transistor radio.

One afternoon, spurred on by an uncharacteristic desire to do some housework, Marie was hoovering and dusting when she almost tripped over a Tonka truck on the kitchen floor. She picked it up and went into the lounge, where the boy was playing with a Fisher Price toy telephone, rotating the dial over and over, and laughing at the ringing noise.

'For God's sake, Donny, I just trod on this!' Marie waved the toy at her son, but he was busy playing with the telephone and didn't even acknowledge her. 'You could really hurt Mummy leaving your things laying all over the place!' She looked at the truck and turned it in her hands. Made of cold-rolled steel, it was pretty heavy, bright yellow in colour and almost the size of a shoebox; she couldn't comprehend how on earth she hadn't seen it. 'I could have broken my effing neck,' she muttered irritably. 'And *you* don't care, do you, sausage?'

Setting the toy down on the coffee table, she lifted Donovan up onto the sofa and surveyed the things strewn all over around the room. 'It's no good,' she sighed, 'you've got *far* too much stuff. I'm going to put it all in a box and take it to the jumble sale before somebody has a nasty accident.' It was an idle threat, of course, but she went around the house gathering up everything she could find and stacked it all away in the closet in Donovan's room.

Later that afternoon, she was watching TV when Harriet appeared in the doorway. Since she'd stopped going out, she never bothered to get dressed and today she was a vision in pink, wrapped in a garish matching fuchsia corduroy bathrobe over a cotton chemise and fluffy slippers.

She cleared her throat to get her niece's attention, but Marie ignored her.

'You've tidied up,' Harriet said with a note of gratitude. Marie didn't respond. 'I said...'

'I heard you.'

'Well, thank you. The place looks so much better for it, don't you think?'

Marie didn't turn her head. She shrugged. 'Someone had to do it, didn't they? It was pretty flippin' obvious it wasn't going to be you. And I don't want you coming accusing me of not doing anything round the house.'

Harriet looked at her niece sadly. She loved her dearly, but something had gone very wrong between them and she couldn't for the life of her understand what or why. She cleared her throat again. 'I've been thinking, dear, we haven't been getting on very well lately. I know it's all my fault, but I'd really like for us to be friends again.'

Marie didn't answer.

'If you would too, I mean.'

Still Marie didn't answer. She was staring blankly at the television.

Harriet tried again. 'Perhaps we could get a takeaway this evening. Chinese maybe. We haven't had that for ages. Then we could put on a film.'

Marie picked up the remote control and raised the sound on the TV.

'You could choose which one,' Harriet offered hopefully.

'Actually, I'm going out tonight.'

'Oh.' Harriet looked disheartened. 'Maybe tomorrow instead then? Or another night?'

Marie pressed a button on the remote and the TV shut off. 'I've got to get ready.'

A thought suddenly crossed Harriet's mind. 'If you're going out, dear… I mean, what's happening about Donny?'

Marie glanced at her aunt contemptuously. 'Don't worry, I wouldn't trust you to look after him again if you were the last person on the planet. I'm taking him with me. It's a Mums and Toddlers get-together, the one that got cancelled just before Christmas because everyone seemed to have gone down with something. You remember.'

Harriet nodded, but she didn't really remember at all. But then she didn't seem to be able to remember very much any more. 'That will be nice.'

'I doubt it.' Marie got up and, taking Donovan's hand, walked him out into the hall. He resisted, but she managed to get him into his little blue coat and strap him in the pushchair. As she put on her Parka, she became aware that Harriet was standing in the doorway watching her. '*What*?'

'Nothing. Have a lovely time with your friends.'

'They *aren't* my friends, I just happen to know a couple of them, that's all. But anything's got to be better than sitting around this place all evening.'

When Marie had gone, Harriet switched the television on and selected Channel 4. She watched the last twenty minutes of *Countdown* and turned it off. Beginning to feel hungry, she went out to the kitchen to make herself some beans on toast. Marie hadn't closed up the loaf of bread she'd opened at the weekend and it had gone stale; *It'll do for toast, I suppose*, Harriet thought. However, the last can of beans was sitting on the counter where it had been left, empty and dribbling tomato sauce. She picked it up and dropped it in the pedal bin, then got a cloth and wiped the surface clean. 'Just toast then,' she said, sighing. She took out two pieces of bread and opened the fridge door to get the butter, but, as she did so, she put her foot on something down on the floor. With a grinding sound, whatever it was shifted and rolled away from beneath her. Stumbling and crying out with surprise, she caught her temple a glancing blow on the open fridge door as she went down hard and lay still on the floor.

Oblivious to the accident it had just caused, the bright yellow Tonka truck trundled across the linoleum, bumping against the skirting board beside the kitchen door and coming to a stop.

CHAPTER 15

At a quarter past eight, as soon as she opened the front door, Marie heard the voice call out and her blood ran cold. It wasn't loud, but the word was distinct and it came from the kitchen:

'Help!'

'Wait here a moment,' Marie said to Donovan, parking the pushchair at the bottom of the stairs and hurrying down the hall to the kitchen, where she found her aunt laid flat on her back on the kitchen floor in front of the fridge. 'Oh my God!'

Harriet slowly turned her head and looked up. 'Marie,' she said weakly. 'I can't get up.'

Marie knelt down beside her. 'What happened?'

'I can't exactly remember,' she said unsteadily. 'I wanted to make beans on toast, but I couldn't find the beans…'

'I opened the last tin for Donny at lunchtime.'

'Well, I decided to just have plain toast and the next thing I knew I was laying on the floor.'

Marie shook her head. 'Don't worry about that now. Let me see if I can get you up.'

As she moved around, she caught sight of a smear of blood on the linoleum beneath her aunt's head. Then she saw the cut and the bruise on her temple. 'God, you've bashed your head. Hang on a second…'

With some effort, she managed to hook her arms underneath Harriet's armpits. 'Are you ready?'

Harriet didn't answer.

'Harri, are you *ready?*' she repeated.

Harriet grunted an unintelligible reply.

'Okay. One... two... three.' As soon as she started to lift her, Harriet let out a frightful scream of agony and Marie hastily lowered her back onto the floor. Out in the hall, presumably in response to the scream, Donovan began to cry.

Marie scrambled around to her side. 'Harri, I'm just going to hurt you if I try to lift you up and I don't want to do that.'

Harriet had started moaning quietly.

'I'm going to call an ambulance, okay?'

Harriet mumbled something indistinct.

'Can you understand me, Harri? I'm going to call for an ambulance.

'I don't need an ambulance, dear, but just check that the toast isn't burning, would you?' Harriet mumbled, almost inaudibly.

Marie glanced over at the counter where there were two slices of bread laid out on a plate. 'I will.' As she got up, she spotted the toy truck beside the door. Quickly grabbing it up, she hurried through to the living room, dropped it out of sight behind the sofa and made the emergency call. Then she went out into the hall and unstrapped Donovan from the pushchair. 'Cartoons?'

At the sound of the word, the boy stopped crying. 'Toons, toons!'

Depositing Donovan on the sofa in front of the television, she hurried back out to the kitchen. 'The ambulance is coming. It'll be here really soon.'

149

Harriet seemed to have come around a little and she was shivering. 'I want to go to bed. I'm cold.'

'Hang on.' Cursing under her breath, Marie ran upstairs to Harriet's bedroom and returned a minute later with her duvet. 'Here, this will warm you up,' she said, gently laying it down over her aunt's prone body so that only her head remained uncovered.

The ambulance arrived a little under half an hour after Marie had made the call. With an embroidered display of concern, she explained to the two attending paramedics – a young woman and an older man – that she knew nothing other than the fact her aunt had fallen. Then she stepped out of their way and listened from outside the door while they spent the next twenty minutes assessing Harriet. The diagnosis was that she was suffering from a possible mild concussion and, of greater concern, was experiencing severe pain in her pelvis. Explaining to Marie that her aunt needed to be admitted to hospital for further assessment, they carefully lifted Harriet onto a stretcher and took her out to the ambulance.

When the man returned to collect the medical kit from the kitchen floor, Marie asked if she could accompany Harriet in the ambulance. She had Donovan in her arms and the man looked at her apologetically.

'Sorry, my love, not with the little'un.'

Marie almost sobbed. 'But I need to be with her!'

'Is there someone else who can look after him?'

'No.'

Seeing how upset she was, the man attempted to offer her some consolation. 'There won't be anything you can do tonight anyway. You'll just be sitting around while she's in with the doctors and it might be some while. What I'd suggest is you call after eight in the morning and they'll know more. Your aunt will be on a ward by then and you can come in and see her.' Marie didn't answer and the man gave her a smile of encouragement. 'Don't worry, we'll look after her. She's in perfectly safe hands.'

When the ambulance had gone, Marie went into the living room and sat Donovan on the carpet. He watched her retrieve the toy truck from behind the sofa and put it down beside him. 'Be a good boy and play with vroom-vroom for a minute. Mummy's got a call to make.' Sitting down on the sofa, she picked up the telephone and called home.

After several rings her father answered. 'Hello?'

'Dad, it's Marie.'

There was a brief silence, followed by a click and the soft burring noise of the dialing tone.

Marie tried again and this time it rang and rang with no answer. 'Damn you!' she exclaimed, banging the receiver down on the cradle.

Marie rose early the next morning and, after eating a bowl of cereal and swiftly downing a cup of tea, she called the hospital. The staff nurse she spoke with was very helpful. She explained that Harriet had broken her hip, she'd been given pain relief and had a settled night. They were intending to operate that afternoon, but for now she had been made comfortable on Primrose Ward. As there was no restricted morning visitation, Marie was welcome to come in immediately if she wanted to.

When she finished the call, Marie tried phoning home again, but, as had been the case the night before, it rang for over a minute without an answer.

'Come on,' she said crossly, strapping Donovan into his pushchair. 'We'll have to get the bus.'

'Is it okay if I take my son in with me?'

'Ah, so *this* is young Donny is it?' The plump nurse on the desk on Primrose Ward gave Marie a cheerful smile. 'Your aunt was telling us all about him while she had her breakfast this morning.' She got up and came around the desk. 'And he's every bit as cute as she said you were.' Squatting down, she tickled Donovan under his chin. 'Yes you are.'

'So is it okay?' Marie said with a hint of impatience.

The nurse nodded and stood up. 'She'll be over the moon to see him. She's in bed five at the end by the window'

All of the beds on the ward except for one were occupied. Most of the patients were quietly reading, one was knitting and another was staring miserably into space. As Marie wheeled the pushchair through, she felt all the eyes following her. The bed at the end had a curtain pulled around it to the halfway point and Marie tentatively peered in. Harriet had her head turned away and Marie could see the small plaster on her temple covering the cut.

'Hello.'

Harriet looked round. It appeared to take her a moment to recognise Marie, but when she did her mouth formed into a wide smile. 'Oh, my dear, have you come to take me home?'

'No, but I've brought someone to see you.' Marie manoeuvred the pushchair round and parked it under the window.

Donovan spotted Harriet and he grinned broadly. 'Haweee- Haweee!'

'Oh, bless him,' Harriet said. 'Come and give your Hawee a kiss.'

Marie lifted the boy out of the pushchair and carried him over. 'Careful now. Hawee isn't very well.'

After he'd given Harriet a slobbery kiss on her cheek, Marie put him back in the chair and pulled out the bag from the rack underneath. 'I've got a wash kit, some undies and a couple of clean nighties for you, but I wasn't sure what else you might need.'

'I won't need anything else, dear. I think I'm coming home tonight.'

Marie's brow furrowed. 'Who told you that?'

'The doctors.'

'I don't think so, Harri. You've damaged your hip and they told me you need to have an operation.'

'I know all that, but then I can come home can't I?

'Well,' Marie said, bending and putting the carrier bag away in the bedside closet, 'they'll be operating this afternoon, but I imagine you'll be in for at least a few days so they can keep an eye on you.' She seated herself in the bedside chair.

Harriet rolled her eyes. 'Oh, tsch, I don't need anyone keeping an eye on me! Get back to my own bed and I'll be right as rain.'

'I'm sure you'll be home before you know it. Let's just see how things stand after the operation, yes?'

Harriet thought for a moment and then nodded. 'Very well. And when is that again?'

'This afternoon.'

'This afternoon,' Harriet repeated, as if she was trying to process the information. 'Oh, well.' She smiled. 'Anyway, I must say, it's lovely to see you. I'm sorry to be such a burden to you.'

'Hey, that's enough of that! You *aren't* a burden. Listen, I'm just going to go and find someone I can have a word with, okay? I'll only be a minute. I'll leave Donny here.'

'As you wish, dear. Then are we going home?'

Marie went back out to the reception desk and waited for the plump nurse to finish on the phone.

She hung up and looked up at Marie. 'Is everything okay?'

'I'm not sure. My aunt doesn't seem to fully understand what's happening.'

'How do you mean?'

'She seems to think she's coming home today.'

'Just a moment.' The nurse called up Harriet's records on her computer screen. 'The overnight report says Doctor Devlin has her on forty milligrams of morphine for pain, twice daily.'

'Is that a lot?'

154

'It's the maximum we prescribe. It may be making her a little disoriented, it's perfectly normal. I'll come in and check on her in a minute.'

'She banged her head when she fell though. The ambulance guy said something about concussion.'

The nurse consulted the screen again. 'It says here that she suffered a minor abrasion which has been treated, but nothing about concussion.'

Marie sighed. 'Okay.'

'Don't worry,' the nurse said, smiling. 'She's in the best possible place.'

'Sure. Thanks.'

While Harriet drifted in and out of sleep, Marie sat on the bedside chair making small talk, repeating old stories of her time in Australia; the few years that she lived there felt *so* long ago now. After an hour she said it was time for her and Donovan to make tracks, but promised she would return the following afternoon.

'Is there anything at all I can bring?'

'If there are any of those nice minty chocolates left over from Christmas, I'm quite partial to those.'

Marie remembered finishing off the box on New Year's Day. 'I'll see what I can do.'

On her way out through the lobby, she spotted a payphone and stopped to make a call.

Her mother's voice came on the line. 'Hello?'

'Mum. Don't hang up!'

'Why would I do that?'

'Well, Dad did last night.'

There was an awkward silence, then her mother said, 'He told me.'

'Listen, that doesn't matter. I thought you should know Harri is in hospital.'

'No! Why on earth didn't you tell Dad last night?'

'Er, maybe because he hung up on me and when I tried calling back nobody answered?' Marie said sarcastically.

'You could have come round!'

'Just so as he could leave me standing on the doorstep? I don't think so.'

'Alright, Marie, let's not get into that now. What's wrong with Harriet? Is it her heart?'

'No, nothing like that. She had a fall last night. I was out for a bit and when I got back I found her flat out on the kitchen floor. She's broken her hip.'

'Oh, good Lord, that's awful. Where is she? The General?'

'Yes, she's on Primrose Ward.'

Marie explained that she had just visited and that the surgeon would be operating the following morning. Her mother said that she would call her father at work and let him know and that they would visit as soon as they could.

CHAPTER 16

When Marie telephoned the hospital that evening, she was told that Harriet had been on the operating table for several hours and there was good news: the break wasn't severe and a mooted potential hemiarthroplasty to replace the ball joint in her hip was fortunately deemed unnecessary.

Marie asked the staff nurse to pass on her love to her aunt and tell her she would visit the following morning.

Having had difficulty folding the pushchair when she boarded the bus, she reached the hospital in a foul mood; the mentality of uncooperative bus drivers, who would rather sit impatiently watching a young mother struggle with a pushchair than take two seconds to get out of their seat and help is beyond comprehension.

The plump nurse who Marie had spoken to the day before was coming along the corridor when she arrived. She spotted Marie and called out.

'Hello there. You're visiting Mrs Palmer?'

'I am. Is everything okay?'

'Absolutely fine. Her operation went smoothly. I just wanted to warn you she's a little confused again this morning. She seems to think she's going home. The nurses have explained she'll be here for a few days before we can discharge her.'

'Okay, I'll speak to her. Is there any idea how long she's likely to be here?'

'It's far too soon to say. It's different in every single patient. It'll be a minimum of a week, but more often it's closer to two.'

'That long?'

'Possibly even longer. The older the patient, the longer we would expect the recovery time to be.'

Secretly celebrating the realisation that she would have the house to herself for at least a fortnight, Marie adopted a serious expression that she hoped would relay deep concern and said solemnly, 'Of course. I understand. Thank you.'

Marie only spent twenty minutes with Harriet. The nurse had been right: she was very sleepy and seemed to be even more confused than she had been the day before. Nevertheless, Marie did manage to make her understand that she would have to remain in hospital for a couple of weeks. She also mentioned that her parents would probably be visiting soon and promised that she and Donovan would come every day. On the way over, she had stopped at the newsagents near the hospital and bought a box of After Eight mint chocolates – the nearest thing she could find to the luxury peppermint creams they'd had at Christmas – along with a couple of women's magazines and a crossword puzzle book. Harriet didn't show any interest in her gifts and Marie put it all on the bedside cabinet, cross with herself for having wasted the money. As an afterthought, when she got up to leave she tucked the chocolates back in her bag.

Despite intensive physiotherapy to get Harriet fit and mobile, it turned out that her recovery was slower than anybody expected and she was still in hospital three weeks later. And, naturally, Marie took full advantage of the situation. She had friends over every night and, funded by an oblivious Harriet, they partied into the early hours.

With increasing reluctance, Marie visited her aunt every day, although more often than not, within ten minutes of arriving, she would be making her excuses to leave. One morning when she was waiting for the bus to take her to the hospital, one of Harriet's friends saw her from across the street and crossed over.

'You're Harriet's niece aren't you?'

'Yes,' Marie replied, looking at the woman blankly.

'I thought it was you. Harriet showed us a photo of you and your little one.' She looked down at Donovan in his pushchair. 'He's adorable.' Looking back at Marie, she saw the puzzlement on her face. 'Oh, I do apologise, you've no idea who I am. My name's Deborah, I'm one of her friends. She's part of our little coffee morning quartet. That is to say, she *was*. We haven't seen anything of her for a while. How is she doing? Well, I hope?'

'I'm afraid not. She had a fall a couple of weeks ago and broke her hip. She's in hospital.'

Deborah looked at her with dismay. 'Oh, I'm so sorry. Poor old Harriet.'

'She'll be fine. They operated and she's having physio to get her moving about, then she'll be coming home. I'm just going to see her now actually.'

'Oh, bless you, dear. You have a good heart.'

'I wouldn't have it any other way. Besides, it's the very least I can do. Harri's been good to me and Donny.' Much to

159

Marie's relief, the bus appeared in the distance. 'Anyway, you'll have to excuse me, my bus is here.'

'Well, do please tell her that Deborah and the ladies all send their love and wish her a speedy recovery. We miss her.'

Two stops along, Marie was delighted to see Cassandra waiting to board. She acknowledged Marie's wave and came up the aisle to sit with her.

'Alright, babe?' Cassandra said, plonking herself down on the seat next to Marie.

'Yes, you?'

'Still got a hangover from Tuesday night! God, how much did we get through?'

'I lost count after the fifth bottle.'

Cassandra laughed. 'What are we like, eh?' She patted Donovan on the head. 'Morning handsome.'

The boy laughed and tried to grab her hand.

'You heading into town?'

'I wish.' Marie rolled her eyes. 'I'm going to the hospital – again!'

'That's too bad. I'm meeting Trish and we're gonna get something to eat and have a girls' shopping day. Sure you don't want to come with?'

'God, I'd love to.' Marie sighed. 'Honestly, Cass, going up there every day has become a real fucking pain in the arse.'

'Why do it then? From what you said the other day, she doesn't even know you're there half the time.'

'Sometimes she does, sometimes she doesn't. It's the morphine they're giving her.'

Cassandra shook her head. 'I wouldn't bother if I were you.'

'Yes, well, I have to keep in with the old bag, don't I? If she thinks I can't even be bothered to visit her when she's sick, she might get antsy and turf me out when she comes home.'

'She wouldn't!'

'No, probably not. But she *might*. What the hell would I do then?'

'Fair point.' A thought crossed Cassandra's mind. 'Hey, you could always come and meet us after the hospital, you know. We'll be in the Black Bull until at least two.'

'Yes, okay.' Marie grinned. 'If I keep it *really* short, I can probably be with you by twelve.'

Four weeks had passed since Harriet's fall and one morning when Marie dutifully arrived to see her, one of the nurses called her to one side and told her the Discharge Coordinator wanted to speak with her about Harriet.

'Discharge Coordinator?' Marie asked, unable to disguise a note of gloom. 'Does that mean she's ready to come home?'

The nurse looked at her sympathetically. 'It's best that Ms Crowther explain.'

The nurse escorted Marie up a floor in an elevator and along to a private office bearing the blue and white plastic nameplate: **PAULINE CROWTHER**. She tapped the door.

Ms Crowther looked up from her computer. 'Come in.'

'Miss Shaw is here to see you,' the nurse said, ushering Marie into the office.

161

Ms Crowther offered her a seat, and when the nurse had gone, she explained the reason for wanting to speak with her.

'You are Mrs Palmer's next of kin?'

'I suppose so, yes. What's happening?'

'I'm afraid her recovery hasn't been going quite as well as we might have hoped. She's responding well to the physiotherapy and her hip is improving in leaps and bounds – no pun intended.'

Marie frowned. 'So what's the problem?'

'We have concerns over her mental health. She's sometimes confused.'

'I'm aware of that. She's been like it for ages.'

Miss Crowther looked at Marie inquiringly. 'Ages?'

'A while. Look, what's this got to do with her discharge?'

'You said ages. Can you elaborate a little?'

Marie shrugged. 'I don't know. She's been behaving erratically for months. Forgetting things she *has* done. Thinking she's done things she hasn't. Oh and there were a couple of times she was supposed to be looking after my son, Donny… and… well, it doesn't matter now.'

'Please, go on.'

'There was an accident. Harri – sorry, I mean Harriet – left boiling water on the cooker and Donny got burned. And another time she fell asleep and I came home just in time to find he'd got hold of a pair of scissors.'

'Hmm,' Ms Crowther said noncommittally. She pulled a notepad from her desk drawer and scribbled something on it. After a minute, she said, 'This might seem like a difficult question to answer, but in your opinion, would you say Mrs Palmer is capable of looking after herself at home?'

Suddenly realising where the conversation might be going, Marie felt her heart jump. Hoping that her face wasn't divulging the overwhelming rush of excitement she was feeling, she pretended to think for a moment. 'I'm not sure.'

'Well, let me be more specific. Let's say you were out and your aunt was at home on her own, would she be capable of preparing some lunch for herself?'

Marie shook her head sorrowfully. 'No, I don't think she would.'

'Tell me, does she have an upstairs bedroom?'

Marie nodded.

Ms Crowther made a note on her notepad and looked at her compassionately. 'I'm sorry to have to ask you all this, I realise how hard it must be for you. The point is, it's my job to assess certain patients for discharge – those who no longer need to be in hospital, but aren't necessarily quite ready to go home. Your aunt falls into that category.'

'Okay.'

'So we're looking at arranging some respite for her.'

Marie frowned. 'I don't understand what you mean,' she lied. 'Respite?'

'She'll move into a rest home. We're looking at The Larches.'

'Never heard of it.'

'It's very nice and it's not far from here. The thing is, she'll be extremely well looked after and she can stay there for a bit until it's determined that she's fit enough to come home.'

163

'You said a *bit*. How long is that?'

'A few weeks. A month perhaps. Maybe longer. I can't really say. It all depends on how much progress she makes. Are you agreeable that we move forward on this?'

'I suppose there's not a lot of choice.'

'Not really. Unless you're in a position to take care of your aunt yourself, which I assume you're not?'

'No.'

Ms Crowther looked at Marie sympathetically. 'Then temporary respite is the best option for her ongoing wellbeing. Provided she makes a full recovery then obviously we'd love nothing more than to send her home,'

Marie lowered her head and looked sadly at her feet. 'I suppose I agree then.'

Ms Crowther spent the next fifteen minutes outlining how she would proceed, but Marie didn't really take any of it in. When they had finished talking, Marie stood and waited for the elevator to take her back down to the ward. As she stepped inside and the doors closed, she let out a little squeal and punched the air. 'Yes!'

CHAPTER 17

Ms Crowther had told Marie that, once a placement for Harriet at The Larches had been cemented, she would receive a letter furnishing her with all the necessary details. It duly arrived eight days later. Marie didn't bother to open it for another two. When she did, and she took in the words under the subheading "Payments", her jubilation that her run of the house had been extended was immediately quashed. As she read on, it became apparent that Harriet was to be means tested and, if she had substantial savings, she would be required to pay for her own care.

Marie's blood ran cold.

The previous summer, when Harriet had one day asked Marie if she minded picking up some things at the supermarket, she had discovered she had hardly any money in her purse. Instead, in good faith, she gave Marie her bankcard with carte blanche to draw however much she thought would be needed. Marie drew more than was necessary and pocketed the extra. Harriet subsequently neglected to ask her to return the card and Marie had no intention of handing it back unrequested. At first she used it to draw cash only sporadically when she needed to support an evening out, or if there was a new CD released that she wanted. But since Harriet had been in hospital, she had been using it more freely and she hadn't a clue how much she had frittered on alcohol and food to entertain her friends. Were anyone to pry, it might flag up as unusual spending.

Harriet had hundreds of thousands stashed away and there was no doubt she would be funding her stay at The Larches. But would an investigation into her financial affairs show how much Marie had been spending?

After her initial alarm subsided, it occurred to her that, should anyone nose about, there had been no suspicious withdrawals of lump sums. She consoled herself that any means test would surely only be looking at what was in the account now. After all, what would be the point of probing retrospectively? What she had spent, although it might total a considerable sum, had been drawn in small, irregular amounts over a period of months, long prior to any mention of paid-for respite.

She nevertheless decided that she wouldn't use the card for anything more other than essentials. If anyone did query anything, she would swear blind that Harriet had endorsed her use of the card, which she had done – initially, at least. And if someone asked Harriet herself about it... well, Marie would cross that bridge if she came to it. It would ultimately be her word against that of a confused old lady. Who were they likely to believe?

Harriet was transferred from the General Hospital to The Larches in patient transportation on the 23rd of March. Her room, with en-suite facilities, was on the ground floor of the building. Although there were signs of practicality – bars fitted to the bed to prevent a tumble, a handrail alongside the toilet – it also had quite a homely feel to it; the cream wallpaper was dappled with small daisies and there were bookshelves and a display cabinet where, Harriet was told, she could keep a few of her own things if she chose to.

'I'll not be here long enough for that,' Harriet had retorted flatly.

The day following Harriet's arrival, Marie made the bus journey over to see her. She found her sitting in an armchair in the communal room.

A young woman with a tea trolley was in the midst of serving Harriet a cup of tea. 'There you go, my love.'

'Thank you, dear' Harriet said.

'How are you this morning, Mrs Palmer?'

'Splendid,' Harriet said, taking the cup from her with a grateful smile.

The woman wheeled the trolley away as Marie and Donovan came across the room. As soon as the boy set eyes on Harriet, he cried out excitedly. 'Haweee!'

She smiled when she saw them, but it seemed forced and there was disquiet in her eyes. She gave Donovan a kiss on his brow. 'Thank God you're here,' she said quietly as Marie took a seat beside her and perched Donovan on her lap.

'Everything alright? You seemed chirpy enough just now.'

'You have to be, don't you? Or they take a disliking to you.'

'That's silly. What's wrong? Are you not settling in?'

Harriet leant over and lowered her voice to a whisper. 'No. It's like *Prisoner Cell Block H*, except with men as well as women.'

Marie began to laugh, but then she saw the look on Harriet's face and realised she wasn't joking. 'Oh, come on,

167

it can't be all that bad.' She cast a look around. There were three other residents in the room – a man and two women. All of them appeared uniformly unmotivated, staring blankly at a TV set in the corner; the sound was muted and, on the screen, a celebrity chef was flamboyantly preparing some noodles and vegetables in a wok. 'Mingle a bit. You might find you make some new friends.'

'Are you mad?' Harriet whispered. 'Look at them, they're like zombies!'

'You just need to give it time. After all, you only got here yesterday. It seems a nice enough place to me.'

'You're not the one who has to stay here. I want to go home.'

Marie smiled. 'Don't worry, I'm sure you'll be home soon enough.' She attempted to change the subject. 'How did the ride over from the hospital go?'

'Okay I suppose.'

'What about the food. Is it good?'

Harriet shrugged. 'Edible.'

'Well, that's alright then. What did you have for dinner last night?'

'I can't remember.' Harriet looked imploringly at Marie. 'You will come and visit every day, won't you?'

'Of course.'

'Do you promise?'

Marie drew an invisible cross over her heart. 'Promise.'

Harriet's recovery was less successful than anyone could have anticipated. Aside from her ongoing battle with arthritis, due to which she was finding it increasingly hard to

168

pick up everyday objects, with the aid of a walking cane she was relatively mobile. But her mental health went into steep decline. Since the death of her husband she had largely been used to looking after herself; the enforced stay at The Larches – which, when talking to Marie, she would alternatively liken to Colditz, Cell Block H or "that one from *Porridge*" – had an adverse effect. She started to spend more and more time in self-imposed solitude and slid into a deep depression. As she receded ever further into her shell, it reached the point where she hardly left her room at all, not even to eat. On those days when she refused to go along to the dining room, a member of staff would deliver meals to her room, but they would often be left on the table to go cold.

It was a regular occurrence for the respite home to arrange entertainment for their residents. There were twice-weekly bingo nights. Two local singers alternated Saturday evenings; a man who performed all "the old songs" and a woman with a more contemporary repertoire. Children from the nearby junior school would come in and sing. And, very occasionally, there would be visits from the local animal sanctuary. Despite some gentle cajoling of Harriet to join in, she was having none of it.

Her mental state became a growing concern for everyone. Everyone, that is, except for Marie, who continued to enjoy the liberty of Harriet's home for her own agenda. The party didn't come without a price, however. The means test outlined in Ms Crowther's letter had determined that she had more than sufficient private funds to pay for her care, and

Marie had no choice but to bite the bullet and make the necessary arrangements with the bank.

A difficult conversation took place one afternoon early in June when Marie was invited in to speak to The Larches' Head of Patient Care.

'We're rather worried about your aunt.' The man sitting across the desk from Marie, wearing a badge with name **Dr Vernon Enright** on it, looked suitably concerned. 'Physically speaking we couldn't be any more delighted with her progress. If that were the only issue, I'd say she was ready to come home.'

Marie's face fell. 'Come *home*?'

'Yes. But her hip isn't the only issue. Up here...' – he tapped his brow with the tip of his index finger – '...she's not doing not so well. I'm aware you're very loyal to your aunt – I've worked here for almost ten years and I don't think I've ever known anyone else visit *every* single day.'

'She's my aunt. I love her.'

'Of course you do. And I'm sure you've noticed a wane in her mental faculties.'

Marie nodded. 'Are you saying she'll be here a bit longer?'

The man shifted in his chair. 'The fact is, Marie... May I call you Marie?'

'Sure.'

'The fact is, Marie, there's nothing more we can do for her here at The Larches. This is primarily a short-term rehabilitation facility and, as I say, in terms of your aunt's hip, she's as well now as she'll ever be.' He afforded Marie a trace of a smile. 'Nimble even. But it's time to consider moving her on.'

'I'm, sorry, move her on? You *are* talking about sending her home, aren't you? Listen, *I* can't look after her. I mean, I would if I could, obviously but I've got my little one to think about, and if she's losing her marbles…' Marie trailed off. 'Sorry, that sounded awful. Obviously I'd do *anything* for her, but…'

Dr Enright held up a hand. 'Please, Marie, don't worry. She won't be coming home. Not just yet anyway. A home environment wouldn't be in her best interests. What we are talking about is a move to a care home where she will be looked after by professionals round the clock, twenty-four-seven.'

'Okay. That sounds expensive.' Marie caught herself sounding unsympathetic. 'Not that that's a problem,' she added hastily. 'Just, well, you know… twenty-four seven care.'

The doctor opened a drawer in his desk and removed an A4-sized brown manila envelope. 'The place that would be best suited to her needs is called Archer's Grove. They have the necessary facilities to assess your aunt's needs and implement the requisite care. I don't expect you to commit now.' He slid the envelope across the desk to her. 'You should find everything you need to know is in here. Take it away with you and have a good read through, then we'll talk again. Obviously if you have any immediate questions that need answering, you can telephone. If I'm not available, one of my associates should be able to help you.'

171

Archer's Grove turned out to be a long-established assisted living and nursing facility located in a leafy, wooded neighbourhood. A good forty-minute bus ride from the house, Marie didn't much relish the thought of making the trip daily, yet keeping well in with Harriet had become more crucial than ever now. The fees for accommodation at Archer's Grove were considerably more than they had been at The Larches too.

A few days after Harriet moved in, Marie and Cassandra were sitting on the sofa at home one evening, drinking and listening to music, and the subject of Harriet's situation came up.

Cassandra emptied her glass and held it out towards Marie. 'I need refilling.'

'As the actress said to the bishop.'

Cassandra guffawed. 'Dirty cow!'

Marie picked up the bottle of vodka from the coffee table and mixed her another drink. 'Seriously though,' she said, topping up her own glass and setting the bottle down, 'it costs a bloody fortune, that place. Her account is going to be hemorrhaging money!'

'What you worried about? It's not you paying for it.'

'It kind of is though. It might be my inheritance one day.'

Cassandra rolled her eyes. 'You wish.'

'Who else is she going to leave it to then? The way things are going, if she's in there for any length of time, there won't be anything left! Then the government will just have to cough up.'

'After they've taken the house first.'

'Yeah right.'

'No, straight up.'

Marie nearly choked on her drink. '*What*?!'

'Trust me, they'll make her sell the house.'

'You're winding me up!'

'No, seriously. You remember that guy I went out with a couple of times, Calvin?'

'Creepy Calvin?'

'God, he was a weirdo. Anyway, yeah, it happened to his Nan. She had some sort of dementia and they bunged her in a care home. She didn't have much savings, but she owned her own home. It had to be sold and the proceeds were used to pay the home's fees. She was in there about six years before she died and by then every single penny was gone.'

As Marie listened, her face grew longer and longer. 'Where the hell am I supposed to go if Harri has to sell this place?'

Cassandra laughed. 'They won't give a toss about you, babe. You ain't their problem.'

'But I haven't got a penny to my name. What am I supposed to live on?'

'How about your parents?'

'You're having a laugh, aren't you? They'd see me in the gutter first!' Marie cast an eye around the room. 'I guess I could sell some of these ornaments.'

'They don't look all that. I doubt they're worth much.'

'No but there's some much better ones upstairs. Harri put them away because she was worried Donny might break them.' Marie took a swig of her vodka. 'And there are a few bits of jewellery which might have some value to them. It's not going to be a fortune though.'

'But it's a start, something to be going on with.' Cassandra held out her glass for another refill.

'I'll tell you what,' Marie said. 'There are some china dogs that used to be on the fireplace that Harri stashed away. They're heirlooms or something, I bet they would fetch a bit.'

'They weren't ugly looking spaniels with chain leads on were they?'

'Yes, that's them.'

'My Gran had some like that. They were a bit chipped, but she always said they were valuable. But do you think it's right to go selling her stuff?'

Marie took a sip form her glass. 'What use has she got for them now? She won't even notice they're gone.'

'A bit out of order though, isn't it?'

'Well, Donny starts nursery soon, he'll be needing some new stuff. I've got to keep the meter topped up. And we both have to eat! Actually, it's been on my mind for a while, I was thinking I might get a part time job once Donny's at nursery. You know, just mornings.'

Cassandra sniggered. '*You*? *Work*?'

'Oi, you cheeky mare!' Marie batted her friend's arm. 'I'll have you know I worked bloody hard when I was waitressing in Oz.'

'Yeah, like three years ago. I haven't seen you doing much since you moved into your life of luxury here.'

'Whatever. I was walking past the laundrette down the road the other day and there was a sign in the window that said they're hiring. Of course, that's not going to see me alright for the rest of my life. Whilst Harri's in that care

174

home, the money's going to keep on dwindling away. The last thing I want is for us to lose this roof over our heads!'

'Do you know if Harri's made a will?' Cassandra held out her glass and Marie refilled it for her.

'The subject's never come up, but I suppose I'd better find out.'

'Yeah, babe. Put your mind at rest on that at least.'

Marie drained her glass. 'I'm going to see her tomorrow. I'll raise the subject.' She refilled both their glasses and grinned. 'I'll take those awful dogs with me and drop into the antiques shop in town on the way over. You never know, I might just get enough for them to cover the bloody bus fare!'

The two women exchanged smiles and clinked glasses.

'Yamas,' Cassandra said.

'Eh?'

'It's the Greek word for cheers. I learned it when I was on holiday in Corfu.'

Marie smiled. 'Yamas.'

CHAPTER 18

Sat on the bus, Marie opened her purse and smiled to herself at the wad of notes she'd received from the antique dealer for the awful Staffordshire dogs. It made the miserable journey more tolerable.

When she arrived at Archer's Grove she was surprised to find Harriet up and dressed and sitting beside her bed. She was much more communicative than she had been for some time. There was still an undercurrent of despondency evident, but she seemed to have accepted that she wouldn't be going home any time soon, and as residential care homes went, Archer's Grove had a pleasant enough ambience about it.

'So, do you want to hear my news?' Marie said, trying to inject some enthusiasm into her voice.

'What's that, dear?'

'I'm thinking about getting a job.'

'That's nice.'

It really isn't, Marie thought. 'Now you're living here, the money's disappearing like water and, well, it doesn't grow on trees, does it? There's all the bills to pay, and mouths to feed – I tell you, Donny seems to have turned into a little eating machine.'

Harriet appeared to notice for the first time that Donny wasn't with her. 'Where is he?'

'Oh, Mum's taken him to the park. Dad still doesn't want anything to do with him – or me – so she only gets a chance to see him every few weeks.'

176

'Maybe bring him tomorrow?'

'For sure. Hey, he'll be starting nursery next month too. Can you believe it? I don't know where the time has gone.'

Harriet smiled. 'Bless him.'

'That's going to cost a packet too. So, yes, I thought I'd try to get a little something part-time.'

'Good for you, dear.'

Marie stood up and walked to the window. The room had a lovely view out across hedgerowed fields to a woodland beyond. 'It's quite nice here really, isn't it?'

Harriet didn't reply.

'Harri…' Marie began tentatively.

'Yes, dear?'

'Can I ask you something?'

As if it were clearly a rhetorical question, Harriet looked at her niece waiting for the question.

'I've been thinking about the house.'

'What house?'

'Your house. In Ogilvie Crescent.'

'Oh, yes. What about it?'

'I was wondering, when you're gone…' – she turned to face her aunt – '…which won't be for a *very* long time yet, obviously, but when you *are*, what's going to happen with the house?'

Harriet smiled warmly. 'Don't you go worrying yourself about that dear. It's all been taken care of.'

Marie felt a wave of elation and relief course through her. She came back over and sat down beside Harriet. 'Really?'

The old lady reached out a frail hand and the arthritic fingers curled around Marie's knee. Her eyes twinkled. 'Really.'

Marie placed her hand over Harriet's and gave it a little squeeze. 'Thank you.' Leaning forward, she kissed her cheek. *All that you have to do now is hurry up and die.* She smiled. 'I love you, Harri.'

Marie was still reveling in how much money the doddery old codger at Fanning Antiquities had handed over for the pottery spaniels. Two hundred and fifty pounds for those manky old things! Incentivised by the notion that there might be even more value in her aunt's dusty trinkets than she had given credence, as soon as she got back to the house that afternoon, Marie went up to Harriet's room and had a good sort through her drawers. She picked out a necklace, several pairs of earrings and two bracelets that looked as if they might be worth something. Harriet had a magnifying glass on her bedside table, which she always used for crossword puzzles. Marie took the jewellery to the window and used the glass to examine each piece in the light to see if they had hallmarks. Squinting, she could see some indistinct etchings, but she didn't have a clue whether they were indicative of any value. Dropping them in her pocket, she went downstairs to make herself a cup of tea.

Just as she got to the bottom of the stairs, the doorbell rang. She glanced at her watch and frowned; it was only just after three and her mother had said she'd bring Donovan back around four. Quickly depositing the pieces of jewellery on the kitchen table, she went to the front door to find an elderly woman standing on the step holding a bunch of flowers.

The woman smiled. 'Hello again.'

It took Marie a moment to recognise her. It was the woman who'd collared her at the bus stop several months earlier. 'Margaret?'

'Deborah.'

'Sorry, Deborah.'

'How are you?'

'I'm fine.' There was a pregnant pause. The woman was looking at Marie expectantly. 'Sorry, please come in.'

The woman smiled sweetly. 'Just for a moment then. I won't stop.'

Marie showed her through to the living room, quickly picking up some dirt laundry and throwing it over the back of the sofa.

'We heard on the grapevine that Harriet's been moved to Archer's Grove.'

'That's right. She's not doing so well, I'm afraid.'

Deborah looked at her sympathetically. 'You dear soul. You must be so worried.'

Marie nodded sadly. 'Very.'

'We weren't sure if we would be allowed to visit her or not.'

'I'm sure she'd be pleased to see a friendly face.'

'Do you think?' The woman looked a little awkward.

You don't actually want *to visit her, do you?*, Marie thought. 'Why not give them a call?'

'Perhaps I will. But in the meantime, we wondered if you'd be kind enough to take her some flowers from us? Just a token gesture to let her know we're thinking about her.'

'That's very kind. Of course I will.' At that moment the phone rang. 'Excuse me a sec.' Marie picked up the receiver.

While she exchanged a few words with whoever was calling, Deborah waited and surveyed the room.

Marie hung up. 'My Mum,' she said, as if an explanation were necessary. 'She's got my little boy with her today. They've just missed a bus, so she's going to be a bit late bringing him back. Sorry, you were saying…'

'Flowers for Harriet.' Deborah handed them over. 'I'd better be off.' Crossing to the door, she paused and looked back at the hearth. 'I couldn't help noticing while you were on the phone: Harriet's lovely dogs are gone.'

'Oh, those old things...' Marie thought quickly. 'Yes, they got broken.'

'Both of them?'

Was there a hint of suspicion there? Marie could feel herself colouring up. 'Yes, my son did it. They got smashed. I had to throw them away.'

'What a shame. Harriet did love them so.'

Marie ushered her to the front door.

'Give Harriet our love, won't you?' Deborah said as stepped out.

'Will do.'

Marie shut the front door and took the flowers out to the kitchen. Removing the small card stapled to the cellophane wrapping, she scornfully read it aloud: 'Dear Harriet. We miss you and we hope you'll be feeling well again soon.

Coffee and cake awaits! Love from Deborah, Claire and Martha. Kiss kiss *kiss*.' She screwed up the card and dropped it in the pedal bin. Looking at the flowers – a mix of pretty pink and white roses interwoven with gypsophila – she smiled. 'Harriet will like these. They'll make for a lovely little gift from me and Donny.'

On the following Monday morning, Marie went into the Suds'n'Spin launderette to find out about the part-time position that had been advertised on the window. It turned out it was going to be ideal; three-hours each morning, five days a week would dovetail perfectly with Donovan's hours at the crèche.

The owner of the premises, Dennis Savage – he told Marie it was pronounced "So-varje" – was in his early sixties, with long, evidently dyed, jet black hair that he kept tied back in a ponytail. He was wearing a scruffy tracksuit and had a discernible problem with body odour. When Marie said she wouldn't actually be able to start for another three weeks, he dithered over offering her the position, explaining he'd really been looking for someone who could start immediately.

'I saw the sign in the window *weeks* ago,' Marie said sadly. 'Couldn't you maybe wait just a little longer?' She smiled coquettishly. 'It would mean so much to me.'

Savage seemed to ponder her words for a moment, then his mouth formed a thin smile. 'I'm sure I can make an exception for a pretty little thing like you.' He afforded Marie a wink that crossed the line between friendly and lecherous and it made Marie feel a little uncomfortable. But she thanked him for his kindness and three weeks later she found herself in gainful employment again for the first time since her return from Australia.

The nursery wasn't too far from Suds'n'Spin and Donovan seemed to thrive on interacting with dozens of other children. They soon had a routine going from which they seldom deviated. Marie would drop him off at eight-fifty every morning, make the mad dash to the launderette to be ready to start at nine, leave at twelve and dashed back to collect him, then hop on a bus to Archer's Grove. The work at the launderette wasn't exactly demanding, but having not had to exert herself for some time, Marie initially found it hard going and she would get home exhausted.

Her primary task at work was dealing with service washes, washing, drying and folding clothing – and sometimes bedding – brought in by customers, ensuring it was all ready for collection at the agreed time. Between times she was responsible for keeping the machines clean, wiping down surfaces and mopping the floor to make sure there was no danger of customers slipping. Dennis Savage spent most of the day in his small office at the back of the premises, but on those occasions when he did put in an appearance, his flirty, often lewd line of chit-chat became tiresomely predictable. Marie quickly learned that the best way to deal with him was feign interest enough to keep him sweet and hold on to the job, but not so much interest that he misread the signs and misconstrue anything she said as a come-on.

As the weeks passed by, Marie found that she was usually left to tend the shop floor alone and she got to know the regulars. Some she wasn't keen on, others she grew to like. There was one in particular who Marie got on really well with, an elderly lady named Doreen who would come in several times a week on a mobility scooter with her Pomeranian, Archibald, nestled in a basket attached to the front. Doreen liked to chatter away about anything and everything while she drank tea and watched the drum hypnotically spinning her smalls around, and she never failed to make Marie laugh. Once a week, the kindly woman would bring in cream cakes from the bakery two doors down and stealthily pass one to Marie with a twinkle in her eye: 'Don't let that boss of yours see you eating it!'

After Marie had been working at the launderette for a couple of months, things seemed to get busier and eventually Savage employed another girl to help out on Tuesdays and Thursdays. Laurie Harris wasn't much of a conversationalist, preferring to keep herself to herself, and Marie didn't really take to her. Nevertheless, she grew to prefer the days when she was in because she acted as a handy diversion for Savage's lascivious eye.

When she started at Suds'n'Spin as a temporary answer to threatening money problems, there was no way she could have predicted how long she would be there. Nor that Harriet would be very much alive and kicking, still living at Archer's Grove, and the savings account that had been funding her care would have dwindled to virtually nothing.

CHAPTER 19

It had been over two years since Marie started working for Dennis Savage. When Donovan started infants' school, he had generously increased her hours to full days. Although she didn't have the title officially, Marie decided the fact that she was there from nine to five every day gave her managerial status and she used it to push the part-timers around. Laurie had left some six months earlier, but there were now three others working various different shifts throughout the week: Vijay, Kerry and Bonnie.

The increased working hours meant that Marie wasn't getting to visit Harriet as often as she had, but the old lady never seemed to notice that three or four days had passed by since she'd seen her, or if she did she never mentioned it. For her, one day melted into another; an endless hamster wheel of waking, obliviously enduring a day of eating and dozing, then returning to bed until it was time to get up and do it all over again.

Marie's job at Suds'n'Spin was bringing in more money, but with the demands on her from the school – uniform, P.E. kit, dinners, shoes that Donovan seemed to grow out of every three months – it was never enough. She had sold everything she could find in Harriet's house that had any value and it was helping to keep the electric meter fed, but looking to the horizon she could see dark clouds forming. Harriet's savings were getting threateningly low.

One Friday morning, she was offloading her woes on Doreen over a cup of tea and a chocolate éclair.

'I tell you, D, I'm not going to be able to survive much longer on what flippin' Dennis pays me. It's pauper's wages!'

Doreen looked taken aback. 'It would be a shame if you leave. Who would me and young Archibald have to chat to?' Doreen always referred to her dog as "young" Archibald, but the dear little thing was in fact quite elderly.

'I've got to find something else before I can think about leaving. God knows what though.' Marie sighed. 'I haven't exactly had a lot of work experience. Other than serving tables in a bar in Australia when I was just out of school, this is the only job I've ever had.'

'Australia! How exciting! You've never mentioned that before.'

Marie shrugged. 'Not much to tell. Anyway, it feels like a lifetime ago now.'

'So, tell me, if you could choose to do anything, what would it be?'

'Crikey, D, what a question! I haven't a clue. Just something that isn't too taxing, I suppose. As long as it provided a bit of security for me and Donny, at least until the house is mine and…' She trailed off. 'Anyway, it's pie in the sky, isn't it? It's a bit like money, decent jobs don't grow on trees.' Doreen had been listening to Marie with a trace of a smile at the corners of her mouth. She noticed 'What are you grinning at?'

Doreen winked. 'What would you say if I told you I know of a little job coming up that might suit you right down to a t?'

'I'd say keep talking.'

'It's a cleaning job.'

Marie smiled. 'I can do that. I keep a very clean home.'

'Probably a bit of cooking, washing, helping with day-to-day chores. All that sort of thing. I'm not exactly sure to be honest, but I can find out for you if you're interested.'

'Listen, D, if the money's good and the hours fit around Donny's schooling, I'm interested.'

'Okay, well, it's some dear friends of mine, the Campbells. Clive and Geraldine, lovely couple. Their current cleaner is leaving. Yvette, a nice girl, she's French… or is it Dutch? Doesn't matter, she's only been with them a couple of weeks and it's not really working out, not exactly sure why. She's heading back home to… wherever. The thing is, they'll be wanting to take on someone else. Geraldine isn't well, you see. Poor dear. It's ever such a sad story. They've not been married that long, ten years maybe? Not sure. Clive's a bit younger than Gerri, I think there's about five years between them. Anyway, earlier this year Gerri was diagnosed with M.E. A tragedy, my dear, a *real* tragedy. She's still capable of doing the odd bits and bobs around the house, but she's finding it harder and harder, you know what that M.E. is like, drains the life out of you. She's got very exacting standards, in fact come to think of it, that's probably why things aren't working out with Yvette, she's not doing things the way Gerri wants them done. Anyway, what do you think?'

'As I say, if the money's good.'

'If there's one thing that Clive and Geraldine Campbell aren't, it's short of a few bob! If you work hard I think you'll be duly rewarded.'

186

'It does sound good. I don't suppose you'd put a word in for me, would you?'

'Of course. Better still, let me give you their number.' Doreen rummaged around in her bag and found her address book. She flicked through the pages, scribbled down a telephone number on her shopping notepad, tore out the sheet and handed it to Marie. 'Give them a call. You can mention my name if you like.'

'Thanks, D.'

'Anything to help, my love. I will miss our chats if you leave though. And young Archibald will miss you too. Won't you, my lovely boy?' Doreen tickled the dog under it's chin; it made a little whimpering noise and enthusiastically licked her hand.

Marie winced; she didn't particularly like dogs. Doreen looked up at her and she quickly adopted a smile.

'Did you hear him? He just said yes!'

'Aww, bless.'

Marie cut her visit to Harriet short that evening. The old lady was tired and the conversation became one-sided, to the point that there was nothing left to say. Donovan started playing up and she wanted to telephone the Campbells before it got too late anyway, so she made an excuse and headed home.

Donovan was still being awkward when she put a plate of fish fingers, chips and beans in front of him.

'I don't like fish fingers.'

'Don't be ridiculous,' Marie said wearily. 'They're your favourite.'

'Not any more. I want a burger.'

'Well, you can't have a burger. I've got to make a phone call and there's nothing else, so you can eat the fish fingers or starve, it makes no difference to me.' Marie spotted a Beanie Baby unicorn on the table. 'Honestly, Donny, how many times have I told you, no toys at the meal table!' She walked over to take it and, in an instant, Donovan picked it up and threw it at her; the soft toy bounced off her shoulder and dropped to the floor.

'I don't want it anyway,' Donovan said stroppily.

'You little sod!' Marie lashed out and slapped the boy hard across his cheek. He burst into tears. 'Get upstairs to your room *immediately*!'

'But you said to eat my fish fingers,' Donovan howled.

Grabbing him by the arm, Marie hoisted him off his chair and dragged him across the kitchen. 'Don't you dare defy me. You can go without!' She pushed him up the stairs. 'Go on. And don't come down again until I say so!'

Grizzling, Donovan scampered up the stairs and slammed his bedroom door.

'Little bastard. They talk about the terrible two's,' Marie muttered under her breath. 'But what about the bloody sevens?' She poured herself a vodka and lemonade and sat down on the sofa to compose herself. 'Right then.' She picked up the phone and dialled the number Doreen had given her.

It rang and rang, and Marie was about to hang up when someone answered. 'Sunnycatt seven three five double nine.' It was a young woman's voice and there was a slight, indefinable accent. For a moment Marie was thrown, but then she remembered what Doreen had been waffling about.

'Is that, er… Yvette?'

'Yvonne.'

'Oh, sorry, I was told Yvette.' Doreen hadn't even got *that* right.

'Who is this please?'

'My name's Marie. I'm calling about the cleaning job.' She suddenly realised how callous that must sound; she had no idea of the circumstances under which Yvonne was leaving, and she might just as well have said "I'm calling about becoming your replacement". Oh well, too bad. 'Is it possible to speak to Mr or Mrs Campbell please?'

'Just a moment.'

She could hear a muffled conversation, then a man came on the line.

'Clive Campbell speaking.'

'Hello, Mr Campbell. My name's Marie. I'm a friend of one of your neighbours, Doreen Mullins.'

'Is she alright?' The voice sounded concerned.

'Oh, sorry, yes. I was speaking to her today and she was telling me that you and your wife might be looking for a new cleaner.'

'Ah, I see.' Now there was relief in the voice. 'I thought for a moment you were going to tell me something had happened to her.'

'No, no, she's absolutely fine.'

'Glad to hear it. So, yes, the job. It's more of a housekeeper we're looking for actually, there's a bit more to it than just cleaning.'

'That's fine.'

'We're losing our Yvonne, sadly. She came over here a few months ago, but she's not coping being away from home, so she's going back to Denmark in a couple of weeks' time.'

Marie rolled her eyes. 'Sorry to hear that.'

'So are we. I don't know if Doreen mentioned it, but Gerry – that's my wife, Geraldine – she isn't at all well.'

'She did say something about that.'

'It's M.E.,' Clive said solemnly. 'Gerry simply isn't able to do as much around the house as she used to, you see, and Yvonne has been a little diamond. I don't know what we're going to do without her.'

Employ me, Marie thought. 'Well, as I said, that's why I'm calling. I was wondering if I might be able to replace her... well, not *replace* her, obviously, but maybe if I could meet... I mean if *we* could meet...' Marie suddenly found herself getting tongue-tied. 'Sorry, what I'm trying to say – and making a fool of myself – is I'm looking for a job and was hoping you might consider me.'

Clive chuckled. 'Don't apologise, you're not making a fool of yourself at all. Listen, I don't want to dissuade you, but I have to stress that Gerri isn't well and the job entails more than just flicking a duster around.'

'I'm used to that,' Marie said, crossing her fingers. 'My Aunt has dementia and I've been caring for quite a while.'

'Oh, you poor girl.' There was genuine compassion in Clive's tone.

'It's been tough,' Marie said sadly, simultaneously smirking. 'But I do what I can.'

'Are you going to be able to take something like this on if you're looking after your aunt?'

'It's not so much of a problem now, we have carers coming in. And to be honest I could really use the money.'

'Okay, let me see now.' Clive thought for a moment. 'We're going to be out tomorrow morning, but maybe if you could come over about two?'

'Ah.'

'Problem?'

'Yes, sorry, it's Saturday and I don't have anyone who can look after my son. I could come on Monday. If that's convenient for you both.'

'Monday works for us. Do you have a pencil to hand? I'll give you the address.'

Marie looked around but there wasn't a pen and she had nothing to write on. She'd just have to remember it and write it down later. 'Okay, fire away.'

'We're at number two, Honeydew Lane in Sunnycatt.'

Where the hell *is Sunnycatt*? Marie thought. 'Perfect,' she said.

'It's a bit out in the sticks, I'm afraid. I hope that won't be a problem for you.'

'No, not at all,' Marie said, wondering where she was going to find a map.

'Splendid. Does ten-thirty-ish on Monday suit you?'

'Thank you, Mr Campbell. I'll see you then.'

'We'll look forward to meeting you.'

CHAPTER 20

At breakfast on the following Monday morning, Donovan was playing up again. He had made a fuss about getting dressed – there was nothing unusual there, he was like it most mornings – and was sitting at the breakfast table banging his spoon on the side of his cereal dish.

'Can you please stop doing that and eat your breakfast?' Marie sounded exasperated.

'Why?'

'Because I told you to. What's the matter with you lately? Can't you *please* just behave for five minutes?'

Donovan's response was to flick a spoonful of cocoa pops at her.

'Just *stop* it!' Marie slapped him hard and the boy began to sob. He looked up at her reproachfully.

Marie had been hitting him more and more frequently lately. 'Come here.' She sat down at the kitchen table and lifted him over onto her lap. 'I'm sorry I smacked you, but you have to stop being naughty all the time. I've got an important interview for a job this morning and I need you to eat up your breakfast like a good boy so I can get you to school a bit early. I've a long journey to make.'

Marie had needed to go to the library to find a map of the county and she had been alarmed to see that Sunnycatt was a small rural village. Getting there only entailed a ten-minute bus journey, but there was a good twenty-five minutes' walk along a narrow country lane once she got off. At first she had been tempted to telephone Clive Campbell and tell him she'd changed her mind. But she had already called Savage and arranged the day off, and Doreen's words had been playing on a loop in her mind: *'If there's one thing that Clive and Geraldine Campbell aren't, it's short of a few bob.'* This could be a golden opportunity to get out of the launderette and make some decent money.

Having asked the driver to let her know when they got to the right stop, Marie alighted the bus beside a fenced-off paddock opposite the junction for Honeydew Lane. There was a solitary horse standing on the far side of the enclosure eating grass. Casting a wary eye up at the dark clouds, she crossed the road and set off at a good pace. She had seen on the map that the small gathering of properties was about a mile-and-a-half along the winding lane through open fields. She had only been walking for ten minutes when the skies opened. It had been sunny when she left home and she hadn't bothered to bring a coat; by the time the first house came into sight, she was drenched through. Typically, the brass plate on the gatepost announced that it was number eleven, which meant an even longer walk to get to the Campbells.

The wrought iron gates fronting number two opened onto a narrow, gravel driveway lined by Leylandii that curved away to the right. 'Jesus Christ,' Marie muttered. 'How much further?' The rain had more or less stopped, but her shoes were sodden and they squelched as she crunched along the gravel.

'Can I help you?' The voice came from somewhere off to her left, giving her a start.

193

'I've come to see Mr Campbell,' Marie said, peering to see who had spoken. 'He's expecting me.'

'Is that so?' A young man bundled up in a raincoat appeared from between the trees. He smiled at her amiably. 'You picked a fine old day for it, didn't you?'

Marie rolled her eyes. 'Didn't I just!'

'You'd better get on inside.' The man gestured at the sky. 'I reckon this is only a temporary reprieve.'

The two-floor house was much bigger than Marie had expected. As she walked past a silver Mercedes-Benz and approached the oak-beamed porch, generously wide, curtained windows looked down at her from brickwork coated with ivory-coloured masonry paint. At the front door, she pushed her bedraggled hair out of her face and knocked. As she waited for someone to come, Marie became aware her breathing was elevated and she suddenly felt nervous. *Calm down, girl and breathe*, she thought. *You've got this.*

A few moments later, the door opened. A man wearing a navy polo-neck sweater and beige chinos greeted her with a broad smile. 'You must be Marie. God, look at you, you're half drowned.' He beckoned to her. 'Come in, come in.'

Marie stepped into the hallway and Clive closed the door. 'Don't tell me you walked here?'

'I got the bus as close as I could. But, yes, I walked from the main road.'

'You should have said the other night you didn't have a car. I could have picked you up at the bus stop.'

'It's fine, I didn't mind walking.'

Clive frowned. 'Where are my manners? Let me go grab you a towel so you can dry yourself off.'

'I'm fine, really.'

'Nonsense, you're soaking wet.' Clive hurried up the stairs and, while she waited for him to return, Marie stood on the doormat and took in her surroundings. The exposed floorboards were a polished golden brown and the white-painted plaster walls were dotted with framed watercolour paintings of birds.

Clive reappeared brandishing a bath towel. 'Here you go.' He handed it to Marie. 'Not that I think it's going to help much.'

While Marie dried her hair as best she could, Clive stood with his hands in his pockets. 'I'll definitely run you back to the bus stop.'

'Thank you. Can I ask, there was a man in your garden when I was coming up the drive...'

'Oh, that's Fletcher. I suppose you'd call him our handyman.'

Having got herself as dry as possible, Marie handed the towel back.

'Would you mind taking off your shoes?'

Marie looked down at her wet trainers. 'Oh, of course not.'

She kicked them off and Clive opened a door on the right. 'Come on through to the lounge and meet Gerri. It would have been nice if you could have met Yvonne too, but she's gone into town to get some groceries.'

Geraldine Campbell was sitting in an armchair next to the window doing some cross-stitch. 'Filthy day,' she said, removing her spectacles and looking Marie up and down.

'Looks like you caught the brunt of it.' She motioned to the brown leather sofa. 'Have a seat.'

'My jeans are a bit wet.'

Geraldine smiled. 'Don't worry about that. Would you like a coffee to warm you up?'

'No, thank you,' Marie said, perching herself on the edge of the sofa. Clive sat down on the other end.

'Well, let's get right to it then. Clive tells me you're interested in the vacancy we'll have when Yvonne leaves us.'

Marie nodded. 'That's right.' She was enjoying the feel of the soft, thick pile of the carpet between her toes.

'Did he explain what it entails?'

'No.'

'It'll involve making the beds, washing, ironing, occasionally cooking, but primarily keeping the house spotless. And I *mean* spotless. I have very precise standards. Are you good at housework?'

'I am. And I have high standards too. You say *occasional* cooking?'

Geraldine nodded. 'Yes, that would be light luncheon, but only for Clive. I don't eat much at lunchtimes. It wouldn't be every day either, just when you're asked. Clive is a bit of a fussy eater…'

Clive had been letting his wife take the lead, but he interjected, 'No I'm not!'

Geraldine gave him a knowing look. 'You are too. You like your eggs cooked just right.'

Clive looked a little sheepish. 'Well, *that's* true, but who doesn't?'

Rubbing her arms, Marie smiled. 'That's fine. I can cook eggs any way you want them.'

Geraldine returned her smile. 'You look cold. Are you sure you wouldn't like that hot drink?'

Marie nodded. 'Actually, I wouldn't mind some tea if you're going to have something yourself.' A thought crossed her mind. 'If you show me the kitchen, I'm happy to make it.' *Bonus brownie point, Marie!*

'That's very gracious of you, but you aren't working for us.' Geraldine gave her an encouraging smile. 'Not yet, anyway.' She stood up. 'Clive can get the kettle on while I show you around and explain exactly what will be required of you.'

The house turned out to be even bigger than it had first appeared from the outside, with four upstairs bedrooms, the master being en suite and a bathroom. After Marie had been given a whistle-stop tour, she sat drinking tea and making small talk with the Campbells as they all got to know more about each other. Not that there were any particularly probing questions, but Marie was guarded, making sure she answered as vaguely as possible.

Eventually, Clive asked, 'So what do you think then, Marie? Are you up for the challenge?'

'Yes, if you want me.'

'I think we do.' Clive looked to Geraldine for endorsement.

She smiled, but didn't commit. 'As Clive will have told you, I have this pesky little illness called M.E.'

Marie nodded. 'Yes, he did. I'm so sorry.'

Geraldine waved a dismissive hand. 'Don't be. I'm finding I get fatigued very easily these days. It's a bit of a nuisance, but I still do what I can around the place. If we do take you on, it would be on a trial basis to begin with. I think a month would be fair, don't you, Clive?'

Her husband nodded. 'Yes, I think so.'

'Then, if you pass muster, we can make it permanent. Now, you'll be wondering about money.' Before Marie could respond, she continued, 'We'll start you off on five pounds an hour and after the month – provided we're happy and you're happy – that will raise to seven. Does that sound reasonable?'

Marie almost choked on her tea; she was only earning three pounds an hour at Suds'n'Spin. Hoping the expression on her face wasn't disclosing her exhilaration, as noncommittally as possible she said, 'Yes, I think so.'

'Excellent,' Geraldine said, clapping her hands together. 'We would like you to start on the twenty-seventh.'

Feeling distinctly satisfied with herself, when Marie visited Harriet that evening, she couldn't wait to impart her good news. Her aunt was sitting up in bed, her head propped on a pillow, and while Donovan sat quietly reading a book, Marie made small talk. She told the old lady about her unremarkable weekend, a television programme she'd enjoyed the night before and that she'd just heard that train drivers were threatening to strike. As had become the norm, Harriet stared with glazed eyes at the shape of her feet under the blankets, listening in silence; it was almost as if she wasn't even aware her niece was there.

Only when it was almost time to leave did Marie mention the Campbells. 'Oh, by the way, I've got some really *fantastic* news!'

Harriet didn't stir.

'I've been getting a bit fed up with things at the launderette, so guess what?'

Still Harriet didn't react.

Marie knew she was wasting her breath, but she continued anyway. 'I took myself off for an interview for a new job this morning. Annnd…' – she paused for dramatic effect – '…I got it!'

Almost imperceptibly, Harriet's eyelids flickered.

'There's this really nice couple called the Campbells. They've got a huge house out in Sunnycatt. And yours truly is going to be their new housekeeper!'

Harriet sniggered.

Marie's face filled with surprise. Leaning forward, she studied the vacant face closely as she continued, 'It'll be a month's trial to begin with, but I don't think there's any question they'll be keeping me on. I'll be doing a bit of cooking, a bit of cleaning, that sort of stuff.'

Harriet sniggered again, more loudly this time.

Rather than feeling pleased that she'd elicited a reaction from her aunt for the first time in weeks, Marie suddenly felt affronted. Was the old witch belittling her good news? Not really expecting a response, she asked indignantly, 'What's so bloody funny?'

Harriet's head slowly turned on the pillow and she looked Marie right in the eyes. 'I hope your cleaning skills have improved, dear.'

199

Marie sat bolt upright in her chair. She was so taken aback, she was rendered speechless.

Harriet turned her head away and her face glazed over again.

CHAPTER 21

Three weeks later to the day, Marie started work at the big house on Honeydew Lane. Clive and Geraldine Campbell had proven very amenable and her hours had been arranged to fit around the obligation to drop off and collect Donovan from school. All the same, Marie would make a concerted effort to arrive early to begin the chores, and more often than not left ten minutes after the agreed finish time; doing so meant a jog to catch the bus, but if it gave the Campbells the impression she was more dedicated than she actually was, it made it worthwhile.

Geraldine's health was worse than she had initially let on and she actually did very little in the way of housework. Marie was fine with that; she was kept busy and the hours flew past. She worked harder than she had done in her entire life, going above and beyond the call of duty to ingratiate herself with the Campbells. She ensured she carried out every duty handed to her to a level that surpassed exemplary and regularly volunteered herself for things that hadn't been requested; upon leaving every afternoon she would habitually ask if there was anything Geraldine needed that she could bring with her the next morning. Usually there wasn't, but, regardless, she would occasionally arrive with fresh strawberries and cream, which Geraldine was particularly partial to, or custard doughnuts, which were one of Clive's little weaknesses.

Clive had an office at the back of the house where he worked from home. Marie wasn't sure what he did – it was something in finance – and she learned when it was best not to disturb him. But he liked to have a coffee and a sandwich at lunchtime, which coincided with Geraldine taking her regular nap. Marie would prepare Clive's lunch and, at his insistence, make herself a cup of tea and join him for twenty minutes. Their chats were rarely about anything of importance, but one day she saw yet another opportunity to get her feet under the table.

Clive was talking about Geraldine's declining health. 'She used to be such a sharp, intelligent woman,' he said sadly. 'But this M.E., it's having a drip-drip effect on her faculties. Slowly but surely it's stealing her away from me.'

'It's really awful,' Marie said. 'But how are *you*?'

'*Me*?'

'Yes. How are *you* coping, Mr Campbell?'

Clive looked at her as if it wasn't something that had really crossed his mind. After a moment, he said, 'I hadn't really thought about it.'

'Of course, because you're a decent, selfless man. But nobody ever consider the spouses. How *are* you coping?'

Unexpectedly, Clive suddenly put his hands over his face and made a small sobbing noise. For a moment, Marie thought she'd gone too far, but then he lowered his hands and looked at her apologetically. 'I'm so sorry.' There were tears in his eyes.

'Oh, God, no, *I'm* sorry!' Marie exclaimed. She put down her tea. 'I honestly didn't mean to upset you.'

'You haven't,' Clive said reassuringly. 'It's just it's *so* hard watching your wife fall ill, slowly changing from the person you fell in love with to become something...' He trailed off. 'Oh, I don't know, it's just very stressful sometimes. And what you said is right. Nobody ever asks how I'm managing. You're the first person who's shown me any compassion since Gerri was diagnosed.'

'You're such a good man.'

'And you're a very thoughtful young lady.'

On the desk, there was a framed photograph of a much younger-looking Clive with his arm around the shoulders of a young girl.

'Who's that in the photo with you?' Marie asked, leaning to get a closer look.

Clive smiled. 'My daughter, Phoebe.'

'She's very pretty.'

'Thank you, she is.' Clive picked up the photo and looked at it wistfully. 'That was on her sixteenth birthday.' He sighed. 'Long time ago now.'

'Do you and Mrs Campbell have any other children?'

'Oh, no, Phoebe isn't Gerri's. She's my daughter by my first wife, Pam. Gerri wasn't able to…well, you know, there were complications.'

'Sorry,' Marie said. 'I didn't mean to pry.'

'Not at all.' Clive returned the photograph to his desk and adjusted the angle so that it was facing him. 'Phoebe lives in Spain now. It must be… oh, two years or more since she was last over. Hopefully you might get to meet her some time. She's about the same age as you, I'm sure you'd get on famously.'

'I'd like that.'

Clive finished the last bite of his ham and tomato sandwich and brushed the crumbs off his shirt onto the desk.

'Right,' he said, scooping them up and emptying them onto the plate. 'I'd better get back to the grindstone or I'll end up sitting here chatting all day.'

Marie gathered up his empty plate and the two mugs. 'I'll leave you to it.'

She was about to close the door when Clive said, 'Marie.' She turned back to look at him. He was smiling at her warmly. 'Thank you.'

'What for?'

Clive smiled. 'Asking after my wellbeing.'

At the end of the month-long trial period, Geraldine told Marie that she had surpassed their expectations and her position with them was secure.

As Geraldine succumbed ever further to the grip of M.E., she became less able to do anything herself around the house. She was permanently tired – even getting up in the mornings was proving increasingly taxing – and she suffered a plethora of other symptoms, among them joint and muscle pain, crippling headaches, dizziness and occasional sickness.

Marie's duties increased accordingly. When the mother of one of Donovan's little friends said she would be happy to take him after school for a couple of hours, she bit the woman's hand off; she was subsequently able to increase her hours at Honeydew Lane and, by extension, her income.

Geraldine had a sister, Nancy, who religiously traveled down once a week from her home in Lincolnshire to visit. She carried an irksomely air about her and, from the first time Marie met the woman, she didn't like her.

Nor did Nancy like Marie. She was always condescending and appeared to eye her with distrust. Although she fully appreciated her sister's health was in steep decline, she couldn't understand why they needed to have a young girl flitting round interfering in Geraldine's care. Marie got the feeling Nancy didn't entirely trust Clive and her suspicions were confirmed when she overheard her warning him to be sure he keep his wandering eyes to himself.

Clive and Geraldine seemed happy enough together, but Marie pondered whether there might have been an indiscretion in the past. Still, it had nothing to do with her. She kept her head down, worked hard, and went out of her way to be exceptionally helpful whenever Nancy was around.

One afternoon, Marie was serving Clive, Geraldine and Nancy with tea in the living room. As she poured the tea, Geraldine took a bite into a chocolate-coated choux bun and a blob of cream dropped onto her blouse. She didn't seem to notice, but Marie did. She picked up a napkin from the tea tray and was about to attend to it when Nancy snapped at her.

'Leave that! Clive can do it.'

'It's fine,' Marie said. 'I can do it.'

'Clive's not an invalid!' Nancy spat back at her. 'Clive! Don't just sit there like a lemon. Make yourself useful and help my sister.'

Clive jumped out of his chair and, casting Marie a rueful look, took the napkin from her and wiped away the cream from his wife's blouse. Geraldine, who had been oblivious to the spill, appeared a little surprised. 'Oh!' she exclaimed. 'Clumsy me.'

Marie looked at Nancy apologetically. 'It wasn't a problem. I didn't mind.'

'Well *I* mind,' Nancy responded curtly.

Clive sat back down. 'Please, Nancy, it doesn't matter.'

Nancy glared at him. 'Don't undermine me, Clive. She's just a housekeeper. She needs to learn her place.'

'I'm sorry,' Marie said. 'I didn't mean to upset anyone. I'll be in the kitchen if you want me.' She left the room, pulling the door to, but rather than going to the kitchen, she loitered in the hall and listened to the conversation in the living room.

'Honestly, Clive, I don't like that girl one bit.'

'Well, Geraldine and I like her, and that's all that matters. Isn't it, Gerri?'

Geraldine had been having a bad day and she looked as if she was half asleep, but she nodded.

'That's beside the point,' Nancy said. 'What *exactly* is her role here? Is she qualified to look after my sister?'

'Look *after* her?'

'Well, she was fussing around her like I don't know what, and I didn't like it. Caring for Gerri is *your* job.'

'And I do! Honestly, Nancy, I don't see what you're making such a fuss about. She was just trying to be helpful. She's a nice girl.'

'Exactly! A mere slip of a *girl*. And just don't you forget that.'

There was a moment of silence. Then Clive said, 'Don't start on with that nonsense again. This is my house and I won't stand for it.'

Marie crept up the hall and went into the kitchen. She had just filled the washing up bowl, when Clive appeared behind her with an empty plate in his hand. 'I'm sorry about that just now,' he said. 'Nancy means well, but sometimes she can just be a little... I suppose you'd say abrupt.'

Marie smiled. 'It doesn't matter.'

'Yes it does. You work your backside off for us, and you certainly don't deserve being spoken to like that for trying to help.'

Without thinking, Marie leant forward and gave him a little kiss on his cheek; for a moment she couldn't read the look on his face – was it surprise or annoyance? – but she instantly regretted what she'd done and quickly took a step back. 'Oh my God, I'm *so* sorry! I don't know why I did that!'

'Please, don't apologise.'

Marie realised the expression on his face was one of embarrassment.

'No harm done,' he added. There was an awkward silence, then he smiled and said, 'Anyway, I think I'd better go back in before our Nancy comes looking for me!'

A few days later, Marie was carrying the rubbish from the kitchen pedal bin out to the dustbin at the back of the house. There was a small portico outside the door and, as she took the single step down onto the chequerboard tiles, her foot caught something and she stumbled. The rubbish

207

scattered across the floor and she had to grab the doorframe to stop herself falling. Cursing, she bent to gather up the rubbish and scowled as some indefinable sticky substance ran through her fingers. Looking back towards the door, she saw a pair of muddy Wellington boots beside the step, one of them laying on its side.

She took the rubbish to the dustbin and bundled it in. As she turned to go back inside, a cheerful voice called out. 'Morning, Marie!'

She looked round and saw the handyman, Fletcher, coming up the garden path towards her. Glancing at his feet, she saw he was wearing Doc Marten shoes with the laces flapping loose. 'Are those *your* boots outside the kitchen door?' she asked irritably.

Seemingly oblivious to the note of hostility in her tone, Fletcher smiled. 'That they are. I'm just going to change in to them actually. One of the fence panels needs repairing at the end of the garden and the ground is muddy as a swamp down there.'

'Would you mind *not* leaving them there in future? I just tripped over them.'

Fletcher grinned. 'You should have a word with your optician then.' He saw the look on Marie's face and realised the levity had been misjudged.

'It's not funny. I could have broken my neck!'

The smile dropped from Fletcher's face. 'I always leave them there. It's never been a problem before.'

'Well, it's a problem *now*. Move them.'

Fletcher frowned. 'I don't know who you think you're talking to, but I don't like your tone. I've been working here tor six and a half years and I've parked my boots in the portico since day one. You've been here five minutes and you're throwing your weight around.'

Marie put her hands on her hips and glared at him. 'Are you going to find somewhere else to keep them or not?'

'*Not*,' Fletcher said firmly.

Still glowering at the man, Marie spun round and flounced back into the house, slamming the kitchen door behind her.

Fletcher stood speechless for a moment, not quite sure what had just happened. Then he stepped into the portico and kicked off his shoes. 'Bloody nerve of her,' he grumbled as he slipped on the Wellingtons. 'I'll keep my boots where I damned well like!'

That same evening, Marie invited Cassandra over for drinks. They had only seen each other twice since Marie started working for the Campbells, but it was Friday and they made up for the infrequency of their girls' nights with a takeaway curry and copious alcohol.

'It's so intense working there,' Marie said as she forked the last of her rice from her plate and into her mouth. 'I don't get a second to sit down.'

Cassandra laughed. 'They ain't paying you to sit down, babe.'

'Ha-bloody-ha. Really though, it's much harder than I expected. The house is huge! By the time I get home every night I'm flipping knackered.'

The living room door opened and Donovan appeared, rubbing his eyes. 'Mummy, I don't feel well. My tummy hurts.'

'You should be in bed,' Marie snapped. 'This is Mummy's time. Can't you see me and Cass are busy?'

'But I don't feel well.'

'Just go back to bed.'

Snivelling, Donovan did as he was told.

Cassandra looked at Marie in disbelief. 'Don't you think you should check to be sure he's alright?'

'No, he pulls this nonsense all the time. He'll be fine.'

Cassandra stood up. 'I'll go and see to him, I don't mind.'

'No, just sit down! He's fine. What was I saying?'

Cassandra shrugged.

'Oh yeah,' Marie continued, 'this job. It's wearing me out.'

'What do you expect?' Cassandra said. 'It's a cleaning job. I'm sure they aren't exactly tyrants.'

'No, not really. But like I told you before, she's ill and she was used to doing things a very particular way. Now she can't, I've got very precise standards to meet. He's a bit more relaxed about it though.'

'It doesn't sound so bad. You want to try working in a call centre. *That's* shite work.'

'But you get to sit down!'

Cassandra laughed. 'True!' She finished her curry and took a long draft of her vodka and lemonade. 'So what's actually wrong with the wife?'

'Geraldine. She's got M.E.'

'What's that?'

'It means Myalgic something or other, I can't pronounce the second word. But it's the same thing as Chronic Fatigue Syndrome.'

'Oh, God, a woman I work with, her son's got that. It sounds awful too.'

'It is. She's only in her mid-fifties and she's dying.'

Cassandra smiled. 'Here, if this Geraldine is gonna croak, you could be well in there, babe.'

'What are you on about?'

'Rich widower and all that. You said the place is huge.' She rubbed her thumb and forefinger together. 'Bet he's loaded!'

Marie screwed up her face. 'Oh, give over. He's like fifty years old!'

'So? I reckon a fifty-year-old bloke would enjoy the attention of a younger woman. Is he good looking?'

'I never really noticed. Average, I suppose.'

'Aww, too bad. Never mind, you ain't all that yourself.' Cassandra giggled. 'Just open your legs, close your eyes and keep thinking about all that dosh!'

'That's *disgusting*!' Marie scoffed.

'Your face!' Cassandra spluttered between fits of giggles. 'Have another drink and calm down. I'm only winding you up!'

'Well, you can talk. How many years exactly between you and that new fella of yours?'

'Danny's actually only five years older than me. No more than six.' Cassandra saw Marie smirk. 'Okay, maybe seven. Eight tops!'

'Cradle snatcher then.'

'Oi, watch your sass!'

When Marie went to bed that night, she lay awake for over an hour thinking about what Cassandra had said. Clive Campbell? Sure, he was nice enough. And she knew far less appealing looking men; that idiot Fletcher for one. But the house… now *that* was truly amazing.

CHAPTER 22

Once a month, Clive had to drive Geraldine to the hospital for a check-up and assessment. It was no more than routine, but she always became irascible on the days she had to go: 'I'm dying and there's sod all they can do about it. What is the point of keep going up there just to be poked about?'

One Wednesday morning, before they set off, Geraldine lost her temper with Marie over two trivial matters. At breakfast she said that her toast had been cold and, just as they were going out the door, she complained about a smudge on her dressing table mirror that she claimed had been left unattended to for two days: 'Make sure it's gone by the time we get back please!'

Clive, who was standing behind his wife, gritted his teeth theatrically at Marie and she had to bite the inside of her lip to stop herself smiling. She wasn't concerned, she knew the toast had been freshly made and warm, and a smudge on the mirror wasn't anything to get all het up about in her opinion. Besides, she was used to Geraldine's little outbursts on appointment day. 'I'll deal with it immediately,' she said apologetically.

When the Campbells had gone, she went up to the master bedroom. It took very close inspection to find the offending smudge on the mirror. It looked like it might be hand lotion or something similar, and it came off easily with the wipe of a tissue. 'Christ, she could have done that herself,' Marie muttered. As she bent to throw the tissue into the wastebasket, her elbow caught the red leather jewellery box sitting on the dressing table. It flew off and the lid popped open, depositing some of the contents onto the carpet. As she scooped it up, her eyes widened at the sight of a beautiful diamond ring.

She put the box on the bed and sat down beside it. She knew the house was empty, but she impulsively glanced back over her shoulder anyway and then started sifting through the contents. Inside there was a compartmentalised tray lined with black velvet. It was filled with a selection of stud earrings. Marie picked up a pair shaped like butterflies. She held them to her ears, looked at her reflection in the mirror and pouted. Rolling her eyes, she dropped them back with the others and removed the tray. Beneath it there was a tangle of various items; several pendants, a number of rings and brooches and a couple of bracelets. Looking through, Marie picked out a small, gold crucifix on a fine chain. She held it to the light for a moment. *This should fetch a few quid*, she thought, and – spontaneously glancing behind her again – she hastily pushed it into her back pocket. An attractive gold ring with a setting of tiny diamonds and rubies caught her eye. 'Nice.' Putting it into her pocket with the necklace, she replaced the tray of earrings and shut the lid.

As she got back downstairs, she heard the noise of the tap running in the kitchen. Fletcher was at the sink running a glass of water. She thought the house had been empty and the sight of him standing there gave her a start.

'What are you doing sneaking about?'

Fletcher and Marie hadn't had much to do with each other since she'd first come to work for the Campbells. He thought she seemed nice enough and they got along reasonably well. But the way she had spoken to him a few days earlier had come out of left field. He looked at her now with vague amusement. 'Sneaking about?'

'You know what I mean.'

Fletcher frowned. 'No, I don't as it happens. I've been working hard and I'm thirsty.' He held up the glass of water. 'You got a problem with that too?'

'Just make sure you wash the glass and put it away when you're done.'

Fletcher feigned a little curtsey. 'Yes, ma'am, whatever you say.' As Marie started to turn away, he said, 'You know, I thought you were alright when you showed up here looking like a drowned rat. Doesn't speak well for my judge of character, does it?'

Marie paused and looked down at his feet; he was wearing his Wellington boots and there was a trail of muddy prints across the lino leading to the back door. 'For Christ's sake, look!' she exclaimed angrily.

Fletcher glanced down. 'Oops, sorry about that,' he said without an iota of sincerity.

Marie's eyes blazed. 'Just get out!'

'Keep your hair on, it's just a bit of dirt.' Fletcher washed out his glass and put it upside down on the draining board. 'You've changed,' he said, strolling nonchalantly to the back door. 'You might act all superior like, but just remember you're the same as me round here: staff.'

Marie waited for him to leave, then she ran a bowl of hot water and got down on her knees to clean the floor. She could hear him out in the portico banging around, but by the time she'd finished and tipped the dirty water down the sink, it had gone quiet. Opening the door a sliver, she peered out. Fletcher appeared to have gone. Beside the back step, exactly where she had asked him not to leave them, were his Wellington boots.

'Fletcher?' she said. There was no reply. She repeated it, louder the second time. Nothing.

Satisfied he was gone, she picked up one of the boots. It smelt of sweaty feet. Holding it at arms length, she carried it upstairs. She bent down outside the door to Clive and Geraldine's bedroom and carefully lowered the boot onto the carpet. Applying some downward force, she lifted it up again and examined her handywork. The mud had dried out a bit and it wasn't quite what she'd hoped for, but the mark was distinctive enough to serve its purpose; the zig-zag pattern from the sole of the boot was unmistakable. Smiling to herself, she made a similar print at the top of the stairs, then went back down and returned the boot to its place alongside its partner in the portico.

Later that day, Marie was in the hall, putting her coat on to leave, when Clive appeared from the living room. 'Marie, can I have a quick word?' he asked quietly.

She looked past him into the living room and, as he pulled the door to, she caught a glimpse of Geraldine, asleep in her armchair.

'Everything okay?'

'Yes. I mean, no, not really.' Clive and Geraldine had been very quiet since returning from her appointment that morning.

'Oh no. Was it bad news at the hospital?'

'It's not about Gerri. It's about you.'

He was looking at Marie with a worryingly serious expression on his face and she felt herself go hot and cold. The jewellery! She had taken a couple of pieces from the mélange in the bottom of the case on the assumption they probably wouldn't be missed – for some time, at least, if ever. Had they actually noticed already? Surely it couldn't be that... could it?

'What's the matter?' she asked, trying to think of something else she might have done wrong.

'When we got back at lunchtime, I went upstairs to put Gerri's medication away.'

Shit! Marie thought. *It is the jewellery.* She could feel her palms beginning to sweat. *Here it comes...*

'You do a really great job and we feel lucky to have you working for us, but...'

Marie opened her mouth to speak, but Clive held up a hand to silence her.

'...but, you know we expect all our staff to take off their shoes around the house.'

Marie was almost lost for words. She hadn't expected that at all. 'Excuse me?'

'There was mud on the landing from a Wellington boot.'

'Oh! I don't wear Wellington boots.'

'Of course not, it's obviously Fletcher. You should have cleaned it up though.'

Marie could feel herself bristling, but she kept her poise. 'I did do upstairs, he must have gone up after I'd done it.'

217

Clive smiled. 'It's okay, we don't hang, draw and quarter our employees round here. I think the last time that happened in Sunnycatt was five hundred years ago.'

'I'm sorry,' Marie said. 'I'll go and clean it up now.'

'It's okay, I did it myself before Gerri caught sight of it. She might not have been as merciful as me.' Clive winked at her. 'We'll keep it between us, eh?' He reached out and ran the back of his hand briskly up and down her arm. 'It looks like it's going to rain. Let me give you a lift to the bus stop.'

The sound of the telephone ringing woke Marie with a jolt. She tried to focus on where she was and blinked at her bedside clock; the glowing red digits said three-twenty-three. 'What the…?'

Swinging her legs out from under the blankets, she went out onto the landing. It was the phone in the living room that was ringing. But she had just reached the foot of the stairs when it stopped.

'Damn it!'

As she turned to go back up, the ringing started again. She dashed into the living room and grabbed up the receiver. 'Hello?'

Nobody expects a ringing phone in the middle of the night to be anything other than a harbinger of bad news.

Marie sat perched on the edge of the sofa and listened in silence as Quinn, one of the nurses at Archer's Grove explained that, most unexpectedly, her Aunt Harriet had passed away peacefully in her sleep at two-fifty-seven. He asked her if she would be able to come in the next day to discuss the necessary arrangements that needed to be made

218

and – he apologised profusely for seeming indelicate – collect Harriet's things. When Quinn had finished, Marie said she would be in the next morning, thanked him for calling and hung up. Then she filled a shot glass with neat vodka and consumed it in one gulp.

Marie didn't manage to get back to sleep. Her mind was buzzing with excitement. There wasn't a lot of money left in Harriet's savings account – her extended stay at Archer's Grove was responsible for that. But all fear of the house being taken were gone, and now it was all hers!

She rose at six and had a light breakfast, waiting until seven-thirty to ring the Campbells. Sounding sleepy and a little irritable, Clive answered. She apologised for giving him such short notice, but explained that she needed to take the morning off. Clive was exceedingly sympathetic, offered her his sincere condolences, understood she had a lot to do and insisted she take a few days off.

Next, almost as an afterthought, she called her parents. Her father answered. Not giving him the chance to hang up on her, Marie blurted out, 'Harri's dead.'

There was a moment's silence on the end of the line, then her father said, 'Okay, thanks for letting me know.' There was a slight tremor in his voice. Before Marie could speak again, there was a click and the dialing tone sounded.

It transpired that the cause of Harriet's death had been heart failure. The meeting at Archer's Grove went as well as a meeting under the circumstances could. Marie sat and listened as the manager, Mr Perin, explained the legal requirements following a death to her. He finished by asking if she had any questions.

Without thinking, Marie said, 'What about the will?'

Mr Perin looked slightly taken aback. 'Are you referring to your aunt's last will and testament?'

'Yes.'

'I'm afraid that's nothing to do with us.' There was disrespect in the man's eyes. 'You would need to speak with her solicitor about that.'

When Marie went to leave, one of the nurses appeared and handed her two bulging carrier bags. 'Will you manage?'

'Sure.'

Marie didn't bother to look to see what was inside. On the way back to the bus stop, she passed a house where there was some building work being done. Making sure she couldn't be seen by the two men up on the scaffolding, she tossed the two carrier bags containing Harriet's final worldly possessions into a skip.

That evening, she telephoned Cassandra. 'I've got news!'

'Go on.'

'The old bat is dead!'

'Harri?!' Cassandra exclaimed.

'Yep!'

'Oh, God, I'm so sorry.'

'Don't be.' Marie smiled. 'It's the best thing that could have happened.'

'Well, at least that means you're quids in now.'

Marie grinned. 'Yep. Want to come over and celebrate?'

CHAPTER 23

Harriet's funeral took place on the 14th of October, 1997, one week to the day following her death. It was a relatively small affair.

Harriet had chosen to be cremated. It was preceded by a short, humanist service in a tiny chapel annexing the crematorium. Gareth and Lynda Shaw were sat on one side of the chapel with Marie's brother and sister. Marie herself sat on the other side with two of the nurses from Archer's Grove who had been particularly fond of Harriet, her coffee morning cronies – Deborah, Claire and Martha – and a pleasant old man with his slightly spiky wife in tow; he approached Marie just before the service started and told her that he and Harriet used to work together many years ago. Cassandra, although she had barely known Harriet, had also offered to come as moral support for Marie. The celebrant delivered a moving memorial speech based upon Gareth Shaw's memories of his sister when they were children. Swept up in the moment, even Marie was briefly moved to tears.

After the service, everyone converged at The Green Man pub nearby, where finger food and drinks had been laid out. Marie found herself cornered by Deborah.

'Hello there. Lovely service.'

'Hmm,' Marie muttered noncommittally.

Deborah pulled a face. 'Well, as lovely as these things *can* be. What I mean is, for a funeral. Obviously funerals aren't lovely, but…' She trailed off, and, realising she was digging a hole, hastily changed tack. 'You didn't bring your little boy with you?'

'No,' Marie said. 'I don't think a funeral is appropriate for a child. He's still very upset.'

'Oh, poor dear. Yes, young children don't really understand, do they?' Deborah took a bite out of a sausage roll. 'I think you probably did the right thing.'

I don't give a monkey's what you think, Marie thought, but she smiled. 'Yes, he went to school as normal. He's staying over at a friend's tonight.'

'That'll be nice for him.' Deborah was clearly struggling to find something else to say, yet seemed reluctant to move away. She sighed. 'Yes, things certainly won't be the same without her.' She popped the last of the sausage roll into her mouth and licked the flakes of pastry from her fingers with the tip of her tongue.

'No,' Marie said solemnly.

'So where will you be living now?'

Before Marie had a chance to answer, Claire and Martha appeared at Deborah's shoulder.

'We're going to make a move, Debbie,' Claire said. 'Are you ready for the off?'

'I am,' Deborah said, putting down her empty plate on a nearby table. She looked back to Marie. 'Again, we're so sorry for your loss.'

Claire and Martha nodded in agreement.

Marie smiled at them sweetly and watched them heading for the exit, huddled together and whispering amongst themselves. At the door, Deborah glanced back for an instant, then she was gone. *Nosy bitch*, Marie thought.

Gradually, the few remaining mourners filtered away until only Marie and her family were left.

'Well, that's that over and done then.' Mr Shaw finished his pint of Guinness. He rose and looked at his wife. 'I'm going to settle the bar bill, Lynda. Get your coats on, kids.'

Lucy and Thomas did as they'd been told.

Spotting her father at the bar and her mother on her own for the first time since they had arrived at the pub, Marie asked Cassandra to wait for her outside while she had a quick word with her.

'Sure,' Cassandra said. 'I'll wait in the car. Don't be too long though, eh?'

'I won't.' Marie stepped over to where Mrs Shaw was putting on her coat. 'He hasn't spoken two words to me all day, Mum!'

'Well what do you expect, Marie? The situation isn't going to change, so you'd better get used to it.'

'I don't actually care, I just thought that today of all days…'

Glancing towards the bar where her husband was talking to the barman, Mrs Shaw took Marie's arm and led her out of earshot to a table beside the window. 'The fact is, he couldn't get his head around why Harriet took you in when you came back from Australia. He thought she had undermined him. He thinks you abused her kindness too.'

'Abused her kindness? I did everything for her. Right up until she had that fall and ended up in hospital, I'd looked after her as best I could.' Marie's voice had got louder. 'How *dare* he suggest I abused her kindness?'

223

Mrs Shaw shooshed her. 'Don't cause a scene. Not here. Not today.'

'Well, honestly!'

'Look, it doesn't matter whether he's right or wrong, that's what he thinks. He's as stubborn as a mule and he always will be.' Mrs Shaw afforded Marie a weak smile. 'A bit like his daughter, eh?'

Marie shrugged. 'Whatever.'

Mr Shaw reappeared, tucking his wallet into his jacket pocket. 'Seventy-three bloody quid! For drinks and a few savouries. Bloody scandalous!'

Mrs Shaw exchanged glances with Marie.

'Right.' He patted his trouser pocket to feel for his car keys. 'Ready then?'

'Aye.' Mrs Shaw smiled at Marie. 'Give Donny a kiss from us.'

Later that afternoon, after she'd eaten, Marie gave the Campbells a call.

As usual, it was Clive who answered. 'Marie. How did the service go today? We were thinking about you.'

Marie sighed. 'It was very sad.'

'Of course. It must have been awful for you.'

Marie noticed the nail on the end of her finger was broken and she idly started chewing on it. 'Yes, I tried not to cry, but I couldn't help it. I still can't believe she's gone.' She looked at the end of her finger; annoyingly, the nail was still rough.

'It will take a while. These things do.'

'I suppose. But it was a nice service though and the celebrant said some lovely things.' Finally the little piece of nail came away and Marie spat it out. 'I got to meet some of Harri's friends at the wake too, so that was nice.'

'I'm glad. As I say, you were in our thoughts.'

'That's very kind. Anyway, I wanted to call to let you know I'll be back to work tomorrow.'

'Oh, really? Well that's good news. But, listen, we're actually going to be out tomorrow all day. An old associate of mine is retiring and they're holding a gala dinner for him at Dauncey's.'

'That sounds nice.' Marie had never heard of it, but just from its name it sounded posh.

'Yes, so the thing is, it might be best if you leave it till Thursday.'

'Oh, okay.'

'Yes,' Clive continued. 'Take the extra day. You probably still have quite a lot on your plate to sort out.'

'No, not really. All the legal stuff is in the hands of Harri's solicitor now.'

'Well, take the day anyway, even if it's just to unwind. You've been through a lot.'

'Okay, thanks, Mr Campbell.'

'Excellent. We'll see you on Thursday then, yes?'

'Absolutely.'

When Marie arrived for work on the Thursday morning, she found Clive seated at the kitchen table nursing a mug of coffee.

'I'd have happily made that for you if you'd have waited,' Marie said, slipping off her coat. Clive didn't reply. Sensing that something wasn't right, she crossed to the sink and washed her hands. 'How did your dinner go?' she asked breezily.

'Very well. It was good to see some of the old faces. Listen, I know you've been through the ringer this week, but would you mind taking a seat for a moment? There's something I need to ask you.'

Marie sat down beside him. 'Everything okay?'

Clearly it wasn't.

'When we were getting ready to go out yesterday, Gerri went to her jewellery box for one of her pendants.'

Marie felt her stomach tighten, but her face remained expressionless.

'A gold crucifix on a chain,' Clive continued.

'That sounds nice.'

'It's nothing special, but it belonged to her mother, so it has sentimental value.' Clive's eyes were studying Marie intently, searching for a reaction, but he wasn't getting one. 'The thing is, it wasn't there. Gerri had a good look through and a diamond and ruby ring was missing too.'

Marie thought about the down-payment on driving lessons that she'd made using some of the money from the sale of the jewellery. 'Are you sure?'

'Sure about what?'

'That it's missing. Maybe she put them somewhere else, in a drawer maybe, and simply forgot.'

'We've looked high and low and there's no sign of them.'

Marie exhaled and shrugged. 'I'm sorry, I don't really know what to say.'

'I'm not accusing you of taking them or anything like that,' Clive said awkwardly. 'It's just, I was wondering if maybe you'd come across them when you were doing the housework.'

Marie shook her head. 'No, sorry, I haven't.'

'Hmm.' There was a moment's silence. Clive was still looking her in the eyes.

You bloody are *accusing me*, Marie thought.

'You're absolutely certain.'

'One hundred percent. I don't know what else to tell you, Mr Campbell.'

Clive frowned. 'Well, they can't have vanished into the ether. There's only yourself and Fletcher have free access to the house, and…'

'Fletcher!' Marie exclaimed.

'What about him?'

'Remember you said you found a footprint from his boots last week?'

'Well, yes, but…'

'I thought it was odd at the time he'd be tramping around upstairs, but the boot mark was there, so…'

'Woah, slow down a moment.'

Marie looked at Clive. She could almost hear the cogs turning in his head. 'Sorry,' she said meekly. 'He probably just wanted to use the bathroom.'

Clive shook his head. 'He uses the facilities in the utility room downstairs. I can't conceive that he'd steal from us, but there's no reason for Fletcher to be upstairs.' He seemed to

227

come to a decision. 'I think I'm going to have to have word with him.'

'I feel awful.' Marie looked at Clive imploringly. 'I didn't mean to make it sound like I was accusing him, it's just it suddenly occurred to me...'

'You did the right thing. He's not working today, but I'll give him a call later.'

'Please don't say anything to him about what I said.'

'Don't worry.' Clive put a hand on her arm. 'It's strictly between you and I.' He looked at her uncomfortably. 'Er, listen, Marie, I'm very sorry.'

'What for?'

'To be honest, I couldn't think of any other explanation than theft. Just by asking you, it must have seemed like I was being accusatory.'

Too right, Marie thought.

Clive sat back in his chair and puffed out his cheeks. 'Why didn't I make that connection with the muddy boot print?' he thought aloud. 'Fletcher though, I still can't quite believe it. He's been with us for years. I've treated him like the son I never had.' He looked at Marie. 'Did you know he's a single father?'

She shook her head.

'Yes, his wife passed away just before he started here. Tragic. I think the boy's about nine now.'

'It isn't easy being a single parent,' Marie said, trying to sound compassionate. 'Maybe he's got money problems. Perhaps he saw an opportunity and... well, desperation can drive people to do silly things.'

'Be that as it may, we can't have a thief in the house,' Clive said. 'If he has financial difficulties, he could have come and spoken to me. He knows that.' Draining his mug of coffee, he stood up. 'Anyway, don't you worry about it any more.' He smiled. 'It's good to have you back.'

The following day when Marie arrived for work, Clive collared her in the hall.

'I just wanted to let you know that I telephoned Fletcher last night and he's not going to be working here any more.'

'Oh!' Marie tried to look surprised. 'So he admitted the theft?'

'No, sadly not. He flat out denied it. Tried to tell me it had to be you. But I know a lie when I hear it.' Clive inhaled deeply. 'It's a bloody shame. The ring didn't matter quite so much, but I was really hoping we might get the pendant back. It means a lot to Gerri.'

'It's incredible. After all you said you'd done for him, I can't believe he'd steal from you.'

'Neither can we. Just goes to show that you never really know someone as well as you think you do. Anyway, listen, Gerri's having a lay in this morning, so try to be as quiet as possible with the housework.'

'Of course, Mr Campbell.'

Clive winked at her. 'Isn't it about time you started calling me Clive?'

'I'm not sure that would be proper.'

'Nonsense.' He brushed Marie's arm. 'It would please me if you would.'

Marie smiled. 'Okay. Clive.'

'Excellent. Right, I'd better get on.'

Clive retreated to his office and Marie went out to the portico. She picked up the pair of Wellington boots from beside the step, went out into the garden and dropped them into the dustbin.

CHAPTER 24

One Saturday morning, three weeks later, Marie was clearing away the breakfast things and Donovan was watching cartoons on the TV, when the letterbox clattered. Donovan heard it and went out to hall to pick up the post. There were three official-looking letters and he carried them out to the kitchen.

'Post, Mum.'

Marie was running water into the washing up bowl. 'My hands are wet. Drop it on the table, I'll look in a minute.'

Donovan did as he was asked. 'Can I have a biscuit?'

'No, you can't, you've only just had breakfast.'

Donovan screwed up his face. 'Not fair!'

'Nor is me having to stand here washing the dishes, but life *isn't* fair!'

'Didn't really want one anyway!' Giving his mother a filthy look, Donovan stomped back into the living room.

When Marie had finished doing the dishes, she sat down at the table to see what had arrived. Since Harriet's funeral, she had received so much mail containing paperwork that she struggled to understand, she was sick to death of it all. But then a black ink stamp on the back of one of the envelopes caught her eye: **Petrescu & May, Solicitors**.

Marie felt her heartbeat quicken as, with trembling fingers, she tore it open and pulled out the neatly folded letter inside. Expecting it to confirm the bequeathal of the house and all Harriet's worldy goods to her, as she read the letter, her excitement was dampened. Brief and worded very formally, it read:

Dear Miss Shaw,

As per the wishes of the late Mrs Harriet Palmer, you are cordially invited to attend the official reading of her last will and testament at the offices of Petrescu & May (see address above) on Monday 1st December at 10.00 a.m.

I look forward to receiving you.

Yours sincerely,
(Following the letters p.p., there was an illegible signature, presumably that of a secretary, then a typed name)
Michael Petrescu, LLB (Hons)

'The first of December!' Marie exclaimed aloud. *That's another month!*, she thought. *And I've got to go all the way to* – she looked at the address on the letterhead – 'London?! Oh, for Christ's sake, that's insane! All that way just to be told what I already know!'

As she irritably folded the letter and returned it to the envelope, it crossed her mind that she might not be the only person there. Like something out of an old movie, she imagined a fusty, poorly-lit room and an antique leather-topped desk, behind which was an old man with a bushy white beard, peering contemptuously over the top of his half-moon spectacles at the gathering of expectant vultures seated opposite him. She shook off the image.

232

Well, there was no point dwelling on it now; she would find out when she got there.

'The first of December,' she muttered bitterly as she tucked the letter away in the kitchen drawer. 'Bloody ridiculous.'

As the day of the reading of the will approached, Clive was very gracious in letting Marie take time off and even offered to drive Marie into London. She thanked him, but politely declined.

Having dropped Donovan at school, on December the first she boarded the eight-forty-six train into the City. It was inexplicably held just outside Waterloo, and almost ten minutes passed before it finally got moving again. When it arrived on the platform furthest from the exit, she had to run to catch a bus. She just missed it, but, checking the timetable at the stop, she was relieved to see there would be another along in ten minutes.

The offices of Petrescu & May were situated in a small building off The Strand. There were tiny flecks of snow in the air as Marie arrived, and she stepped inside at five minutes to ten.

A woman seated behind the desk in the small lobby looked up and smiled. 'Good morning.'

'Hi, I'm here to see Mr Petrescu.' Marie pulled the letter out of her bag and handed to the woman, but she shook her head.

'That's fine, I don't need to see that. You must be Miss Shaw.'

'That's right.'

'Mr Petrescu's is expecting you. You're the last to arrive, but you're still in good time. Let me show you straight up.'

As the woman led the way up a narrow staircase, her words echoed in Marie's mind: *The last to arrive.* At the top of the stairs was a short corridor, brightly illuminated by a strip light, its walls dotted with gold-framed certificates. There were two doors, one on either side, and the woman tapped lightly on the one to the left and opened it. 'Miss Shaw is here, sir.'

Marie heard the voice from inside: 'Splendid. Show her in would you?'

Marie stepped into the room to be greeted by the sight of five chairs arranged in a semi-circle in front of a desk. The one nearest to her was empty, but the other four were occupied. She bristled at the sight of her parents sitting in the two farthest from her near the window; why hadn't her mother mentioned that they'd received an invitation too? Both her mother and father avoided making eye contact with her. Also present was Harriet's friend Deborah and, sitting nearest to her, a man whose face was familiar, but who Marie couldn't at first place. Then it came back to her: he was Harriet's old work colleague, he'd been at the funeral.

There was a young man sitting on the other side of the desk – nothing like the starchy Victorian gent Marie had imagined – and he got up and came towards her with his hand outstretched.

'Mike Petrescu.' He shook her hand enthusiastically. 'Delighted to meet you, Miss Shaw.' He gestured to the empty chair. 'If you'd like to take a pew, we can get started.'

He returned to his chair and Marie sat down.

'Thank you all for coming,' Petrescu said, smiling pleasantly at the assembly of people in front of him. 'It probably all seems a bit Alfred Hitchcock, the big family gathering for the reading of the will. All we really need are a few cobwebs and a flash of lightning to take out the power.' He chuckled and waited for a response, but aside from Deborah, who smiled politely, he was met with blank faces. He cleared his throat. 'Anyway, obviously it's not really common practice to do it like this any more, but as I explained briefly in my letter, it was Mrs Palmer's wish that it be carried out this way. She obviously had a bit of a flare for the dramatic.'

'A flare for *something*,' Gareth Shaw muttered. Lynda Shaw nudged him with her elbow to be quiet.

'Right then, let's get on with it, shall we?' There was a blue loose-leaf folder on the desk. Petrescu flipped it open and withdrew what appeared to be no more than three sheets of foolscap paper, held together with a staple in the top lefthand corner.

'Can we just skip the formalities and cut to the chase?' Marie's father asked impatiently.

Petrescu looked a little chagrined, but he nodded. 'Provided everyone else present is in agreement...'

There was a mumble of approval.

'Very well.' He folded over the paperwork to the second page. 'As you'll have realised, you've all been invited here today because you're beneficiaries in the Last Will and Testament of Harriet Palmer, née Shaw. I shall read through in the order that Mrs Palmer was very specific about.' He looked at Deborah and smiled, then consulted the stapled papers. 'To Deborah Caldicott, as a sign of my affection, and immense gratitude for her years of friendship, I leave my pair of Lladro porcelain figurines.'

Marie breathed a sigh of relief. The figurines were among the few ornaments in the house she hadn't sold. She knew she had put them away in a box somewhere, but at that moment she couldn't recall precisely where.

'That's lovely,' Deborah said, although from the expression on her face she had clearly expected something more.

Petrescu turned his attention to the man seated next to Marie. 'To Fred Pilson, in remembrance of the happy days we spent working together, I bequeath my painting of the stag in the mist as he admired it so.'

Pilson looked suitably pleased. He nodded gratefully. 'She was a lovely lady.'

Petrescu looked up. 'There is an additional bequest here for Mrs Palmer's neighbour, Brenda Taylor. Regrettably she couldn't be with us today. The bequest is for her precious Jade plant. Mrs Palmer says here...' – he glanced back down – '...Please look after it for me.' He smiled. As he turned to Marie's mother and father, she felt her heart rate elevating. 'To my brother, Gareth Shaw, and his wife Lynda, I leave dear Old Mabel (my Jeep Cherokee), and the sum of two thousand pounds. And to their children, my niece and nephew, Lucy and Thomas, the sum of three hundred pounds each.'

Mr Shaw didn't look too happy. He shook his head, but remained silent.

Good luck with the two grand, Dad, Marie thought. There might be enough remaining in Harriet's account to cover the six hundred pounds for Thomas and Lucy, but only just. Marie felt a little peeved about the car – she'd been intending to use it when she passed her driving test – but it didn't really matter.

'And finally…' – Petrescu turned to face Marie – '…to my niece, Marie Shaw…'

Here it comes, Marie thought. *At last!*

Petrescu suddenly had a coughing fit. He reached for a glass of water and took a sip. 'Sorry about that,' he said. 'The price one pays for smoking cigars.' He looked back down at the paper work and read aloud, 'To my niece, Marie Shaw, I also leave the sum of three hundred pounds, along with my two beloved fireside Spaniels.'

For a fleeting moment, Marie's throat constricted and she was unable to speak. Then she managed to splutter, '*And*…?'

'Sorry, yes,' Petrescu continued, looking back down at the paperwork. 'And, once any expenses and outstanding bills have been cleared, all other assets, including my house at number nine Ogilvie Crescent and those possessions not otherwise gifted, are to be sold. The proceeds, along with any monies that may be remaining in my bank account, are to be donated to the donkey sanctuary in Sidmouth.'

The silence in the room was deafening. It was broken when Mr Shaw sniggered.

'*What*?!' Marie exclaimed. 'That has to be a joke! She told me everything had been taken care of.'

'And so it has,' Petrescu said, returning the paperwork to the folder. 'Mrs Palmer told me personally some years ago

237

that she and her late husband, Frank, visited the donkey sanctuary in Sidmouth on their honeymoon back in the late nineteen fifties. She said they were so moved by the work being done there, they pledged that whichever of them went last would ensure everything they owned was donated to the sanctuary.'

'Didn't you say those dear little dogs got broken?' Deborah asked.

Marie shot her a look and saw a faint smirk on the woman's lips. 'Shut up!' she snapped, suddenly feeling sick. She leant forward and tried to take the paperwork from the desk. 'Let me see that.'

Petrescu slid it away out of reach. 'I'm sorry,' he said. 'By law, you're at liberty to contest it. But I wouldn't advise wasting your time.' He tapped the folder with his index finger. 'It's *very* specific.'

'Good old Harriet,' Mr Shaw said, chuckling.

Marie could feel her blood rising. 'It's not funny, Dad!' Marie said, struggling to contain her rage.

'It actually is though,' her father replied. 'Come on, Lynda, I'm hungry. Let's go and splash some of our inheritance on a fancy lunch.'

CHAPTER 25

Marie spent the train journey home in a state of mild shock. Petrescu had asked to her to stay back while everyone else left and informed her that the house on Ogilvie Crescent had to be vacated and on the market within one month of the reading of the will; essentially, she had to move out on or before January the first. But move *where*?

She was bent over wiping down the bath at the Campbells' house the next morning when Clive appeared in the doorway. 'Good morning.' Marie looked round at him and he immediately realised something was wrong. His smile faded. 'What's the matter?'

Marie perched herself on the edge of the bath. 'It looks as if I'm going to be homeless. My aunt told me she was going to leave me her house, but she didn't and I have to move out by New Year.'

'That's terrible news! Why on earth would she do that to you after everything you did for her?'

'I don't know.' She felt the tears burning in her eyes and she lowered her head and began to cry.

For a moment Clive was lost for words, then he came over and sat down next to her. 'Come on now, don't cry.' He put an arm around her shoulders and she buried her face in his chest and sobbed.

'But what am I going to do?'

Clive gave her shoulder a gentle squeeze. 'You have a little boy to take care of. You can't just be thrown out on the street. There'll be some sort of recourse available to you, I'm certain of it.'

'The solicitor told me I have to be out by January the first. My aunt wants the place sold off on behalf of a flippin' donkey sanctuary.'

''It's always darkest before the dawn. We all feel as if we're on our own when life turns against us, but I assure you, you're not. Gerri and I will do whatever we can to help.'

At that moment, Geraldine appeared in the doorway, tying the cord on her robe. 'Do whatever we can to help who?'

'Marie has just been told she has to vacate her home.'

Geraldine looked suitably shocked. 'How awful! Who said that that to her?'

'Her aunt's solicitor. You remember, Marie went to the reading of the will yesterday?'

Geraldine looked at Marie sympathetically. 'What are you planning to do?'

Clive reached out for a spare toilet roll sitting on the top of the cistern and gave it to Marie. 'I have no idea.' She sat up, tore off a few sheets and handed the roll back. 'Thanks.' She blew her nose.

'I was just saying we'd do what we can to help,' Clive said. He looked at Marie. 'I'm sure we can find you legal counsel. It might take a bit of time, of course, but there are often loopholes in these things, and if we can forestall your eviction, even if it's just in the short term…'

Geraldine huffed and shook her head. 'Honestly, Clive, stop waffling. We can do far better than that.'

Her husband looked at her blankly.

'Marie can move in here with us.'

'Of course!' Clive exclaimed. 'We have plenty of room.'

'And we owe Marie a debt of gratitude for exposing that thieving snake Fletcher,' Geraldine added.

Marie shook her head tearfully. 'That's really good of you, but I couldn't.'

Geraldine beamed. 'Give me one good reason why not.'

'I have my little boy, and...'

'What's the problem with that?'

'It would be an imposition.'

'Nonsense. As long as you don't mind sharing the spare room together. You've seen, it's full of nick-nacks, but Clive can clear out. It's actually quite spacious when it's empty.'

Clive nodded. 'Some of it can probably be dumped anyway. I'll move everything else into the attic.'

'And there's a lock on the door,' Geraldine added. 'You can keep the key, so you can maintain your privacy.'

Marie shook her head. 'I don't know what to say.'

Geraldine smiled. 'Say yes. Honestly, it would bring a breath of fresh air to the place having you both here, wouldn't it, Clive?'

'It would,' Clive said, nodding his agreement. 'There hasn't been a youngster around here since Phoebe left home.'

'It would be an additional benefit for you not having to bus back and forth every day too,' Geraldine continued.

Marie reached over and dropped the toilet paper in the waste bin. 'I suppose.'

'Look, I'll not lie to you, Marie. You'd be doing me a favour living-in. I'm on the way out…'

241

'Gerri, please!' Clive said, pulling a face.

She gave her husband a dismissive glance. 'Well, I am. There's no getting around it, Clive, I'm not going to be here forever. It would give me peace of mind to know the old place is in good hands.'

'Please don't speak like that, love,' Clive said. 'You're not going anywhere any time soon.'

'Of course not! But we can't ignore the cold facts. We all have to go sometime.' She looked at Marie. 'It'll be rent free accommodation and you can have your own space. Weekends can still be your own too, of course, as long as you don't mind stepping into the fray in the event of an emergency. As I'm finding it more and more difficult, if you'd be willing to prepare the evening meals too, that would be appreciated.'

Marie appeared to give the matter some thought; she had no intention of turning down Geraldine's offer, but she didn't want to appear overly eager. After a moment, she smiled gratefully. 'You're both so kind. How can I refuse?'

'That's settled then,' Geraldine said with a note of finality. 'You can move in as soon as you wish.'

'I ought to wait until after Christmas, let you guys have the time to yourselves.'

Clive smiled. 'You're more than welcome to spend Christmas here if you'd like to. It's only usually the two of us and Gerri gets fed up staring at my old face all day.'

Geraldine laughed. 'He thinks he's joking!'

They were both looking at Marie, waiting for her to respond.

'Well,' she said. 'If you're absolutely sure, then I'll bring a few of my things in at the end of the week.'

'Tell you what, I'll bring the car over on Friday night and we'll pile her up with as much as we can fit in. How does that sound?'

Marie put her arms around him and gave him a hug. 'That would be amazing, thank you.' She stood up and gave Geraldine a hug too. 'Thank you, Mrs Campbell. *So* much. You're both life-savers!'

'There's just one proviso if you're to move in,' Clive said.

Geraldine and Marie both looked at him questioningly.

'No more of this Mr and Mrs Campbell. From now on you're please address us as Clive and Gerri.'

Marie smiled and nodded. 'I think I can manage that.'

On the Saturday before Christmas, Marie had been out doing some Christmas shopping. She returned home quite late in the afternoon to find the house empty. She was a little surprised – the Campbells usually told her if they had plans to go out..

She had bought a few decorations to put up in the living room, but Geraldine had requested hotpot for dinner, one of her favourites: 'Nothing quite like it for warming the old tummy on a cold winter's day!' It was going to take a good ninety-minutes to cook, so she decided that putting up the Christmas stuff could wait until the following morning. Sitting Donovan down at the kitchen table with a colouring book, she got on with preparing the meal.

Twenty-minutes later, she heard the front door slam. She cocked an ear, but couldn't hear voices. 'Stay away from the oven, Donny,' she said, and went through to the lounge.

Clive was sitting in Geraldine's armchair beside the window with his head in his hands.

'What's wrong?'

Clive lowered his hands and looked up at her. His eyes were red. 'She's gone.'

It took Marie a moment to process what he meant. She put a hand to her mouth. 'Oh, my God.'

Donny appeared in the living room doorway. 'What's going on?'

Marie quickly hustled him out into the hall. 'Just go back to the kitchen, there's a good boy. I'll be out in a moment.'

'Can I have a biscuit?'

'Yes, alright, but only one.' Marie returned to the living room. 'What happened?'

'She went up to the bathroom mid-morning and took a fall. I heard her cry out. I managed to get her up, but she refused point blank to let me call an ambulance. She seemed to be okay, so I let it go. We were having a sandwich at lunchtime and she started complaining about head pains. She relented and let me to take her to A and E. She got seen quite quickly. They took her into an assessment room. I waited for about fifteen minutes, then a doctor appeared and called me in to a side room…' Clive faltered and swallowed hard. 'He told me that while they were checking her over she had a seizure and…' – lowering his head, he let out a strangled sob – '…died.'

Marie stared at him. 'God, I'm *so* sorry, Clive. I don't know what to say.'

'There's nothing *to* be said. My Gerri's gone and there's nothing anyone can say or do to bring her back.' Clive looked up at her. 'Would you mind just leaving me alone for a bit please?'

'Of course. Just call me if you need anything.'

Marie went back to the kitchen. Donovan was sitting eating a fruit shortcake biscuit. The packet lay open on the table in front of him. Marie ignored the fact that he'd clearly had more than one. She sat down beside him.

'What's up, Mum?'

Marie didn't answer. She pulled a biscuit from the wrapper and absent-mindedly took a bite. Her mind was racing; with this unexpectedly sudden turn of events, were her days living in Sunnycatt numbered?

CHAPTER 26

In the days that immediately followed Geraldine's unexpected death, Clive didn't leave the house. When he wasn't on the phone dealing with the fallout, he spent most of the time in his office with the door closed, choosing to bury himself in work. Marie only saw him at mealtimes and, even then, conversation between them was scant.

Marie's own mood wasn't too good either; her driving lessons weren't going well, and she desperately wanted to broach the matter of her own future at the house, but the opportunity hadn't presented itself. She had also wanted to put up the festive decorations she'd bought for the living room, if only for Donovan's sake, but it now felt slightly inappropriate; she resigned herself to the fact that Christmas was going to be a dismal affair.

As it turned out, it was quite to the contrary.

On Christmas Eve, she was in the kitchen preparing the turkey for the following day when Clive appeared.

'Listen, Marie, I owe you an apology.'

She was genuinely mystified. 'What for?'

'For being intolerable to be around the past few days.'

'Please don't apologise for *that*. You've just lost you…' Marie cut herself short.

'It's okay. You can say it.'

'What I *meant* was, it's perfectly understandable. I've been in a bit of a state wondering what to say or do to help.'

'Honestly, you've helped by leaving me alone.' He smiled. 'And making sure I didn't starve. You're a Godsend.'

'Speaking of that,' Marie started tentatively, 'I'm sorry to bring it up, but it's been playing on my mind and, well, I know I was taken on mainly to help out because of Gerri. Are you… I mean, will you be letting me go?'

Clive looked genuinely astonished by the question. 'Good Lord, no! I've got used to having you around. Provided you're comfortable here, you're welcome to stay on as long as you wish.'

'Thank you, Clive. It's a weight off my mind. Not so much for me as Donny.'

'You really should have said something sooner if it's been worrying you. Again, I suppose that's my fault for making myself seem unapproachable.'

'Please, you've *nothing* to apologise for. And I'm glad to have been a support for you, however insignificantly.'

'Keeping a grieving man fed isn't insignificant.' Clive patted his belly. 'Life must go on, eh? But, listen, I really appreciate it that you care.'

'Of *course* I care.' Marie sighed. 'I just wish I could have done more to help.'

'There *is* something you could do now actually.'

'Go on.'

'It's Christmas Eve. I've been cooped up in this bloody house all week. There's a nice little pub up the road and I'd consider it a great honour if you'd let me take you out for a drink.'

247

Marie looked at him doubtfully. 'I'd love that, but I've got tomorrow's dinner to prepare.'

Clive nodded approvingly. 'And don't think I don't appreciate it. But don't worry about it now. You can do it later. Or not at all. We can have egg and chips if it comes to it. I was never that fond of turkey, it's a bit dry for my taste.'

'But there's Donny to think about.'

Clive looked at her apologetically. 'Sorry, that was a bit selfish of me, wasn't it? If you and the lad like turkey…'

'No, I meant I can't leave him on his own.'

'Oh! I see. Well, the Old Oak is kid-friendly. He can come too and have a lemonade.'

'Well, if you're sure you feel like it then.'

Clive nodded. 'One hundred percent.'

So it was that, contrary to Marie's expectations, Christmas turned out to be very enjoyable. Clive was a little subdued first thing on Christmas Day, but Marie could tell he was making a concerted effort to maintain a convivial atmosphere. Dinner was a success and Clive even remarked that Marie had changed his opinion on roast turkey.

While Marie was clearing the table, the telephone rang. It was his daughter, Phoebe, calling from Spain. Ushering Donovan to come and help her in the kitchen, Marie left Clive to his call.

'Merry Christmas, Dad!'

'And to you, my darling. How's your day going?'

'Quiet. Just as I like it. How about yours?'

'The same. Obviously it feels strange not having Gerri around, but having Marie and her little boy here helps.'

'I'm glad. She sounds really nice, Dad. Wish her a Merry Christmas from me, would you?'

'I will. You'll get to meet her when you're over in a couple of weeks.'

They moved on to the subject of the arrangements for Geraldine's funeral and talked for a few more minutes. Phoebe brought the matter to a close by saying, 'I'll be flying in early that morning. I'll see you at the church?'

'I can't wait to see you, darling.'

'Love you, Dad.'

Clive could feel himself beginning to well up. 'Love you too.'

Marie and Donovan came back into the dining room to find he had laid out some brightly-wrapped packages on the table.

'Just a few token gifts for Donny.' He winked at the boy. 'Don't get too excited.'

Marie smiled gratefully. 'Thank you. What do you say, Donovan?'

'Thanks, Mr Campbell.'

'Shall we move into the other room?' Clive said.

'Sure.'

Clive gathered up the gifts and carried them through to the living room. Donovan sat on the floor and tore open his presents: there was a selection of books and a Meccano set.

'Is Phoebe having a good Christmas?' Marie asked; she wasn't particularly interested, but it seemed only appropriate to ask.

'She split up with her man a few months ago, so she's on her own this year, but, yes, I think so. She said to say Merry Christmas to you.'

'Aww, that's nice.'

Although the boy was initially a bit indifferent to the gifts from Clive, on Boxing Day, they got down on the carpet together, laid out the Meccano and had fun constructing a model oilrig.

Marie sat in the armchair with a box of Turkish Delight, watching the man laughing with her son. She smiled contentedly. It seemed as if things were going to work out very nicely after all.

Geraldine's funeral was booked for January the tenth. Marie didn't want Donovan to attend, so she had bribed Cassandra with a bottle of vodka to have him for the preceding night, take him to school in the morning and collect him after classes and bring him home. Donovan was pleased as punch to be going off on an adventure with Auntie Cass, and he had climbed into her car without even looking back.

Not unexpectedly, Clive was very quiet over breakfast on the morning of the funeral, until something Marie said quite matter-of-factly almost caused him to break down.

Marie happened to ask him whether he wanted the regular chunky marmalade for his toast, or the lime variety.

He stifled a sob. 'Geri used to love the lime. She refused to have anything else on her toast.'

Marie kicked herself. 'Oh, God! I should have stopped to think.'

Clive hastily wiped each of his eyes with the back of his hand. 'It's not your fault.'

'No, really, that was really insensitive of me. I'm sorry.'

'No, *I'm* sorry.' Clive composed himself. 'I'm wound tight as a spring this morning.'

Marie rested a comforting hand on his arm. 'It would be unnatural if you weren't. It's a big day ahead.'

'I'll make no bones about it, I'll be glad when today is over.'

Marie picked up the jar of lime marmalade to return it to the cupboard.

'Wait,' Clive said. 'I will have some.' He scooped a big dollop of the preserve onto a slice of toast. 'We first had this on our honeymoon in the Lake District.'

Marie saw an opportunity to lighten the conversation. 'Oh, I've always wanted to go there.'

'You should. It's very beautiful; I can heartily recommend it. We stayed in a little guest house in Ambleside at the head of Lake Windermere.'

Clive became quite animated as he chatted away, telling Marie about the places he and Geraldine had visited in Cumbria. After breakfast he disappeared upstairs to change for the funeral.

There were around thirty people due to be coming back to the house after the service, Clive had entrusted Marie with doing the food for the wake and she didn't want to let him down. Quickly putting the finishing touches to the savouries that she'd prepared the previous evening, she went upstairs to get changed.

She came down fifteen minutes later to find Clive standing in front to the hall mirror, muttering to himself and fiddling with his tie. He paused when he saw Marie. She was dressed in a black strapless dress, black tights and black, patent leather shoes. 'My word, you look lovely,' he said.

'So do you,' she replied.

Clive returned his attention to his reflection. 'I might do if I could sort out this bloody thing.' Marie noticed his fingers were trembling. 'I never could do up a tie,' he continued. 'Even when I was a kid. Luckily I don't wear one that often any more. If I had to, Gerri used to help.'

Marie smiled. 'Here, let me.'

Clive turned and stood still while she deftly crossed the two ends, threaded the long end through the loop and tied the perfect knot.

He turned and inspected the results in the mirror. 'That's amazing!'

Marie smiled. 'I used to have to do my brother's school tie for him. I got to be a bit of a dab hand.'

'You can say that again,' Clive said, adjusting the knot to cover his top button.' He turned back to face her. 'Would it be alright if I gave you a hug?'

Marie didn't quite know how to respond and she hesitated just long enough to inadvertently make Clive feel awkward. 'Forgive me,' he said. 'I've embarrassed you.'

Smiling, Marie stepped forward and put her arms around him and he reciprocated. She could feel the warmth of his breath on her neck and his aftershave smelt good. She closed her eyes. It was the first time she had been embraced by a man since Kai.

Clive released her and stepped back. There were tears in his eyes. 'I really needed that. Thank you.' He glanced at his watch. 'Right then, ready for the off?'

'Ready for the off,' Marie replied.

CHAPTER 27

Geraldine Campbell's funeral was a burial in a small churchyard a mile from Sunnycatt. She had clearly been well-loved, for the church was filled to capacity with in excess of a hundred mourners. Marie thought about the food she'd readied for the wake and began to worry there wouldn't be nearly enough. For that matter, how would so many people fit into the house?

As everyone filed out into the churchyard after the service, she managed to have a word with Clive and he put her fears to rest.

'It's fine,' he whispered. 'I don't even know who some of these people are. There won't be more than thirty coming back to the house.'

It was a bitterly cold morning and there was a sheen of white frost on the ground, but otherwise the weather couldn't have been kinder. The sun glittered down from cloudless blue skies, fighting the chill air to melt the tiny rows of icicles hanging from the branches of an ancient yew tree.

Everyone huddled around in silence in a wide circle as Clive and Phoebe took up position alongside the elderly vicar beside the grave. Marie found herself standing next to Doreen, who had parked her mobility scooter on the narrow path that ran between the rows of graves and hobbled with the aid of a walking cane over to join her.

Marie was genuinely delighted to see the old lady. Even though she lived near the Campbells, they had only bumped into each other twice since Marie had been working there, and on both occasions Doreen had been on her way out and hadn't had much time to stop and chat.

'I didn't see you in the church,' Marie said quietly.

'I stayed at the back near the door, just in case I had to make a quick exit.' She motioned to the mobility scooter where her little Pomeranian, Archibald, was peering out at them from the cosy folds of a thick crocheted blanket in the basket. 'Archie's a good boy, he wouldn't have caused a fuss, but he'd got a bit of a dickey tummy at the moment – too many rich treats over Christmas – so I thought it best to…' She stopped and made a zipping motion across her mouth with her pinched thumb and forefinger as the vicar started to speak.

Clearing her throat, the vicar read a few words from the Bible and then, as the coffin was lowered slowly into the ground, Clive – who was struggling, but failing epically, to maintain his composure – threw a dusting of earth onto the lid. The vicar intoned a few final words, after which everyone began to move quietly away.

Marie walked Doreen back to her scooter. 'Are you coming back to the house?'

'I am,' Doreen replied with a smile. 'We can have a good old chinwag there.'

'Well, all I can do is repeat how *very* disappointed I was with the whole thing,' Nancy said, suspiciously eyeing up the vol-au-vent in her hand. 'What actually *is* in this?'

'Chicken,' Clive said flatly. Everybody else was standing in little groups chatting amiably, and he had to get saddled with *her*!

255

Clive had never cared for his wife's sister at the best of times. She was a selfish, spiteful woman and her weekly visits had never been less than endurance tests. She had cornered him as soon as they got back to the house and made it very clear that, in her opinion, the arrangements for her sister's funeral had been substandard and became excessively vocal about the fact she hadn't been consulted on anything...

The flowers on the coffin wouldn't have been her choice: ('Orchids are all very well,' she sniped, 'but Gerri liked Snapdragons, you know that, Clive!')

In the photo on the cover of the Order Of Service booklets, Geraldine looked a bit gormless ('Couldn't you have found something nicer than that?!')

The font inside the Order Of Service was too small: ('I had to strain my eyes to read it!')

And the vicar had failed to enunciate properly: ('She was a mumbler! I was at sitting at the front and even *I* couldn't hear half of what she said! *God* only knows what the people at the back must have thought!')

In her final summation the whole funeral had been "a complete shambles".

Nancy was still looking at the vol-au-vent critically. 'Did you *buy* these things?'

'No, Marie kindly made them herself – from scratch.'

'Oh!' Nancy sounded genuinely offended. 'Well that explains it then.' She dropped the pastry back onto the serving plate. 'I'll not be eating any of that muck.' She looked at the row of plates filled with a variety of sandwiches. 'They don't look very fresh.'

256

'Well, they are.'

'Look,' she picked up a triangular salmon and cucumber sandwich and held it out. 'The crusts are all curled at the edges. And why *are* there crusts? If you know the first thing about finger food, you know you cut the crusts off.'

'Does it *matter*?' Clive said irritably. 'Marie worked really hard on all this and as far as I'm concerned she's done an excellent job.'

'You *would* say that! If you hadn't been so tight-fisted, you'd have paid to get experienced caterers in. Even the wine is inferior. I suppose your precious Marie chose that too?'

'Don't be facetious. I chose it. It was one of Gerri's favourites.'

Nancy scowled. 'Whatever. Gerri deserved so much better. You should be ashamed of yourself.'

Clive sighed. 'If you don't like it, just don't eat it.'

'Oh, I see, that's how it is, is it? You'd have me starve at my own sister's wake would you?' Nancy hissed.

'That's not what I meant and you know it. There are some crisps and nuts over there, they came straight out of the packets, so you can fill you face with those safe in the knowledge Marie didn't make them.'

At that moment, Phoebe – who had been talking with Marie and Doreen – stepped over and appeared at her father's shoulder. Her auburn locks were pulled back taut and tied with a black ribbon. She had no make-up on her face, which was pale and dappled with light freckles. 'Everything going okay, Dad?'

'It most certainly is *not*,' Nancy answered for him. 'I was just telling your father that this food is inedible.'

'Really? I think Marie prepared a lovely spread.' Phoebe picked up a ham and tomato sandwich and took a bite. 'Mmm. Really good.'

'Don't *you* start!' Nancy snapped. 'Marie this, Marie that.'

Phoebe was slightly taken aback by the venom in her step-aunt's tone. She had been chatting to Marie for the past ten minutes and found her to be quite lovely. She looked at Clive quizzically. 'Have I missed something here?'

'It's alright,' Clive said. 'She's not too happy that I didn't splash out on caterers.'

'It's far more than that,' Nancy said curtly. She looked Phoebe in the eye. 'You need to have a word with your father, young lady. She's so far up your backside, it's hard to tell where one begins and the other ends!'

Phoebe laughed. 'That's a bit over the top, isn't it?'

'*Is* it? If you ask me, that girl doesn't belong here. I can't put my finger on it, but I didn't take to her when I first met her, and now Gerri's gone I trust her even less.'

'What are you getting at?' Clive said.

'Are you really so stupid, Clive? She's a gold-digger, plain and simple and, you mark my words, she'll have her grubby hands on everything you own just as soon as look at you!'

Clive looked at Nancy angrily. 'Alright, that's enough!' he barked. 'How *dare* you come into my house and disrespect me and my housekeeper?' He wagged a finger at her. 'I'll tell you this for nothing: Marie was Gerri's choice

258

and she really liked her. And she's been an absolute Godsend around here since she died. I'd have drowned in my own misery if it weren't for her taking care of me. To suggest she has ulterior motives is downright offensive. Besides which, I owe her more than you'll ever understand, and her price is *far* above rubies.'

Nancy laughed theatrically. 'You're quoting the Bible at me now? You're a blind fool, man, and it's going to cost you dearly.'

Clive glared at her. 'Right, nobody's forcing you to be here. I suggest you find Melvin and leave.'

Nancy scowled. 'Don't you worry about that. I wouldn't stay now if you paid me!'

'I saw him out in the garden having a cigarette a few minutes ago,' Phoebe offered helpfully.

Without uttering another word, Nancy pushed past Clive and Phoebe and headed off in the direction of the kitchen.

'What the hell was all that about?' Phoebe asked incredulously.

Clive shook his head. 'No idea. She was a bit wound up that I hadn't consulted her on the funeral arrangements and that escalated to criticising the food and Marie.'

'She certainly seems to have a bee in her bonnet about her.'

Clive chuckled. 'You could say that.'

'Well, I really like her. She's sweet and she obviously cares a great deal about your well-being. For my money you couldn't ask for a better housekeeper.'

Clive planted a kiss on top of Phoebe's head. 'I'm, glad you approve. Come on, let's get you another drink.'

That evening, after the last guest had finally departed, Clive sunk down on the sofa and exhaled heavily. 'Thank *God* that's over! If I'd had to smile cheerily at one more sympathetic face I think I'd have screamed.' As the words left his mouth, his chin dropped onto his chest and he began to cry.

Marie came over and sat down next to him. 'It's okay. Let it out.' She put her arm around his shoulders and held him while he sobbed. After a few minutes he pulled himself together. 'Sorry about that – *again*,' he said, blowing his nose. 'I seem to be constantly having to apologise to you at the moment.'

'I told you before, you've no need to apologise.'

Clive reached out and tapped his fingers on her knee. 'And *you*, my dear, can be very proud of yourself. You did a magnificent job with the buffet.'

'Well, not everyone seemed as impressed as you.'

Clive frowned. 'You heard that?'

'Some of it, yes.' Marie grinned. 'It was kind of hard not to.'

'I don't know what to say. I'm so sorry. Nancy was completely out of order.'

'It's fine, really. It's been an emotional day for everyone.' Marie had actually felt quite nettled about what she'd heard Nancy saying, but she quickly changed the subject. 'Hey, Phoebe is really nice. She was telling me all about her job. She's a real grafter by the sound of it. Turns out we're both big fans of *Neighbours* too.'

Clive chuckled. 'Good Lord, she was absolutely obsessed with that bloody show when she was a kid.'

'She was seriously impressed that I'd named Donny after Jason.'

Clive looked at her blankly. 'Who?'

'Jason Donovan.'

'The singer?'

'Yes, but before he launched his singing career, he played Scott Robinson on *Neighbours*.'

'Oh, okay.' He frowned. 'You know, I don't think you've ever told me that before.'

Marie smiled. 'I suppose there's no reason I should have. Anyway, Phoebe is lovely. I didn't ask why she's not staying here.'

'She's sleeping over with an old friend she hasn't seen since she first went out to Spain. She did ask if I minded, but what was I going to say? No?'

Marie smiled at him warmly. 'You're a good Dad.'

Clive raised his eyebrows. 'I don't know about that. Anyway, she's flying back tomorrow, but we are going to meet up for an early bite of lunch first.'

'That's good.'

Clive suddenly realised he still had his hand on Marie's knee. She hadn't seemed to notice either, but he casually withdrew it and stood up. Stretching and yawning, he said, 'I'm going upstairs to get this clobber off.' He winked at her. 'If you're putting the kettle on, I could murder a cup of tea.'

CHAPTER 28

It was five days after the funeral and Clive was at the desk in his office as Marie entered with his morning coffee. She put it on the table along with a long, white envelope.

'This just came in the post.'

Clive picked it up and tore it open. 'Bugger! I'd completely forgotten about this. We paid for them weeks ago.' He held up two tickets. 'For the local pantomime.'

Marie put down the mug on a coaster on his desk. 'That's cool. What is it?'

'I'm not sure actually.' Clive picked up the envelope again and inspected the tickets inside. 'Let's see. Oh, yes, *Snow White and the Beanstalk*.'

'Snow White and the *what*?'

'The beanstalk.' Clive smiled. 'Sunnycatt's am-dram group like to put their own spin on things. Last year's was *Robin Hood and the Headless Horseman*. It was hilarious actually.'

Marie looked unconvinced. 'Is it children doing it?'

'No, no, it's adults. They're a bunch of nutters, but it's all done for charity. Supporting them was a tradition for me and Gerri. We always made sure we went to the final night.' He dropped the envelope on the desk. 'I won't be going now anyway.' A thought crossed his mind. 'Hey, look, it's a shame to waste the tickets. It's this Saturday night. Why don't you take Donny?'

Marie smiled. The one time her parents had taken her, Thomas and Lucy to a pantomine she had been bored to tears, and she couldn't actually think of anything more mind-numbing than sitting through two hours of forced merriment with an audience of braying kids. 'That's very kind of you, but I couldn't take your tickets. Isn't there someone else you could ask?'

'Like who?'

Marie's mind was racing. 'What about Doreen? She might like to go.'

'She'll already be there selling programs and sweets.' Clive held out the envelope to her. 'Here, take them. It's only a five-minute walk to the village hall, and if it's raining I'll drive you.'

Forcing a smile, Marie took the envelope from him. 'How can I refuse?'

When she told Donovan, he reminded her that he had a sleepover planned with a school friend for the Saturday night. Relieved that she had a get-out, she went to return the tickets to Clive, but he was having none of it.

'It'll have to be you and me then,' he said. 'We'll drop the lad off at his friend's, grab an early bite to eat, and we can be at the hall for seven. Sound like a plan?'

Marie forced a smile. 'Oh, er, yeah, okay. Why not?'

Despite her apathy towards the whole idea, at the end of the show on Saturday night, Marie's sides were hurting from laughter and she joined in the applause with gusto. As the lights came up, she turned to Clive. 'I really enjoyed that. That guy playing Snow White was *hilarious*. When he was hanging upside down off the beanstalk and his wig fell off, I could hardly breathe for laughing.'

'I told you they were good. I'm glad you had a nice time.'

'Thank you for bringing me.'

'And thank *you* for being such good company.' Clive suddenly looked sad. 'Gerri would certainly have loved it.' Not wishing to dampen the evening, he abruptly stood up. 'Lord, these seats are hard,' he said, rubbing his bottom briskly. 'Okay. Home then?'

On the walk back to the house that night they didn't say much, but as the weeks passed, the atmosphere of vague gloom that hung over the house gently eased. Clive still had occasional dark days – and Marie knew well enough when it was best to leave him be – but they became notably fewer in number. Having Donovan in the house appeared to be spurring Clive to make a more concerted effort to be in good spirits than he might otherwise have done.

He decreed that Fridays should henceforth be takeaway night; it saved Marie the chore of cooking once a week and it became a ritual for Clive and Donovan to hop in the car at five-thirty and return half an hour later with mouth-watering fish and chips from the takeaway in town.

Marie was pleased to see the two of them getting along so well, not leastways because it seemed to ignite a spark in Donovan. Clive also started taking him out on Sunday mornings to the local football match to watch Sunnycatt Rangers play, which gave Marie a little time to herself.

As February rolled over into March and Easter loomed on the horizon, the outings became more frequent. To celebrate his fifty-first birthday, Clive treated the pair of them, along with one of Donovan's friends, to a day at London Zoo. On a couple of occasions, he took them to the cinema. Clive was a pillar of generosity, and if Marie offered to pay for everything, he would habitually say: 'Just you put your money away. This is my treat.'

For Marie, it felt as if the three of them had become a happy little family unit and, although he never said anything to indicate so, she was convinced that Clive felt the same. If Donovan needed anything for school, Marie would find a way of casually dropping it into the conversation and Clive would insist on paying. She would always put up a half-hearted argument, but still took the money when it was handed to her. In June, when a weekend away on the Isle of Wight with Donovan's class came up, once again, Clive readily opened his wallet.

Following Fletcher's dismissal, the Campbells hadn't got around to employing anyone to replace him, and Clive had initially taken it upon himself to potter in the garden, discovering in the process that he had a latent green thumb. As much as anything, because she didn't like the idea of anyone else intruding on the life she was making for herself on Honeydew Lane, Marie had encouraged him to keep it up and most Saturdays would find him out mowing the lawn, or tending the myriad of plants in the herbaceous borders. On the odd occasion when he made noises about it all becoming too much and mooted seeking a new handyman to do it all, Marie would compliment his efforts and point out how lovely he'd made the grounds look. Sometimes flattery did the trick, sometimes it didn't. But if he still wavered, she would offer to help out if he needed her to; the words were empty and never converted into any practical support.

One afternoon in September, Marie was in the kitchen ironing Donovan's school shirts when Clive marched in fuming. He had caught his padded gilet on an overhanging branch, tearing a gaping hole in the shoulder.

'Gerri bought me this jacket. It's my favourite too!'

Marie stepped out from behind the ironing board. 'Here let me see.'

As she reached out to take a look, Clive pulled his arm away. 'Just leave it! It's bloody ruined!'

'Honestly, I'm sure it's not completely beyond repair. Take it off and let me see what I can do.'

Scowling, Clive slipped out of the gilet and thrust it at her. 'Knock yourself out.'

Marie found some dark blue thread in Geraldine's old sewing kit, which, rather than having been disposed of, had been stored away upstairs in a cupboard with some of her craft supplies. Managing to repair the tear, she found Clive sulking over a crossword in the living room. She held out the gilet. 'There you go. Not quite good as new, but the next best thing.'

Clive took it from her and inspected the repair. He nodded approvingly. 'You've done a lovely job.' Rising to his feet, he said 'Listen, I'm sorry I snapped just now. It's just that Gerri gave it to me for my birthday a couple of years ago and it's very special to me.'

'It's fine,' Marie said. 'I get it.'

'Well, thank you.' At the same moment that Clive moved to give her a peck on the cheek, Marie turned her head ever so slightly and their lips brushed and remained pressed together for a second longer than they ought to have. Then Clive took an abrupt step back, his face filled with embarrassment, and they stood staring at each other in awkward silence for a moment, neither of them quite sure what to say.

Then Marie said, 'Anyway, I'd better get back and finish the ironing.'

'Indeed,' Clive said. He was patently avoiding meeting her eyes and he picked up his newspaper and sat down. 'Dinner at six as usual?' he muttered, staring fixedly at the crossword.

'Of course.'

When Marie had left the room, Clive realised he'd been holding his breath. He exhaled a long, deep sigh. Putting the tip of his index finger to his lips, he couldn't help smiling.

Out in the kitchen, Marie was doing exactly the same thing.

The conversation over dinner that evening was unusually inconsequential, neither of them seemingly wanting to mention what had happened. But finally, after Donovan had retreated to the living room to watch TV and they were having coffee at the table, the subject was finally raised.

Just as Clive opened his mouth and said, 'What occurred this afternoon…', simultaneously Marie said, 'About earlier…'.

They looked at each other and both laughed nervously.

Clive smiled. 'Go on.'

'No, after you.'

'Very well. I just wanted to say I hope I didn't embarrass you earlier.'

Marie shook her head. 'Not at all.'

'I wouldn't want you to think it was intentional.'

'I didn't. It's just one of those things.'

'It was. And I wouldn't like to think you'll be feeling uncomfortable around me.'

'I won't.'

'Well... that's good then.'

'If I'm, honest,' Marie added casually, 'I was quite flattered.'

'Oh!' Clive's face filled with surprise and he looked as if he didn't know how to respond. He shifted in his seat. 'The thing is...' He trailed off and started again. 'What I mean to say is, I quite liked it.' Expecting a rebuttal, he took a breath and held it, expecting the worst.

'So did I,' Marie said, smiling at him coyly.

'*Really*?' Clive's eyes were searching hers, looking for any hint that she might be mocking him.

'Truly.'

Clive breathed a sigh of relief. 'Can I be honest with you?'

'Of course you can.'

'I know this will sound wildly inappropriate, especially with Gerri only being gone for eight months, but... the fact is...' He seemed to be struggling to find the right words. 'I've developed feelings for you.'

Marie thought she knew exactly what he was trying to say, but she said, casually, 'Well I really like you too, Clive.'

'I mean, *strong* feelings.' Clive was staring at his tightly interlocked fingers. 'I find you very attractive and I... I've fallen in love with you.'

The one thing Marie hadn't been expecting was the L-word. Not quite so soon anyway. Standing up, she came around the table and stood in front of him. He looked up at her, his cheeks flushed. He opened his mouth to speak, but she put a finger to his lips. 'I feel the same,' she said. 'I've felt that way about you for the longest time.' Then she bent and kissed him passionately.

'Hey, Clive!' Donovan's voice sounded from the hall.

Clive and Marie parted and she quickly returned to her seat as the boy appeared in the doorway. 'That movie you said we could watch together is just starting. Are you coming?'

'We're just going to clear the things and we'll be right there,' Clive said huskily.

Smiling, Donovan disappeared back into living room.

'Donny's going over to his friend's tomorrow afternoon,' Marie said.

'That's right.' Clive nodded. 'I said I'd drop him off and pick him up. What of it?'

'He'll be out for at least three or four hours.'

Clive looked at her, slightly baffled. She was smiling at him. Then the penny dropped. 'Ohhhh, you mean...'

She nodded. 'I mean.'

Marie had lied when she said she felt the same way about Clive as he did for her. Although she could never imagine herself falling in love with him, she liked him well enough and now he was hers, and the *house* was hers – or at least as good as hers – she had no intention of letting go.

In the days following that fateful kiss, they took every opportunity that presented itself to make love. Clive was considerate and attentive, putting what he perceived to be Marie's needs before his own, but for her it was – as Cassandra had jovially remarked – a case of laying back and thinking of "all that dosh".

CHAPTER 29

Marie hadn't seen Clive so happy since before Gerri passed away, and it actually made her feel happy too. But for every yin there's a yang and that joy didn't come without a cost.

One evening when they were sitting on the sofa watching TV, Clive mentioned to Marie that he'd been thinking about telephoning his daughter and wanted to tell her that they were now together. In spite of the fact Marie suggested it might not be the best idea so early in their relationship, he was insistent:

'You've made me feel things I haven't felt in a very long time and I want to shout out to the whole world how much I love you,' he said, looking at her affectionately. 'But Phoebe will do nicely for a start, and she'll be really happy for me.'

Much to Clive's disappointment, the phonecall didn't go at all well.

They didn't call each other often and, as was always the way when they did get to speak, Phoebe enthusiastically reeled off her news first; she had just returned from a couple of days away with a girlfriend in Cádiz, where she'd bought the most divine neckscarf; she had been seeing new guy – Miguel – and she was sure Clive would absolutely adore him; and a promotion opportunity had come up at work and she was certain she would get it. Clive was happy to listen until, finally, she got around to asking, 'So how are things with you?'

'Very good actually, my darling. I've got some news of my own.'

'Go on.'

'It's about Marie.'

'Housekeeper Marie?'

'Yes. Well, she was, but… well, she still is I guess. Oh, I'm waffling.' Clive took a small breath. 'The thing is, Marie and I are courting.'

'You're what?'

'Courting. You know, seeing each other.'

Phoebe laughed.

'What's so funny?'

'You're joking, right?'

'Absolutely not.' Clive smiled. 'We've been dating now for a few weeks and…'

'Whoa, slow down. Marie? The young girl you employed to clean the house? The one I met at Gerri's funeral?'

'Yes, Marie.'

'Dad! She's the same age as me!'

Clive frowned. He had been convinced Phoebe would be pleased that he was happy. 'Age is just a number, darling.'

'Don't spin that crap, Dad! She's *half* your age!'

'Not quite. Anyway, Marie makes me happy, and surely that's what's important? I thought you liked Marie when you met her.'

'I do… I mean, I *did*.'

'Well what's the problem then?'

'*Seriously*, Dad? Gerri's hardly even cold in her grave and you're messing around with the bloody housekeeper!'

Clive winced. 'That hurt, Phoebe.'

'Well, it's true! What did you expect me to say? Well done for shagging the hired help?'

272

'Don't be so coarse! Firstly, Gerri has been gone almost a year...'

'Ten months.'

'Okay, ten months. But secondly, she wasn't even your mother. What are you getting so het up about?'

'Because I loved her like a mother – and you know that.' There was anger in Phoebe's voice now. 'I can't believe this!'

'Look, Pheobe, it isn't imperative that I have your blessing on this, but it would have been nice. I was hoping you'd be pleased that I've found someone who makes me happy.'

'Well, I'm not. If you think there's any future in this, you're a fool.'

Clive bristled. 'Please don't speak to me that way, Phoebe. I wasn't very happy about it when you moved to Spain, I thought it was a mistake. But did I try to stop you? No. Because you had your mind set on it and your happiness means everything to me. I hardly ever see anything of you, and now you think you can denigrate *my* life choices? You'd rather I was on my own and lonely and miserable?'

'Of course I wouldn't,' Phoebe said quietly. 'Look, I don't want to argue with you, so I can't see the point in talking about this any more. I'm going to hang up now. I'll call you next week.'

Before Clive could answer, there was a click and she was gone.

Two days later over breakfast Clive mentioned to Marie that he'd received an email from an old friend.

'I've not seen Tom for ages,' he said through a mouthful of muesli. 'It must be two years at least. He asked me if I fancied getting together for a game of golf.'

'You're not going to go are you?'

'I said I would.'

'I didn't even know you played golf.'

'You never noticed the set of clubs in the closet?'

Marie shook her head.

'Yes, well, I pretty much stopped playing when Gerri fell ill. She used to try to encourage me to go, but I'd kind of lost the spirit for it.'

'I never understood the appeal,' Marie said with a hint of derision. 'Grown men bashing little balls around with sticks.'

Clive chuckled. 'There's a bit more to it than that.'

'When is this happening then?'

'Tom? Thursday afternoon.'

Marie frowned. 'Not Thursday.'

'Why not?'

'I thought we might take a walk along the river to Abbottshill.'

Clive smiled. 'We can do that any time.'

'I wanted to go on Thursday. It'll be lovely with all the colours in the trees at the moment.'

Clive looked a little bemused. 'It'll be just as lovely on Friday.'

'They say it's going to rain Friday.'

'Another day then.'

Marie pouted. 'If you don't want to go with me, just say.'

'Don't be a goose. Of course I want to go with you. But I haven't seen Tom for ages.'

Marie looked at him sadly. 'I thought it would be really romantic as well, just the two of us. But if that's how you feel, forget it.' She got up from the table and went to the sink to run some water into her empty cereal dish.

Clive sighed. 'What would you have me do? Cancel Tom?'

'Not if you'd rather be with him than me,' Marie said petulantly.

The conversation was reaching beyond ridiculous, but Clive didn't want to upset her. 'You're right, I'm being selfish. I can play golf with Tom any time. I'll go and email him in a moment and you and I will go to Abbotshill.'

Marie turned around to face him. She was smiling. 'We could stop at The Bridge and get some lunch too. You know how much you enjoyed the ploughman's last time we were there.'

'Sounds good to me.' Clive rose, stepped over to the sink and put his arms around her. 'I love you, my darling.'

Marie smiled and kissed the end of his nose. 'I know.'

It was the first time that she intervened in Clive's plans to spend time with friends.

It wouldn't be the last.

One Saturday evening early in November, Clive had a dinner date with an old colleague and he told Marie that he wouldn't be back until late. She had been systematically chipping away at and subtly breaking down Clive's relationships with his circle of acquaintances. But on this occasion, only because it suited her own agenda, she was happy to see him go; the fact was that she had been aching to

275

tell Cassandra about the developments between her and Clive. As soon as he'd left the house she got on the phone.

'Fancy coming over for a drinky or two tonight? I've got news.'

'Sorry, babe, I can't tonight,' Cassandra replied. 'I've got a date with Scott.'

'Can't you come up with an excuse and cry off just this once? We haven't seen each other for weeks.'

'I know, but since Scott got his new job at Iceland, his hours are all over the place and I only get to see him on weekends.'

'Come on, Cass. You won't believe what's happened.'

'Why can't you just tell me now?'

'Because I can't.' Marie's eyes narrowed. 'I thought we were besties.'

'Don't go playing that card!' Cassandra said irritably. 'Of *course* we're besties. It's just I was looking forward to seeing Scott, that's all.'

'Who's more important to you then? Me, or some bloke you've only known five minutes?'

'You, but…'

'Suppose I order in some food too? My treat.'

'Won't Clive be there?'

'Nope. We've got the place to ourselves until at least eleven, I reckon.'

'Hmm. Your treat, eh?'

Marie could tell Cassandra was wavering. 'That's what I said. My treat, *your* choice.'

Cassandra sighed. 'Yeah, go on then. But this news had better be good. I'll have to call Scott and cancel and he isn't gonna be a happy bunny.'

Marie laughed. 'Just promise him he'll get double-lucky next time.'

'Dirty cow! Okay, what time do you want me?'

'Soon as you can get here. We've got the place to ourselves for the evening.'

Cassandra picked up the framed photograph from the mantelpiece and looked at it. It was one that Clive had taken of Marie and Donovan on one of their days out. 'This is nice.'

Marie was filling their glasses. She glanced over. 'God, I tell you, Clive takes his camera *everywhere*. He's worse than David Bailey!'

Cassandra laughed and accepted the glass that Marie handed her. 'Anyway, come on, what's your news.'

Marie smiled. 'It's about Clive. He kissed me! I mean, it was an accident, but…'

Cassandra's jaw dropped open. 'He kissed you by accident? Yeah, right.' You are *fucking* kidding me!'

'No, seriously!' Marie said. 'It's insane, isn't it?'

Cassandra screwed up her face. 'I mean, like, ewwwww!'

Marie laughed. 'It wasn't *that* bad!'

'*Double* ewwwww!'

'Honestly, it was quite nice.'

'You want to watch yourself, girl. Before you know it, he'll be expecting the housemaid to play the pink oboe!' She moved her clenched fist back and forth in front of her mouth and pushed her tongue into her cheek.

'And what would be so terrible about that? I could do far worse.'

Cassandra burst out laughing. 'You have *got* to be kidding me!'

'Why?'

'It's okay if you don't mind waking up with Bruce Forsyth every morning, I suppose.'

'He's not *that* old.'

'*Seriously*, babe? He's old enough to be your dad!'

Marie had come out fully prepared to reveal to Cassandra that she and Clive were having sex, but now she thought better of it. 'Whatever. It was just a kiss.'

After she had finished her drink, Marie feigned a burgeoning headache and asked Cassandra to leave.

Although Marie and Clive kept the propinquity of their relationship low key, if they took a walk in the lanes – which became something of a Sunday afternoon routine – he would often hold her hand.

And in a small village like Sunnycatt, tongues will inevitably wag.

One morning a few weeks later, Marie was getting out of the car outside the gate to the driveway following yet another difficult driving lesson when a voice called out.

'Coo-ee!'

She turned saw Doreen trundling up the lane towards her on her mobility scooter, waving frantically.

'How lovely to see you,' the old lady said as she pulled up in front of her.

'Likewise,' Marie replied. She noticed the empty basket on the front. 'No Archibald today then?'

'Oh! I suppose I haven't seen you since…' Doreen put a hand to her mouth. 'Well, no, I had to have the poor dear put to sleep.'

'Oh, no!' Marie had never liked the dog, but she offered a few suitably sympathetic words. 'Will you get another?'

Doreen beamed. 'As a matter of fact, it's in hand. There's a lovely poodle at the rescue, Barnaby. He's a bit older than I would have liked, he's almost eight, but he's a dear. I registered my interest last week, I'm waiting to hear back from them.'

'I hope it works out for you.'

Doreen smiled. 'We can but hope.' She raised her hand and crossed her fingers. 'I'm surprised we don't bump into each other more often. Living so close, I mean. If it wasn't for the fact Georgina across the way said she's spotted you out and about with Clive a couple of times, I'd have thought maybe you'd moved on.'

Marie smiled. 'No, still here toiling away.'

'So I see.'

The expression on Doreen's face indicated she wanted to say something more, but Marie wasn't in the mood to chat. 'Well, lovely to see you, D. I'd better press on.'

'Yes, of course. Er, Marie…' Doreen was looking at her awkwardly. 'You're okay, are you?'

Marie frowned. 'Fine.'

'And Clive? He's alright, is he?'

279

'Yes, he's fine too.'

'Getting on okay without Gerri?'

Marie started to feel annoyed. 'Yes, like I say, he's fine.' She turned to walk away.

'That's good then. The thing is... Georgina was telling me that she caught sight of you both near the river at Monks' Fields a week or so back.'

Marie faltered in her step. 'Possibly. We take a walk up there sometimes to get some fresh air.'

'Yes, it's really lovely. Only, well, she said she saw you and Clive kissing.'

'She was mistaken.'

'Georgina seemed very sure. I know her eyesight isn't what it used to be, but...'

'She was *mistaken*,' Marie repeated firmly.

Doreen didn't look convinced, but she decided it was best to back off. 'In all honesty that's what I thought,' she said. 'Clive's such a nice, honorable man and he was devoted to dear Gerri. I couldn't quite believe he would sully her memory by... well, you know what I mean.'

'Oh, I know *exactly* what you mean,' Marie said, trying to maintain her equanimity.

'I probably shouldn't have even mentioned it,' Doreen said. 'But I suppose I thought you deserved to know what people are saying.'

'What people are *saying*?' Marie glared at her. 'What you said just now is right, D. Clive *is* a decent man. And he deserves far better than having a bunch of silly old biddies tittle-tattling about him behind his back.'

Doreen looked taken aback at the indefinable, but palpable threat in Marie's tone. 'I couldn't agree more,' she said, now seriously regretting having opened her mouth.

'Then I suggest you tell Georgina – and anyone else who's spreading these spiteful lies for that matter – to mind their own damned business and show a grieving man some respect!'

Before Doreen could say any more, Marie spun on her heels and walked away.

The next day, Clive told Marie he was taking her and Donovan out; he wouldn't say where, only that it was a surprise. It turned into a memorable day for all the wrong reasons.

After a long drive they arrived at Hampton Court Palace.

'They always deck it out on the lead-up to Christmas,' Clive said excitedly. 'It's magical.'

Marie didn't have the heart to tell him that she'd visited as a child, hated every moment of it and if she *never* saw the place again it would still be too soon. Instead she put a half-hearted smile on her face and they spent hours dragging around the chambers in the palace. Clive was enthusiastically pointing out his favourite paintings and sharing his knowledge of the artists with Donny, who wasn't the least bit interested. Marie was equally apathetic; all she wanted to do was go home. Clive, who had brought his new camera and was eagerly shooting everything in sight, seemed to be enjoying himself immensely and didn't notice the air of dissent.

Clive insisted on taking them into the maze too, but while they were still inside trying to negotiate their way out, the skies clouded over and it started to rain and they all got a soaking; a fitting end to a thoroughly miserable day.

On the way back to the car, there was a muddy puddle and Donovan jumped into it feet first, splashing filthy water all over Marie's jeans. 'For Christ's sake, Donny!' Marie shouted furiously and, as she raised her hand to strike him, Donovan flinched.

Clive was staring at her with a shocked expression on his face. 'Don't do that, Marie. He's just a kid having a bit of fun.'

'He's my kid, not yours,' Marie snapped, lowering her hand. 'Don't try to tell me how to raise him.'

Clive looked a bit sheepish and didn't respond, but by the time they reached the car the moment had passed.

Marie hadn't told Clive about her encounter with Doreen the previous day, but they had almost reached home, and Donovan had fallen asleep on the back seat, when she finally decided she would tell him. He listened patiently while she repeated what Doreen had said someone called Georgina had told her.

When she had finished, he smiled. 'It's a small village. People like to wag their tongues. The men are just as bad as the women, if not worse. But why should we care what they think?'

'It just *really* irritated me that they're talking about us behind our backs and making up stories. Nosey bints.'

Clive chuckled. 'But she – what was her name again?'

'Georgina.'

'Well, this Georgina *wasn't* making up stories, was she? It's pretty likely we *were* holding hands over at the river. And what if we were? Let them gossip if it makes them, happy.'

'It's *your* reputation they're dragging through the mud.'

Clive chuckled again. 'I couldn't care less if I tried. I have no reputation to drag anywhere. Not here in Sunnycatt at least.'

'Well, *I* care. We have to live among these people. Anyway, I gave Doreen a bit of a mouthful.'

'Don't be hard on the old girl,' Clive said as he swung the car into the driveway. 'She and Gerri used to get along very well. And besides, we owe her big time.'

Marie frowned. 'For *what*?'

They pulled up in front of the house and Clive switched off the engine. 'For introducing us to each other. Without doddery old Doreen, I'd never have met you and we wouldn't be sitting here having this conversation right now. And, more importantly, I would never have fallen in love with you.'

Marie felt herself stiffen. She knew how Clive felt about her, but she still hated it when he vocalised those feelings, mainly because a silence always that all but commanded her to echo the words. She turned her head and saw that even now he was looking at her expectantly, waiting for her response, with that soppy expression on his face that irritated her massively. She forced a smile and said, 'I love you back.' Feeling the fleeting tension subside, she smiled inwardly; every time she said the words back to him, it became easier and easier to live with the lie.

Clive leant over and gave her a peck on the lips. 'Anyway, my trousers are soaked through and yours must be too. Let's get inside and jump in the shower together. Then we can either have some dinner, or...' he trailed off and placed a hand on her knee and gave it a squeeze.

Marie pretended not to have registered what he was implying. 'Yes, I'm starving actually. There's a Hawaiian pizza in the freezer too. Sound good?'

Clive was about to respond when Donovan, who had just woken, answered for him. 'Yes! Pizza!'

III

CHAPTER 30

The day after Donovan's fourteenth birthday, Marie received a call from the school secretary asking her to come in to speak with the Headmistress. The woman was infuriatingly vague, telling her only that there had been "an incident in CDT" between Donovan and another boy.

It wasn't the first time she had received such a call. Only the week beforehand he had been hauled up before the Headmistress for spitting at a teacher and, throughout the year, there had been a countless succession of detentions for all manner of infractions. He had become the epitome of what the Headmistress referred to as "a difficult boy".

Wondering what she was going to be faced with when she reached the school, Marie sped down the lane out of Sunnycatt in her brand new Toyota Camry, heading towards the main road.

Just a month earlier, she had taken her driving test and passed. It was her fourth attempt, the first for almost three years; during the disastrous third, she had mounted the kerb on a bend – coming within a few inches of hitting a pedestrian and almost giving the examiner heart failure – resulting in an automatic fail. It had knocked the confidence out of her and she had lost all enthusiasm and given up for a while. After all, Clive was always happy to drive her wherever she wanted to go. Nevertheless, as a reward for eventually trying again and actually passing, Clive had bought her the lime green Camry, and the freedom it had granted her was priceless.

Twenty-five minutes later, Marie was sitting across the desk from Mrs Banning. The rotund woman was dressed very formally in a two-piece Navy blue trouser suit that only seemed to accentuate her bulk, and her mousey hair, flecked with grey at the temples, was pulled back tightly, held in place at the back by a tortoiseshell-effect claw clip.

Seated beside Marie, sporting a bruise on his cheek, was Donovan.

Mrs Banning adjusted her spectacles and addressed Marie in a clipped accent that needlessly annunciated the Ts. 'You have to appreciate, Mrs Shaw, Grimthorne Secondary cannot – and *will* not – tolerate behaviour of this sort.'

'Miss.'

'Excuse me?'

'It's Miss. Not Mrs.'

Mrs Banning gave Marie a withering look. 'The point is, this isn't the first time Donovan has got into a fight over a trifling matter.'

'Of course, and I'm very sorry,' Marie said wearily.

'It wasn't trifling,' Donovan muttered.

Mrs Banning's tongue flicked out across her plump lips. 'Hitting someone else merely because they whistled the *Neighbours* theme tune is not an excuse for raising your fists.'

Marie looked at Donovan irritably. 'Really, Donny? *That's* what this is about? *Again*?'

'It's okay for you,' Donovan grumbled sullenly. 'You don't have to put up with it. He does it all the time to wind me up. I fucking *hate* him!'

'Watch your tongue!' Marie snapped.

'Ahem!' Mrs Banning cleared her throat and tapped her fat fingers on the desk to reclaim the conversation. 'You broke Gary's front tooth, split his lip and threatened him with a chisel. There is absolutely no justification for that. You're fortunate that his parents have said they won't be taking legal action. Nevertheless, Mrs Shaw, it's my duty to officially inform you that your son is suspended for ten days.'

'It's *Miss* Shaw,' Marie said touchily.

Mrs Banning ignored her. 'This also constitutes his final warning. If there's another incident like this, regardless of the reason, Donovan *will* find himself facing expulsion.'

287

'Again, I can only apologise,' Marie said. 'I assure you it won't happen again.' She shot Donovan a warning look. 'Will it, Donny?'

Donovan shrugged, but he said, 'No.'

'Very well.' Mrs Banning glanced up at the clock then looked back at Donovan. 'I suggest you spend the coming week giving careful consideration to your future, young man. And when you return a week on Monday I trust it will be with a suitably adjusted attitude.' She rose from her chair and extended her hand. 'I appreciate you coming in, Mrs Shaw. I trust we'll not be meeting under such circumstances again.'

Marie took the outstretched hand; it was cold and damp. 'We certainly won't.' She shook Mrs Banning's hand. 'And it's Miss.'

'I was picked on myself when I was at school,' Clive said, setting down his empty coffee cup on the kitchen table. 'A kid named Tony Hanleigh took a disliking to me. I've not got a clue why. My face didn't fit or something, I suppose. Anyway, he made it his mission to make my life hell. It was never anything particularly dramatic, it was just the steady drip, drip, drip effect. I remember how horrible it felt. If I'd had the courage, I'd have done the same thing as Donny.'

Marie looked at him as if she couldn't believe what she was hearing. 'For Christ's sake, Clive, he threatened another boy with a chisel!'

'I didn't mean I'd have done *that*, obviously. I was talking about punching Tony Hanleigh slap bang in the middle of his smug little face. Sometimes you have to stand up to a bully to reset the status quo. Sadly, I just didn't have it in me.'

'I can't believe you're sticking up for him. What Donny did is inexcusable. We're lucky we don't have a bloody lawsuit on our hands.'

'I'm not sticking up for him. I'm just saying I can understand why he did it.'

Donovan, who had been sent to his bedroom as soon as they'd got home, appeared in the kitchen doorway. 'Mum, is it okay if I still go round Darren's tonight?'

Marie glared at him. 'No, it damned well isn't. You're grounded.'

'But he's got a new PlayStation and we were going to play *Resident Evil*.'

'I don't care. You're not going out.'

'It's *so* unfair!' Donovan said, in the whiny voice that always made Marie even angrier. Turning away, he clumped back up the stairs to his room.

Clive shook his head. 'He's becoming a bit of a handful, isn't he?'

'You're telling me!' Marie said, as she took their empty cups to the sink. Somewhere outside a dog started barking. 'Christ, I wish that dog would shut up!'

'It's only Barnaby, he's harmless enough,' Clive said amiably.

'I know who it is! But Doreen needs to put a muzzle on it. Every damned night, yap, yap, bloody yap!'

'Come on now,' Clive said, 'you're getting yourself into a state.'

'Can you blame me? Not only do I have to listen to Doreen's dog barking incessantly, I've got a kid who answers me back all the time.'

'He's going through that phase. We all did. Maybe you could cut him a little slack?' Marie turned to look at him. He was smiling at her. 'Let him go. It'll give us the evening on our own. We could have an early night.'

'Forget it,' Marie said flatly. 'And stop trying to undermine me.'

Clive's smile faded. 'I wasn't. I just thought…'

'Well *don't!*'

It had turned eleven-thirty when they switched off the television.

Clive stretched and yawned. 'I think it's that time.'

'I'm just going to have a word with Donny before we turn in,' Marie said, standing up. 'He's been very quiet up there tonight.'

'Probably still feeling sorry for himself,' Clive said, patting Marie on her bottom. 'Don't be too long.'

The reason for the peace quickly became apparent: Donovan wasn't in his room.

'Clive!' Marie shouted.

'What?' he called out from the bedroom.

'Donny's gone!'

Clive came out of the bedroom onto the landing. He had already stripped down to his underpants and socks. 'What do you mean, gone?'

Marie was standing in the open doorway to Donovan's room. 'How else do you want me to put it, for Christ's sake?' she snapped. 'He's not in his room!'

'He must be.'

'Oh, really, Sherlock?' She pushed the door open wider. 'Perhaps you'd like to take a look.'

'Well where's he gone then?'

Marie scowled. 'Isn't it obvious? To see his mate. He must have snuck out the back way while we were watching the movie.'

As the words left her mouth, they heard the sound of a car crushing up the gravel drive at the front of the house. Marie went to the window at the end of the landing and looked out. She recognised the car as that of Darren's parents. It pulled to a stop, the passenger door opened and Donovan stepped out. She saw him smile and say something to the driver, then he shut the door and waved the car off.

'Right!' Marie exclaimed. 'Wait until I get my hands on him!'

As she passed Clive, he grabbed hold of her arm and she spun round to face him. Her eyes were blazing.

'Why don't you let me talk to him?' Clive said calmly.

'How many times do I have to say it? He's *my* kid, not yours!'

'I'm well aware of that,' Clive said. 'But he's a headstrong lad and you're angry…'

Marie opened her mouth to speak but he held up a hand.

'…and quite rightfully so. I just don't want you to say something you might regret in the heat of the moment. Perhaps a few words from me might help avoid a row and pave the way to a more level-headed conversation in the morning about the rights and wrongs of what he has done.'

The fire appeared to go out in Marie's eyes and she sighed. 'There *are* no rights,' she said as they heard the back door close. Despite herself, she knew Clive was right. If she spoke with Donovan now, they would inevitably argue, he would be his usual obstinate self and she would end up even more livid. 'I'm at my wits' end what to do with him.'

Clive rested a hand on her shoulder. 'Then let me speak to him. Please?'

'Alright,' Marie said simply. 'But don't let him think what he did is okay.'

'I won't.' Clive hadn't really thought that she would back down. He smiled at her warmly and reached round the bedroom door and retrieved his robe from the hook. 'You go on to bed. I won't be long.' He bent and kissed her forehead. 'It'll be fine.'

When Clive got downstairs, he found Donovan sitting at the kitchen table eating a bag of crisps. 'Evening, young man.'

Donovan paused mid-munch, but he didn't seem particularly surprised to see Clive. 'I thought you'd be in bed,' he said, then resumed crunching and swallowed.

'We were just about to turn in. Your Mum wanted a word with you and you weren't in your room.'

'Obviously,' Donovan said. There was a hint of ridicule in his tone.

Clive sat down at the table next to him. 'Did you have a good time with your pal tonight?'

Donovan hadn't expected that. He shrugged. 'I s'pose.'

'That's good then.'

'Yeah.' Donovan tipped up the packet and emptied the remaining fragments into his mouth. 'I'm going to bed,' he said through a mouthful of crumbs. 'Good talk.' He started to get up, but Clive put a hand on his arm.

'Listen, Donny. Your Mum loves you very much.'

Donovan sat back down and looked at Clive curiously. 'And?'

'And she worries about you. When she asks you to do something – or *not* do something – it's always for a good reason. Defying her wishes isn't... cool.'

'*Cool*?' Donny was looking at him mockingly and Clive immediately regretted using the word.

'You behaved very badly at school today and, under the circumstances, I think you got off very lightly. I think the least you could do is show a little contrition, and not go sneaking out late at night to see your friends behind your mother's back.'

Suddenly, Donny laughed. 'Did she put you up to this?'

He is *mocking me*, Clive thought. 'No. Your Mum's upset and it just occurred to me that it might be nice if we had a little chat, man to man. When I was a boy...'

Donovan cut him off, and his words hit Clive in the face like a sharp slap.

'You might be shagging my Mum, but that doesn't give you the right to try to lecture me. You're not my Dad, you know.'

Clive was lost for words. Of course he wasn't Donovan's father, but since he and Marie had become a couple, he'd always treated the boy like the son he'd never had, going out of his way to ensure he wanted for nothing.

Clive had come down to speak to the boy brimming with confidence. Now he felt completely deflated. 'I know that,' he started, 'but…'

'Is that it then?' Donovan stood up. 'Talk over?'

'Yes,' Clive said quietly. There was nothing else he *could* say. 'Best get yourself to bed.'

CHAPTER 31

When Marie asked Clive what had been said between him and Donovan, he replied simply, 'I think he understands how wrong it was to defy you. Best not mention it to him again, eh?' The truth was, Donovan's attitude had left him feeling bruised, and he was unusually quiet the next day. Marie noticed, but it didn't concern her unduly and she didn't ask if anything was wrong. It was a couple of days later when they went out for dinner and, over dessert, the subject came up, that he revealed what Donovan had said, omitting the coarse remark about his intimate relationship with her.

Even in its toned-down version, Marie couldn't quite believe that Donovan had spoken to him that way; her subsequent apology was born more of what impact it might have on her future in the house than how ungrateful and insulting her son had been to Clive.

'I'm *so* sorry! You should have told me all this the other night.'

Clive sighed. 'I didn't want to exacerbate the situation. You were angry and the lad wasn't happy. It just seemed easier to let it pass.'

'But he had no right to speak to you like that, not after everything you've done for him. I'll speak to him when we get home.'

'No, really, it doesn't matter now.'

Marie looked at him earnestly. 'It *does* matter. You're such a good man and it means everything to me that you and Donny get along. I know he's going through an awkward stage at the moment, but I'm worried that if you get fed up having him around…' – she picked up a napkin and exaggeratedly dabbed it to the corner of her eye – '…you'll get fed up with me too.'

'Hey.' Clive placed a hand over hers. 'Never.'

'But you can't know that. And what would become of us if you and I split up?'

'We're not going to.'

Marie sniffed. 'But what if we *did*? Me and Donny would be homeless and…'

'We *aren't* going to split up,' Clive said firmly. 'So you can banish any such notion from your pretty little head.' He brushed the back of her hand. 'I love you.'

'And I love you too,' Marie said. 'But it does worry me. I can't help it. I've already been made homeless once and I don't want to even think about a nightmare like that again. I'm never going to be able to afford a place of my own.' She made a little sobbing noise.

'I'll tell you what.' Clive sat back in his seat. 'How would it be if half the house was in your name? Would that put your mind at rest?'

Gotcha! Marie thought. She looked up at him with sad eyes. 'I don't understand.'

'What I'm saying is, we make an appointment to go and see my solicitor and we get the deeds to the house altered so that your name is on them.'

Marie gasped. 'Seriously?'

Clive smiled. 'Completely'

'But… but… You'd do that for *me*?' Marie stuttered, silently congratulating herself on her acting skills.

'In a heartbeat. And maybe it's about time I gave some serious thought to amending my will too.'

'Oh, Clive, you can't!'

'Try and stop me. It would make me very happy to know that you and Donny are taken care of when I shuffle off.'

'Don't talk like that. You're not going *anywhere*, and…' Marie trailed off and shook her head. 'Just a minute though. Won't Phoebe be expecting to inherit?'

'What Phoebe expects is neither here nor there.' Clive pursed his lips. 'We haven't spoken since I told her about us. You know she didn't approve. Not that I need her approval, of course, but the things she said were very hurtful. Besides, she's doing alright for herself, she'll never go wanting.'

'I don't know what to say.'

'Of course…' Clive hesitated. 'Of course, it would make things better still if we were…' He hesitated again. 'Married?'

'Married?' Marie wouldn't have married Clive if he were the last man on God's earth, but she feigned a coy expression. 'Are you proposing to me?'

He grinned. 'Yes, I suppose I am. I mean, I'm afraid I haven't got a ring yet or anything, and getting down on one knee is out of the question, but…'

'Yes.'

'Sorry?'

Marie smiled at him. 'Yes, I *will* marry you.'

Clive's face lit up. 'You will?'

'I will.'

297

'Gosh.' Clive shook his head in disbelief. 'I've been wanting to ask for weeks, but I was worried you might turn me down. Now it's me who doesn't know what to say.'

'Just tell me again how much you love me.'

Clive lifted her hand to his mouth and gently kissed each of her fingers, punctuating each peck with a single word: 'I. Love. You. Very….' – he reached the thumb – 'Much.'

'I love you too.'

Clive smiled at her warmly. 'Do you want coffee, or shall we head for home and have one there?'

'Never mind the coffee. Let's go home and have an early night. I'm feeling naughty.'

Clive felt himself stir. He arched an eyebrow. 'Is that so? How naughty exactly?'

Marie gave him a cheeky grin. 'Very. And maybe in the morning you can call the solicitor and make an appointment about the house.'

Clive nodded. 'Let me get the bill.'

'I think tonight should be my treat.'

'I don't think so.'

'But you pay for everything. I am working, you know. I've got a very nice boss as it happens.' Marie paused and smiled. 'In fact, technically you *will* be paying for the meal.'

Clive laughed. 'You can pay next time.' Pulling his wallet from his inside jacket pocket, he raised a hand to catch the waiter's eye. 'This one's definitely on me.'

Clive was as good as his word and, the following morning he telephoned his solicitor and made an appointment to go in on Friday. He hadn't bought Donovan much for his birthday, and over dinner that evening he suggested they might all go together. And, after the meeting with the solicitor – provided Donovan promised to make an effort to keep his head down and work hard upon his return to school the following week – they might stop by Curry's and see what was available in the way of PlayStations.

Donovan hadn't shown much interest when Marie told him that Clive had proposed to her, and he had been moping around the house all day. Having been hunched over his plate at the table, picking at his food in silence for fifteen minutes, he suddenly became animated. 'A PlayStation! *Really*?'

'If you promise me you'll start studying harder at school and try your darnedest to make your Mum proud of you, yes.'

'Do you promise?' Donovan asked excitedly.

'Yes, but the point is, do *you* promise?' Clive retorted.

'Cross my heart.'

'That's a plan then,' Clive said.

Their eyes met and an unspoken apology passed between them. 'Thanks,' Donovan said. Then, as an afterthought, he added, 'Dad.'

Marie looked at Clive and silently mouthed 'Awww' at him.

Clive got up. 'Okay then. Help your Mum clear the dishes and we can all watch a movie together.'

On the Friday morning, the three of them went into town as planned. Marie and Clive had a ten-forty-five appointment with his solicitor, George Haworth. Clive gave Donovan

299

some money for a burger and suggested he have a mooch around the shops for an hour or so and they would meet him outside Curry's at midday.

Forty minutes later, with all amendments having been implemented to the deeds for the house and Clive's will, he was about to sign and date it when Marie put a hand on his arm to stop him.

'Are you absolutely sure this is what you want, darling?'

Although she was a hundred percent sure that giving him pause wouldn't change a thing, it was a calculated risk, but still one worth taking to put on a show for the solicitor; it was possibly just in her head, but she was almost certain the man had eyed her with suspicion when Clive outlined his intentions.

Clive smiled at her. 'It is.'

He had decided against leaving Phoebe anything, and they emerged ten minutes later with Marie not only now half-owner of the house, but the sole beneficiary in Clive's will.

'I'm sure that guy was looking at me funny,' Marie said.

'George?'

'When you were telling him what your wishes were, he had a real supercilious expression in his face. Like he didn't exactly trust me or something.'

Clive chuckled. 'I wouldn't worry about George. He had a bit of a soft spot for Gerri. I could have been leaving my money to the Queen and even she would have got the stink-eye.'

Marie laughed.

'Besides,' Clive continued, 'what I choose to do with my money is none of his business. What he may or may not think is irrelevant, he's paid to do as I ask. Anyway, come on, let's go and see about getting Donny his PlayStation.'

On Saturday afternoon, Clive said that he'd forgotten to pick up something at the hardware store the previous day and disappeared off for an hour.

He and Marie had discussed going out for a meal that evening; a new Thai restaurant had opened in town a few months earlier and Clive was keen to visit. Donovan asked Marie if she minded him staying at home, and would it be okay if Darren came over to play on his new games console. Pleased at the prospect that she and Clive would get to have a quiet evening to themselves, she readily agreed and Clive was more than happy with the arrangements.

The lighting in the restaurant was low and the waiter escorted them to a table at the back of the room away from all the others.

'This is nice, isn't it?' Clive said, as they took their seats.

Marie raised her eyebrows. 'I'll have to take your word for it, I can hardly see anything.'

They were studying their menus in the light from the candle in the middle of the table when the waiter reappeared at Clive's shoulder carrying a tray. On it were two champagne flutes and an ice bucket containing a large bottle with a foil wrapped top.

'Your champagne, sir.'

Marie looked up from her menu. 'Sorry, we didn't order that.'

'No, madam,' the man said, setting the tray down on the table. 'Sir did.'

Puzzled, Marie looked at Clive. 'Did you?'

The waiter popped the cork on the bottle and filled the two glasses.

Clive smiled. 'I requested it when I rang through to book the table earlier. I thought it was appropriate.'

'For what?'

'Are you ready to order, sir?' the waiter asked.

'Just give us a couple of minutes would you?' Clive said.

Giving him a polite nod, the waiter made himself scarce.

'Come on, what's with the bubbles?' Marie asked.

Clive reached inside his jacket and pulled out a small, black leatherette box and set it down on the table. 'I picked this up in town this morning.' Flipping it open, he withdrew a circular band of gold inset with an exquisite diamond and ruby cluster. 'I thought we should make it official.' He reached over and took hold of Marie's left hand. 'Marie Shaw. Will you marry me and make me the happiest man alive?'

Smiling, Marie blew him a little kiss. 'I will.'

Clive beamed and slipped the ring onto the fourth finger of her hand. 'It's a little loose. I feared it might be.' He smiled nervously. 'We can take it in and get it adjusted.' Picking up the champagne flutes, he handed one to her and they clinked them together. 'Here's to us.'

Smiling, Marie turned her finger to the candle and the gems glittered in the flickering flame. 'To us,' she repeated.

Clive sipped his drink. 'Hey,' he said, 'I was looking at the pictures again today that I took when we went to

302

Hampton Court. Made me smile. We've had some lovely romantic times together, haven't we?'

Marie looked down at the table and rolled her eyes.

Clive noticed and frowned. 'Did you just roll your eyes?'

How did he see that in this light? Marie thought. 'No, I…'

'Please don't mock me. I don't have as long left on this planet as you do. I like to savour every little thing.'

'I wasn't mocking you. It's just… Hampton Court? *Really*?'

Clive smiled. 'Yes, okay, I'll grant you it wasn't one of the better ones. But we've still had some very memorable times together.' He picked up the bottle. 'More?'

Marie had been doubtful that Donovan would make the effort he'd promised, but when he returned to school and the weeks passed, there were no further incidents.

The run of best behaviour came to a jarring end one Friday in March when Clive had dropped Marie in town to meet up with Cassandra for a girls' shopping afternoon. He'd took himself off to the pub for a quick pint and then, not having to pick up Marie until five, decided to head for home for a couple of hours.

It was just after two and, as soon as he walked through the front door, he smelt an unpleasant pungent aroma. He went into the living room and his face darkened as he saw Donovan, laid back on the sofa with his eyes closed and a pair of headphones in his ears, listening to the iPod they had bought him for Christmas. Hanging loosely between the fingers of his right hand was a cannabis joint.

'What the hell is going on here?!' Clive exclaimed.

Donovan jerked and abruptly sat up, pulling out the earphones. 'God, you made me jump!'

'What do you think you're doing?!'

'Just chilling,' Donovan said indifferently.

'It's two o'clock in the afternoon. Why aren't you at school?'

Donovan looked a bit sheepish. 'They sent me home.' He saw the look on Clive's face. 'It wasn't my fault. This teacher, Mr Holloway, he's a right wanker and he's been giving me earache all week, so I told him where to get off.'

Clive held up a hand. 'Actually, I don't want to hear it. How did you get home?'

'They tried calling Mum but she wasn't answering. I had to get the bus to the bottom of the lane and walk.'

Clive pointed to the marijuana joint. 'And what's that?'

Donovan grinned. 'Don't you know?'

Clive glared at the boy. 'Where exactly do you get off thinking it's okay to smoke cannabis in my house?'

'I don't know what you're getting so wound up about. It's just a doobie.'

'Where did you get it?'

'A friend.' Donovan leant over and flicked some ash into a saucer on the table.

Clive's eyes widened and he pointed at the saucer. 'Where did you get that?'

'The cabinet.'

Clive turned his head looked over at the display cabinet in the corner of the room, which contained Geraldine's hand-painted Royal Worcester tea set. The door was open.

304

'How *dare* you touch Gerri's things?'

Donovan smirked. 'What would you rather, I flick ash on the carpet?'

Clive was apoplectic. 'I credited you with more sense than that! Those...' – he pointed to the cabinet – '...are *incredibly* valuable. If you *had* to behave like a delinquent, you could have got a plain saucer from the kitchen cupboard.'

'You need to calm down. You'll give yourself a heart attack.' Donovan put the joint to his lips and sucked in the smoke. Breathing it out in a thin plume, he held it out to Clive. 'Here, have a puff.'

Clive snatched it off him.

'Oi! Give that back!'

'You promised you were going to keep your nose clean.' Clive crossed the room and paused at the door. 'Just get out of my sight before I do something I'll regret.'

'Here,' Donovan said, as a look of devilment crossed his face. 'Don't forget this piece of crap.' Picking up the saucer, he hurled it at Clive, who had to duck to avoid being struck in the face with it.

Resisting the urge to strike the boy, Clive glowered at him. 'You're out of control, lad. Carry on like this and your days in this house are numbered.'

Clive arrived a few minutes late to pick up Marie and it had just started to rain. He pulled up at the kerb and she dropped two carrier bags onto the back seat, slammed the door, and ran round to the passenger side.

305

'I was starting to think you'd forgotten me,' Marie said breathlessly, pulling the door shut and leaning over to give Clive a peck on the cheek. 'You got here just in time, it looks like it's about to chuck it down.'

Clive was staring directly ahead with his hands gripped tightly around the wheel. The fact that he hadn't spoken seemed to have gone over Marie's head; she was smiling at him cheerfully, evidently pleased with herself. 'I got you a little surprise. You'll never guess what it is. When I saw it I just had to buy it for you. It's…' She trailed off as she finally saw the look of thunder on his face. 'What's the matter?'

'Your son.'

The smile vanished from Marie's face. 'Oh God, is he okay?'

'Is *he* okay? Yes, he's absolutely fine and dandy.'

Marie frowned. 'Don't talk in riddles, Clive. What's happened?'

As the rain started hammering down on the windscreen, Clive finally turned to look at her. 'Where do you want me to start?' His expression was grim. 'Being sent home from school for cheeking a teacher? Sitting on my sofa smoking bloody cannabis? No, I'll tell you what, let's start with throwing one of Gerri's dishes at me.'

Marie stared at him. 'Is this some kind of joke?'

'Do I look like I'm joking?'

'I don't believe it. He's been doing so well.'

'Believe it, Marie. There's something wrong with that boy. You need to get him to a counsellor.'

'He doesn't need counselling!' Marie exclaimed. 'He's just at that awkward age. You as good as said it yourself. He'll come through it. I'll speak to him.'

Some of Clive's anger seemed to dissipate. 'Make sure you do before he does something that gets him into serious trouble. He's out of control.'

A thought flashed into Marie's mind. 'Where is he now?'

'I sent him to his room. I didn't know what else to do with him.'

As soon as they got home, Marie summoned Donovan downstairs and Clive left the two of them seated opposite each other at the kitchen table.

Rather than reading the riot act, Marie calmly tried to impress on the boy, not only how unacceptable his behaviour was becoming, but how he was putting their lives on Honeydew Lane at risk.

'Clive would have chucked us both out in a heartbeat today. What do you think would happen to us then?'

Donovan shrugged.

'I know you probably don't see it, but Clive really cares about you. I've never told you much about your Dad, but he was an unkind and selfish man. The only good thing to come out of our time together was you.' Marie moved round the table, sat down alongside him and put her arm around his shoulders. 'But you can take it from me, he wouldn't have been a good father to you. Clive isn't trying to take the place of a Dad, but he's a very loving and caring man. Just look at everything he's done for us. Think about the fun you had together redecorating your bedroom. Honestly, all he really wants in return is a little respect.'

Resting his head against Marie's chest, Donovan broke down in tears. 'I don't know why I do it,' he sobbed. 'I just feel so angry all the time.'

Marie held him tightly to her. 'You're a boy who's turning into a young man. You're going through all sorts of changes. It's normal, you're growing up, it happens to everyone your age. But that anger will go away, I promise. For now, when you feel it building up inside you, you have to try extra hard to work through it. Don't let it get the better of you and damage the respectable young man who's going to make his Mum proud.'

Sitting up, Donovan apologised and promised faithfully that he would endeavour to conduct himself properly in future.

Marie knew in her heart it wouldn't last, but for now it was all she could ask. 'Alright then. Let's go and find Clive and you can say sorry to him too.'

It became routine for Clive and Marie to dine out on a Saturday night, while Donovan stayed at home, usually playing on his games console with his friend, Darren.

One evening several months later, having enjoyed a pleasant meal out, Clive and Marie got back to Sunnycatt just after eleven. As they rounded the bend in the drive and the house came into view, Marie immediately sensed something was wrong.

'Where's my car?'

Clive's brow furrowed. 'Wasn't it in the garage? I didn't really register when we left.'

'No, it was on the drive.'

'Are you sure?' Irritatingly, Clive appeared unconcerned.

'Of course I'm sure. I gave it a spray-wash while you were in town and I hadn't put it away.'

They pulled up, and before Clive had even shut off the engine, Marie had the door open and was climbing out. She pointed at the ground. 'Look, the gravel's all churned up.' She was panicking now. 'It's been stolen!'

Clive got out and looked down. Sure enough, there were deep furrows in the gravel. His eye followed the tracks towards the far side of the house. 'Wait here,' he said; there was a discernible note of apprehension in his voice now. He crunched across the gravel and when he reached the corner of the house, he squinted into the darkness and his eyes fell upon the Toyota. It looked as if it had been parked between two apple trees on the far side of the garden.

Marie appeared behind Clive and she saw it too. 'What the bloody hell...?'

'Go inside and get the flashlight from under the sink,' Clive said firmly.

Marie started to protest.

'*Please*, just get it.'

She scurried off to do as he'd asked and Clive warily crossed the grass towards the car. He stumbled once and looked down to see there was a deep rut in the grass. What the hell was going on? As he got closer, it he saw that the car wasn't parked between the two trees at all; it was wedged front first.

Clive walked around to the driver's side. Even in the darkness he could see the long scrape marks scoring the paintwork, A check of the passenger side revealed the same thing, only much worse.

Marie appeared holding the flashlight. 'What happened?' she asked breathlessly. She was waving the light around and it shone directly into Clive's face.

He put up a hand to shield his eyes from the glare. 'How the hell should I know?' he said sharply.

'Did someone try to steal it?'

'You'd have to be pretty thick to try and steal a car and take it across the garden instead of out of the damned gates. It looks like some moron has been buggering around. Have you seen the state of my lawn?'

Marie shone the light back across the grass. From where they were standing now, the full extent of the damage became apparent; there were a series of deep-cut circular ruts where the grass had been churned up. She returned the light to the car and saw the chunks of turf dangling from the bumper and the mud spray on the bodywork.

'My God!' Marie exclaimed. 'Who the hell did this?'

'Who do you think?'

Marie turned the light back on Clive, making sure to keep it out of his face. He was staring at her with an expression on his face she had never seen before. 'Your *fucking* son!' he said through gritted teeth.

Marie was almost as shocked at hearing Clive utter the F-word as she was that he was accusing Donny; frankly, she wouldn't have thought him capable of ever being angry enough to use such an expletive. She looked at him wide-eyed. 'You can't be serious! Donny would *never* do something like this!'

'Who *did* then? The fucking Sugarplum Fairy?'

As much as she couldn't believe that Donovan would have done such a thing, in her mind she knew that he had to be right. Who else *was* there? She looked at him, lost for words, but he snatched the flashlight from her and marched off in the direction of the house.

'What are you going to do?' Marie cried out as she took off after him.

'Ask him!' Clive shouted back. 'Let's just hear the little bastard deny it!'

'Please, Clive, don't be too mad. If it was Donny, there has to be a reasonable explanation.'

Clive stopped so abruptly that Marie almost ran into him. He spun round, eyes filled with rage. 'Come on then, let's hear it!'

Again Marie was lost for words.

'Exactly,' Clive said. 'There isn't one.'

They went into the house and Clive stopped at the bottom of the stairs and roared, 'Donovan! Get down here right now!'

There was no reply and he was about to go up when the living room door opened slowly and Donovan, looking very sorry for himself, came out into the hall. He hung his head. 'It wasn't me.'

'*What* wasn't you?' Marie said, trying to control her own anger.

'The car,' Donovan said quietly.

Clive shot Marie an angry look that said "told you". 'What the hell did you do?' he said.

'It was Darren. We were playing *Grand Theft Auto* and he said it would be fun if we had a go in a real car.'

'And that seemed like a good idea to you, did it?' Clive seethed.

Donovan was still staring at the carpet. He shook his head. 'No.'

Marie looked at him incredulously. 'He can't even drive – can he?'

Clive looked at Marie as if he couldn't believe what she's just said. 'That's a stupid question, of course he can't. He's fourteen fucking years old!'

'Fifteen,' Donovan said. 'And he can drive a bit.'

'*Seriously*?' Clive fumed.

'Well, he knows how to turn the engine on.' Donovan looked at Marie. 'I did tell him you'd be cross but he insisted.'

'And you do everything Darren says, do you?' Marie spat back.

'We didn't mean any harm, honest. We were only going to take it to the end of the drive and back. But as soon as Darren put it into gear, he kind of lost control.'

'And tore up my lawn!' Clive exclaimed.

'That was when he was trying to do donuts.'

Clive stared at the boy. 'You just said he lost control!'

'He did. *After* the donuts.'

'You're lucky you didn't kill yourselves, you stupid boy,' Marie said angrily. 'Where's Darren now?'

'He ran off.'

'Ran off?' Clive spluttered. 'Ran off *where*?'

Donovan shrugged. 'Home I guess.'

Clive shook his head in disbelief. 'I'm not listening to any more of this crap tonight.'

'What about Darren,' Marie said, looking at Clive imploringly. 'Shouldn't we go and look for him? He lives two miles away. What if something happens to him? What will his parents think?'

'I don't give a shit about Darren,' Clive said. He looked at Donovan. 'You, get up to your room. I'll decide on your punishment in the morning.'

'I'm sorry,' Donovan said miserably.

'Sorry doesn't cut it this time. We'll be taking that PlayStation back for a start. We can use the money to go towards repairing your Mum's car.'

Donovan finally raised his head. 'That's not fair!'

'Don't you tell me what is and isn't fair,' Clive snapped. 'Now get your arse back up those stairs!'

Donovan looked at Marie imploringly, but she shook her head. 'You've crossed the line this time, Donny. Just go to bed.'

They watched in silence as the boy retreated up the stairs and then Clive went through to the living room and poured himself a large brandy.

Marie meekly sat down on the sofa beside him. 'Please don't do anything you'll regret.'

Clive scowled at her. 'Like asking you to marry me?' he said sourly. He knew it was an awful thing to say, but he didn't care.

Marie put a hand to her mouth. 'You don't mean that!'

Clive didn't reply. He took a slug from the glass of brandy and swallowed. 'That kid is out of control.'

'Of course he isn't. He's just… boisterous.'

'It's far more serious than that and you know it!' Clive scoffed. 'Boisterous is scrumping for apples, playing knock and run, or bunking off science class. Not wrapping a bloody car round a tree! He's lucky he didn't end up in the pond! What next? Burning the house down because Darren…' – he made little air quotes – '…thinks it's a good idea to play campfires? I tell you, Marie, he needs taking in hand before he does something that ends him up in borstal.' He emptied his glass.

'What can I do?'

'It's not my problem. As you've reminded me on countless occasions, he's *your* son, not mine. But something has to be done. I can't have him in my house, worrying about what he might do next.'

'*Our* house,' Marie said.

Giving her a dismissive look, Clive got up and poured himself another brandy. He was standing with his back to her. 'Yes, well, that's something else I should have given a bit more consideration before acting so rashly,' he muttered.

Marie looked up at him in alarm. 'Don't say that.' She rose from the sofa and walked up behind him. 'I can understand why you're angry. Hell, I'm angry too, it's *my* car that got all smashed up. Donny *will* be punished.' She wrapped her arms around his waist. 'But please, don't let this thing come between *us*.' She dropped her right hand down and he tensed. 'There are more important things in life than a car.' She could feel him through his trousers. Squeezing

314

gently, she nuzzled her face into the back of his neck. 'Why don't we go to bed and talk it over when we've both calmed down.'

Gruffly brushing Marie's hand away from his crotch, Clive stepped out of her arms. 'I'm going to sleep in the spare room tonight.' He set down his glass and crossed to the door. 'And you need to have a long, hard think about the way you handle that boy. I mean, what sort of kid thinks for one second he can trash his mother's car without facing *serious* consequences?'

'He knows he did wrong.' Marie said defensively. 'He said he was sorry.'

'Oh, well, that's alright then,' Clive said sarcastically.

'I'm sure he meant it.'

'There you go again, defending him. You're a bad mother, Marie. If it was left up to you he'd get away with murder!'

CHAPTER 32

Sleep eluded Marie for a long time that night. Alone in the bed, she lay awake in the darkness thinking long and hard, exactly as Clive had suggested. But what was spinning through her head couldn't have been further removed from what Clive had suggested. Sure, the things he said were spouted in anger, but they carried an underlying threat that rocked the foundations of her future, and she had worked far too hard to let it all slip through her fingers because of her wayward son.

She eventually drifted off and fell into a deep slumber that was broken by the sound of a car engine revving. She looked at the beside clock: it read nine-twenty-three. Getting out of bed, she went to the window and looked out across the garden.

Down below, the Toyota, it's back wheels spinning and spitting up mud, reversed out from between the two apple trees. As it swung away to the left, she could see Clive was at the wheel.

Quickly dressing, she hurried downstairs and, as she reached the kitchen, the back door swung open and Clive came in. He looked at her and, without speaking, went to the sink and washed his hands.

Marie stood looking at him awkwardly. 'Is it as bad as it looked last night?'

'Worse.' Clive reached for a tea towel and dried his wet hands. 'It's going to cost a fortune to sort that out.' The rage of the previous evening was gone and he spoke matter-of-factly. 'It's not just the car got damaged either. One of my trees came out of it the worse for wear. There are a couple of branches I'm going to need to attend to.'

'I'm sorry we argued last night,' Marie said tentatively.

Clive turned to face her. 'So am I.' He came over and put his arms around her. Holding her tightly to him. 'I said some unforgivable things. You do know I didn't mean any of it?'

Marie didn't answer, but she nodded.

Clive took a step away and looked her in the eyes. 'You still want to marry a grouchy old bugger like me then?'

Marie smiled and nodded, but again she didn't offer verbal affirmation. She crossed to the cupboard and pulled out a box of cereal. 'Let's have some breakfast, then we can speak with Donny.'

'I've had my breakfast and I've spoken to him already.'

Marie felt herself bristle. 'You spoke to him without waiting for me?'

'Don't worry, it's fine.' Clive smiled. 'I didn't get cross, honestly. We had a really good heart to heart actually, and he completely knows how wrong what he and his friend did was. He swore blind he'd never do anything so stupid again.'

Of all the things Marie expected to wake up to, this wasn't one of them. 'And that's the end of it, is it?' she said suspiciously.

'No, he realises that actions have consequences and accepts that he'll be sacrificing his PlayStation to help make amends.'

'It wasn't *all* him,' Marie said. 'It was Darren too.'

'I know. And we're going to take a run over later to have a word with his parents.'

317

'We?'

'All three of us.'

Marie frowned. 'Where is Donny now?'

'He's out.'

'Out?' Something suddenly didn't feel right. Marie looked at Clive in puzzlement. 'Out *where*?'

'We needed some milk. He volunteered to go down to the store and get some.'

'He's *walking*?'

'It'll do him the power of good. Give him time to think about what he did.'

Marie frowned. 'When did he go?'

'About fifteen minutes ago. He'll be back in an hour or so.'

'Okay. But I think I need to have a word with him about all this when he gets back.'

'Absolutely.'

Something about this turn of events didn't feel right, but there was nothing Marie could do about it now.

'Look, I'm going to get up a ladder and lop those damaged branches,' Clive said. 'The ground is a bit soft and even with the thing open to full length I'm going to have to stretch. Come and hold it steady for me will you?'

Marie nodded. 'Sure. Let me get my shoes on.'

Clive hadn't exaggerated; the tree was at a distinctly slightly skewed angle and there were several torn branches hanging loose about ten feet up.

'Shouldn't the whole thing come down?' Marie asked as she surveyed the damage.

'Inevitably, yes,' Clive said, slipping on a pair of gloves and ascending the ladder. 'For now I just want to get these branches off in case the wind brings them down.' He reached the third rung from the top and rested a hand against the trunk to steady himself. 'Bugger,' he muttered, observing the nearest of the two damaged branches. 'This is as high as I can go safely. Probably could have done with a chainsaw really.'

Marie stood at the bottom of the ladder looking up at him. 'How are you going to do it then?'

'Brute force, my darling.'

'What do you mean?'

Clive looked down at Marie and grinned. 'They should come away easily enough with a bit of encouragement.' Reaching out for the branch closest to him he grabbed hold of it and pulled. There was a splintering sound and the branch broke easily away, dropping to the ground a few feet away from Marie. 'That was easy enough,' he called down.

'Except it almost hit me!' Marie said irritably.

Clive chuckled. 'Sorry!' Gripping the top of the ladder with his left hand, he said, 'Hold on really tight now, I'm going to have to stretch to get the other one.'

As he leaned outwards Marie released her grip on the ladder and it rocked an inch sideways.

'Hey!' Clive exclaimed, scrambling to get his balance. 'I said hold tight!'

'I am,' Marie said, resting her hands lightly on the sides of the ladder.

'I mean *really* tight,' Clive said shakily.

'Got it,' Marie said.

As Clive leaned out again and got a hold of the branch, Marie took a step back and glanced up to be sure he wasn't looking. Moving forward again, she put her full weight against the ladder and pushed. It lurched to the right and, as it fell, Marie quickly turned her head away and closed her eyes, waiting for the accompanying bone-breaking crunching sound as Clive hit the ground.

But it didn't come.

She turned and looked up to see him dangling from the branch by both hands. 'What the hell are you doing?!' he screamed. 'Get the bloody ladder back up!'

No sooner had the words left his mouth than there was an almighty cracking sound and the branch broke free from the trunk. With a petrifying shriek, Clive plummeted downwards. In the blink of an eye he hit the ground, rolled once and cracked his head hard on one of the rocks surrounding the pond.

For a fleeting moment, time seemed to stand still as Marie stared at his splayed body with a mixture of stark horror and unbridled elation. Then, somewhere across the way, Doreen's dog started barking. With her pulse racing, Marie rushed forward and stood over Clive

He was laid on his front with his face turned away from her. The left leg, clearly broken, was jutting out at an unnatural angle from the knee and, almost comically, the boot on his right foot had come off and was sitting upright on the grass a few feet away.

Marie was unable to stop herself sniggering. *Wellington's last stand*, she thought. She leaned forward. 'Clive?'

He didn't stir.

'Clive!' she repeated with faux heightened urgency. Moving around to the other side of his body, it was then that she saw the pool of crimson spreading out from beneath his head. The eyes were half open, staring lifelessly at a stone frog sitting on the rockery.

An eerie stillness seemed to descend on the garden, as if the birds that had been twittering in the trees, the koi splashing in the pond, even the leaves rustling softly in the light morning breeze had taken a moment of silence to pay their respects.

There was no doubt in Marie's mind that Clive was dead, but she got down on her knees anyway and put her ear close to his nose, listening. There was nothing to hear but the rapid thumping of her own heartbeat.

As she got to her feet, she happened to cast a glance up towards the house and she did a double-take; had the curtain in Donovan's bedroom window just moved?

Marie raced across the lawn and kicked off her shoes at the kitchen door. She ran barefoot across the kitchen out into the hall, stopping at the foot of the stairs with her heart beating out of her chest. 'Donny?' she called breathlessly.

There was no reply.

Marie fought to calm her breathing. 'Donny, love. Are you home?'

Silence.

Marie went upstairs and tapped lightly on Donovan's bedroom door. 'Donny?' Taking a small breath, she pushed it open.

Donovan was sitting on the end of his bed, hunched over with his back to her.

Marie stared at him, momentarily lost for words. Then she spoke. 'Donny?'

The boy turned his head to look at her. 'Mum.'

Marie tried to force a smile, but it wouldn't come. 'Clive said you'd gone to the shop to get, er...' Her mind blanked.

'Milk.'

'Er, milk, yes. You must have run all the way.'

Donovan shrugged. 'I got as far as the main road and I realised he hadn't given me the money.'

Marie's stomach tightened. She managed to raise the smile. 'That was a bit daft of him. And you walked all that way, just to have to turn round and...'

'Is Clive okay, Mum?'

Marie felt the bile rise in her throat. She stared at her son, lost for words.

'Is he?' Donovan asked again, lowering his head

Marie's mind was racing. She shook her head sadly. 'No. There's been a terrible accident. He wanted to clear some split branches from the apple trees. I asked him to wait for me to come and help, but he went out and started without me. I heard him yell and I ran out, but...'

'I saw what happened,' Donovan whispered hoarsely.

Marie felt her knees go weak and for a second she thought she was going to pass out. She put a hand on the door to steady herself.

There were tears in the boys eyes. 'Why did you do it?'

'Oh, sweetheart.' Marie went over and knelt down on the carpet in front of him. 'I didn't mean to. It was an accident.'

'I saw you push the ladder.' Donovan was avoiding making eye contact with her. 'Why did you do that?' he said shakily.

There was no point in trying to lie. The boy had evidently seen the whole thing. Marie put a hand on his knee. 'For us. I did it for *us*. Clive was threatening to throw us out because of what you did. I couldn't let that happen. We would have been destitute.'

Donovan sniffed. 'Is he… is he…?'

'He's dead.'

'Then you killed him.'

'Because there was no other way, sweetheart. Surely you must see that?'

Donovan shook his head. 'You killed him,' he repeated, almost as if he was still trying to process the magnitude of what he'd witnessed.

'Stop *saying* that!' Marie felt her fear being eclipsed by annoyance. 'Whatever you saw, or *think* you saw, is irrelevant. You need to get it through your head that it was a terrible accident. There are going to be questions to answer, but as far as you're concerned you don't know anything. How could you? You weren't even here. You'd gone to the shops to get milk so I could make a cake.'

Marie stood up and Donovan looked up at her questioningly. 'A cake?'

'That's what I said. I'm going to go downstairs now to call for an ambulance. You stay here and when it arrives you keep quiet and stay out of sight.'

Before making the call, she went out to the kitchen and calmly put the kettle on. Then she methodically laid out the ingredients to make a cake on the kitchen table and by the time she'd done that, the kettle had boiled. She prepared two mugs of tea and set them down on the table. Casting a last look at the scene that would provide an alibi should it be needed, she went out into the garden with her mobile phone. Rapidly breathing in and out a dozen times to make herself breathless, Marie made the 999 call, inflecting her voice with precisely the right level of panic. After hanging up, she went to the side of the house to watch the driveway.

The First Responder arrived in a car ahead of the ambulance just a few minutes later. As she heard the car coming into the drive, Marie dashed back across the lawn and took up position beside Clive's body. She had focused on working herself into a frenzy and when the woman – sporting short hair dyed purple and clad in a medic's uniform with an ID badge that read **WALSH** clipped to her breast pocket – came across the lawn, Marie looked every bit the part of the distraught wife.

She stood back, her arms wrapped tightly around herself, watching in silence while Walsh checked Clive for any vital signs.

'Is he…?' Marie sobbed.

Walsh got to her feet. 'The paramedics will need to check him properly.'

Surprising even herself, Marie burst into tears. It wasn't the outpouring of grief that the sudden death of a loved one would naturally kindle, rather it was an all-consuming sense of release; her display of emotion had the desired effect.

Walsh looked at her sympathetically. 'Let's go back indoors and wait for them to come.'

Marie made herself scarce while the crew carried Clive in a body bag out to the ambulance. Walsh found her standing in the kitchen, staring listlessly out of the window.

'The ambulance is ready to leave. Would you like to accompany your husband to the hospital, ma'am?'

Marie didn't turn round. 'We weren't married.' She let out a little sob. 'We were planning for a big wedding next year...'

'I'm really sorry for your loss. But if you'd like to accompany the body...'

Now Marie turned to face her. 'No. If it's okay, I'll make my own way.'

'Of course. It might be an idea to have a hot drink before you do. It'll help calm your nerves.' Walsh cast a look around the kitchen and saw the baking ingredients on the table beside the two cups of cold tea.

Marie saw her looking. 'I'd just made tea when I heard Clive cry out.' She stifled another sob. 'I thought he said he'd call me to come and hold the ladder when he was ready. If only he'd listened and waited...'

'You mustn't blame yourself, ma'am,' Walsh said. 'It was an accident.'

Marie nodded and blew her nose.

Walsh gave her a comforting smile. 'Have that tea and follow on when you're ready. There's no hurry.'

When Walsh and the ambulance had gone, Marie went back upstairs. She found Donovan still sitting on the end of his bed. He looked up at her as she came into the room and softly closed the door behind her. His eyes were red; it was obvious he had been crying.

'Okay, listen to me, Donny. This is what's going to happen.'

CHAPTER 33

A year before Geraldine had fallen ill, she and Clive had visited a Funeral Director and made the necessary arrangements for their send-offs. With negotiation, a double plot in the churchyard outside Sunnycatt had been secured. At the time, they had joked about how long it would probably be before they would be occupying them. They couldn't have possibly foreseen that they would both be dead within three years.

Clive Campbell was buried in the churchyard next to Geraldine two weeks after the fall from the ladder that killed him.

Marie had telephoned to the Funeral Director to see if there was anything that could be done to prevent one or two specific people attending; Phoebe and Geraldine's sister, Nancy. They were in the process, as per Clive's instructions, of sending out details of the funeral to the list of people he had given them.

'Clive had a terrible falling out with his daughter, and I know he wouldn't have wanted her there.'

'I'm sorry,' the well-spoken but slightly bemused man on the end of the line told her. 'Mr Campbell's last registered wishes are very specific.'

'But when did he give you them?'

'With all due respect, madam, that's irrelevant. They *do* constitute his last wishes and we are legally bound to follow them to the letter.'

Marie huffed. 'So you're saying there's nothing I can do? I know he would have changed it if he'd had the opportunity.'

'It may not be much consolation to madam, but just because Miss Campbell is furnished with the details of her late father's funeral, it doesn't necessarily follow that she will attend. In fact, if they were estranged as you say, I would suggest it is likely that she won't.'

Marie held her ground on the fact there wasn't going to be a wake, putting quite a number of noses out of joint in the process.

On the day, Nancy had called to say that she regrettably wouldn't be coming because she was unwell. Unsurprisingly, Phoebe did attend.

Inside the church, she sat in the second row of pews directly behind Marie. They acknowledged each other with a nod, but didn't speak. Throughout the entire service – which felt as if it went on forever – Marie could feel Phoebe's eyes burning into her neck.

After the burial, when everyone was filing out of the churchyard into the lane, Phoebe sidled up to her. 'I suppose you'll be sitting pretty now then.' There was an abruptness in her tone.

Marie didn't even turn her head. 'What's that supposed to mean?'

'I'm sure my foolish, infatuated father named you as a beneficiary in his will.'

'I really don't know. But, yes, I would imagine he will have made sure his future wife was taken care of in the event of his death.' The look of shock on Phoebe's face told her what she had suspected; although Clive had never broached the subject, Marie was fairly sure he hadn't told his daughter they were engaged. 'Oh, sorry,' she said with a glint of spite in her eye. 'Didn't your Dad tell you that we were engaged and planning to be married next year?' She reached out and rested a conciliatory hand on Phoebe's arm. 'Don't worry, I'm sure you'll get what's coming to you too.'

Phoebe was clearly struggling to maintain her composure. She moved closer. 'You're a nasty little bitch, aren't you?'

Marie smiled at her sweetly. 'Pot and kettle come to mind.'

Phoebe opened her mouth to fire back, but appeared to think better of it; she had just seen her father buried, now wasn't the time to cause a scene. Regaining her composure, she said, 'What exactly happened that day in the garden?'

'You already know everything there is to know.'

'Tell me anyway.'

'Really? Okay, Clive went into the garden to cut down some damaged branches from one of the trees. I'd asked him to wait until I could come out and help, but he went ahead without me. That's it. He was your Dad, you know how headstrong he was.'

'Dad wasn't the headstrong type at all,' Phoebe said flatly.

Marie looked at her dismissively. 'Well then, maybe you didn't know him as well as you thought you did. Now if you'll excuse me, there are a few other people I want to catch before they leave.' Turning away, she walked over to see Doreen, who had been sitting on her mobility scooter waiting patiently for her to finish speaking with Phoebe. The old lady saw her approaching and smiled warmly.

'Hi, D. Thanks so much for coming.'

'Hello, my dear. That was a very fitting service.'

'Did you think so?' Marie muttered noncommittally.

'I can't stop long, old Barnaby gets a bit antsy being left alone in the house. He can bark up a real storm when he gets going.'

'I know,' Marie said sourly. 'We hear him all the time.'

The note of annoyance in her voice appeared to go over Doreen's head. 'How are you holding up?'

'Not great. But it's hit Donny *really* hard.'

'Oh, poor lamb,' Doreen said sadly. 'I noticed he wasn't here today.'

'He couldn't face it. He was too upset.'

Doreen sighed. 'Well, I'll be sorry to see you go.'

Marie's brow furrowed. 'Go where?'

'Leave, dear. Now Clive's gone, I assume you and the little boy will be moving on.'

The friendliness disappeared from Marie's face. 'Why don't you just mind your own damned business?'

'Excuse me?'

Marie glowered at her. 'I said stop interfering in my affairs and get yourself off home before Barnaby eats your couch!' With that, she turned and walked away.

A woman standing nearby had overheard the tail end of the conversation and caught Doreen's eye. 'That was a little harsh wasn't it?'

Doreen forced a smile. 'It's perfectly understandable though. She's under a lot of pressure and she's grieving, poor lass.'

Cassandra had offered to pick Marie up and drive her to the funeral. She was waiting for her beside her maroon Vauxhall Corsa, parked up at the end of the old stone and mortar wall that fronted the churchyard. She smiled as Marie approached, then saw the look of annoyance on her face. 'You alright, babe?'

'Not really. Let's just get out of here.'

'Okay. Wanna go for a drink?'

'No, I don't feel like it. Just run me home.'

'Sure.'

They got into the car and Cassandra turned the key in the ignition. On the third attempt, the engine sputtered into life. 'I guess that place is all yours now.'

Marie smiled. 'Well, the will hasn't been read yet. But, yes, trust me, it's all mine.'

After Clive's death, Marie had telephoned Donovan's school and explained to the secretary that he wouldn't be in for a while. 'I can't say how long it will be,' she had told her. 'He was very close to his stepfather and he's heartbroken.' The woman was very sympathetic and offered her condolences, asking that Marie please keep them appraised as to when Donovan would be returning. Marie promised that she would, but she had already decided he wouldn't be attending school again – ever.

As soon as Marie arrived home following the funeral, she made a cheese and pickle sandwich and a glass of fruit squash, then she went upstairs to see Donovan.

The boy was laying on his bed reading a comic book. As he heard the key turn in the lock, he threw it aside and propped himself up on his elbows.

Marie came in and set down the snack on his bedside table. 'Do you need the bathroom, sweetheart?'

Donovan got up off the bed. 'Yeah, I'm busting.'

Marie waited outside the bathroom door while he went, then took him back to his room. 'We'll need to get you something so you can go in here.' She saw the look of disgust on her son's face. 'If I'm out for any length of time and you need to, obviously,' she added, crossing to the window and staring out across the garden towards the apple trees. She exhaled deeply. 'Thank God it's over and done with.'

Donovan picked up the plate and took a bite out of the sandwich. 'Did it go okay?'

'No, it was awful. You should be glad I wouldn't let you come.'

'I still would have liked to.'

'You'd have hated it.' Marie came over and sat down on the edge of the bed. 'I've come to a decision about school.'

'Am I going to be allowed to go back now?' Donovan asked hopefully

'No.'

The boy's face fell. 'But it's been, like, two weeks. I'm missing my mates.'

'You won't be going back at all,' Marie said firmly. 'I shall be home schooling you from now on.'

'*What*?'

'You heard me. I'd have thought you'd be pleased. I don't think that school was doing you any good anyway. You were always getting into trouble and your choice of friends was questionable – to put it mildly.'

'But what about Darren?' Donovan protested. 'I haven't seen him since…'

'*Especially* Darren!'

Donovan screwed up his face. 'This is rubbish. You can't do this.'

'I can and I *am*.'

'But I'm supposed to be working towards my exams.'

'Don't worry, you'll pass. I've checked on the requirements, all I need to do is speak to the council and get hold of the national curriculum, then just let the school know you'll not be going back.' Marie was almost thinking aloud now.

'Mum…'

'Yes, sweetheart?'

'I was wondering if I might be allowed to go out for a bit. I've been locked up here for ages now. I promised I wouldn't say anything to anyone about what happened.'

'I've told you before, it's for your own good. Grief is a very unpredictable thing; it affects everyone differently.'

'I'm not grieving, Mum, honestly.'

Marie smiled. 'Of course you are, sweetheart. You just can't see it yet. And that's why staying here in the house is the best thing for you right now. Safe and warm, where your Mum can look after you.'

'But…'

'That's enough now. Finish your sandwich and you can have a nap.'

Donovan looked at her petulantly. 'I don't need a nap. I want to go out.'

'Have you forgotten whose fault it is that Clive is dead?'

'How's it my fault?'

'If you hadn't taken the car and damaged the trees he wouldn't have been up that ladder in the first place!' Marie got up and crossed to the door. She paused and smiled at him sweetly. 'I'll bring you your dinner later. It's chicken pie, your favourite.'

'Please, Mum,' Donovan started, but she closed the door on him and he heard the rattle of the key turning in the lock.

The following afternoon Marie had an appointment at the bank. Driving Clive's Mercedes was significantly different to being in her Toyota; although she was still getting used to the feel of it, she thrilled at the surge of power when she pressed down on the accelerator and, with the roads being relatively quiet, she got into town in record time.

When she left the bank an hour later, she was standing waiting at the lights to cross the street when someone spoke to her. 'Marie?'

Marie idly turned her head and saw a young woman standing behind her. She looked to be about the same age as her and there was something vaguely familiar about the face, but she couldn't quite place it. Then the penny dropped and her eyes widened. 'Emily?'

Emily smiled at her. 'I thought it was you. I mean, I wasn't entirely sure for a moment, but, yeah, I was right.'

'Oh my God, I haven't seen you since…'

'When you went off to Australia.'

Marie remembered the bitterness of their conversation the last time they'd spoken. 'How are you? You look well.'

'I'm good, yeah. What about you?'

'Yes, I'm okay I guess.'

The traffic lights turned red and the cars came to a halt. The little green man lit up and the signal to cross bleeped. They crossed over and stopped outside a Costa coffee shop.

Emily smiled thinly. 'Well, it was nice to see you.'

'Listen, I don't suppose you fancy getting a coffee, do you?'

'Er…' Emily looked at her watch. 'I don't know. I've got to collect the twins from school in an hour and I've got some bits to pick up first.'

'Just for twenty minutes. It'd be so good to catch up.'

Emily patently wasn't keen, but she nodded. 'Go on then. Twenty minutes.'

Costa was busy and noisy, but they managed to find an empty table in the corner and sat down.

'What are you having?' Marie asked.

'Cappuccino please. A small one.' Emily reached into her bag for her purse.

'It's okay, I'll get them.'

Marie went to the counter and returned a few minutes later with their drinks.

'So you have kids?'

'Three. The two boys, Jacob and Matthew, and a baby girl, Natasha. She's with Mum this afternoon. You?'

'Just the one. Donny.' Marie smiled. 'It seems only yesterday we were kids ourselves. Who'd have ever thought we'd end up with kids of our own? And little Emily Marks has got three!'

'I'm not Marks any more. It's Emily Bird.'

It took Marie a moment to register the name. 'You married Mickey Bird?!'

'I did.'

Marie laughed. 'That's insane!'

Emily didn't smile. 'Not really.'

'I didn't mean that rudely. I'm pleased for you, really I am.'

'He's not the delinquent we knew at school any more. He's a good man.'

'I'm sure. What does he do for a living?'

'He's a delivery driver. It's not ideal, but he works hard to provide for us all. Coupled with the part-time hours I do in Asda, we get by.'

'Gosh, *so* much has happened since I last saw you. I…' Marie trailed off as the tears welled in her eyes.

'What's the matter?' Emily was looking at her a little bemused. Marie had always had a knack for turning on the waterworks, and she had never quite been able to ascertain when it was genuine and when it wasn't.

Marie pulled a tissue from her bag and blew her nose. 'Sorry.'

'Don't apologise. What's wrong?'

336

'I've had an awful time of it recently. My fiancé, Clive died a few weeks ago and we had the funeral yesterday.'

'Oh, God.' Emily reached out and put her hand on Marie's. 'I'm *so* sorry.'

'It's fine. I just feel like I'm walking on an emotional knife-edge at the moment.'

'That's understandable.' Despite their past differences, Emily was genuinely sorry at what she was hearing. She took a sip of her coffee and tried to change the subject. 'So how old is your boy now?'

'Fifteen.'

'Crikey. Won't be long until he leaves school then. How's he getting along?'

'Okay. Clive's death has hit him hard though. He saw him as a father and they loved each other so much. He refuses to leave the house now.'

'Not even for school?'

'No. I've spoken to them and explained and they've been incredibly patient and understanding. It's all I can do to get him to leave his room. I try to encourage him, of course, but most of the time he won't even come down for meals. He just sits up there on his own, day in, day out. If I say anything, he gets into a strop and won't even speak to me.'

'Poor boy,' Emily said. 'I wish I knew what to suggest.'

'There's nothing you can suggest I haven't already tried. I just can't see an end to it. Clive was Donny's whole world and now he's gone he can't cope.'

'How did you meet your Clive?' Emily asked, hoping to lighten the conversation. 'If it's not prying,' she added hastily.

'Oh, well, that's a long story.'

Emily smiled. 'Start at the beginning then.'

Marie returned the smile. 'Okay, I'll try to keep it short though. When I got back from Oz I moved in with my Aunt.'

'I heard that,' Emily said. 'Ogilvie Crescent wasn't it?'

'That's right.'

'I've got a friend who lives just round the corner from there. June Gibbs?'

Marie shrugged, as if to say "so what?". 'Never heard of her.'

'No reason you should. I was just saying.'

Marie frowned. '*Anyway*. When my Aunt died I thought I was going to be homeless. She'd promised to leave me the house, but when it came to it, she went and left it to a bloody donkey sanctuary instead, if you can believe that! Fortunately I had a really decent job in finance at the time and I'd managed to stash quite a bit away. It meant I could get a mortgage on a place of my own, ended up with a nice place up in Sunnycatt.'

'Wow!' Emily looked genuinely impressed. 'Mickey's boss was hoping to get a place out that way a couple of years ago, but he said the prices were ridiculous.'

'Yes, it's nothing fancy,' Marie said matter-of-factly, 'but it's comfortable enough, you know? Anyway, what was I saying? Oh, yes, the job. Well, I had quite a few clients and one of them was Clive. The day he first walked into my office… well, you'd laugh if I said it was love at first sight, but honestly, it really was. For both of us. He asked me out and we had an amazing night and after that we started dating regularly. And the sex… it was, like, phenomenal.' Emily

338

looked a little uncomfortable at that, exactly as Marie knew she would; she was relishing every minute of the fiction she was spinning. 'Anyway, he was living in a flat at the time, and after a few months it made sense that he moved in with me and Donny. We had over a year together, until... well, you know.' There was an awkward silence, then Marie smiled. 'I've missed you, Em. I thought I'd never see you again.'

Emily looked at her dispassionately. 'You could have got in touch when you came back. If you'd really wanted to.'

'I *did* want to. But after the last time we spoke, I didn't think you ever wanted to see *me* again.'

'I'll be honest with you, I didn't.' Emily sighed. 'You really hurt me you know, Marie. We were as close as two friends could be, then you swanned off to Australia and didn't so much as look back. How do you think that made me feel? How would *you* have felt if I'd done that to you?'

Marie looked at her old friend sadly. 'I know it doesn't count for much now, but I'm really sorry.'

'You're right, it doesn't.' Emily had been looking at Marie coldly, but then, unexpectedly, she smiled. 'But it's a start I guess. I missed you too, you know.'

'Really?' Marie said sadly.

'Of course. We were best mates. We did everything together. That sort of thing doesn't just become insignificant in the blink of an eye.' Now it was Emily's turn to well up. She found a tissue and dabbed at her eyes. 'Anyway, I'm going to go and pick up my boys before I make a fool of myself in the middle of Costa. Hopefully we'll bump into each other again.' She rose.

Marie smiled up at her. 'I'd like that. But, look, let's not leave it to chance, eh? Let me give you my number and you can give me a shout when you're free and maybe we can go somewhere a bit nicer than Costa next time. What about next Monday?'

Emily shook her head. 'I'd love to, but I've got to take the boys to the dentist first thing. Mickey's got the day off too, so we're going to DFS to look at new sofas.'

'So you haven't got time for me then?' Marie said tersely.

Was that a touch of the old Marie petulance? Emily squinted at her. 'Don't be daft.' She wasn't actually sure if Marie was joking or not, so she decided it was best to let it pass. 'We can do it another day.'

'If you can find time to squeeze me in I suppose.'

Emily put her arms round her and gave her a hug. 'Of course I can.'

CHAPTER 34

Over the weeks that followed, Marie and Emily met up several times and the friendship that had been dashed on the rocks years beforehand was rekindled.

Even when they were children, Marie had thrived on the edge of superiority she felt she had over her friend. Emily had always been the underdog in their relationship, and here they were, years later, and nothing had changed. For Marie, it wasn't so much that she enjoyed spending time with Emily, so much as she delighted in seizing every opportunity to crow about her life achievements to someone who seemed happy to listen. And Emily was; Marie's stories about her successful career, her numerous relationships – *so* numerous in fact that she often couldn't remember the names of the men – and her lovely home in Sunnycatt made Emily's own life feel positively mundane by comparison, but she was genuinely happy for her.

Even though Marie had told Emily the house was hers, on the day she received the official letter confirming that Clive had bequeathed it to her, she took Emily out to lunch in the swankiest restaurant in town.

'What are we celebrating exactly?' Emily asked, as the sommelier set down the bottle of chilled Chablis on the table.

'I got a rather unexpected letter from a solicitor today. Clive always said he was going to leave me his money, but I never took it very seriously, I thought it was talk. I mean, it's not like I needed it. Anyway, he never said, but it turns out he did actually change his will. He left the lot to me!'

Emily's eyes widened. 'Wow!'

'Well, I say the lot, but most of it anyway,' Marie continued. 'There was a few grand in it for his daughter – not that the slimy little bloodsucker deserved it, honestly you wouldn't believe what a conniving bitch she is – but the rest is all mine.' Marie took a sip of her wine. 'Mmm, that's good.'

Emily tasted hers and agreed. 'So how much are we talking about, if you don't mind me asking? Life-changing?'

'Not life-changing. It's only just over three hundred grand.'

Emily almost choked on her drink. 'My God, that's incredible!'

'Yes, it'll make for a little bit of pocket money.' Marie grinned. 'Better than a kick in the teeth, I suppose.'

Emily shook her head in disbelief. 'Crikey, how can you be so blasé about it? Me and Mickey could only ever dream of having money like that. It would certainly change *our* lives.'

Marie laughed. 'You should have found yourself a man who'd amount to something then!' She saw the look of hurt cross Emily's face. 'Sorry,' she said, although she wasn't. 'I was only joking. You couldn't have chosen better. Honestly, love, you're lucky to have Mickey and he's *really* lucky to have you.'

The plates of steak and chips they'd ordered arrived and they ate quietly for a couple of minutes. It was Marie who broke the silence.

'You're a proper Mrs Domesticated now, aren't you?'

Emily almost choked on a chip. 'I wouldn't put it quite like that.

'I would,' Marie said flatly. 'All cosy and settled with a husband and three kids.'

Emily didn't like the tone in Marie's voice, so she steered the subject back to her. 'So, when am I going to get an invite to see this lovely house of yours?'

Marie looked thoughtful. After a moment, she finished chewing and cleaned her palate with a mouthful of wine. 'I've been thinking of redecorating actually. Top to bottom. It wasn't in the greatest shape when I moved in, the previous owners' tastes were a bit nineteen-forties. But what with one thing and another I haven't got around to it. Best wait until it's done and come then.'

Emily smiled. 'I wouldn't judge you.'

'I'm sure, but I'd like the place to look respectable.'

'You should see the state of our place! Honestly, Marie, it doesn't matter a jot what the pattern on the wallpaper is. And I thought maybe I could get to meet your son.'

'Oh, no,' Marie said flatly. 'That's out of the question. I told you, he's become a bit of a recluse.'

'Well, just to see your home then,' Emily persisted. 'I'd love to see where you're living now.'

'I don't think so.'

Emily looked at Marie mockingly. 'Is it because you've made it all up and you're really living in a hovel?'

'Don't be so ridiculous!' Marie snapped. 'Do you think I'd make up stories about where I live?'

'Pardon me for joking,' Emily said, taken aback by the vitriol in her friend's voice.

343

Marie forced a smile. 'Sorry, I didn't mean to get shirty. I've got a lot on my plate at the moment. There's an important client coming into the office next week and a lot rests on me securing the account. It's very stressful.'

'I can believe it.' Emily crossed her knife and fork. 'I couldn't handle that sort of pressure.' She chuckled. 'It's stressful enough for me on the tills in Asda! Where is it you work again? Actually, I'm not sure you ever said.'

'I'll tell you what,' Marie said, dodging the question. 'I'm off work for a couple of days. Why don't you come over to the house tomorrow morning for coffee? I can give you the official tour.'

'Oh! That would be lovely.' Emily grinned. 'I won't be counting the cobwebs, I promise. What time would you like me?'

'About ten suit you?'

Emily drained her glass and retrieved a little notepad from her handbag. She slid it across the table. 'Jot you address down and I'll be there.'

When Marie arrived home, she went up to see Donovan. Even before she got to the top of the stairs, the acrid smell of faeces caught her nostrils. Unlocking the bedroom door, she found Donovan sitting on the bed looking sorry for himself. She put a hand to her nose and scowled at him with disgust. 'Couldn't you have waited?'

'I was desperate, I've got an upset tummy.'

'Well go and empty the pot before I'm sick!'

Getting up, the boy picked up the chamber pot from the floor beside the bed and carried it through to the bathroom.

Marie went and opened the window an inch to let in some air and went back out onto the landing to wait beside his bathroom door.

The toilet flushed and a moment later Donovan reappeared.

'Sorry, Mum,' he said sadly.

'I should damned well think so. The pot is only supposed to be for wee. You know that. Anything more, you hold it till I get home.'

They went back through to the bedroom and Donovan dropped the pot back beside the bed. 'I couldn't help it.'

'It's not even like I've been out all day, It's only been a couple of hours.'

'If my door wasn't locked all the time, I could go to the bathroom when I need to.'

Marie's expression softened. 'How many times have I told you? I don't want you getting any ideas about wandering off.'

'I wouldn't...'

'And it's for your own protection. It's an unkind world out there and it's getting worse.'

'You said that, but…'

'Just try bloody harder to hold on next time,' Marie said with a tone of finality that suggested the subject wasn't open for further discussion.

Donovan sighed. 'I will.' He slumped down on the bed. 'Did you have a nice time out?'

'It was okay. But it was ruined by what I was listening to on the radio on the way home. Remember those terror attacks in London last summer?'

Donovan nodded.

'There have been more, but they weren't restricted to London, it's happening in cities and towns everywhere. Hundreds of people died.'

Donovan looked at his mother with trepidation. 'Near us?'

'Not that far from here. That's another reason why you're safer not going out. If you're here with me, I can protect you from all the horrors going on out there.' Marie sat down on the edge of the bed. 'Okay, listen. I've got a friend coming for coffee tomorrow morning for an hour or so. It's important that you stay quiet.'

Donovan frowned. 'Can't I come down and meet them?'

'No, you can't. It's an old friend from when I was a girl, but she's not a very nice woman.'

'Why did you invite her then?'

'What does it matter?' Marie said irritably. 'I got cornered into it. The thing is, I want to avoid any awkward questions, so as far as she's concerned you're in bed sick.'

'What awkward questions?'

'Questions that might lead to someone finding out what you did. And how damaging those trees makes you responsible for Clive's death. Is that what you want? Because that's what could happen if you don't just do what I say.'

Donovan frowned. 'I don't understand. Why would your friend ask questions about Clive?'

Marie huffed. 'We may have inherited this house, but we could lose it in a heartbeat if people found out what you did. If it hadn't been for you, we wouldn't be in this situation in the first place. So for God's sake, stop asking stupid questions and just do as I ask.' A thought crossed her mind. Although, following the incident with the Toyota, Clive had confiscated the boy's games console, it had been sitting in the cupboard under the stairs since that night. 'I'll tell you what,' she said, 'I'll do you a deal. If you promise to stay completely schtum while Emily is here, you can have your PlayStation back. You can use the headphones.'

'They make my ears hot,' Donovan said petulantly.

Marie flared. 'Do you want the damned PlayStation back or don't you?'

Donovan looked at her apologetically. 'Yes please.'

'Alright then. But if I hear a single peep out of you while she's here, it's going straight back in the cupboard and it'll stay there permanently.' Marie stood up.

'Oh,' Donovan said. 'While you were out there was someone at the front door.'

Marie frowned. 'Who?'

Donovan looked at her as if to say "seriously?". 'I couldn't see, could I?'

Marie detected the note of sarcasm in his voice. 'Probably just as well. We weren't expecting anyone. I'll be up with your dinner later.'

'What are we having?'

'I've not decided yet.' With that Marie left the room, locking the door behind her.

She slept badly that night. There were fireworks going off and they triggered a barking frenzy over at Doreen's house. When the time came round to get up, she felt exhausted. She briefly considered cancelling Emily's visit, but ultimately decided it might be best just to get it over and done with.

It was almost ten-thirty. Marie had started to think her friend wasn't coming when the doorbell finally rang.

'Wow, this place is amazing!' Emily stepped through the front door into the hall and wiped her feet on the mat. 'I knew the houses up here were big, but I didn't realise *how* big.'

Marie smiled. 'It's alright I guess. I'll probably be looking for something bigger next year.'

Emily removed her coat and shoes. 'Oh, really? I thought you said you were going to redecorate.'

'*Thinking* about redecorating. I haven't made up my mind yet.' Marie held open the living room door. 'Come on through.'

'Sorry I'm a bit late,' Emily said. 'There's been an accident on Deacon Street. A van and a car collided by the looks of it, there was fuel all over the road and the traffic was all snarled up. The diversion took me all out round the back lanes.'

'That's not good. Was anyone hurt?'

'I don't think so. From what I could see it wasn't *that* serious.'

Marie showed Emily around the ground floor of the house and took her out into the garden.

'It's huge!' Emily exclaimed.

'It could use a bit of a tidy up. I used to have a guy do it for me, but I caught him thieving and had to let him go.'

'That's awful,' Emily said. 'You can't trust anyone these days.' She looked over towards the pond and gasped. 'You've got a pond too! Are there fish?'

'Koi.'

'Gosh, Marie, you're so lucky. What with the kids' trampoline, there's barely enough room on our lawn to put two deckchairs out.'

Across the way, Doreen's dog started barking and Emily saw Marie pull a face.

'What's up?'

'That dog drives me nuts. All it does is bark.'

Emily grinned. 'That's what dogs are supposed to do, isn't it?'

'It's not funny. This one's incessant. Day and night. It used to make Clive so mad. He absolutely loathed the thing. You should have heard it last night. Someone was letting off fireworks and…'

'Oh, we took the kids to a little display last night. They loved it.'

'Waste of damned money if you ask me. And when they start dogs barking it's the last straw. I hardly got a wink of sleep.'

'What sort of dog is it?'

Marie shrugged. 'A black one.'

Emily laughed. 'I meant what breed, not what colour.'

'A poodley type thing I think. Who cares? All I know is it does nothing but yap. Come on, lets go inside and have our coffee.'

Marie put the kettle on and leant back against the counter waiting for it to boil. 'I won't show you upstairs today if you

349

don't mind. I told Donny you were coming and he threw a strop.'

Emily looked a little dismayed. 'Oh, I hope me coming over hasn't caused friction.'

'It's fine.' Marie added a little weary sigh to suggest it really wasn't fine. 'Honestly, I told him you were a close friend from when I was his age and how lovely you are, but he wasn't having it.' She shrugged. 'There's nothing I could do about it.'

After their coffee and Emily had left, Marie went up to see Donovan. She unlocked the door and stepped in. The boy was sitting on the end of his bed with his back to her, staring at the screen in front of him, on which he was steering a virtual car through rough woodland terrain.

Donovan had headphones on and hadn't noticed Marie enter the room. 'She's gone,' she said. He didn't respond. 'My friend has gone,' she said more loudly.

With a start, Donovan turned. When he saw Marie, he pulled the headphones off his head. 'Has she gone?'

'Yes. And think yourself lucky you didn't come down to meet her; she was asking all sorts of questions about how Clive died.'

Donovan looked at her fearfully. 'Did you mention me?'

'Of course not. I told you, I'm here to protect you. Nobody needs to know it was your fault.'

A look of relief crossed the boy's face. 'Is she coming back?'

'Maybe. But don't worry about that. What would you like for lunch?'

'Beans on toast?'

Marie smiled. 'Okey doke.' She paused at the door. 'Oh, there was something else Emily told me. She got diverted on the way over. Apparently a terrorist bomb went off in a van on Deacon Street. Six people blown to smithereens. It just isn't safe anywhere any more.' Smiling inwardly, she closed the door behind her, turned the key in the lock and returned downstairs to make Donovan's lunch,

Later that afternoon, the front doorbell rang. Marie peered out of the living room window and saw Doreen's mobility scooter parked on the gravel and the woman herself standing on the step holding a large box.

God, what does she *want?* Marie thought. She opened the door.

Doreen beamed at her. 'Hello, dear. Here's your parcel.'

Marie frowned. 'I'm not expecting a parcel.'

'Didn't the man leave a card?' Doreen rolled her eyes. 'He said he would. You can't trust them, can you?' She held out the box and Marie took it from her. 'He tried to deliver it yesterday but you were out. He came round and asked me if I minded taking it in for you. I thought you might come over to get it last night. But obviously if you had no card, you wouldn't have known.'

Marie looked at the label on the box; it was addressed to Clive. 'Must be something Clive ordered ages ago.' She shook the box. 'No idea what. Anyway, thanks D.'

Marie was about to close the door on her, when Doreen said, 'I hope Barnaby didn't disturb you last night.'

Marie smiled sweetly. 'No? Why?'

351

'He had a little freak out at the fireworks going off and I couldn't calm him down.'

'Never heard a peep.'

'Oh!' Doreen looked surprised. 'That's good then. He gets so worked up sometimes and the man at number seven had a right old go at me the other day. Like it's my fault!'

Marie shook her head. 'I don't think I've heard him once. Maybe when I was in the garden the other day, but it's just background noise, I didn't pay any attention. Anyway, thanks for the parcel – *again*.'

She started to close the door and Doreen stopped her again. 'And how are you coping dear? Without… you know.'

'It's hard. I miss him a lot.'

'That's only to be expected. It takes time. I know when I lost my Arthur…' She trailed off. 'It's so sad thinking about you rattling around this place on your own. Have you got any friends around here?' She smiled. 'Present company excepted I mean.'

Why don't you just piss off? Marie thought. She didn't return the smile. 'One, but she's got a family of her own to think about,' she said with a note of impatience. 'Was that everything?'

'Actually, no. You know that I volunteer with the W.I. in town?'

Marie nodded.

'Well,' Doreen continued, 'we're holding our annual Christmas fete this weekend and everyone seems to be going down with flu. Only this morning Georgina called to cry off.

What we really need is an extra pair of willing hands. And I was thinking…'

Marie shook her head. 'That's not for me, sorry.'

'It's nothing taxing. We just need someone to come along and sell a few Christmas cards or look after the cake stall. We've got a group of children from St Boniface's coming to sing carols this year too.'

Marie looked at her apologetically. 'Sorry, no.'

Doreen wasn't about to take no for an answer. 'Please give it some thought. We could really use the help. The ladies are a lovely bunch, I'm sure you'd like them. Mrs Dixon's husband, he's got a friend works at the *Gazette* and he always comes along to take photos of us for the paper. It's all rather prestigious, but then it's for a such good cause you see: Cancer Research.'

Marie still didn't look convinced.

'Anyway, all I can ask is you think about it. It'll be a terrible shame if we can't find someone, we'll end up having to sacrifice one of the stalls. You'd be saving our bacon if you'd say yes.'

'Saving your bacon?' Marie said.

'Totally.' Doreen smiled. 'It would only be a couple of hours and you'd be our hero.'

Marie smiled. 'A couple of hours, eh?'

'Three at the most.'

'Well, I can't really say no then, can I? Not if it's going to save the day.'

'Really? Oh that's splendid! Thank you *so* much, dear. The ladies will be delighted when I tell them.'

CHAPTER 35

When she had finally got rid of Doreen, Marie carried the parcel through to the living room and opened it up. Inside there was a set of six books filled with pastel drawings of birds by an artist named Alphonse Mead. Mystified, she examined the accompanying receipt and saw that books had been on backorder since Clive paid for them over two years ago. She flipped through the pages of one of them. The pictures were nice enough, but the books weren't of the least interest to her. Dropping it back into the box alongside the other five volumes, she made up her mind to donate them to the W.I.

It had been agreed that Marie would collect Doreen in the Mercedes at eight-thirty on the Saturday morning and they would go to the hall together. Doreen had mentioned that she had a few things to take along, but much to Marie's annoyance it turned out to be eleven heavy boxes filled to the brim with bric-a-brac.

'I pick up bits and pieces throughout the year whenever the opportunity arises,' Doreen remarked cheerfully, completely oblivious to the fact that Marie was struggling. 'My stall always goes down a storm.'

It was tipping with rain and Barnaby was hanging around Marie's legs while she loaded up the car. By the time they actually got moving, she was irritable beyond words and cursing herself for having agreed to help out.

Doreen was in full-on chatty mode and barely pausing for breath all the way to the hall.

'I would have liked to have brought Barnaby with me, but Sadie – she's our senior member – she isn't too keen on dogs. I put some food down for him and I'm hoping he'll behave.'

'I'm sure he will,' Marie said, thinking quite the opposite.

'Actually, I thought your little boy might have wanted to come along today. I haven't seen much of him around recently. I used to see you or Clive taking him off to school in the morning.'

'He's still very upset about Clive's death, so I'm home-schooling him for now.'

'I don't envy you that. It must be hard.'

'Not at all. There's a curriculum we follow and he's doing very well.'

'That's good to hear. It's still a shame he didn't want to come today. We've got a Santa coming and he'll be getting all the children to sit on his knee to tell them what they want for Christmas. Well obviously, it's the verger, Frank Tanner really, but you know what I mean. I'm sure Donny would have liked that.'

'He's a bit old for that sort of malarkey, D.'

'You're never too old to sit on Santa's knee, dear,' Doreen cackled. 'I would myself, except with my size I'd probably break his legs!'

When they reached the hall, Marie was irked to see that the car park at the rear was almost full, with people buzzing back and forth from their cars, carrying goods inside.

Letting Doreen out beside the back door to save her legs, Marie circled twice and she managed to find a spot between a van and a Land Rover that she missed first time round. As she got out, a man wearing a raincoat and a flat cap came hurrying towards her.

'Morning,' he said cheerfully. 'Lovely day for it! Doreen says you've got her stuff. Let me give you a hand to get it all inside.' He held out a hand. 'I'm Ivor. My wife Sadie organised this shindig.' Marie shook his hand and opened the back door. When the man saw the boxes stacked seat to roof, he rubbed his hands together gleefully and grinned. 'Looks like she's done us proud again this year.'

'There are more in the boot,' Marie said.

She kept a close watch on Ivor to make sure the paintwork on the Mercedes wasn't getting scratched, but he appeared to be taking care and between the two of them they unloaded the car and got all the boxes inside in ten minutes. Grabbing up Clive's books from the back seat, she hurried inside.

Doreen had a double table set up at the back of the hall and Marie felt obliged to help her to lay out her wares. As they were finishing, an elderly woman with a blue rinse and overlapping teeth that appeared to be too big for her mouth approached them.

'Looking very impressive over here, Doreen,' the woman said, surveying the array of bric-a-brac on the table.

Doreen looked pleased with herself. 'Thank you, Sadie. It should go well this year.'

The woman looked at Marie. 'And you must be the little life saver Doreen was telling us about.' She extended her hand. 'Sadie Beavis. Our Doreen has been singing your praises and I can't tell you how grateful we are to you for digging us out of a hole.'

'Well, it's for a good cause and I appreciate the opportunity to help. What would you like me to do?'

'I was going to have you man the cake stand, but Violet has turned up after all.' She lowered her voice and spoke out of the corner of her mouth. 'She's our resident hypochondriac. A decent sort though.' She laughed loudly; the sound reminded Marie of a donkey braying, which, combined with the mouthful of outsize teeth, completed the picture.

'Okay. So shall I help Doreen then?'

'No, no, Doreen is a past master, she'll manage. But if you'd like to sell some Christmas cards, that would be a huge help. Georgina was going to do it, but she's gone down with flu.'

Marie smiled. 'Just show me where.'

'Excellent!' Sadie hee-hawed. 'Come with me.'

'Oh, just a moment,' Marie said, picking up Clive's books from under the table where she'd left them. 'I thought you might like to have these.'

Sadie took them from her. 'My word, darling, these look rather lovely. Are you sure you want to part with them?'

'It's just a small donation, the least I could do.'

'How terribly kind you are.' Sadie beamed. 'We'll add them to the raffle. Someone will be delighted to win these. I'll leave them here and come back for them in a moment.' She set down the books on the end of Doreen's table. 'Let me show you where you're going to be.'

357

'Good luck,' Doreen said as Sadie led Marie away. 'See you in a bit.'

As they weaved between the laden tables, Sadie paused to speak to a woman laying out scented candles. 'Remember not to light any this year, Carrie!' The woman smiled and nodded and they moved on. 'We had a minor panic last year when she set the tablecloth on fire,' Sadie said. 'Not her fault really, she's a decent sort, meant well.'

'I'm sure.'

They got to a table nicely set out with packets of Christmas cards positioned near the front door.

'This is Liz,' Sadie said, introducing Marie to the wizened little woman on the adjacent stall. 'She's our tombola queen, aren't you Liz?'

The woman looked at her a little blankly.

Sadie leant in close to Marie. 'A touch Mutt and Jeff,' she said from the corner of her mouth. 'She's got an aid, but always forgets to wear it. Still, she's a decent sort.'

Is there anyone here who isn't "a decent sort"? Marie mused.

'Liz, this is Marie,' Sadie said, enunciating every word. 'She's doing the cards. I was just telling her you're our tombola queen.'

'That's right,' Liz said proudly. 'I've done it every Christmas for the past thirty-three years.'

'Wow!' Marie pretended to look impressed.

Sadie grinned. 'Bless her. Anyway, listen, darling. We'll be opening the doors in fifteen minutes.' She motioned to a margarine tub with a pile of one-pound and fifty-pence coins in it. 'That's your float, there's twenty-pounds there. The packets of cards are two-pounds fifty each, two for four, four for seven-fifty. Do you think you'll manage alright?'

'Two-pounds fifty each, two for four, four for seven-fifty,' Marie repeated. 'It sounds straight forward enough.'

'Good-oh! If you need me I'll be over at the serving hatch selling hot drinks and mince pies. I'll bring you something over. Do you prefer tea or coffee?'

'Either or.'

The donkey laugh sounded again. 'My Ivor always says that.'

When Sadie returned a couple of minutes later with tea and a scone, Marie eyed the Styrofoam cup in her hand. 'Oh, don't you have any proper cups?'

'Sorry, only the disposables, darling.' A look of concern crossed Sadie's face. 'Wait, you're not allergic are you?'

Marie forced a smile. 'No, it's just that I like a proper cup. Not to worry.'

If she'd been honest, what with the weather being so rotten, Marie hadn't really been expecting many people to turn up; she was very much mistaken. Spot on ten o'clock, Ivor Beavis opened the doors and a surge of people flooded in, pleased to get out of the rain.

One of the first people through the door, an elderly man with a pronounced stoop and walking awkwardly with the aid of a stick, came straight over to her table and bought two packs of cards. He handed her a five-pound note and, as Marie went to give him his pound coin change, he brushed it aside. 'Keep it, sweetheart. It's all for a good cause, isn't it? My Heather passed away two years ago from the big C.'

'I'm sorry,' Marie said sympathetically.

359

'Don't be. She was a right old nag!'

'Oh!' Marie didn't know how to respond.

The man gave her a toothless grin and winked. 'I'm joshing you, sweetheart.'

Marie wasn't sure whether to laugh or not. 'Okay,' she said with a thin smile. 'Well, thank you for your donation. Merry Christmas.'

'And you, sweetheart.' Carefully placing the packets of cards into his Tesco carrier bag, the man moved on.

As Marie dropped the coin back into the tub, a thought crossed her mind. She was a pound up on her first sale. But did anyone really need to know that? She glanced at Liz, who was engaged in selling two women a tombola ticket. Casually taking the pound coin back out of the tub, she slipped it into the hip pocket of her jeans.

It turned out that the old man's generosity wasn't unique. Over the next hour, six other people gave more than they needed to – two of them parting with a ten-pound note for four packs of cards instead of the seven-pounds fifty – and Marie had accumulated ten pounds extra. She took the pound coin out of her back pocket, dropped it into the tub and took out two fivers, which she surreptitiously tucked into her hip pocket.

The fair ended at two o'clock. When the last of the stragglers – a woman with two small boys who were arguing over a stuffed giraffe – finally left and Ivor closed the doors, Marie had pilfered quite a bit of cash, so much in fact that she'd lost count.

Sadie came over to see Marie and smiled to see the half a dozen remaining packs of cards on the table and the tub full of money. 'It looks like you've done us proud, darling.'

'Not too bad,' Marie said, attempting to sound modest. 'I really enjoyed it.'

'Not too bad? You've done far better than Georgina did last year.' Sadie grinned at Marie. 'Not that we'll tell her that, obviously. We don't want to put her nose out of joint. She's a decent sort, you know. Anyway…' – she riffled through the money in the tub – '…this is marvellous. Cancer Research is such a worthy cause, don't you think?'

'I do.'

'I know it benefits everyone, but it's always the little children I think of. Especially at Christmas.'

'Oh, me too,' Marie said earnestly, brushing her hand over the small bulge in her hip pocket.

I do hope you'll come back and help us again.'

'If you'll have me,' Marie said.

Sadie hee-hawed. 'Of course we'll have you, darling! We're talking about doing a summer one for the first time next year. Perhaps we could lure you to assist with that?'

'Let's see, shall we?'

Doreen seemed to have done exceptionally well too. 'What are you going to do with these?' Marie asked, as she helped load the unsold nick-nacks back into the boxes.

'It's the starting point for next year.' Doreen chuckled and picked up a small wooden elephant. 'Although I might be tempted to keep this little fellow for myself.'

Marie said that she would load up the car and pick Doreen up at the front. Before starting the car, she fished out

361

the fistful of notes from her hip pocket and greedily counted them. It had been a profitable morning; there was forty-pounds. She smiled to herself. *I'll definitely be volunteering for that summer fayre*, she thought.

A few days later, Marie was woken just after midnight by the sound of Barnaby barking. It took her ages to get back to sleep, and when it happened again two nights later, she'd finally had enough. 'That *fucking* dog!' she muttered, throwing a pillow over her head to drown out the noise.

First thing the following morning, with the sound of barking still continuing in sporadic bursts, she dressed and went down to the kitchen. She had bought a couple of pieces of steak for dinner the night before and Donovan hadn't wanted his; when she told him it was that or nothing, he had ended up with the latter.

She took the plate out of the fridge and set it down on the table, then got down on her knees in front of the cupboard beneath the counter.

A couple of years earlier, when Fletcher had been working for Clive, they'd had cause to buy some rat poison. She was sure she'd seen the tin when she was looking for something a while back and, as she moved aside some cleaning products, sure enough, there at the back was a tin labelled **RODENTICIDE**.

Pulling it out and prising off the lid with a table knife, she carefully sprinkled a coating of the white powder onto the steak.

Returning the tin to the cupboard, she put on her overcoat and went out into the portico. It quickly became apparent that Barnaby was out in Doreen's garden. Marie knew that, regular as clockwork, the old lady went out early to Suds'n'Spin on a Wednesday, and the dog could be destructive. But even so, she couldn't quite understand the thinking behind leaving the thing out in the garden.

It was a cold morning, but the winter sun was shining brightly. Marie slipped on her shoes and hurried across the garden, skirting the pond to get to the fence. The barking was much louder now. Peering over the top of the fence, she could see Barnaby snuffling around in some bushes. 'Pssst,' she whispered. 'Here boy.' Barnaby jerked his head around and saw her looking at him. His tail started wagging and he started towards her. 'Num-nums,' she whispered. Before he had even reached the fence, Marie tossed the piece of steak at him. 'Merry Christmas, you little bastard,' she hissed and, without waiting to see whether he even showed any interest in it, she darted back across the garden and into the house.

No more than an hour later, Marie was in the kitchen washing the dishes when the doorbell rang. She had only just got out to the hall when it rang again. 'Alright, I'm coming!' She opened the door to find Doreen standing on the step, looking distraught and cradling Barnaby's limp body in a blanket.

'What's happened, D?' Marie said, trying hard to sound concerned.

'I've no idea,' Doreen replied, sobbing. 'I was going to do my laundry and I couldn't leave him inside on his own, not after the mess he made of my hall carpet. It was such a nice morning and I was only going to be an hour or two, so I thought I'd put him out in the garden. I got home just now to find him laying beside the rhododendrons. There was a puddle of sick nearby, I think he's had a heart attack.'

Marie had to bite her lip to stop herself laughing. 'Oh God, surely not! Is he still breathing?'

'Yes, but it's awfully weak. I don't suppose you'd be a dear and take me to the vet's would you? I'm in such a state I'm not fit to drive.'

'Hang on,' Marie said. 'I'll get my coat.'

By the time they reached the surgery, Barnaby had stopped breathing. The veterinary nurse took the body away and Marie sat with Doreen in the waiting room until she returned.

'Mrs Mullins.'

Doreen looked up at the nurse tearfully and reached out to clutch Marie's hand for comfort.

'I'm very sorry for your loss,' the nurse continued. 'I've given Barnaby a through check and it's conclusive that he's consumed rat poison.'

Doreen's face dropped. 'Not a heart attack then?'

'No. Thankfully it's not a commonplace occurrence, but sadly we have seen cases like this before.'

'I don't understand. I…' Doreen trailed off and put a hand to her mouth. 'Oh no.'

'What is it, D?' Marie said.

'It's all my fault!'

Marie frowned. 'Don't say that.'

'But it *is* my fault! I put down some rat poison under the shed a couple of weeks ago. I'd seen mice about in the garden, you see. And Georgina recommended rat poison. She had a similar problem last year and said it worked a treat.' Doreen started to cry. 'Poor little Barnaby. I'll never forgive myself.'

The nurse looked at her sympathetically. 'You really mustn't blame yourself, Mrs Mullins. You didn't do anything wrong. It's just very unfortunate. If you'd like to speak to the receptionist, she'll give you the options for cremation. And once again, my sincere condolences.'

'I'll do that. Thank you, nurse.' Doreen fished a tissue out of her bag and blew her nose. She turned to Marie. 'Then, please, just take me home.'

365

CHAPTER 36

Although Marie and Cassandra had spoken on the phone several times, they hadn't actually seen each other since Clive's funeral. The truth of the matter was that Marie had grown tired of her; Cassandra could be a bit of a loose cannon and was always quick to stand her own ground. Emily Bird, on the other hand, was more malleable and easy to subjugate and Marie was pleased they'd reconnected. So it was that, whenever Cassandra raised the subject of getting together, Marie made an excuse, usually stating Donovan's home-schooling as a reason for postponing.

The week before Christmas her mobile rang and Marie sighed inwardly when she saw Cassandra's name on the screen. She hesitated, but answered anyway, and immediately wished she hadn't; Cassandra had just had a major falling out with her latest boyfriend and wanted to offload.

'Now he doesn't ever want to see me again,' Cassandra concluded miserably. 'I just don't know what I did wrong.'

While she was listening, Marie had been idly leafing through a magazine and an advertorial feature on a new range of make-up had caught her eye. 'If you ask me, you're better off without him,' she said, trying to sound sympathetic while studying the colour chart showing the various shades of lipstick available. 'You'll meet someone who'll appreciate you one day.'

'When is that gonna be though? I'm thirty-one next year. I know we'd only been together a few weeks and it sounds mad, but I really thought Yusef was the one.'

'All men are bastards, Cass. We both know that.'

'I guess. Hey, listen, maybe we could meet up for a drink this week? I haven't seen you for ages.'

Marie pulled a face. 'I'd really love to, the thing is, Donovan's not well and what with Christmas coming I've got so much to do. I'm volunteering with the W.I. now.''

Cassandra sniggered. 'Who am I talking to here? Could you put the real Marie on the line please?'

'Very funny.'

'That's an old lady's thing!' Cassandra spluttered.

'It's for women of all ages.' Marie thought about the CDs she'd purchased using the money stolen from the Christmas fair. 'And it's *ever* so rewarding.'

'Whatever turns you on, I guess. So, you can't spare a couple of hours to see your best mate then? I've got a prezzie for you.'

'Don't keep on, Cass. I told you, I'm all tied up.'

'Well, pardon me for wanting to see the person I *thought* was my friend.' Cassandra sounded affronted now. 'Every time I've suggested meeting recently you've come up with some feeble reason or other why you can't. Why don't you just come out with it and say you just don't *want* to see me?'

'Okay. I don't want to see you.'

The line went silent for a moment. Then Cassandra said, 'You don't mean that.'

'You told me to say it, so I said it.' Marie sighed. 'If you want the truth, Cass, I'm seeing someone else now.'

'You've got a new feller?' Cassandra exclaimed. 'Well, why didn't you say?'

'Not a feller. A girlfriend.'

There was another brief silence while Cassandra tried to process what Marie had just said. 'Hang on, babe, are you trying to tell me you've switched teams?'

'Don't be absurd,' Marie scoffed. 'Why am I not surprised you'd think that?'

'You said girlfriend!'

'Yes, as in a girl who's a friend. She's someone I've known for years and we're very close.'

'Not as close as you and me though, surely.' There was hurt in Cassandra's voice.

'Closer actually. We have real history. We've been friends since we were at school.'

'How come you've never mentioned her before?'

'It never came up. Besides, I don't see how who my friends are has anything to do with you.'

'Woah, wait a minute, what's happening here?' Cassandra sounded tearful. 'Now you've got a fancy house and flash car and enough money to see you never have to work another day in your life, you're dumping me, is that it? Just like that.'

'If you want to put it that way, I suppose, then yes,' Marie said coldly.

'What other way is there?' There was rising anger in the voice now. 'And there was I thinking I actually meant something to you!'

'Don't flatter yourself.'

'You spiteful *bitch*!' Cassandra exploded. There was unharnessed rage now. 'And after everything I've done for you.'

'Your choice. Nobody made you.'

'Fuck off. Just fuck off!'

There was a click and the line went dead.

Marie smiled to herself. *I guess being dumped by Yusef won't be hurting quite so much now*, she thought. Looking at the magazine spread, she mused aloud, 'I think either the Forbidden Fuchsia or the Electric Orchid. Actually, why not both?'

As she got up to go out to the kitchen, her phone rang again. It was Emily.

'Hi. How's things?'

Marie wedged the phone between her chin and her shoulder and reached for the kettle. 'Still got my hands full with Donny, but not too bad I guess.'

'That's good. Listen, what plans have you got for Christmas?'

'Nothing special.' Marie took a cup down from the cupboard. 'Why? Do you fancy going out for a drink beforehand?'

'I'm a bit snowed to be honest, but me and Mickey were talking last night and we had an idea. How would you like to come and spend Christmas Day with us? Donny too, obviously, if he'd like to.'

'Oh, that's ever so sweet of you, Em, but I'll be with Mum and Dad.' Marie tore the end off a sachet of chocolate powder with her teeth and emptied the contents into the mug.

369

'Ah, okay. Only from a few things you've said I kind of got the impression you don't see much of them and I figured you might be on your own.'

'No, not at all,' Marie replied, trying to recall what she had said. 'I mean, we don't always see eye to eye on stuff, they try to interfere with my life a bit too much, but Christmas is Christmas, isn't it? Tradition and all that.'

'Absolutely. Okay, well, maybe we can go for that drink in the new year?'

'Deffo. We'll sort something out.'

'I'll give you a call after Christmas then. Have a good one.'

The kettle boiled and Marie finished making her hot chocolate. For the life of her she couldn't remember what she'd actually said to Emily about her parents. Taking the mug and a packet of chocolate digestive biscuits with her, she went back to the living room to put her feet up.

On Christmas Eve, Emily had to go into the post office to collect a parcel. As she turned away from the counter, the hanging toggle on her coat caught on the shoulder bag of a woman leaving the next window. There was an awkward moment as they tried to unhook each other and, as Emily apologised profusely, she looked at the woman's face.

'Mrs Shaw?'

Lynda Shaw clearly didn't recognise her. 'Yes?'

'It's me, Emily Bird. Well, I used to be Emily Marks.'

Lynda's lips broadened into a smile. 'Emily! Well blow me down. Haven't you grown up?'

Emily smiled. 'Just a bit.'

370

The man behind Emily in the queue harrumphed loudly, and they stepped to one side.

'So how have you been? I heard you got married, is that right?'

'It is. I've got three youngsters now too.'

'*Three*?' Mrs Shaw chuckled. 'I bet you're run off your feet.' Mrs Shaw shook her head. 'Where has the time gone? It only seems like yesterday that you and Marie were playing dolls' tea party in our garden.'

After a couple of minutes spent reminiscing, Emily said, 'I'd better go, I'm meeting my Mum for coffee. It was really good to see you.'

'You too.'

They walked outside and stopped on the pavement. 'Have a lovely Christmas with Marie and your grandson then.' She saw the smile on Mrs Shaw's face fade. 'Sorry, have I said the wrong thing?'

'We haven't spoken to Marie for years.'

'Oh, I'm sorry to hear that.'

Mrs Shaw looked at her sadly. 'Yes, it's her father really. The pair of them just don't get along. I'm not happy about it, but it makes for a more peaceful life just to let things lie.'

'Sorry again.'

'You weren't to know. Thomas and Lucy are doing their own thing this year too. We'll be seeing them Boxing Day, but it'll just be me and Gareth tomorrow.'

'Well, you have a good one anyway.'

Emily watched Mrs Shaw cross the road and disappear among the throng of last minute shoppers. *I knew Marie told me they'd had a falling out*, she thought. *I bloody knew it!*

Marie's lie about spending Christmas Day with her parents was still playing on Emily's mind when she was having coffee with her mother. 'Why do you think she would have lied like that, Mum?'

Mrs Marks finished her drink. 'There could be all sorts of reasons, love. But I'd say she was probably a bit embarrassed.'

'About what? We were only being kind asking her over for some dinner.'

'I'm sure she appreciated the offer. But she might have felt awkward admitting she doesn't have anything to do with her folks any more.'

'I suppose you're right. But that's the thing, I already *knew* that. She told me a while ago. It's like she was only saying it because she didn't want to spend Christmas with us.'

Mrs Marks sighed. 'Don't take it to heart, love. Whatever her motives were, it was very considerate of you to invite her. But if you really want my opinion, you'll have a much nicer time without her. You know what I said when you told me the two of you had patched things up?'

Emily nodded glumly.

'Well, my opinion hasn't changed. She treated you very badly all those years ago.'

'That's all water under the bridge now, Mum.'

'Be that as it may, I think that woman is bad news. And the less you have to do with her the better.'

Having woken on Christmas morning to a light dusting of snow, Marie was feeling benevolent and, ensuring the doors in the house were securely locked, she allowed Donovan to come downstairs to open the new PlayStation games she had bought for him. But his spirits were low and all he was interested in was trying to get her to allow him to go outside for a while. Marie couldn't be bothered to prepare anything fancy for lunch, so she had purchased a couple of complete frozen Christmas Dinners in a box. After they'd consumed their food in silence, she asked Donovan to return to his room and he meekly complied.

It was almost a month later that Marie and Emily finally got together for a drink at Costa. Christmas was already a distant memory for Marie. But not for Emily. Despite her mother's interpretation of the lie Marie had spun, she had been brooding on it ever since. Why would her friend have lied to her?

'So, how was Christmas then?' Emily said, stirring a teaspoonful of sugar into her coffee.

'Oh, you know, same old same old. Yours?'

'I bet your Mum was pleased to see Donny.'

'She spoilt him rotten, of course.'

'I bet. What about your brother and sister? How are they doing?'

'Yes, they're fine. I don't see much of them, so it was nice to catch up. Thomas badgered us all into playing Trivial Pursuit and it ended in an argument.' Marie smiled. 'But it wouldn't be Christmas Day without arguments though, eh? Still, I won, so that showed Thomas! Did you have a good one?'

Why are you lying to me? Emily thought. She sipped her drink. 'And your Dad? Are you getting on better with him now?'

Marie laughed. 'What is this, the flippin' Spanish Inquisition?'

'Sorry, it does sound a bit like that, doesn't it? No, it was just that you said you don't see eye to eye and I was hoping you managed to get through the day without...'

'We got on fine.' Marie put down her mug and squinted at her friend. 'How about you? How was *your* Christmas?'

'Quiet, I guess.' Was that suspicion on Marie's face now? Had she pushed too hard? Emily chuckled nervously. 'Or as quiet as it can be with three kids off their heads on chocolate!'

'Oh, tell me about *that*! I'm surprised Donny wasn't sick.'

Much to Emily's relief, the awkwardness seemed to dissipate and she decided not to pursue the matter of Christmas any further; it was more than clear that Marie was spinning lies.

They finished their coffee and Marie suggested that Emily come over for lunch the following week. She gratefully accepted the invite, but when she got home an hour later she was still pondering Marie's story about Christmas. Unless Mrs Shaw had been lying – and what possible reason would *she* have had for that? – it wasn't just a case of being economical with the truth; Marie had sat there, looked her in the face and flat out lied to her. And, if she had been bare faced enough to do so about something as insignificant as how she spent Christmas, what else was she being untruthful about?

Despite Marie's initial reluctance to be involved with the W.I. Christmas fair, it had proven to be a lucrative move and she had since attended several of the group's gatherings. It had meant sitting through boring talks on, amongst other topics, lepidoptery, heraldry and baking the perfect granary loaf, but it had also enabled her to cosy up with one member in particular, the scented candle lady, Carrie.

An affluent widow with an estranged son, Carrie was very friendly with Frank Tanner, the verger at the church – and it was she who had persuaded him to don the Father Christmas costume for the W.I. fair. She didn't have many friends beyond Frank though, and she was tickled pink by the attention and companionship she was receiving from Marie, the group's newest and indeed youngest member.

The day after her catch-up with Emily, as had become routine, Marie picked up Doreen to take her to the Thursday evening meeting. On the drive over, the subject of Barnaby's death came up.

'Do you know, I still dream about him? Almost every night?'

Marie looked at Doreen sympathetically. 'Oh, that must be very upsetting.'

'No, quite the opposite, dear. It's always lovely to see him. I often dream about Archibald too.'

I wonder if their damned yapping wakes you up? Marie thought, turning her head away so that Doreen couldn't see her smirk. 'That's nice,' she said.

375

'It gives me great comfort to feel as if they're here still with me.'

'Do you think you'll get another?'

'No, I've decided not. I still can't forgive myself for what happened to Barnaby. And besides, you get so attached, don't you? Then you have to go through all the heartbreak when you lose them.'

'That's so true.'

'But I've been thinking I might get a parrot instead. Just for the company really. What do you think?'

'It sounds like a wonderful idea,' Marie said, relieved to hear there wouldn't be another barking dog disturbing the neighbourhood.

Frank Tanner was the group speaker that evening. It was one of the most tedious Marie had yet endured, as he droned on for almost half an hour about the aesthetic rewards to be derived from the pastime of brass rubbing. Everyone else seemed to enjoy it and, when the talk was over, there were even more questions from the ladies than usual.

Leaving them all to coo over the examples of his hobby that Frank had brought along with him, Marie quietly sloped away to the kitchenette. She switched on the radio and, turning the sound low, she set about washing up the tea things. She had almost finished when Sadie appeared.

'Thank you for doing that, darling. I'm heading off in a minute, Ivor isn't well and I promised I'd make it a short one. Wasn't Frank's talk good?'

'Fascinating,' Marie said, taking the drying up cloth from the hook beside the sink.

'A real treat. He's promised to come back next month and tell us about his collection of vintage brass horse buckles.'

Marie smiled. 'It's all about brass with our Frank, isn't it?'

Sadie didn't seem to notice the hint of sarcasm in Marie's voice. 'Indeed. Anyway, Georgina will be locking up in a minute. I must dash.'

When Marie came out into the hall a couple of minutes later, the only person there was Doreen, who was waiting patiently for her on a chair near the door.

'All done, dear?'

'Yes.' As Marie closed the kitchenette door, her eye caught sight of a suede handbag on the windowsill nearest to her. It was navy blue with gold embroidery on the side and she immediately recognised it as belonging to Carrie.

'Actually, I just have to pop to the loo, I don't think I can hold on till I get home.' She crossed the room and offered Doreen the car key. 'You can go on out to the car if you like.'

'That's okay, I'll be fine here.'

'No, really, it's best you go and wait in the car. It's getting cold in here now the heating's been turned off.'

Doreen took the key from her. 'See you in a minute then.'

When Marie got to the toilet door, she glanced over her shoulder and saw Doreen hobbling out. Turning back, she hurried across to the windowsill and picked up the handbag. Looking towards the door again to make sure the old lady was gone, she popped the clasp on the handbag and looked inside. There wasn't much to see; a purse, a make-up compact, a lipstick, a diary and two pens. Glancing over at the door again, she opened the purse. There were only a few loose coins inside, but when she opened the zip on the note wallet, her eyes widened as she took in the sheaf of twenty-pound notes. Hastily removing them, she was about to tuck them into her pocket when she heard the floorboards creak. Her head shot up and she saw Frank standing in the doorway.

'Oh, you startled me!' she exclaimed, dropping the money back into the bag.

'I see you found Carrie's handbag,' Frank said as he approached her.

'Oh, yes, she must have left it up here while you were showing us your brass rubbings.'

'I'm giving her a lift home.' Frank stopped a few feet away from her. 'We got a hundred yards up the road and she realised she'd left it behind.'

'I didn't realise she'd already gone. I was just about to come out and try to catch her.'

'Were you now?' Frank was looking at her accusatorily, but he spoke calmly. 'Was that before or after you stole her money?'

'Excuse me?'

'I *said*, were you going to return her bag before or after you took her money?'

Marie attempted to sound affronted. 'What exactly are you implying?'

'Implying? I'm implying nothing. We both know what's going on here, so don't deny it.' He held out his hand. 'Give it to me.'

Marie couldn't see any point in maintaining the façade. She passed the handbag to him and watched him look inside, return the money to the note wallet and zip it up. 'Did you take anything else?'

'Honestly, I didn't.'

Frank looked her in the eyes, as if trying to discern whether she was telling him the truth. 'Very well then.' He snapped the clasp shut and started to turn away.

'What are you going to do?'

'*Do*?'

'Are you going to tell Carrie?'

Frank's face darkened. 'Just you listen to me, young lady. It just so happens that Carrie thinks very highly of you. She's a lovely lady and I wouldn't want to go causing her any upset.'

'So you won't tell her?'

'I'll have to think about it. But one way or the other, I expect you to get in touch with Sadie and tender your withdrawal from the W.I.'

Marie frowned. 'How am I supposed to explain it?'

'*How* you do it is no concern of mine. Just be sure you do it.'

By the time he reached his car, Frank had already decided not to say anything to Carrie about what he'd seen. He knew she would be upset enough if Marie left the group and he didn't want to be responsible for upsetting her now.

'Thank heavens.' Carrie smiled with relief as he climbed in and handed her the bag. 'I'd forget my head if it wasn't screwed on properly.'

379

As Frank started the car, he wondered if he had been too quick to judge Marie. Beyond the fact she had a nice place next door to Doreen out in Sunnycatt, he didn't really know much about her at all. Having a big house wouldn't necessarily preclude financial worries. Of course, there was no excuse for theft, but it would at least explain what he'd witnessed. Deciding that he had possibly been too hard on the girl, he made up his mind that he would telephone her the next day and give her an opportunity to explain herself.

By the time Marie dropped Doreen off at home, she had come to a decision of her own. She wasn't going to be pushed around by anyone, and she knew exactly what she intended to do about Frank Tanner.

CHAPTER 37

As soon as she got up the next morning, Marie telephoned Sadie.

'Hello, darling,' Sadie said chirpily. 'What an unexpected surprise. You're not calling to check on Ivor, are you? What a sweetheart you are.'

Marie rolled her eyes. 'How is he this morning?'

'Bright as a button. There's hardly any trace of that filthy cold now.'

'Actually, Sadie, I was calling about Frank too.'

'Frank? Oh, wasn't his talk last night wonderful? Almost made me want to do some brass rubbings myself.' Sadie heehawed.

'Listen, about Frank. After you left last night, I'd finished in the kitchen and…' – Marie caught her breath and made a little sobbing noise – '…sorry, this is really hard for me.'

'What is it, darling?'

'There was only me and D left and I needed to go to the toilet, so I gave her the keys so she could go and wait in the car. When I came out…' Marie trailed off and made another sobbing noise. 'Sorry.'

'It's fine. Don't get upset, just take your time.' Sadie's usual cheerful demeanour was gone and she sounded concerned.

'So, when I came out, Frank was waiting for me. He asked if I'd enjoyed the talk. I said that I had and I was looking forward to the next one. He said he had something else he wanted to show me and he opened his coat and...' – she faked another sob – '...his thingy was hanging out.'

Sadie sounded baffled. 'His *thingy*?' Then what Marie meant registered. 'Oh, good grief, really?'

'I couldn't believe it!' Marie was trying her hardest not to laugh now. 'He had me cornered by the toilet door, and I tried to step around him, but he said, although he enjoyed brass rubbing, it was much more fun rubbing his... you know. And he asked me to touch it.'

'Dear God. What a revolting creature!'

Marie put a hand to her mouth to stifle a snigger. 'I pushed past him and as I got to the door he shouted after me to say if I changed my mind...'

'I feel sick just thinking about it! You poor darling.'

'I didn't know whether I ought to say anything or not, and I've hardly slept a wink thinking about it, but after what I saw at the Christmas fair too...'

'What?'

'I think I've said too much already.'

'Tell me. What did you see?'

Marie had to hold the phone away from her mouth as she snorted.

'Hello? Are you still there?'

'Yes, sorry, it's just this is so upsetting.'

'What did you see at the Christmas fair?'

'I had to nip out to get something from my car and, as I passed the lovely little Santa grotto you'd set up in the corner, I glanced inside and Frank was in there with a little girl on his knee...'

'Oh, please don't say what I think you're going to say!' Sadie whispered. She sounded tearful.

'It was horrible. She can't have been more than four or five-years-old and he had his hand up her dress. I had to do a double-take to be honest. He looked up and saw me standing there and quickly pulled out his hand. He saw the look on my face and…'

'Why on earth didn't you find me and say something?'

'Because it all felt so unreal and it happened so fast that afterwards I started to doubt that I'd even seen it.'

'Are you saying it's possible you *didn't* see it then?' There was a note of desperation in Sadie's voice.

'That's what I thought. But when we were packing up at the end, I caught him looking at me kind of funny; he knew I'd seen him, and he knew *I* knew what he'd been doing. Even so, I convinced myself I must have been mistaken. After all, he's the verger, as well as a long-standing and respected friend of the Women's Institute, and I know he's given a lot of his time to helping out behind the scenes. Of course, I feel stupid now, I fully realise I should have said something, but at the end of the day it would have been my word against his. And how could I have proved it? Like I say, you've known him years, you'd only just met me.'

'This is awful. Just *awful*!'

'But then last night, after he exposed himself, I was in no doubt that what I thought I'd seen at the fair was real too.'

After a moment's silence, Sadie exhaled heavily. 'Can I be candid with you, darling?'

'Of course.'

'Strictly between us two, I've never cared much for Frank Tanner. To my knowledge, he's never been married, which I always thought was a bit suspicious. As in, I honestly thought he might be...' – she spelt it out – '... G - A - Y. But after what you've just told me, it's all suddenly very clear. He's just a dirty old man. I'm going to have to speak to Ivor and see what he thinks we should do, but I dare say we'll have to involve the police.'

'He's bound to deny it,' Marie said.

'I've no doubt. These preevert types always do, don't they?'

Preevert? Marie bit her lip to stop herself laughing. She could imagine Sadie's ashen face. 'If the police get involved, the press might get hold of it too. It might not reflect well on the W.I. if that happens.'

'Oh, good Lord! That hadn't occurred to me!'

'Perhaps if you dealt with it yourselves and had a quiet word with Frank? As I say, he'll deny it, but you can just tell him you don't want him coming round any more. And if he protests, just tell him he's lucky you haven't told the vicar, let alone the police.'

'You're right, darling. That's what I'll suggest to Ivor. He'll have the final say, of course, but I'm sure he'll see the sense in handling the matter discreetly and not besmirching our little group.'

'You won't mention my name, will you?'

'Don't worry about that, darling. We'll be the quintessence of tactfulness.'

'You'll let me know what happens though?'

'Definitely.'

Marie sighed. 'I'm really sorry I've caused you so much trouble,' she said, trying to sound earnest.

'I realise it can't have been easy, but I'm grateful to you for plucking up the courage to open up before Frank does something else sickening.'

Later that day, Sadie called back to say that she and Ivor had been to see Frank. They had thought it better not to raise the incident in the hall the night before, for that would have openly implicated Marie as their informant.

'At Ivor's suggestion, we decided we would stick to the incident at the Christmas fair.'

'What did he say?'

'Exactly what we expected him to, darling. He vehemently denied it. He wanted to know who had said such a scurrilous thing about him and, if it had been a genuine complaint, why it had taken so long to come out?'

'What did you say?'

'We obviously told him we couldn't say who had made the complaint. He became extremely indignant and defensive, but I've got a good sense for these things and I could see it in his eyes; he knew he'd been caught. Ivor, bless him, he was an angel, he managed to calm Frank down and told him he had two choices: either he tender his resignation to the vicar immediately, or we go straight to the police. After all, we can't have a monster like him representing our church, can we? Not to mention all the little boys in the Sunday choir, it doesn't bear thinking about!'

'How did he react to *that*?' Marie asked cautiously.

'Obviously he realised he didn't have any choice. He broke down and cried, but that just confirmed what we already knew: guilty as sin! It wasn't remorse either; it was nothing more than crocodile tears as far as we were concerned. Before we left, he promised faithfully he would resign.'

'How can you be sure he will?'

'He knows if the police get involved he'd be arrested and up in court in the blink of an eye. I shudder to think what might have come out then!'

Marie sighed. 'And what about our group?'

'Oh, don't worry about that, he'll not be darkening our door again.'

When Marie ended the call, she cheered aloud: 'Yes!' The annihilation of Frank Tanner had been simpler than she could possibly have hoped.

Having given it some thought, a couple of days later Marie called Sadie again and told her that she wouldn't be coming to any more meetings in the foreseeable future. She claimed that the whole incident with Frank had shaken her and she didn't feel comfortable. The truth of the matter was, she'd had a near miss and got away with it; next time temptation reared its head, she might not be so lucky. Sadie's promise that nothing like what had occurred with Frank would ever be allowed to happen again didn't change things. She said the word had already got around about Frank's behaviour at the Christmas fair and every one of the ladies had told her they'd never been entirely relaxed in his presence.

'Nobody knows it was you who reported him,' Sadie assured her. 'And they never will, you have my guarantee on that.'

'So how has the word spread so quickly?'

'No idea, darling, but you know how people love to gossip. Are you sure I can't change your mind?'

'Sorry, no. Not at the moment.'

'Well all the ladies will miss you, especially Carrie – she's very fond of you. Just know that you're welcome back any time.'

Emily was due over for a bite to eat that evening and Marie briefly toyed with the idea of cancelling; she wasn't in the mood for conversation, besides which Emily had more or less guilted her into it and invited herself anyway. But she knew if she put it off, it would only be delaying the inevitable. She spoke to Donovan and warned him that he needed to be quiet for a couple of hours; securing his silence with the promise that she would get him a new game for his PlayStation if he did as he was asked. Then she set about preparing a light meal, and by the time Emily arrived she was feeling more positive about the evening ahead.

After they'd eaten, Marie opened a second bottle of wine and they moved into the living room.

'How are things going with your W.I. lot then?' Emily asked as she stretched out in the armchair.

Marie scowled. 'Don't ask.'

'I thought you were really enjoying it.'

'I was, but there were a couple of incidents that shook me up a bit, so I won't be going back.'

'What sort of incidents?'

As Marie relayed her elaborate fabrication about Frank's behaviour – first at the Christmas fair, then on the night he'd caught her trying to steal from Carrie – Emily's eyes got wider and wider.

'And he asked you to *touch* it?' Emily shuddered. 'That's so gross!'

'Trust me, it was *nasty*!'

Emily made a little gagging noise. 'What the hell could have been going through his head? I mean, he can't really have expected you to actually do it.'

Marie shrugged. 'Just a dirty pervert trying his luck I guess. Or a preevert, as Sadie called him.'

'Who's Sadie?'

'Oh, she's the head of the group. Malicious piece of work she is too. Do you know, she wouldn't believe me at first when I told her what had happened. She defended him to the hilt.'

'I suppose that's understandable – to a point anyway. From what you said, it sounds like he was an upstanding pillar of the community as far as everyone was concerned.'

'I know, but why would I make something like that up? Anyway, after she and her husband confronted him, he broke down and admitted everything. Practically got down on his knees apparently, pleaded with them not to call the police. Then, of course, she came crawling round me, all apologetic like. But, I tell you, to have had her doubt me after everything I've done for them really hurt. That's why I won't be going anymore.'

Shaking her head, Emily took a sip from her glass. 'Just goes to show you never really know people, I suppose.'

'Do you know, Clive said almost that exact same thing about Fletcher – that was my handyman, I think I mentioned him before – when I told him he'd stolen from me. I'd honestly not have believed it; Fletcher was such a nice guy. I suppose my problem is I'm just too trusting of people.'

'You've got a good heart,' Emily said. 'There will always be someone waiting to take advantage of that.'

Marie nodded. 'I guess.' She picked up the bottle of wine. 'Top you up?'

Emily held out her glass and Marie refilled it for her. 'Well, it sounds like you're better off without the lot of them. Stick to your real friends.'

'I'll drink to that,' Marie said, raising her glass. 'Speaking of real friends, I haven't told you about that one over there, have I?' She nodded her head towards a framed photo on the mantelpiece of herself with Cassandra.

'Oh, I noticed that last time I was here,' Emily said. 'Is that one of your Australian friends?'

'*Her*?' Marie huffed. 'Hardly!'

Emily laughed. 'You can't say something like that and leave it there!'

'She's my *ex*-best friend, Cass. Someone else I trusted who shat on me. Honestly, Em, why do I always seem to attract the bad'uns?'

'What did she do?'

'If I tell you, you have to promise not to breathe a word to anyone.'

'Why would I? I don't even know her.'

'You've got to promise.'

Emily chuckled. 'Okay, okay, I promise.'

'I found out she purposely drove a wedge between me and my boyfriend. I never had quite understood why Yusef dumped me.'

'Hang on, your *boyfriend*?' Emily looked confused. 'I thought you were going to marry Clive?'

'It happened way back before I even knew Clive, but I didn't find about it but until just before Christmas.'

'This Christmas just gone?'

Marie nodded. 'We'd been out for a few drinks and we came back here for a nightcap. We were both a bit tipsy and got into a stupid game of sharing our deepest secrets. She told me she'd slept with Yusef.'

'God, why would she do something like *that*?'

Marie shrugged. 'Oh, it was a long time ago, I guess she thought we were solid enough now that it didn't matter any more. Or maybe she just didn't think at all, as I said, we were drunk and it was a stupid game. But there's more.'

'*More*?'

'She told me she'd only done it because she was jealous. And soon as she'd had him, she dumped him.'

'Crikey, luring your best mate's feller into bed just because you're jealous of her is a bit dramatic.'

'She wasn't jealous of me. She was jealous of Yusef.'

'Of *Yusef*?'

'She admitted she'd always had a thing for me and she hated seeing me with Yusef, and...'

'God, what did you say?'

390

'I was gobsmacked. I couldn't believe what I was hearing to be honest. But then she grabbed me and tried to kiss me and that was the last straw.'

Emily screwed up her face. 'Are you winding me up?'

Marie laughed. 'Don't look so flabbergasted! I've had women proposition me before, you know. Back when I was in Australia.'

'I didn't mean it like that. It just sounds so insane you could be friends for that long without suspecting anything.'

'I know, we spent a heck of a lot of time together too. She was always talking about various guys she was seeing, but with hindsight I realised I never actually got to meet any of them. I suppose she made them up to hide the fact she likes girls. Stupid, trusting me – *again*!'

'What did you do? When she kissed you, I mean.'

'*Tried* to kiss me. Well, I kicked her out, obviously. Haven't spoken to her since and hopefully never will.'

'That's a bit harsh, just because she fancied you. You could have just made it clear you weren't interested.'

'Don't be stupid, it was because she ruined my relationship with Yusef. Who knows where we might be now if that witch hadn't come between us.'

Emily grinned. 'Not in this lovely house for a start.' She caught sight of Marie's stony expression. 'Sorry. I can't quite get my head around this though. If someone had done that to me, I wouldn't keep a photo of them on my mantelpiece. I'd probably burn it!'

'It's such a good one of me though,' Marie said. 'I didn't want to toss it.'

Emily looked at her, trying to work out if she was joking; from the look on her face, she wasn't. 'Anyway, I ought to be making a move in a minute. If I drink any more I won't be fit to drive. Can I use your loo quickly?'

'Sure. Up the stairs, second on the left.'

Before she went into the bathroom, Emily quickly popped her face around the door of the master bedroom; it was every bit the palatial space she had imagined. 'Lucky cow,' she said under her breath.

When she flushed the toilet and came out of the bathroom a couple of minutes later, she heard a small cough come from behind the closed door of the room just opposite. Crossing over, she rapped her fingernails on the door.

'Donny?' she whispered. 'Is that you?'

Her question was greeted by a brief scuffling noise, then silence.

'I'm an old friend of your Mum's.' Emily put her ear to the door and listened, but there was nothing more to hear. 'She's told me so much about you,' she continued quietly. 'I was hoping I might get to meet you at last. Is it okay with you if I come in?' She rested her fingers on the door handle and pushed it down. It moved a few millimetres and stopped. Emily frowned: *Why is it locked from the outside?* As she tentatively applied pressure to turn the key, Marie's voice sounded from the bottom of the stairs. 'You alright up there?'

Quick as a flash, Emily darted back across the landing to the bathroom. 'Just coming,' she shouted, and pressed the flush again.

When she returned downstairs, Marie looked at her suspiciously. 'I was just starting to think I'd have to send out a search party.'

'Sorry.' Emily patted her stomach. 'Bit of a dicky tummy. I'm going to head off now if you don't mind.'

'Of course not. I hope you're feeling better.'

On the drive back, Emily's head was whirling with thoughts of the young boy locked in his room. Marie had told her he was withdrawn and liked solitude, but would he be *so* introverted not to have even answered her when she'd spoken? And why did Marie never seem to encourage him to come down and meet her? Surely she should be doing something to draw the boy out of his shell, not pandering to his neurosis. What hope for the future did he have if Marie let it continue? The whole situation was very strange.

By the time she reached home, her thoughts had turned to her own children. As she got out of the car, she glanced at her watch and smiled; home in time to read them their bedtime story. Hoping that they hadn't played up too much for Mickey, she went inside.

CHAPTER 38

The months drifted past in a blur of innocuousness, the only thing to leave its mark being Doreen's hospitalisation at the beginning of April with renal complications, from which, suddenly and unexpectedly, she passed away. She had no immediate family and she didn't have much money to speak of anyway, but she left a small bestowal of a thousand pounds in her will to Marie, "for all her kindnesses and her loyal friendship". The proceeds on the house she left to be divided up between five of her friends at the Women's Institute and Battersea Dogs and Cats Home.

Marie didn't attend the funeral.

The early warmth of summer filled the air and with it came Donovan's mock exam results; he failed dismally in all subjects. Marie was livid, scolding him for not having tried harder. Confiscating his PlayStation, she warned him he had better knuckle down and make sure he passed the finals.

One morning in early May, Marie's phone rang. It was Emily.

It had been several weeks since they'd seen each other and Emily suggested it would be a nice idea if they got together for a drink to celebrate her birthday the following day: 'My treat.'

Marie sounded surprised. 'Your birthday?'

'You'd forgotten, hadn't you?' Emily said, slightly disappointedly. It was a superfluous question; she was fairly sure that Marie had, and in all honestly wouldn't have expected anything else. It was still a bit upsetting though.

'Of course I hadn't forgotten,' Marie lied.

Emily laughed. 'You had too.'

'I *hadn't* forgotten,' Marie protested. 'It's just my head's a bit all over the place at the moment. If you want to know, I was actually thinking about taking you out somewhere nice.'

'Well, Mickey's taking me out tomorrow.'

'Where?'

'Probably just down to the local Chinese. But maybe we could get together tonight?'

'Tonight it is,' Marie said, thinking quickly. 'I'll take you somewhere special. I can do better for you than the local Chinese.'

'There's nothing wrong with Chinese,' Emily said indignantly. 'We don't go all that often and it's a real treat when we do. Mickey and me both love it. The thing is, we spend most of our disposable money on the kids, so there isn't much left to fritter on stuff like birthdays. And when you get to our age I suppose they don't matter quite so much anyway.'

'Listen,' Marie said, 'my best friend's birthday matters to *me*, okay? Suppose you swing by about six and I can give you your present and card.'

'You got me a present?'

'I bought it weeks ago.'

'Awww, I feel really bad accusing you of forgetting now.'

'Forget it. We can have a swift drinky here while we decide where we're going to eat. And it'll be *my* treat, not yours.'

'Okay.' Emily sounded quite excited now. 'I'll look forward to it. See you at six.'

When the call ended, Marie sat and pondered for a moment. Emily seemed so settled into family life and, although she would never admit it, she resented her that happiness. Making sure she mattered had become more important than ever, and buying Emily a nice birthday present would go a long way to ensuring that.

She went upstairs and told Donovan she was going into town for an hour. As she put on her coat and shoes, her mind was racing, trying to think what she might be able to buy Emily for her birthday.

By the time Marie had parked up in town, she had decided what to get. She popped into Clinton's to buy a card, then crossed over to W.P. Murton, an independent jewellers. She studied the necklaces in the window display. Settling for an inexpensive silver chain with a small bail holding an emerald dangling from it, she went inside.

At the counter, a man wearing an immaculate houndstooth suit was attending to a velveteen-clad tray full of rings. He looked up and afforded Marie welcoming smile. 'Good morning, madam. How may I be of assistance?'

'I'd like one of the necklaces you have in the window please.'

'Certainly. Would madam like to point out which one?'

'It's the silver one with an emerald on it.'

The man smiled approvingly. While he went over and unlocked the glass door at the back of the window to get the necklace, Marie waited at the counter, admiring the rings on the tray. An exceptionally attractive gold band encrusted with sapphires caught her eye. She lifted the tag to examine the price: Three thousand five hundred pounds. Her phone buzzed and she retrieved it from her shoulder bag. There was a text message from Emily on the screen, apologising that she wouldn't able to get to the house until six-thirty.

As Marie sent a text back to thank her for letting her know, the man stepped back behind the counter. Sliding the tray to one side, he laid down a necklace. 'An excellent choice, if I may say so, madam,' he said obsequiously.

'It's my friend's birthday present,' Marie said, setting her phone down on the counter and bending forward to take a closer look at the necklace. 'Emerald is her birthstone.' It looked different to the one she had looked at in the window. She frowned as she saw the tiny one hundred and twenty pounds price tag hanging off the chain. 'That's not the one.'

'It isn't?' The man looked slightly surprised.

'No. I meant the one with the *small* emerald.'

'I see.' The man gave her a withering smile. 'Madam means the *very* tiny one, on special at fifteen pounds?'

'That's it.'

'One moment please.'

As the man hastily scooped up the necklace and went back to the window, Marie cast a glance around her.

There was one other customer being shown a wristwatch by the female sales assistant on the opposite counter, but otherwise the shop was empty. There was a CCTV camera mounted high up on the wall in the corner, but it was pointed at the door.

Without looking down at the counter, Marie casually snaked her fingers over to the tray of rings, plucked out the sapphire-encrusted gold band from its slot and palmed it. Her heart was racing, but she withdrew her hand just as casually and, with a last nonchalant look around to be sure nobody was watching her, she dropped the ring into her open bag.

The man who had been serving her reappeared and set down the cheaper necklace in front of her. 'Very nice,' he said unconvincingly.

Marie picked up the necklace, gave it a cursory look and handed it back. 'I'll take it.'

'Will that be card or cash, madam?'

'Cash.'

'Would madam like to take the additional insurance with that? Guarantees against damage, loss and…'

'No, I'm not interested.'

'Of course.'

Marie could feel herself starting to perspire as the man took an inordinate amount of time to locate the box for the necklace, then proceeded to rummage around in a drawer under the counter for a small gift bag to put it in.

Outside the shop, as she stood at the kerb, waiting for a break in the traffic, she heard someone shout.

'Madam! Madam!'

Glancing round, she saw the man who had just served her emerging from the jewellers, pushing his way past two women who had stopped to talk in front of the doorway. For an instant she froze, then she spun back to face the road. There was still no break in the traffic. She looked back at the man, who was now only yards away.

'Madam!'

Panicking, Marie dashed out into the road, dodging between two slow-moving cars, one of which braked hard and sounded its horn. A young woman, riding her moped up the inside, swerved and Marie caught a fleeting glimpse of an angry face as it flashed past, shouting an obscenity at her. She glanced back towards the pavement, where the jeweller was stood with an expression of confusion on his face. As she turned her back on him and started forward, he raised his arm and waved something at her.

'Madam, wait!'

The driver of the double-decker bus that was running late and moving rapidly along the oncoming lane barely had time to register the woman who ran out in front of him. He slammed on the brakes, but the vehicle was moving too fast and it struck her head on. The woman sitting directly behind the driver's cab screamed as Marie was flipped into the air like a rag doll and dropped like a stone onto the tarmac in a twisted heap.

The man from the jewellery shop stood ashen-faced on the pavement, not really wanting to look, yet unable to tear his eyes away. The traffic had come to a stop now and a number of drivers were already out of their cars, staring in stunned disbelief at the broken body of the young woman that was lying in the road.

A young man shouted out: 'For God's sake someone call an ambulance!'

Turning sadly away from the carnage, the jeweller glanced down at the mobile phone clutched in his hand; it was Marie's, inadvertently left behind on his counter.

Emily didn't reach the house until almost seven o'clock. She had sent a second text to say she would be further delayed, but there had been no reply. Having noticed the absence of the Mercedes on the driveway when she arrived, she had dismissed the notion that Marie might have gone off somewhere in a strop without her. Nevertheless, there was every chance she would be shirty with her. Pondering how she would apologise, as Emily stepped up to the front door and rang the bell, she mentally rebuked herself: *I'm a grown woman and I'm* still *answering to her!*

When nobody came to the door, she bent and peered through the letterbox. 'Marie, it's me. I'm sorry I'm late. Please don't be upset with me.'

Emily looked back to the empty space where the Mercedes was usually parked. 'Surely not,' she muttered. Making her way around the side of the house to the back garden, she pressed her face to the kitchen window, but there was no-one to be seen. This was very odd.

Despite Marie's denial, it had been obvious she had forgotten Emily's birthday. Was it possible she'd gone out somewhere and forgotten they'd arranged to meet? Emily dismissed that idea too. After all, Marie had responded to the first text, surely she couldn't have forgotten in the space of a few hours... could she? Then another thought crossed her mind: perhaps something had happened to Donovan and she had rushed him to the hospital. But then, wouldn't she have at least had the courtesy to send her a text and let her know? Emily rolled her eyes. *Knowing Marie, probably not*, she thought. But that was being too harsh; maybe there hadn't been time. In a panic situation, their dinner date would have

400

been the last thing on Marie's mind. Maybe Donovan had suffered a seizure. Or fallen down the stairs. Maybe he was bleeding badly and …

With all these wildly improbable thoughts swirling around in her head, Emily walked in under the portico, clenched her fist and rapped hard on the back door. It now didn't surprise her that nobody came. Reaching for the door handle, she tried it; although she hadn't really been expecting it to, it opened. She was unsure whether she should go inside or not, but something in her head was urging her onwards and she stepped inside.

'Marie?' she called out. 'It's me, Em. Are you here?'

There was no reply, and scouting around the downstairs rooms confirmed that there was nobody home. She went to the bottom of the staircase and called again. 'Marie?'

Getting no answer, she warily made her way up the stairs. *What would Marie say if she arrived home now and caught me in the house?* she mused.

Her mind flashed to a scene in an old film she and Mickey had watched on TV a few weeks earlier: the detective character, having snuck into a house, went upstairs, only to be pounced on at the top by a madwoman, who slashed him across the face with a carving knife and proceeded to stab him to death. Stopping short of the top step, she called out one last time. 'Marie, it's Em. Is everything okay?'

Still there was no reply. She decided she would ascertain whether Donovan was in his room; if, God forbid, he wasn't, that would suggest one of the awful things that had gone through her mind might have been right. And if he *was* in

401

there? Well, maybe he would be able to tell her where Marie was.

She crossed the landing to his room and tapped lightly on the door. 'Donny?'

Nothing.

'Donovan? It's Emily, your Mum's friend. Are you okay, sweetie?' She reached down and turned the key in the lock. 'I'm coming in, sweetie. There's nothing to be scared of.'

As she pushed open the door, she caught the acrid scent of ammonia and involuntarily recoiled.

The curtains were drawn and the room was in darkness. Putting her hand over her nose, it took Emily's eyes a few moments to adjust and it looked as if the room was empty. So she had been right. Something must have happened to Donovan. As she turned to leave, a scratching sound came from the corner near the window.

Emily spun back. 'Donovan?' Feeling for the switch, she flicked the light on.

Donovan, dressed in his pyjamas, was sitting in the corner, arms wrapped tightly around his knees.

'Hello there. You must be Donovan.' Emily smiled warmly. 'I've heard so much about you. We meet at last.'

Donovan didn't reply. He was staring at her fearfully.

'I'm Emily, your Mum's friend. Maybe she's told you about me?'

Still the boy remained silent.

'Is it okay if I come in?'

Donovan didn't speak, but he nodded cautiously.

'Thank you.' Emily slowly moved forward. 'I've been a bit worried about you. And your Mum. Do you know where she is?'

After deliberating for a moment, the boy shook his head.

'Okay. Well, she and I were supposed to be going out for dinner this evening.' Emily reached the end of the bed. 'Do you mind if I sit for a moment?'

Donovan shook his head. Some of the fear appeared to have vanished now.

As she went to sit on the edge of the bed, Emily felt the dampness on the duvet and she saw the stain. It took her a second to register and she almost gagged again. 'Actually, I'll just stand. Are you hungry?'

Donovan shook his head again.

'Okay. Can I ask you another question?'

Donovan just stared at her.

'Your Mum told me you don't like coming out of your room,' Emily continued. 'But the door is locked from the outside. Does she lock you in here because it's what *she* wants, or because it's what *you* want?'

No reply.

Emily tried another tack. 'Wouldn't you like to get out in the fresh air once in a while? Kick a ball around with your friends?' As she looked into the boy's face, searching for answers that clearly weren't going to be given freely, she saw the single tear roll down Donovan's cheek.

'Oh, sweetie.' Stepping over, she squatted down beside him and, as she put an arm around his shoulders, he started to weep. 'Don't cry.'

There was something seriously wrong, and Emily didn't quite know what else to say. She held the boy close until the tears subsided, then she stood up. 'Okay, listen,' she said. 'I'm going to try and find your Mum. But I *will* be back, I promise.' She crossed to the door and turned back to look at him. His head was down and he was staring at the floor. 'But what do you say we keep this little chat between you and me, eh?' She smiled. 'Your Mum might tell me off if she finds out.'

Slowly Donovan raised his head and looked her in the eyes. 'My Mum killed Clive.'

A little more kindness, a little less speed.
A little more giving, a little less greed.
A little more smile, a little less frown.
A little less kicking a man when he's down.
A little more "We" and a little less "I".
A little more laugh, a little less cry.
A little more flowers on the pathway of life.
And fewer on graves at the end of the strife.

(Mark Twain, *Tom Sawyer*)

THANK YOU FOR READING

FALSE WIDOW

*If you enjoyed it – or any of our books – please
consider visiting Amazon or Goodreads and
leaving us a short review (both would be great!).
It only takes a moment and means so much.*

Acknowledgements:

The authors would like to thank Sandra Watson and Sara Greaves.

We would also like to offer our heartfelt thanks to all the loyal readers
who have supported us on our journey so far.

Cover design by TimBex.

405

STORIES YOU'LL NEVER FORGET

By REBECCA XIBALBA
and TIM GREAVES
All available now in PAPERBACK
and for KINDLE

SELECTED TITLES ALSO AVAILABLE ON AUDIOBOOK

Printed in Great Britain
by Amazon

32912742R00231